WE DARE

AN ANTHOLOGY OF
AUGMENTED HUMANITY

Edited by
Jamie Ibson and Chris Kennedy

Theogony Books
Virginia Beach, VA

Chris Kennedy/Theogony Books
2052 Bierce Dr., Virginia Beach, VA 23454
http://chriskennedypublishing.com/

Publisher's Note: This is a work of fiction. Names, characters, places, and incidents are a product of the author's imagination. Locales and public names are sometimes used for atmospheric purposes. Any resemblance to actual people, living or dead, or to businesses, companies, events, institutions, or locales is completely coincidental.

The stories contained herein have never been previously published, except for "Angel." A substantially shorter version of this story appeared in the U.S. Army Small Wars Journal as "Where Angels Fear." They are copyrighted as follows:

We Dare: An Anthology of Augmented Humanity/Jamie Ibson and Chris Kennedy -- 1st ed.
ISBN 978-1950420278

This book is dedicated to Tim "Uncle Timmy" Bolgeo, whose superhuman efforts brought fans and friends together from all corners of the world.

To my amazingly supportive wife Michelle, and my parents:
all that red ink back in high school is starting to pay off.

—Jamie Ibson

To Sheellah, who is awesome in every way.

—Chris Kennedy

Preface by Chris Kennedy

Welcome to "We Dare!" This book came about when Jamie Ibson asked me one day, "So, when are you going to do something with augmented humanity?" I thought about it a bit and then said, "Right now. How'd you like to be in charge of it?" After picking up his jaw, he accepted the challenge, and he has run with it ever since. While no one knows what people will look like 50-100 years from now, Jamie has put together a great selection of things we *may* do to ourselves to make us "better." Just because we *can* though, doesn't necessarily mean we *should*, and there are some cautionary tales for you in here as well. We dared to put this together for you...now will you dare to read it?

Enjoy!

Chris Kennedy
Virginia Beach, VA

Contents

* * * * *

Kade
by Christopher Woods

A Fallen World Universe Short Story

I awoke with a start.

"Damn this decrepit old bladder," I muttered as I dragged myself out of bed.

"Be a little quieter," Ringold said from the other bed. "Tryin' to sleep here."

"Shut up you old fart." I grunted as I pushed the walker toward the bathroom.

My whole body hurt these days, and I couldn't seem to nail down which part hurt the most. The burning in my groin was almost unbearable, but I made it to the bathroom in time.

"Heh, heh," I laughed. "I beat you this time you bastard."

"Victory!" Ringold yelled from the room.

I pushed the walker back out of the bathroom. "Damn straight."

"Celebrate the victories, Kade." He chuckled. "They're a lot scarcer as you go. Maybe you'll get lucky and kick the bucket before you have to call a nurse every time you need to go."

"Nope." I shook my head. "They'll have to wipe my ass and sponge bathe me for decades before I get to die."

"That's no way to think, Kade."

"Probably won't even send in that pretty redhead. It'll be Carl."

Carl was the size of a Packer's linebacker and wore the face of a serial killer. He was one of my orderlies.

"Damn, Kade."

"Expect the worst, and you'll never be disappointed," I said, then winced as my hip felt like a knife had been jammed into it.

"Damn Dellik Unified and their damn booby traps," I said.

"Hip gettin' you again, old man?"

He'd pried that from me one day while we waited for the nurses to come change the beds, and we got to sit outside for a couple of hours. We were just running a normal patrol in Atlanta when one of their IEDs had gotten my squad. I had been lucky enough to be on the other side of Corporal Jayden. He took the brunt of the shrapnel, but I still got a chunk right through my hip. More frag took me in the knee, effectively removing one Mathew Kade from service. I got shipped back up north to the Reach, part of Virginia.

I remembered when we had been a country of states. Many people still called it such but those of us who served knew better. A lot had changed in my ninety years. Now we were a land of Corporate Territories. Oh, the States were still there, but the dividing lines within this country had become more fluid with the nature of the Corporations, and the Corporations never had enough. They were always participating in a hostile takeover somewhere. Obsidian had become a juggernaut among the Corporate World, and when they settled into any semblance of peace, another would make a play for Obsidian Territory. Then the war would begin again. Dellik Unified had been a rough one, better than six years long.

I had been taken out of that conflict by that IED in the second year. Now Dellik was just a memory, a bad memory for many vets, but a memory, nonetheless. Years ago, I had seen the news vids about JalCom making advances from the Midwest Territories into Obsidian. I had known it wouldn't take long before another made a play for the East.

That conflict still hadn't reached a conclusion yet, but I figured Obsidian had a few tricks left.

"Hey, Ring?"

"What?"

"Look out that window."

"Oh, that's a thing of beauty."

We were looking at a pretty yellow convertible Corvette. Looked like it was from the twentieth.

"Let's go steal it," I said.

"Alright."

He climbed up from the bed, and we pushed our walkers out the door and down the hallway to the side exit. I ran a card across the scanner.

"Whose card did you swipe?"

"Carl's."

"You lifted that big bastard's card?"

"What's he gonna do? Beat up a ninety-year-old geezer?"

"He might," Ringold chuckled.

"He'll have to catch me first."

"Damnit, Kade," he grumbled. "I'm outrunning you. It's not going to be a hard job for Carl to catch you."

"Yeah, but when you passed me I slipped the card in your pocket," I laughed. "Run you old fart!"

"Damnit!"

We rounded the corner beside the Corvette only to see a pretty blonde slip into the driver's seat. The car started, and she pulled away from the curb in our direction. She smiled widely and waved as she passed.

"I reckon that smile was worth the walk out here," he said.

"I'm gonna agree with you, there, Ring."

"Just what are you two doing out here?" A voice said from behind us.

We both turned to find Savannah Garvey standing behind us with her hands on her pretty hips.

"You were going to steal that car, weren't you?"

"Of course not," I said. "What sort of fella do you take me for?"

"We all remember the incident last May, Mister Kade."

"What?" I asked. "What happened in May?"

"You can't tell me you forgot what you two old reprobates did."

"I do well to remember my name if it ain't used pretty regular," I said.

"Who are you?" Ringold asked.

She laughed. "They said that if you stole another car, they'd put you in jail."

"Somehow I don't think they'll jail a ninety-year-old man," I said. "We were gonna bring it back. I just wanted to feel the wind in my hair."

"What hair?" Ringold asked.

"I have a couple left."

"Maybe in your ears," he said.

"Wind still blows through them."

"You only made it ten miles," Savannah said.

"But it was a *fast* ten miles," I said with a grin.

WE DARE | 13

"We would have gotten further but he had to stop and pee."
Ringold laughed.

She smiled and shook her head. "Now, are you going to give me any trouble going back inside?"

"No, Ma'am," Ringold said. "But only if you'll walk in front of us. I'll *follow* you anywhere you want to go."

She looked at him with one eyebrow raised. "Hmm."

She turned and walked toward the door we had exited. I swear she put a little more sway to the hips just for Ring.

"I'd like to bite that butt, develop lock jaw, and be dragged to death," he said.

"Die happy, I reckon."

"Yes Sir. Very happy."

She turned to us as we neared the door and stretched out her hand.

"The card?"

"I don't have a card," I said. "Door was open."

"Here it is, Darlin.'"

I shook my head as Ring held out the card I had slipped into his pocket to the nurse.

"Brave man," she said, looking at the name on the card.

"Wasn't me," he said. "It was that idiot."

"Not all that surprising." She grinned. "I'll try to slip it back to Carl without him knowing."

"He better not mess with Kade," Ringold said. "War hero, and all that. Liable to get kicked in the shins."

"I'm done with all that since I took the arrow to the knee."

"An arrow, Mister Kade?"

"Well, an arrow*head*. Those DU bastards put the damnedest things in their explosive devices. This one had an arrowhead in it with all the other crap. Hit me right in the knee."

* * *

"You have a visitor, Mister Kade," Carl's deep voice came from behind me. "Don't you step too close to me, either, you thieving old fart. I'd like to keep my access card today."

"I have no idea what you're talking about," I said. "Who is the visitor? I ain't had a visitor since Elena passed. Her family finally decide I was someone again? If it's that cousin of hers, Tom, I don't want to see him. He tried to say I'm unfit and take all the money I have left."

"None of her folks, Mister Kade."

"Well, now I'm curious."

"Some fella from corporate."

"They're pissed about the car?"

"No, I mean corporate with all caps, Obsidian Corporation."

"Curiouser and curiouser."

"Do I send him in?"

"I reckon so, since they're the ones paying for my stay."

"He'll meet you in Meeting Room Three, Mister Kade."

"That's the one across the building?"

"Yep."

"Asshole," I said.

"Don't be pickin' my pockets, Mister Kade."

I chuckled. "Guess I had that coming."

"You need the exercise, anyway, old man," Ringold said from the other side of the room. "You're gettin' flabby."

"Look who's talking, you fat bastard."

He laughed as I pushed my walker out into the hall behind Carl. It took some time, and I scowled at the big man's back. But I probably deserved it. After crossing the whole facility, Carl opened the door to Meeting Room Three.

I slapped his shoulder as I went by and said, "Sorry about the card."

He chuckled and walked away as I stepped into the room.

A man stood across the room staring out of the window. Glancing past the guy, my eyes opened in surprise. The car parked outside was *spectacular*. It was an old Camaro from way back in the sixties. The *nineteen* sixties. I hadn't seen one of those aside from pictures. It was a deep candy apple red.

I pushed my walker up to stand beside the man and stare out at the car.

"That's a piece of art," I said.

"That it is," he answered and turned to me. "I'm Nathaniel Bern, OAS." His hand stretched out, and I grasped it. It was soft and his grip seemed weak. But it could just be he was being careful of an old geezer.

"OAS, huh?" I commented. "You're not a grunt. I'd have to say a spook or an egg head."

He laughed. "I'm more of the latter, Mister Kade. Although I'd have to claim both."

"Well," I said. "I have to wonder what a spooky egg head wants with me. Been out for decades. And I'd make it good if I were you.

It's almost lunch time, and they have pudding. Obsidian Armed Services doesn't make a habit of calling on old men."

"Not much for small talk, Mister Kade?"

"Too old for it. Comes a time when you're old enough that every minute is important. There's not as many of them left. So, Bern, let's just get right to it. Today is banana, and I love banana pudding."

"Then I'll get right to it then," he said and motioned to a seat at the table.

I sat down with a sigh. My hip was throbbing.

"You were a damn fine NCO sometime back, and I understand you pulled twenty years in the Service before injuries retired you."

"Yeah, that about sums it up."

"In all that time, I'm sure you heard of the Agent program."

"Yeah I did. Crazy bastards. All sorts of mods to the body. I thought about going that route but they told me I wasn't quite the right sort of person they were looking for. I guess they wanted a bit more moral ambiguity."

"That is one of the prerequisites for the program."

"Sociopaths."

"It is true."

"I'm pretty sure you don't want a ninety-year-old Agent, so I have to wonder what it is."

"You're right and wrong, Mister Kade. We do want a ninety year old to join the program, mostly."

"Mostly? If you're going to take parts, try this blasted hip and knee."

He smiled. "Let me tell you a story."

I sighed and settled back into the chair. I had to admit, my curiosity was piqued.

WE DARE | 17

"Ten years ago, a project began to build what we call an Imprinter. We can, literally, imprint memories into a living mind. Tests began with mice. We ran ten mice through a maze and used the Imprinter to download the memories of all of the mice. Then we imprinted these memories into an eleventh mouse who went straight through the maze without a single mistaken turn. The early tests were such a success that we have now successfully imprinted people. We've given people complete memories from one person to another. We've even begun to build skill packages. They aren't quite as successful. It seems skill packages don't take if the person has no skill at all in the area. We can't give a fisherman unparalleled skill in martial arts. But we can take that fisherman and give him a Marine Biology imprint and he retains the majority of it."

"That's impressive,"

"It is, Mister Kade."

"You want a lab rat," I said.

"In a manner of speaking." He nodded. "We want to make Agents. We want to build Imprints we can use in Agents."

"Unlimited skills for sociopaths," I snorted. "I'm just filled with anticipation when I think of something like that. Wait a minute, maybe that's something else…anxiety, distress? *Are you frigging crazy?*"

"This is why we need you, mister Kade. We don't want to build sociopaths. We want to build complete personalities to fit any situation. We want them to have the skill set to do whatever job needs to be done, and most of all, we need to be able to return the originals back to their bodies after the job is done."

"And what's that got to do with me?"

"Mister Kade, you have decades of experience. You've done things in those ninety years that would allow almost any personality to be built around it. Mister Kade, we want your mind."

"You gotta be kidding me. I'm going to get some pudding."

"Just hear me out." He held out a placating hand.

I eased back into the seat again.

"What I'm offering you is immortality. I'm not talking about removing your brain. Let me tell you about the next step in the program we took."

"Go ahead."

"We started building personalities but none of them were anything more than surface constructs. The mind is much too complicated to just build from nothing. We were almost to the point of shutting the endeavor down and just proceeding with the Education Imprint Program. A couple of us developed a theory, and it has proven itself, up to a point. Several volunteers had their minds Imprinted to the databanks. We used those minds as templates for the personalities. I say, up to a point...because they all went insane," he admitted. "First the minds and then the templates."

"That fills me with all sorts of anticipation...nope, nope. Anxiety again."

"The problem, Mister Kade, is that all of the volunteers were young, healthy and couldn't take the loss of their bodies. In theory."

"So you want to copy a mind of some old goat who is tired of his body."

"Not just that, Sir." He frowned. "I have seen both your medical files and your psyche eval. I know what you've been told, and I know what you've let them see about your mental state. I'm pretty sure no one has seen what your mental state truly is, except yourself."

I grunted. I guess the secret wasn't really a secret.

"I know that your body is failing. And worse, it is just a matter of time until it starts to affect your mind."

"Yeah, those moments I told you about are all that more precious, now."

"I can imagine." He scooted his chair back and stood up, facing the window. "Will you, at least, come and look at the program?"

"I'll tell you what I'll do," I said. "I'm going to go eat some pudding. Then, if you'll help me do something, I'll go with you and look this thing over."

"What can I help with?"

"You help me steal that car."

He looked at the car with a grin, "Done."

"And one more thing," I said.

"What's that?"

"Drop this off at the front desk."

I pulled Carl's wallet from the pocket of my robe and placed it on the table.

Bern raised his left eyebrow.

"Made me walk all the way across the place." I shrugged.

He chuckled. "Done."

It was almost half an hour later when I eased into the driver seat of the Camaro. I grunted as I reached under the seat, looking for a spare key. Always check before trying to hotwire a car. A lot of folks just throw the keys under the seat out of sight. Something jingled, and I raised my head to see Bern holding a set of keys.

My eyes narrowed. "Your car?"

"No, Sir, Mister Kade, *yours*. It would be a shame to damage the steering column."

"No doubt," I said and took the offered keys.

The engine rumbled with power, and I smiled. Immortality? Hmmm.

* * *

"**T**his place looks well-guarded," I said as the Camaro rumbled into the drive of a military compound.

"It is," Bern returned. "The guards don't even know what they're guarding."

"There's plenty of them." I pointed to our left. "Looks like seven posts on the left, four on the right. Then the two guys in the shack."

"Pretty good, Mister Kade. There are six on the right."

"Damn these old eyes," I muttered.

"Pretty good for an old man, Mister Kade," he said. "Stop at the gate."

I stopped at the gatehouse and watched the two guards approach the car from each side.

"Doctor Bern," the guy on the left nodded. "Who is this?"

"If you'll look on the orders in the shack, you'll see I am expected with company."

He grinned. "I did, Doc. Didn't really expect someone so…"

"Old." I chuckled.

"Yeah," he said. "Most of the folks coming in here are a bit more spry."

"I used to be, Sarge."

He smiled as I commented on his rank. "You served?"

"Back when the DU was causing a ruckus. Took some shrapnel to the hip back in forty-two."

"Those were rough years, Sir," he said.

"Don't call me Sir, I worked for a living."

"You're still around after all that," he said. "I'll stick with Sir."

"Guess I'll live with it as long as you don't start thinking I was a lieutenant or something."

"Staff?"

"Gunny," I answered.

"Maybe I should salute." He grinned.

"Been civilian for a long time," I said with a laugh. "I don't think they'll let me re-enlist."

He smiled and waved us through.

"You've been re-enlisted since we left the vets home," Bern said.

"I'll be damned," I said. "Obsidian must be pretty desperate if they're re-enlisting ninety-year-old gunnery sergeants."

"This is the Hail Mary, Mister Kade," he returned. "If this doesn't work, we're back to enlisting sociopaths. I, for one, would like to change that."

"I guess we'll see," I said.

"You're on board?"

"Really, what have I got to lose?" I shrugged as he motioned toward a parking spot near the smallest of the clustered buildings on the base. "Six weeks of hell as my mind begins to go?"

"The report says you have a year and a half before the effects are seen in your mind."

"It says six weeks to a year and a half."

"You may have more time…"

"Expect the worst, Doc. You'll never be disappointed."

"That's a pretty bad outlook, Mister Kade."

"I am almost never disappointed, Doc. Disappointment will eat at your soul."

He chuckled. "Alright, then."

I brushed my hand across the top of the magnificent car as we headed toward the door to the small building. My walker kept us moving at a pretty slow pace.

"Welcome," Bern said as he motioned me inside.

There were three checkpoints along the hallway that made its way around the perimeter of the building before turning in to end at an elevator. The walls were reinforced steel with the standard concrete on the exterior that hid what was inside.

"Hard place to get into."

"It needs to be," he said. "This is the future. What we do here could end the wars. Not the war. The wars."

"You have a lot of faith in this system of yours."

"There's nothing wrong with the system. The hardware is flawless, Mister Kade." He tapped his head. "It's the wetware that seems to be the problem."

"Good luck," I said pointing at my own head. "The noodle you're about to try hasn't ever been considered flawless."

"I think you may surprise yourself," he said.

"Whatever."

I stopped and leaned on my walker. This had been the furthest I had walked in some time.

Bern pushed a button, and the elevator opened. Inside was a pretty redhead with a wheelchair.

"Oh, my stars and garters, that's the most beautiful thing I've seen in years," I said and sat down in the chair. "You're not too bad, either, Miss."

She chuckled. "I thought you might appreciate getting off of your feet, Mister Kade."

"I most certainly do." I turned to Bern. "Let's get this show on the road, Doc."

"Just like that?" he asked. "You're all in?"

"Hell, Doc, I was all in the second we got in the car," I said. "Like I said before, what have I got to lose?"

* * *

There was nothing. I would have smiled but there wasn't a mouth for me to use. I could understand why the others had gone nuts. But there was one huge difference, the pain was gone. I hadn't even realized how much there was until it was gone.

Perceiving something in the distance, or what seemed like a distance, I moved toward it. It was disconcerting as the light that had seemed so far away a moment ago was right there. It was a door.

I walked through the bright white opening into a room. It wasn't an impressive room, just a simple round room with a table and two chairs. Walking toward the table, I realized I had a body in this room. There were none of the normal inputs you would have, though, except the visual. The virtual body moved with the same mental commands as the real body. It seemed to follow the same rules.

"Mister Kade?"

The voice came from everywhere and was just a bit disturbing.

"I'm here, Doc."

"Unexpected, but a good sign."

"Unexpected?"

"I hadn't connected you to the room yet," he said. "How did you find it?"

"Saw a light and moved toward it," I said. "Then walked through the door into this…round room."

"Interesting," he said. "Can you remember everything?"

"I think so," I answered. "How would I know if I don't remember something?"

"True," he said. "Let's go through a few questions."

"Sure."

"What is the most important memory you can think of?"

"That's easy enough," I answered. "Elena."

"And what memory is that?"

"Doc, that's a whole lot of memories. Thirty-two years of them."

"Good."

"How about more recent memories?" he asked. "Do you remember stealing a car?"

"Which time?"

"We'll discount the last one since it was my car and was more of a gift."

"There were a couple of times even without that one. I stole my first car after Elena died. I used the 'Vette I stole to take her ashes to the ocean. She loved this spot out there where we used to go, and I spread her ashes there on the beach. When I came back, I left a bit of money and a note on the seat of the car. No one figured out who took the car for six hours. I was in better then." I chuckled. "They noticed the last one within thirty minutes. I blame Ring. He was with me that time so I might as well blame him."

"Well, it certainly seems to have worked correctly, Mister Kade."

"I like the pain being gone, Doc," I said. "Hadn't realized there was so much of it until it was gone. But it's real dark in here."

"I have some programs that I made for the others to make it seem more hospitable. Programs much like this room."

"Good."

"There are a few things I would like to do differently with this trial that I didn't do with the others. This has to work, or our program is over, so I will be giving you administrative access to the programs. This is as much an experiment as the rest of it, but the fact that you found the room without being tethered bodes well for the interface."

"Okay, Doc," I said. "Let's do it."

"I am inputting a program called Environ. It is a building program that you can use to build an environment around you like this room. It's a rather large program because of the availability of so many aspects. What I don't know is how the interface will work for you since you are inside the system. Your access keyword is HJDRFETY. You may change that after you access the program. I'm going to leave you to examine the program for a bit."

"Alright, Doc."

I said the key aloud, and a console materialized at one side of the room.

"That was easy enough," I muttered and walked over to the console.

"Enjoy the program, Mister Kade."

"Thanks, Doc."

I searched through the console commands to find settings and found my way to the access key. With a few commands, I had the key changed to something I could easily remember, then I signed out. The console disappeared.

I walked out of the meeting room into the dark, moving away from the bright door.

"Who dat? Who dere?"

The console appeared in front of me again. Then I really dug into the different landscapes.

* * *

"You appear to have been busy, Mister Kade."

The Doc's voice came from everywhere again.

"It's kind of fun," I said.

"The gardens are quite splendid."

"Elena loved flowers. She would have loved building something like this."

"It is beautiful. I was planning to leave you alone for a determined amount of time but we have a small problem."

"What is it?"

"You seem to have disappeared."

"I'm right here."

"No, the other you. He got a little upset when I told him we were going to download his mind so that we could update your consciousness inside the machine. I left him be for a little while to calm down and came back to find him gone."

"It must be getting worse," I said. "He knows I'm free of the pain, now. He doesn't want to send his pain to me."

"I thought as much, but it might be needed to continue the experiment. We did this with the others, and it made them worse. They began to miss their bodies much more."

"Doc, I don't miss it and bombarding me with memories of more pain isn't going to make me want to go back. Let me think a minute, and I can help find him."

"Thank you, Mister Kade."

"Call me Mathew, Doc."

"One more thing, Mathew," he said. "He stole a gun."

"Shit."

* * *

"He did, indeed, go where you said he would," Doc said. "We were too late to stop him."

"He's gone, then."

I wasn't sure how I felt about what my old self had done. I had only spoken with him once since I had been downloaded into the machine. I'm *pretty* sure Doc was unaware of the conversation we had. He was beginning to lose some of the memories. Our worst fear had started. The cancer had moved into his brain. We had known it would come at some point, but we both hoped it would kill him before it took that. Most people with this form of cancer die well before it reaches the brain.

"How did he do it?"

"I expected him to suicide, Mathew," he said. "Even after you told me he would not. He went down into the city and found one of the worst sections of town. There, he interrupted a robbery and shot three of them before a fourth managed to shoot him. He lived long enough to shoot the fourth, who is now recovering in a hospital on Grave Street."

"Tough old bastard," I said.

"Yes he was. But now we have no back-up if your program doesn't work."

"We didn't have one left in him, either, Doc. The cancer was into his brain."

"He never said anything about that."

"He told me he was losing memories of our past, Doc."

"Then you expected something like this?"

"Actually, I wasn't. This place has changed the way I think more than I would like to admit. I can look back and see where I would have expected it, but time in here has changed me."

"You have been inside longer than any of the other volunteers made it, Mathew. You feel no longing for the physical world?"

"Not so much, Doc."

"The next experiment will be the one that tells us whether we will succeed or not."

"And what's that?"

"You are going outside for a bit, Mathew. Time to stretch your legs."

"Alright."

I was...*familiar* with the theory of being downloaded into a body. It was pretty anticlimactic when it actually *happened*.

"When are we doing it?"

"It's done, Mathew," he said. "The part where we see if the experiment is a success will be when we upload the copy back into the machine and the two merge."

"That could be interesting."

"Indeed. Here we go. I will speak again with you after you assimilate."

"Okay, Doc. Let me have it."

The memory was as vivid as the memory of building the latest construct in the machine. It was as if I had lived them both, and in a way I guess I did.

* * *

My eyes opened. I felt them this time, and the sensations of the body that I had been missing inside of the machine. There was only a little pain, but the sensations seemed odd to me. I raised my head and looked down.

"Doc?" My voice was much higher pitched, but very soft. A voice I would have enjoyed listening to, once upon a time. "Why do I have boobs?"

I heard a giggle from my left and turned my head to find the red-haired nurse who had met us at the top of the elevator.

"You've changed your hair," I said. "Close to a foot longer."

"It has been some time since you last saw me, Mister Kade."

I looked back down at my chest. "I guess it's *Miss* Kade."

She laughed again. "At least you're a good sport about it. Doctor Bern insists on the first body that one of you are placed into is of the opposite sex. It gets the shock over with."

"One of you?"

"The others who came before you. Some of them handled the transition tolerably well. Some, not so much."

"It's just a body," I said and sat up. I twisted to the side and let my legs hang off of the bed. The wall was mirrored and my eyebrows arched. "An extremely attractive body, certainly."

"Sometimes, the Agent can't be a male."

"I got no problem with that," I said and slipped off the bed to drop a little before my feet touched the floor. "Where is the person who came out of this body?"

"There was no one inside of the body, Mister Kade."

"Now I'm curious."

"Extreme cases in the prison system are sentenced to death. Our mode of execution is much different than it used to be. Instead of killing them, they are sent to us, where we wipe the mind. It is an empty shell. Then we use the bodies for Agents. It's a relatively new system since we have had little success with the 'wetware' up to this point. We have high hopes for you Mister Kade."

"Alright."

The door opened, and Bern entered.

"How are you holding up, Mathew?"

"May as well call me Mattie for the time being, Doc."

"You are handling it well enough," he said.

"These," I patted my chest, "are going to be a distraction. They seem to get in the way."

I twisted and moved my arms, which kept connecting in unfamiliar places.

Red laughed again. "Welcome to womanhood, Mister Kade."

"You may as well call me Mattie, too. At least as long as I'm in this body. Mathew when I'm not. Mister Kade is...*was,* a crotchety old man."

"I can do that."

"Alright, Doc," I said as I turned to Bern. "What's next?"

"I have a job for you, Mathe...Mattie. One you just might be glad to take care of. It is somewhat of a personal matter. I want you to remove someone."

I was silent for a moment. I'd killed many men in my time as an OAS trooper. This seemed different.

"Kill someone," I corrected. "Don't mince words, Doc. *Own* it."

"Yes," Bern said. "I want you to kill the man who killed Mathew Kade."

I watched Bern, closely. He was angry.

"That, I can do," I said. "You guys were closer than I thought."

"He was my friend," he said. "It needs to look like an accident."

"I can do that, too."

"Good. You have all of the tools necessary for the job in that Agent's body. I would suggest you go to the gym and test out what you are capable of before you leave the facility. You will find that you are much stronger, faster, and more durable. You also have many skills you are unaware of. If you think about it, you may remember many years of training."

"What training?"

My mouth dropped open as sixty years of skills and training dumped directly into my memory bank.

"Holy shit," I muttered.

"*That* training."

"Damn, Doc.

"That is how the imprinter works, Mathew. If you have a grounding in any given field, it can be instantly added to your skill set. You have had many years with an affinity for violence. Now you have many years of training to accompany it. Some of it will not last, but some of it will be ingrained into you after this."

"Okay, Doc. I'll hit the gym and then go take care of business."

"Thank you, Mathew."

I nodded to him and turned to Red. "I never caught your name, but can you show me to the gym, and tell me where I can get some clothes?"

"It's Regina," she answered. "And you can follow me. I'll take you to a dressing room first."

I followed Regina out of the initial room where I had awakened. It felt a little weird walking down the hall naked. Even weirder to walk down the hall as a naked woman. There were subtle differences in my gait that seemed off. More movement in the hips than I was accustomed to.

I laughed.

"What is it?" Regina turned to me.

"Walking feels a bit weird." I grinned. "Things move a little different."

She laughed and opened a door. "Step on the scale," she said, then placed her hand out to stop me. "But first, tell me how much you think you weigh."

"How am I supposed to know?"

She cocked her head to the side. "Really?"

"I figure about a hundred and twenty at the most. This body has good musculature which weighs in heavier than it looks."

She smiled. "*Now* step on the scale."

"What the hell? How do I weigh two hundred and forty pounds?"

"The bones and muscle are denser than a normal person. Increased strength and durability. You'll find that you can do things you never would have thought possible."

She pointed toward a locker with the number four stenciled on the front. "The clothes in number four will fit you."

I opened the locker and pulled a lacey pair of underwear from the top of the pile. I paused looking at them as it sank in where I was.

"You're thinking naughty thoughts."

"Just give me thirty minutes," I said.

She laughed and shook her head. "Men."

I chuckled and pulled the panties on.

"That's weird," I said as the thong slid into place.

"I take it you never wore a thong?"

"Yeah, for some reason they wouldn't let us wear 'em at the Vet's."

Next I pulled a pair of thin stretchy pants on.

"May as well just go naked," I muttered.

They *were* really comfortable though.

Glancing to the side, I caught my reflection in the mirror. "Yep, thirty minutes."

Regina laughed again.

I pulled the top from the locker and pulled it on. It was a sort of sports bra-type thing.

"That helps keep the damn things under control," I said and moved my arms around without as much interference.

"The gym is through here," she said with a grin.

I followed her through another door into a large room with lots of exercise equipment and a wide open space in the center. Glancing up, I could see the ceiling was about thirty feet above us.

"The first thing I want you to do is jump straight up," she said.

"Okay." I shrugged and jumped.

I gasped as I realized I had jumped higher than the top of the door behind us.

"Damn."

"That was what you could do with what you expected. Now I want you to jump all the way to the ceiling."

"Really?"

"Absolutely."

I squatted a lot further and really pushed off. The ceiling approached pretty quickly, and I raised my hands to stop myself from hitting it with my head. Then I was falling back down. I remembered my training from the OAS and let my legs bend to absorb the shock. There wasn't as much as I expected though, the body was made to handle things like that.

"Son of a bitch," I muttered.

"Now let's go lift some weights."

* * *

"This is different," I said as I re-lived the memories of slipping into the hospital.

I'd gone out a window and climbed up the side of the building to bypass the guards outside the room of Delmar Maples. He looked up as I slid his window open and dropped into his room.

"Who are you?"

"You killed someone very close to me, Mister Maples."

His eyes widened as I dragged him from the bed he was laying in. His mouth opened, and I clamped my hand over it.

I held him in front of the open window. "What do you see out there? A world of victims? You shot three people and an old man who walked into a bank. The old man was my friend."

I removed my hand from his mouth.

"That old bastard killed three of us."

"Yes," I said. "That glorious old bastard did. And now he's going to kill the last one."

I gave him a small push, and he staggered forward, out the window.

I left the window open and climbed back out. In a few short jumps, I was on the roof and walking calmly toward the roof access door.

* * *

"They said he jumped out the window instead of facing the courts," I said to Bern as my reverie into the past faded.

"Yes, they did," he said. "They closed the case the next day. Not even much of an investigation."

"That seems to have worked out well," I said.

"Yes," he agreed. "I'm curious why it took you so long to return after the mission."

"A gentleman never tells."

I heard a giggle from the speaker. Apparently, Regina was also on the other side of the conversation.

"It seems I need to build a new training ground in here to keep these new skills," I said. "Give me a holler when you need me again, Doc."

* * *

I spent many hours using the fighting techniques that had been imprinted in the previous body, but many of them still slipped away. Not all of them, but some faded. I had hoped to keep them all.

I sat in the garden and read a book from the unlimited library that was held in the computer systems.

"Mathew!"

Doc Bern's voice was frantic.

"We are under attack!"

"Get me a body," I said.

"It is underway," he said. "There won't be time to acclimate. You must get into action immediately!"

"Gotcha."

I waited for something to happen but there was nothing. Then I realized what was happening. They'd downloaded a copy, just like before. I would just have to wait until he returned.

It seemed like a long time as I paced around the gardens.

"Nothing you can do about it, old man," I muttered to myself. Or maybe it was just a thought. It was pretty much the same thing in the machine.

Then everything went dark for a moment.

"That doesn't bode well," I said.

Then there were memories flooding my awareness. I staggered and dropped to the ground in front of the roses I had planted for Elena.

Everything was jumbled up and almost impossible to follow. I was here, but I was there, and at another place. After the memories stopped flooding in, I just sat there in front of the roses and tried to make any sense of what was happening. Then I realized what they had done. I had been downloaded into six different bodies at the same time, and all the memories were clamoring to be first.

"That's enough!" my voice, or thought rang across the gardens and the memories were pushed aside. "One at a time."

I sifted through six different versions of me as they took up the defense of the facility. After a bit, I settled on the one that had awakened as Number One.

* * *

I awoke before they could even get me pulled from the Imprinter. It was a cylindrical device that encircled the body like an old MRI machine or tanning bed...I sat up as the straps holding me to the platform tore.

"Situation, Doc."

"A large force of JalCom troops are flooding into the base, Mathew," he said. "I don't know how they found us."

"How many?"

"Hundreds!"

"Safe to say they found out what's happening here."

"We can't let this fall into their hands, Mathew."

"Load me into all the remaining Agent bodies, Doc." I said as I strode from the chamber toward the locker room. I went straight to the number one locker and pulled clothes on quickly. I saw something in the back of the locker.

"What do I tell them?" Doc's voice came from the comm in my ear. He was still in the control room.

"Tell them to kill anyone that ain't us, Doc."

I pulled the object from the locker and flipped open the straight razor with a smile.

The closest place I would find a gun would be the Armory. This would do until then.

"How long until the others are ready?"

"Number two is downloading."

"Alright. I'm heading for the Armory," I said. "Tell him to grab what he can and join me there."

I was at the door in an instant.

"Damn these Agent bodies are fast," I muttered, and sprinted down the hall toward the ramp that circled the facility.

I saw a group of our guys crouching behind the first checkpoint.

"Hi, guys!" I yelled as I leapt over them and kept running.

Someone in a tan camo uniform rounded the corner and met with the straight razor across his throat. I caught his body in one hand and drew the holstered sidearm on his right. The strap had been over it but I ripped it from his side without much problem.

His body slid to the floor, and I looked around the corner. Three more followed the guy I had killed, about halfway down the hall. I launched myself forward, careened off the far wall, and opened fire with the stolen pistol. Two of them went down before the last got off a shot. I was already halfway down the hall toward him and bouncing like a pinball from side to side. There was a tug at my leg, but I was already too close for him to do anything except die, as my fist folded around the closed razor and slammed into his chest like a pile driver.

There was an audible crunch, and he flew backward.

"Damn!" I mused at the strength behind that blow.

"Doc, tell your guys on Checkpoint One to start moving forward as I clear these out."

"Okay, Mathew. Two is on the way."

"Almost to the armory."

I dropped and peeked around the next corner to see another group of JC's between me and the armory access.

"Alright then," I said as another form approached from behind me.

I glanced back to see Agent Two coming up the hall with what looked like a prosthetic leg gripped in his hand.

I looked at him with one eyebrow arched.

"What?" he asked.

"Nothin.'"

"What are you waitin' for, then, Old Man?"

He sprinted around the corner faster than a human has any right to move, and I followed right behind him. He slammed into the group of four like a football player and started laying them down with the leg.

I shot one of them who looked to be about to raise his rifle.

"Heh, heh," Two giggled.

"Sometimes I have to wonder about myself," I said as I moved past the grinning idiot.

The JCs had killed the four OAS troopers guarding Checkpoint Two on the far side of the Armory access. Glancing back, I saw the guys I had passed earlier, now coming up the hall behind us. I motioned to the other checkpoint.

"Hold that while we get armed."

"Yes, Sir."

Two and I grabbed vests and slid them on. Buckling up, I saw him stick the foot through an adjustable loop.

"You're keeping that?"

"Of course," he said and cinched the loop down to hold the leg along his left side.

The vest had pockets for pistol and rifle magazines; I filled them all. I had holstered a pistol and slung a rifle when I turned around and saw Two cramming grenades anywhere he could put them.

"What?" he shrugged.

"I'll take a few of those."

We left the armory just in time to see one of our guys go down from fire on the other side of the checkpoint.

I pulled the pin and tossed one of the grenades down the hall.

The explosion was deafening in the closed area, and my ears began to ring, but I followed the grenade into the hallway with my rifle firing into the group of JC's. They were disoriented by the grenade blast, and I made short work of them. The ringing in my ears was already easing. Regina had said the bodies healed very quickly.

We were nearing the open area at the front of the building and I knew there would be a lot of JC's in there.

"I'll take the left," I said to Two. "You take the right."

"Gotcha."

"I'll take the middle," A woman's voice said as Four ran past with nothing on but a savage smile. She was carrying two Kukri knives and hadn't even bothered with a gun.

"They'll all be watching her," I said and charged out of the hallway behind the naked Agent. I shot the first two on the left while they were still distracted and ejected the mag to slam another back in its place. I glanced to the right to see Two slam his rifle right through the chest of a JC.

"That's not how you're supposed to use that!" I yelled as my mag ran out again.

Two looked like he was giggling again.

"Shit," I muttered and did the same thing as the JC's got too close.

I didn't even reach for another weapon, I just reached out and grabbed the first JC I could. Pulling him in close with my arm around his neck, I squeezed and ripped his head completely from his shoulders.

"Maybe she had the right idea all along," I said and threw the head into the face of another. Then I was right in among them.

When my fists connected, bones broke, and organs ruptured. There were a lot of screams. Three exited the hall and started shooting from the edge of the room. Every shot meant another dead JC, and soon enough the room was completely empty except for the cooling bodies and pooling blood.

"When we head outside, everyone has to keep moving. Only way they're going to stop us is from a distance." I pointed toward the doors that had been blown open.

"Gotcha."

The three answers came as one, and it was just a little creepy since I know they were all me.

"Distraction time," Four said.

"Go for it," I said.

She grinned and charged out the door with her bloody knives.

"I'd say I was in love, if it weren't me," Two said as he followed her.

"Nothing wrong with that," I said as I went through the door, "I love me."

* * *

It was dark outside, and we moved faster than any of the JC's were expecting. It was the very definition of a target-rich environment, but it only took a moment for them to track us. I felt a fire in my side that seemed to fade into the background as I reached the first soldier. I had seen Four jerk once as she crossed the clearing, and Two had been hit as well.

But then we were among them. My pistol was empty, and I left it embedded in the throat of a woman with beautiful blue eyes.

"Sorry about that," I muttered. Unfortunately, I always had one of those old-fashioned attitudes that demanded respect for those of the opposite sex. Fortunately, when they are trying to kill me, I can work through my issues fairly quickly.

The next one was a young man, barely old enough to shave. It was depressing but had to be done. Then Four was thrown through the air.

She impacted the ground and was back on her feet in an instant. I saw where she was looking, and it wasn't pretty. The man was huge, with grotesque bulges for musculature. He had to be some sort of experiment by the JC's to offset the Agents. It would stand to reason that if they had such a thing, it would be deployed for this.

"Two!"

He looked in our direction and saw the Behemoth. I couldn't think of a better descriptor.

The Behemoth charged toward Four, and I moved in her direction on an intercept course. There was nothing graceful about my charge through the few remaining JC's. I kicked or punched with the force of a pile driver. Two was also on an intercept.

"Come on, Big Boy!" Four yelled and moved forward to meet him.

Then the whole back of the Behemoth's head exploded as Five fired the Barrett from the rooftop.

The giant still made three steps forward before toppling.

A bullet whizzed past my ear and my attention returned to the fight at hand.

"They probably brought ten of those," I muttered as I plowed back into the rest of the JC's.

"They brought two," Five said over the comm as the Barret boomed again.

Why didn't I think of sniping from the roof? I guess maybe I did, if you looked at it the right way.

I chuckled as my open hand contacted the side of a JC's head, spinning it all the way around with a crack.

Four paused beside me.

"Sometimes I worry about myself," she said shaking her head at my apparent amusement.

"I'm not the one running around out here naked," I said.

"Yes you are," she argued.

I shrugged. "I guess I am."

She laughed and moved off to our right, toward the next group of soldiers. They had sent close to five hundred men and women to take the facility, along with *two* Behemoths. They would have rolled right over the thirty-two men and women guarding the place, if not for the six of me.

The four of me on the ground were wounded.

I had taken one to the leg and side as well as several stabs on my arms.

Two had been shot once in the arm and stabbed in the side.

Three had been firing from the entrance to the building, but he had still managed to take a bullet in the shoulder.

Four had been shot, stabbed, and hit by the Behemoth, which left a massive welt on her left side.

Five was on the roof with the Barrett, and Six was protecting Doc Bern and Regina.

All of the JC's were dead.

* * *

"They'll have a Plan B, Doc."

"What do you mean?"

"If the attack fails, they'll have a contingency plan," Two said.

"We do too," Bern said. "We'll move to the northern lab. No one knows about it."

"Then we have to hurry," I said.

"How did they find us?" Bern asked.

The sound of the gun was deafening in the closed space, and my pistol was in my hand without conscious thought. Five bullets and a Kukri knife slammed into the OAS traitor who shot Bern.

"Shit!" I cursed.

Regina had caught the Doc, who lay in her lap with blood spreading across his chest.

"They've killed me, Gina," he gasped, looking up at her.

"Not yet, they haven't!"

I grabbed Bern and dragged him to the Imprinter.

"What are you doing?" Regina screamed.

"Not *me*," I said and pointed at her. "*You* are going to upload him into the database."

"I can't do that!" She shook her head. "He'll go insane!"

"*Or,* he'll die," Four said.

I pushed him into the Imprinter. "Do it now, Regina."

She ran to the console and initiated the machine. "It will take ten minutes. Can he last that long?"

"We'll just have to see," I said and began digging in her purse. "You have any pads?"

"Pads?"

"Gonna tape him up so he doesn't bleed out in the next ten minutes."

"I got it, One," Five said. "You guys patch yourselves up."

He pointed at Four, "And you put some damn clothes on. I've got a reputation to uphold."

She nodded and headed to the locker room.

I nodded to him and turned to the other OAS men. "Prep a truck to move to the north lab, like the doc said. Then you are to report back to your headquarters and tell them what happened here.

"Won't you need us for defense?" Sergeant Malcolm asked.

"We'll be defense until we get there and make contact."

"Yes, sir."

Two was trying to patch one of the wounds on his own back.

"Let me help you with that," I said, grabbing the pad and duct tape. "Three, go help Four get patched up. She had several I know she can't reach."

He grinned.

"Pervert."

"I happen to know you've…"

"Piss off," I said.

I had almost gotten Two taped up when Regina's hand landed on my shoulder. "It's done. He's gone."

I placed my hands on her shoulders. "It had to be done, Girl. It's his only chance to survive."

"I know, but I hate to think I condemned him to insanity."

"Doc may be made of sterner stuff than that," I said. "At least he's not in there alone."

"He will be until I can get the database back up and running in Philly."

"Then we had best get a move on. Get it packed up, and we'll plant the charges."

"Charges?"

"We can't leave all this tech behind," I said and pointed at the Imprinters.

She shook her head. "You're right, Mister Kade."

"It's Mathew," I said. "Now go get me and the Doc all packed up while the rest of myselves get ready to move out. We'll be going north with every damn thing in that Armory."

I could tell she was close to the edge, but she had guts. She took a deep breath and straightened her slumped shoulders. Then she nodded to me and returned to the computers.

"Let's go load some guns in the truck," I said to Two.

"Damn straight."

* * *

"You know, I almost terminated this copy of myself when you put me into that Agent body. Hard to believe it's been close to a year."

Bern moved his Knight toward my Bishop.

"Kind of glad you didn't, Doc."

"Surprisingly, I'm rather glad you talked me out of it," he said.

"You'd miss all of this," I said, motioning toward the surrounding greenery in the virtual garden.

"The periodic updates from the version of myself outside help to keep me straight."

"They've been good for me, too," I said. "I still have all of the memories from them and those from myself. As a matter of fact, there should be a new upload soon from that last copy the other you downloaded. He said he was going to try something new. Didn't elaborate much past that. Have you had an update recently?"

"No, I haven't."

"Oh well." I shrugged. "I guess we'll find out together."

I glanced to my right to see another form walking toward us through the garden.

"That's odd," I said, pointing at the new inhabitant.

He looked up to see me and I recognized those eyes. They were mine.

"That's not the way one of these normally goes," I said.

"Indeed," Doc agreed.

"Hello Mathew," the newcomer said with a precise voice unlike any I would use. "My name is Stephen. These roses are absolutely delightful."

He looked over his shoulder, and I could see dozens of additional people coming. They all looked different, but they all had my eyes.

"Oh, yeah," he said, "I forgot to mention it. I'm not alone."

Things get complicated in this Fallen World.

* * * * *

Christopher Woods Bio

Christopher Woods, writer of fiction, teller of tales, and professional liar, was born in 1970 and spent decades reading books of many genres. One of his favorites is Military Science Fiction. In 2014, he published his first book in the successful Soulguard series. Since then, he has published four more in that series and has two other novels, plus several short stories, published by Chris Kennedy Publishing. He is currently working on The Fallen World series with Chris Kennedy, another book in the Four Horseman Universe's "Legend" series, and a sixth Soulguard novel. He is in the process of transitioning to full time author and looking forward to spending his time doing what he loves, telling stories.

# # # #

Taming the Beast
by Kevin Steverson

A Salvage Title Universe Short Story

Planet Salvage, Salvage System

G unnery Sergeant Ron Harper looked down at the ends of his legs. He would have preferred to look down at his feet, but they were no longer there. Having lost them in the ground actions on planet Barlat when his mech was literally sliced in two by a laser designed to knock fighters from the sky, it had been a long hard road to recovery.

Sure, the emergency nanites used by the combat medic had helped the surgeon with her job. She had closed off the arteries and veins, saved what muscle she could, and ensured enough skin was left to cover the stumps, but they couldn't prevent the damage to the nerves or stop the pain. Every time he put his prosthetics on, it was pure agony. Most days he could take it, but there were some he could not.

Salvage System was still in the early stages of colonization and didn't have any prosthetics on the main planet, but he did have the best in prosthetics. They were made by a specialist in the Tretra System and were the best credit could buy. They had tried many different sockets, but they all still aggravated the nerve endings below his knees.

Maybe it was time to retire. *I'll just stay here on Salvage, watch the Net and hang out in the local bar, Our Bar & Grill, every night*, he thought. Mayla would come home every few weeks for a long weekend. It could be worse. He could have been one of the many that didn't survive.

Gunny looked around his home. It was a nice house with just the right touch of a woman. Not too much, though. After all, Mayla was in the Fleet and didn't feel the need to cover every wall with frilly things. Except for the bed. Like most women, Captain Mayla Opawn had enough colorful pillows to cover the bed…twice. Gunny didn't make a big deal out of it. He had been around long enough to know that you had to pick your battles in a relationship. Your better half's choice of pillows wasn't one of them.

The house was in town and close to everything. While growing at a staggering pace, Bank Town was still small enough one could walk everywhere. Well, if your legs didn't make you want to scream in pain every time you stepped, you could. Except, he couldn't scream. He was the Gunny. Every soldier in the specialty unit, The Bolts, knew him. The marines on the ships of Salvage Fleet, flying between the planets and the system gate, knew him. Most ship crew members knew of him. Though he had retired from the Tretrayon Defense Force, he had retained his rank when he joined Tomeral and Associates and the Salvage Fleet. He was *The Gunny*. Larger than life and indestructible.

Until now.

It had been six months since the injury. Six long months of rehabilitation and strengthening trying to get back, or at least close, to what he was before that mission. It wasn't working. Deep down, he knew it just wasn't going to be. With a sigh, he put his feet on and slowly stood beside his bed. Attempting to ignore the pain, he walked out of the room. Sure, his movements were almost normal, so not many knew of the pain. He knew. He felt it.

* * *

Gunny walked into the front offices of the Bolt's orderly room, and the private behind the front desk jumped to her feet. "Good Morning, Gunny," she said loudly.

"Morning," he said. "Is the captain in?"

"He is," answered the nervous private, her tattoo seeming to dance on one side of her face. All the members of the Bolts had the same lightning tattoo, regardless of race. It was an identifying unit patch like no other, although the blue streaks of lightning could be turned off should the situation dictate, such as piloting a mech, pulling security, on patrol, or on a mission when the tattoos would give away their position.

Gunny went into the office off the back of the room, and its occupant, Captain Nathan Brink, rose to greet him. Technically, the commander of the Bolts outranked the non-commissioned officer, but it was irrelevant. Gunny Harper had been his drill instructor as a trainee, and his respect for the man would remain forever, regulations be damned.

"Gunny!" Brink said, holding out a hand. "I didn't know you were coming by today. What can I do for you?"

"I want to try the Beast," Gunny said, with a determined look as he shook the outstretched hand.

Brink sat down. "Are you sure? You know you don't have to prove anything to anyone."

The Beast was the obstacle course used by the Bolts in training. It was a true monster, and it was as difficult to navigate as any course across the galaxy. For those in initial training, it took weeks of practice to be able to complete it on time before graduation day. For those injured, whether they were members of the Bolts, or marines making up the security platoons in Salvage Fleet, completing the course on time was required before being authorized to go back to duty. It was something he had a hand in putting in place.

"I have to prove it to me, Captain Brink...to me," answered Gunny.

"You look like you're fine, you walk normally, and you can operate a mech again one day. We'll let the maintenance platoon modify one, so it doesn't have any controls operated by feet. You don't need the course," Brink said. "You of all people have earned the right to skip it."

"I can't do that, Nate," Gunny said. It was the first time he had ever called his former trainee by his first name. "You know I can't."

"What does the commodore say about you attempting the Beast?" the captain asked. He was getting angry. Not at Gunny. Never at the Gunny, but at the fact that everyone coming off medical status had to do it. Mad that he had been a part of enforcing the regulations along with Gunny. Mad at the injury that had happened to his own personal hero. Mad at the entire situation.

"He told me I don't owe it to anyone, and whenever I'm ready, my marines are waiting for me on *Windswept*," answered Gunny.

"Well, there you have it," said the Captain. "If Commodore Tomeral says you're good to go, then you're good to go."

"It's not that simple, sir," Gunny said. "I would like to run it this weekend when it's not in use. I don't want to get in your troop's way."

"I'll be here at 0800, the day after tomorrow," answered the captain, resigned to whatever might come of the attempt.

* * *

On the first day of the weekend, at 0800, Gunny stood at the starting line. There was no one around except him and Captain Brink. Gunny hadn't told Mayla he was attempting the course when they spoke on comms the night before. She was out toward the gate in the system, where her task force was going through maneuvers with one of the Kashkal task forces. Most of the repairs had been made to her ships, fixing damage incurred from a mission he had not been part of due to his injuries. He didn't tell her because he knew she would say the same thing everyone else said. "You don't have to prove anything."

Like most days, his legs hurt, but today they were tolerable to an extent. He was glad they didn't protest the moment he put on his feet. Those days he tended to just stay home.

He was wearing a t-shirt, his battle dress pants, and combat boots on his artificial feet. Without the boots, an onlooker would see the shiny metal of his prosthetics. Stretching his arms behind his back, then above his head, that same onlooker would have noted the corded muscles of a man in exceptional shape.

Captain Brink stood near the starting line with a recording slate in his hands. When Gunny stepped across the line, he touched the screen of the slate, and the time started. Gunny breezed through the first two obstacles, crawling under entanglement wire and swinging across a deep mud pit. The third obstacle was the first wall. Gunny grabbed the rope and pulled himself up it.

He scrambled over the top and lowered himself to hang at arm's length, he dropped the final five feet. When he hit the ground, a pain shot through both legs so intensely he dropped to his knees. He stayed on his hands and knees trying to overcome it. Slowly, he stood, and on trembling legs attempted to take a step. It was pure agony, and he sucked in his breath through gritted teeth.

Gunny bent over with his hands on his knees, his entire body shaking. When he felt he had enough control over the pain he took a step. It was too much. Without saying a word, he turned and gingerly walked off the course, stopping every few steps to catch his breath.

Captain Brink stayed silent and watched him walk away. Nathan Brink was a strong man, one who had once led a large street gang and now commanded over two hundred specialty troops of multiple races. A man with several combat actions under his belt, he watched his hero step off a course he helped design…giving up. Once Gunny was out of sight, Brink threw the recording slate at the wall, shattering it. He couldn't see where the pieces landed through his tears.

* * *

"Sir, I don't know what to do for him," Captain Brink said. "He insisted on attempting the Beast. I tried to talk him out of it."

"Gunny's not going to allow himself to come back on duty if he can't complete the course," Harmon said.

The conference call included Commodore Harmon Tomeral, Captain Marteen Yatarward, Brink and Captain Mayla Opawn. Brink had gathered himself and gone to his office to think, trying to figure

WE DARE | 55

a way around the regulation. Realizing he was in over his head, he initiated the call.

"You're right," Marteen agreed. "The day I met him as a brand-new lieutenant, I learned that from him. There is absolutely no way he is going to ask his marines to do something he can't do."

"I love him to death, but sometimes he drives me crazy with his stubbornness," Mayla said. "And I accept that. I would never want to change him. His idea of leadership is leading, not telling. He's an incredible leader and an even better man. If he wants to retire, then I will support it." She paused a moment and then continued, "I will give you some time, Commodore, but my heart will be home with him. I intend to join it there. Especially since some days the pain is almost too much for him to bear."

"I hate to lose the both of you," Harmon sighed, "but I completely understand. I just wish there was a way to do something about the pain."

"The specialists say the nerves were damaged," Mayla said. "The doctor did the best she could, but it was emergency surgery on the ship. Saving his life was the priority."

"I know," Harmon said. "I'm not blaming the Doc."

"I'm going home for the week," Mayla said. "I'll talk to him and see what he wants to do. I'll call you."

"Alright," Harmon said. "I'll think about it some more. There has to be something we can do."

* * *

Harmon leaned back in his chair and put his feet on the conference table. *There has to be something we can do.* He looked over at Clip Kolgct. "What do you think?"

"I don't know, man," Clip said. "All the advances in bionics and prosthetics through the centuries can't help if the nerves themselves are damaged. Maybe they could take off more of his legs above the frayed nerves, but that's above his knees and kinda risky. I mean, it's not like we have the latest technology or techniques out here on the edge of the galaxy, dude."

"That's it!" Harmon exclaimed, jumping to his feet.

"I alwayss get nervouss, when he doess that," Zerith said with his reptilian race's distinctive lisp. He shook his head and went back to eating his mid-morning snack. The Prithmar was always eating something; right now it was a bowl of mixed fruit. "The next thing he'll ssay iss: what can go wrong?"

"His ideas tend to work themselves out," admitted Jayneen. She spoke through the overhead speaker. She was currently in the Defensive Bridge with Bahroot, where the two AI's were attempting to reprogram the guidance programming for the defensive shotgun missiles, giving them greater range.

"You tell them, Jayneen," Harmon said. "It's all about positive thinking. Can you do me a favor and make a direct call for me?"

The Bith Gate, the transportation method connecting systems throughout the galaxy, was the system wide router for the Galaxy Network, and it allowed direct calls between systems. It was extremely expensive to use, but Harmon would spare no cost for what he had planned.

"I can," the AI said. "Who would you like to call?"

"The Mars Bionics Corporation in Sol System," Harmon answered. "Ask for Jerock Guyland, the CEO."

A few moments later, the screen in the conference room lit up and changed to a man sitting behind a huge desk. A young boy of about seven was standing beside him. Harmon could see the red mountain ranges of Mars through the clear-steel windows behind the CEO.

"President Tomeral, this is a nice surprise," said Jerock Guyland. "Meet my grandson, Patton. Patton say hello to President Tomeral. He is the president of Salvage System."

"Hello, sir," the boy said. He held up a picture he had colored. It was in red and vaguely resembled the skyline behind them. "Do you like my picture?"

"I do," Harmon confirmed. "I like how you've exhausted your reds in an attempt to convey the true Martian landscape. The rocks in the foreground are nicely done and provide a good contrast to the mountain range. They draw the eye but don't hold it for too long, allowing the entire scene to be enjoyed. Good job."

"Thanks," Patton said, beaming. "I'm going to show it to my mom and tell her I 'zausted my reds. Bye." He ran off with his picture.

"Thank you for that, Mr. President," the CEO said, smiling. "You are a man full of surprises."

Harmon shrugged. "You're welcome. I like art. Young ones should be encouraged to draw and paint. Please, call me Harmon."

"Certainly, if you'll call me Jerock," he said. "Tell me, what prompts the call? What can I do for you?"

"Well," Harmon began. He spoke with the CEO for quite some time.

* * *

Gunny woke to a pounding on his front door. He was alert instantly; like most in the military, he had the ability to go from a deep sleep to instant consciousness. He sat up and swung his legs over the side to sit up. He reached for his feet when he heard Mayla open the door.

"Hi guys," she said. "You're here early. I just fixed breakfast and was going to wake him up. Come on in."

Gunny stopped in mid reach and tried to remember if Mayla had mentioned visitors coming over today. Nothing rang a bell. When he heard the voices of the visitors, he really got curious. *What are Hank and Stan doing at my house?* he wondered. He finished attaching his feet and stood. *Today isn't a bad leg day*, he thought as he walked out of the bedroom.

"Hi, Gunny," Hank said around a mouthful of eggs. Much to everyone's delight, chickens from Earth had taken to the planet Salvage and settled with no issues, unlike in the Tretrayon System.

"Come eat!" Stan said. He had a huge forkful about to go in his mouth. "Captain Opawn made cake. It is kind of flat, but it is good. She says they are called pans."

Gunny just grinned and shook his head. The brothers, a couple of Leethogs, were of a marsupial race; they looked like large opossums from earth. They were both lieutenants in Salvage Fleet, and, technically, they were some of his employers. As associates, they owned a percentage of Tomeral and Associates, which meant they owned part of the entire Salvage System, including its fleet.

They were both wearing their Earth World War I-era flight helmets with goggles on top. Without laughing, he sat down and had breakfast with Mayla and the brothers. They talked of the fleet, repairs, and about them sharing a ship again, since the frigate *Watch*

This had been destroyed. Hank acted as pilot and Stan sat in the commander's seat because Stan was missing a hand. He had a prosthetic from Leethog, but it didn't really give him the feeling he needed to pilot a warship in combat.

"I'll be back in a minute," Mayla said. She stood up, walked into the bedroom, and shut the door.

"So, what are you two doing here, anyway?" Gunny asked between bites. "I haven't retired yet. The ceremony is not until the end of the month. Are you two going to come see me every now and then when I do?"

"We came to get you," Hank said. "We get to take you to Sol System." He smiled. "All by ourselves."

"Sol System?" Gunny asked. "Why would I want to cross the entire galaxy? I mean, don't get me wrong, it would be…um, exciting, to go on a trip with you two, and I have never been to the home system but…"

"We are going to get new stuff," Stan said, grinning. Every sharp tooth in his mouth was plain to see.

"Stuff?" Gunny asked. "What stuff?"

"You're getting new legs, and Stan is getting a new hand," Hank said, matter-of-factly. "I'm flying the shuttle."

"Mayla!" Gunny called out, staring at the brothers. "Did you know about this?"

Mayla came out of the bedroom with Gunny's go-bag fully packed. "I don't think I forgot anything. If you need anything else, you can buy it there. There should be enough changes of clothing."

"Mayla, I don't know about this," Gunny said. "The feet I have are not a bad design. It's the nerves."

"Ron, you are going to Sol System," Mayla said. "Earth, the home of all humanity. The techniques and technology there are light years ahead of what we have here in our corner of the galaxy. You're going to the Mars Bionics Corporation because they lead the entire galaxy in human bionics. Mr. Guyland has assured Harmon they can work on the nerves and fit you with legs that won't hurt you anymore."

Gunny stood up, kissed Mayla, and looked over at the brothers. "Let's go, guys. Breakfast is over. Get it down and get out!" Both brothers scrambled toward the door like trainees. Gunny grinned at Mayla. "See you when I get back."

* * *

They came through the Bith Gate into a bustling system. None of them had ever experienced anything like it. They were immediately contacted by Sol System Flight Control, and after they gave their destination, they received a flight path and designated speed. Gunny didn't mind. The last thing he wanted was for Hank to fly like he normally did back home.

The brothers were in awe. Among the many ships, huge super-freighters could be seen coming and going. Sol Fleet warships patrolled, helping the system's law enforcement ships maintain order. There were several space ports within hours of the gate, as well as defense platforms. The trip across the system took days, and Gunny lost track of the various types of ships he saw while en route. The three dreadnoughts flying in formation stood out above them all, though. They were by far the largest warships he had ever seen in his career. He figured each must've held a battalion of marines as security.

"There is Mars," Stan said pointing through the clear-steel portals in the cockpit. "Everything inhabited has to be enclosed on the planet."

"I wonder how much power it takes for the gravity plates under the domes," Hank asked.

It was a much smaller planet than Salvage and lacked the greens and blues of most habitable worlds. It reminded Gunny of the planet Joth, though it was red in color as opposed to the browns and tans of the desert planet in the Tretrayon System. Like Joth, water was an issue, and moisture collection was big business on the planet Mars. The domed cities were huge and a lot of water was needed daily.

Hank followed the directions of the star port flight control and slowly came to a hover in front of a large hanger door at their assigned terminal, which extended out of the dome over the city named Rover. The door opened, and he flew the shuttle in like it was the bay on a ship. The door closed behind them, and they watched a huge panel on the wall in front of the shuttle until it showed normal atmosphere in the parking bay. The terminal they had been assigned was for ships their size and below. They had passed other terminals designed for bigger ships on the way in.

Gunny, Hank, and Stan grabbed their bags and exited the shuttle. Hank made sure it was secure before they walked away. It was one of the really nice ones from the cruise ship docked back in their system. Zerith had set up a travel account for Salvage System before they left the system, so Gunny used the codes to pay for the berth. Once the credit was transferred, the outer door to the chamber opened, and they passed through the scanner headed into the terminal.

When they exited the inner lock of the chamber, two armed security officers walked over from a kiosk. One consulted his slate and said something to the other. A hand-held scanner was passed over Stan's arm and both of Gunny's lower legs. After the scan, he nodded and said, "Enjoy your stay on Mars."

Hank and Stan weren't the only non-humans in the terminal, but they still received plenty of looks. Very few humans in this part of the galaxy had ever seen a Leethog. Hank and Stan didn't seem to notice the stares and smiled politely to those they passed; most stepped a little farther away from all the teeth. A large, green multi-tentacled being ambled by, and Gunny noticed that this time, the brothers were doing the staring and stepping away.

"We could never fly that one's ship," Hank whispered. "We only have four limbs."

"I have three and a half," grinned Stan, waving his prosthetic. "You have four. Is seven enough?"

"Let us ask," Hank said, turning back toward the direction the being went.

"Hold it right there," Gunny said, realizing things were about to get out of hand. "You're not asking a complete stranger if you can fly their ship."

"Do not worry, I will introduce myself first," Hank explained.

"Maybe next time," Gunny said, shaking his head. "We need to find the exit to the star port and catch our ride to Mars Bionics. Let's go."

"Perhaps you are right," Hank said, "Besides, it would be embarrassing if its language was not one programmed in our translators."

They caught the magnetic rail train running through the center of the terminal and, minutes later, they were standing in the entry lobby to the star port. Through the floor-to-ceiling clear-steel portal, they could see the city and all of its lights and activity. There were rental rides parked against the walkway and small stands selling all kinds of things from food to souvenirs, even at this time of night.

Across the road, leaning against a wall, were four men. Gunny noticed them immediately because they reminded him of others, ones he grew up with in an orphanage in a city on Tretra. He enlisted in the Tretrayon Defense Force as soon as he could, but they stayed in the city, joined gangs, and he never knew what became of them. When he left the home he never looked back.

They were probably looking for an easy mark. His slight limp, and Stan's obvious metal hand would attract them like zaxs to an outdoor party. Zaxs were a small biting insect on his home world of Tretra, and thankfully, they hadn't been brought to Salvage System when they began colonizing it.

"Guys," Gunny instructed, "don't carry your bags. Put them on your backs and fasten the chest strap, before we go out and look for our ride."

With a shrug at his brother, Hank put his backpack on and helped Stan fasten his. They stepped out into the crowded walkway, and Gunny looked up and down the street. In the distance he saw the area where noncommercial hovercraft were waiting to pick up arrivals. As they started in that direction, Gunny watched the four men out of the corner of his eye. After a moment one of them nudged another, nodding in their direction. The men started keeping pace on the walkway on the other side of the road.

Great, Gunny thought, and here we are in a system that requires all kinds of registration and digital licensing to carry a weapon. Probably should have just hid something nonmetallic on myself and took a chance with the authorities. "Guys, when we get to that pick up area, be ready. I don't like the way those four are trailing us."

"Do you think they will try and take our belongings?" Hank asked, without looking across the street.

"It is the middle of the night in this system," Stan advised. "On Leethog, this is not the time to be out in some areas of the capital. It is the same everywhere."

"We will just have to fight them," Hank said. "No one is taking anything of mine."

"At least one of them will get hit with this metal hand," Stan said, full of confidence.

Gunny grinned and said, "You guys are alright by me. We'll see what they do when we enter the hovercraft area."

The three of them turned into the parking lot and looked for a hovercraft marked with Mars Bionics Corporation. "There it is." Hank said pointing to one on the other side of the lot. "That says Mars Bionics in Earth common."

"You're right," Gunny said. "Let's go."

Gunny glanced at the four followers and saw they were still on the other side of the street, so Gunny headed to the hovercraft. When they got there, Gunny punched the code he had been given into the door, and both sides clicked open. It was an automated vehicle that would take them where they needed to go once they were settled inside. They started to take off their packs when a voice rang out, "You can leave those bags right here. Your slates and comms, too."

Gunny and the brothers turned to see the four men closing in on them. The man that spoke had a knife out. It hummed softly. Two of the others had a hand in their jacket pockets. "You can leave the ear pieces too; translators go for a good price."

"Boys," Gunny said, slowly shaking his head, "you don't want to do this."

Out of the corner of his eye, Gunny saw Hank bend down and put his pack on the ground. He stayed down longer than he should have before standing back up. "Why don't you crawl back under whatever rock you came from?" Gunny asked.

"You're gonna give us what we want, old man," the leader said, "and we'll see who wants to crawl under a rock."

As he continued stepping toward Gunny with the vibro-blade held in front of him, Gunny slung his pack around and threw it at him. The unexpected move caught the four of them off guard. The pack knocked the man back a few paces and when his blade hit the ground, the vibration stopped.

Gunny stepped to the side, prepared to fight. He didn't know if they had other weapons and wanted to put some distance between them. Stan couched low, ready to spring and hit someone. Hank hopped on one foot, then the other, while taking off his unclasped boots.

The leader yelled, "Get them!" and the three men rushed forward. The one in charge bent to retrieve his blade and tried to turn it back on.

The middle man was fastest, and he closed in on Stan. Stan stood his ground, and when the man swung the small piece of pipe now in his hand, Stan blocked it with his prosthetic, making an obvious *clang* sound. He kicked the side of the man's knee, and when the man dropped to his other knee in obvious pain, Stan caught him across the side of the head as hard as he could. The man was down for the count.

The big gang member on the far side thought he had an easy opponent in the five-foot-tall Leethog in front of him, even if he was holding a pair of boots. He led with his knife, a normal steel blade. The man misjudged the distance between them because of the extension in reach the boots gave Hank. He stepped toward Hank, and the heel of Hank's boot caught the back of his hand when Hank whipped it around. The man felt bones break, and he dropped the knife. Before he could scream in pain, Hank brought the other boot up in an uppercut swing, shattering teeth and splitting the man's lips. He hit him one more time in the side of the head for good measure, and the man dropped without uttering a sound.

Gunny's attacker figured he could just fight toe to toe with the limping middle-aged man in front of him. Gunny blocked a wild right by the man and threw a left jab that connected sharply. The man put his hands up in front of his face—like he knew how to fight—to block the next punch. Gunny hit him solidly in the lower ribs with a left and followed it with a hard right hook when the man bent forward and slightly to the side. The man dropped unconscious, like Gunny had long ago in a combatives match against Harmon Tomeral. True to his word, Harmon had taught the move to the older marine.

The leader of the gangbangers turned and ran. Without thinking, Gunny took off to chase him down, but after the fourth step he jumped slightly over the pack he had thrown and shooting pain raced up the leg when he landed. He stopped himself with a grimace and watched the man get away. He slowly walked back over to the brothers, limping badly.

"Hank, call the authorities," Gunny said through clenched teeth. "You can find the number on the Net."

A short time later, law officers secured the three unconscious men and medical personnel revived them, checked them, and loaded them on emergency hovercraft to take them to the nearest medical facilities before locking them up. The lead officer took their statements.

"Wait, wait, wait," the officer said, "Lemme get this straight. Youse beat the big one down with your boots? Did youse kick him or sumthin?'"

"No, sir," Hank said, mindful he was speaking to authority. "I took them off and hit him with the heels. These are the boots I wear when walking on a hull. When fully suited, they can be connected to the suit's power source and magnetized. The soles are heavy."

The man whistled long and low, shaking his head. He looked over at Stan. "What did youse do? Whack one with that metal hand or sumthin?'"

"Yes, sir," Stan said grinning. "But he dented it with that pipe, first. Now some of my fingers will not close. Unless I did that when I hit him. I am not one hundred percent sure which caused the damage, but I am getting a new one, so it is alright. Oh, and I did kick him."

"Jesus, youse two…" the man said, shaking his head. He entered something into his slate and looked over at Gunny. "Alright, your turn, what did youse do to your guy?"

"I gave him the ol' one-two, officer," Gunny answered, nonchalantly.

"You mean youse hit him with your fists and did that?" the man asked. He looked down at his slate. "You say you're from…Salvage System? I don't know what kind of place that is, but I don't know that I'd ever want to visit. If I did, I'd mind my manners, that's for sure, ya know what I mean?"

"Hey, Sergeant," one of his men, standing nearby said, "that's that system the video shows. The one where they tore the invading fleet a new one and somebody put a sound track of really old music to it and put it on the Net. It's *awesome*."

"That was youse guys?" the sergeant asked, putting his slate away. "If those punks woulda' known that, they would have let youse three walk right on by. Enjoy your stay on Mars. Try not to beat anybody else up." He handed Gunny his card. "If youse do, make sure it's somebody I can arrest. To tell ya the truth, I don't want to have to try and put restraints on any one of youse three. It could be bad for my health, and I'm trying to make it to retirement."

They finally got in the Mars Bionics Corporation's hovercraft and the automated system took them to the corporate headquarters' guest housing. After making sure the brothers weren't going to have a pillow fight or anything else crazy in their room, Gunny went to bed. They had an appointment the next day after lunch, and he was eager to learn what could be done for the nerves in his legs.

* * *

Gunny, Hank, and Stan sat in the conference room with several human medical specialists, a Leethog doctor, the chief engineer, and the CEO of Mars Bionics himself, Jerock Guyland. The CEO set up the meeting with Gunny and the brothers after a long day of testing. Normally, he didn't involve himself with patients and clients, but this was different.

"To sum it all up," Jerock said, "The lower legs and feet you have are not bad. A little outdated, but not bad. The same goes for Stan. You can move your feet, rotate the ankles and move each toe. Stan could move his fingers before damage was done to the arm."

He continued, "Now, they don't have our patented synthetic skin, or in Stan's case, fur matching his, but that can be remedied. We can even upgrade to the most modern prosthetics if you would prefer. Doctor Jiltron assures me he can fix the nerve issues through surgery. He has revolutionized the procedure with his technique. Doctor Alice will assist with Stan." He used the shortened version of her Leethog name.

"If that means no more pain, then let's do this," Gunny said.

"But they will still be prosthetics," said the CEO. "You know, you don't have to keep using them. Replacing limbs with functional bionics is common here in Sol system. It has been for centuries."

"Well, yeah, that's what most people use in our corner of the galaxy," Gunny said. "To attach limbs permanently costs quite a bit more than I have saved." Stan and Hank nodded at the statement. They had plenty of credit, but they didn't know if they could afford that type of procedure.

"First, let me assure you," Jerock said, waving his hand dismissively, "your credit is no good here. I am covering all of Doctor Alice's fees for her visit to the Sol System, and we will not accept a single credit from members of your fleet. Period. I may even set up a small operation in your system just for situations like this. I have plenty of employees that would like to rotate through and see a colony grow. It would be a break from their normal work."

"I would go for a rotation," agreed Dr. Jiltron. "I think my wife and kids would love it."

"There is another option," Jerock said. "It involves more…substantial surgery. It has been performed successfully several times now with military members here in Sol System, and on one officer of the law. It is not something that is widely spoken of, you understand. As a matter of fact, if you agree, what you will receive is an upgrade compared to theirs, and it is not to be discussed openly, either."

"Yes!" Stan said. "I'll do it."

"Hold on there, Stan," Gunny said, tilting his head a little and looking across the table at the CEO and specialists. "What exactly are we talking about here?"

At this, the chief engineer leaned forward. "With Stan, we would have to take his arm almost to his elbow and integrate the artificial limb with his nerves. We would replace the entire forearm and hand. It will have synthetic skin and fur. The new hand will have near-normal sensitivity."

"You mean he will actually be able to feel his fingertips?" Gunny asked.

"Yes, well, his brain will think he is," answered Dr. Jiltron. Dr. Alice, the Leethog physician nodded along.

"What does near-normal mean?" Stan asked.

"It means you will have more sensitivity, not less," the CEO said, smiling, "and the bionic hand will be much stronger than a normal Leethog hand. The metal alloy used is as strong as any in the galaxy. The skin will also repair itself if it gets cut, to an extent. If too much damage is done, then you just come back and see us."

"Or the branch of the corporation we put on Salvage," added Dr. Jiltron. He really wanted to go to a frontier planet, at least for a little while. It would be like a six-month vacation.

"I'll do it," Stan said, again. He and his brother were both nodding their heads and grinning.

"What about my legs?" Gunny asked. "How much are we talking about?"

"The nerves are damaged both below and above the knees," De Jiltron said. "If we are going above the knee, then we are talking the entirety of your legs. We normally only replace the legs without going higher than the damage. That is what has been done for centuries. It is fairly common, as we have said. Instead, what we are proposing is the most advanced set of legs we have ever devised. We would replace them from the hips down, and even include the muscles in your buttocks."

"What? Why?" Gunny asked, alarmed.

"As a member of the military, you are familiar with battle armor that is servo-assisted?" the CEO asked.

"I am," Gunny said. "The marines can run faster, farther, and jump higher in them. Kicking in doors is no big deal either."

"Precisely," the engineer said. "In a singular fashion, the legs will be faster and stronger. In order for you to use them properly, the muscles in your buttocks will have to be able to keep up. Yours can't. No humans' can. So, we replace everything from the waist down."

"Everything?" Hank asked, eyes wide, looking at his brother. They both started elbowing each other and hissing in laughter.

"Not that," Dr. Jiltron assured Gunny. "You will be normal in that area. The last thing we need is your wife or significant other demanding to speak to Mr. Guyland about what his corporation did to you."

"Well that's something, anyway," Gunny said leaning back and thinking.

"That is good," Stan said. "Captain Opawn is a Task Force Commander. You do not want her coming here angry."

"No, we do not." Jerock laughed.

"How long will I be down?" Gunny asked. "And tell me about the power sources."

"Four weeks," said Dr. Jiltron. "We will be utilizing the best medical nanites in the galaxy for healing. The last few days, you will be getting used to your new limbs at full power. The limbs will have power cells that are rechargeable. We will, of course, provide extra cells, one of which you can store in a compartment in the thigh area and Stan will have an extra on the inside of his forearm. They last for days before they need to be charged."

"I wish I needed one," Hank sighed. "But I am glad my brother will be able to fly a ship again."

"We replace damaged limbs here," the CEO said. "We will not have any part in replacing perfectly good limbs. Some other corporations may do that, but not Mars Bionics. Sorry."

* * *

Gunny woke up to two Leethogs staring at his face. They were closer than they needed to be, and his eyes crossed trying to see them. Stan held a cup with a straw, and Gunny sipped, thankful for the water. After swallowing a few times, he asked, "How long have I been out?"

"Over a week," Hank said.

"We kept you sedated to give the nanites time to help you heal," said Dr. Jiltron from the other side of the bed. "How do you feel?"

"A little stiff," Gunny said. "My back aches a little from sleeping too long in one position."

"That is normal. How do your feet feel?" the Doctor asked.

"Fine, I guess," Gunny said moving a foot back and forth, "I…hey! I feel the blanket. I can feel the blanket with my toes!"

"You think you can," corrected Stan. "That is what they told me about my fingers."

"I don't care if I really can or I think I can," Gunny said with a grin. "I just know I feel it."

"Tomorrow, we'll have you stand," Dr. Jiltron said. "We'll keep your legs turned down until you get used to them. You will be surprised how strong they are."

"Yeah!" Stan said. "Look at this." The Leethog crushed the metal cup he was holding spilling water everywhere. "Sorry! Hey, that's cold."

"Watch the boots!" Hank said, jumping back. "They are my secret weapons, you know."

Gunny looked closely at the cup in the Leethogs' hand and realized he hadn't even noticed the metal hand was gone. Stan's hands looked the same. He lifted the covers and was amazed to see full legs with the same skin color as the rest of him. *I wonder if they'll tan*, he thought.

* * *

"Why are we leaving in the middle of the night?" Stan asked.

"Because I want to see if our friend learned his lesson, or if he has a new group of thugs with him, waiting on more victims," Gunny said, looking out the clear-steel windows of the hovercraft.

It had been a long month, but it was well worth it. Both Gunny and Stan were fully healed, and the bionics had integrated with their nervous systems with no real issues. They had both been assured, in time, except for recharging the power cells, they would hardly notice their new limbs weren't part of them. They would notice whenever they used the limbs to their maximum potential, however.

"Well, I'm flying the shuttle," Stan stated.

"That will be fine," agreed his brother. "I will enjoy the ride."

"Doesn't look like he's there," Gunny said as they passed the front of the star port's main entrance.

The automated hovercraft slowed to turn into the same place they loaded into it weeks earlier when Gunny saw the man. Gunny grabbed the handle for the door and the hover craft stopped immediately, causing the brothers to lean forward, unprepared for the emergency feature programed in the vehicle. They were stopped in the entry way to the parking area.

On the far side of the lot, the same thug was standing with his hand held out, but they were too far away to see if he had his knife. Six others were with him, surrounding two tall beings of an avian race. It looked like they were handing their belongings over to the men.

"You guys feel like another fight?" Gunny asked, stepping out of the hovercraft.

"Yes!" Stan said and got out right behind Gunny.

"Hold on!" Hanks said. "Let me get my boots off!"

As Gunny and the brothers approached the group, one of the avians saw them coming. Its look alerted some of the men. The leader turned and shouted, "You! You'll pay for last time. There's more of us now! Get them!"

The other six men turned toward them, which was a mistake, because the avian on the left sprang forward and dragged one of the thugs to the ground. As soon as the man hit the ground, the avian and its partner began stomping the man.

The largest of the group ran at Gunny. He wasn't holding a weapon; his size had been advantage enough his whole life. His size didn't matter when he caught a straight kick in the chest from Gunny. He dropped, wheezing with broken ribs, and Gunny ignored him.

Gunny turned and blocked a swing by the next man. He reached in and grabbed the man's jacket and pulled him down, introducing the man's face to Gunny's rising knee. The locals may have been tough, but they'd never dealt with anyone who could actually *fight*. The leader, smarter than the rest and realizing he was still outmatched, turned to run.

While Gunny was fighting two men, Stan stepped toward a man holding a long, flat metal bar, with tape wrapped around one end as a makeshift handle. The man swung hard at Stan's head, and he ducked the blow. He came up fast inside the man's reach, grabbed an offending hand with his new improved one, and squeezed. *Hard.* Shattered fingers turned nerveless, and he dropped the steel before collapsing to his knees, screaming in pain.

Stan looked over at his brother and saw he was handling his own. By this time, a second thug turned and ran, following his leader. Stan grabbed the discarded metal bar and flicked it with a snap of his wrist, sending it spinning the twenty feet into the running man's back. It struck him flat, and he went down hard.

Hank was having a *great* time. Every time his opponent thought he had an opening to cut the smaller Leethog, Hank would whip one of his boots around and slap the man's arm away. He saw his brother throw something out of the corner of his eye and figured it was time to stop messing around. He followed another arm slap with a serious blow from his other boot into the man's side, then hit him hard in the head with the first. The fight went out of that one.

Gunny ran the leader down before he could get to the entrance of the lot. When he caught him, he shoved him into the side of a hovercraft. The man dropped his knife when he hit, and it quit humming when it bounced, just like the last time. Showing a little restraint, Gunny kicked the man, but not hard enough to kill him.

Gunny reached into a pocket and pulled out a card. It was a nice hologram card; they didn't have those in Salvage System. "Hank, call the sergeant and tell him we have some more arrests for him, would you?" He handed the card over. "Let me get that back when you're done. We might be back one day and need it."

* * *

It was bright sunny morning, perfect for a run on the Beast. Gunny was waiting when Captain Brink walked up sipping a cup of coffee. "I tell you, I'm sure glad Bradford talked me into trying this stuff," Brink said. "After last night, I don't think I could function without it today."

"Lightweight," Gunny said laughing at the obviously hungover man.

"Whatever," Brink said, taking another sip. "I don't have years and years of building up a tolerance to drinking. Years...and years. Did I mention a lot of years?"

"If you didn't outrank me, Nate, I'd call you something a little stronger than lightweight." Gunny laughed again.

"Seriously, you look good," the captain said. "I can't see a limp and you're not hesitant when you step off. I see a big difference, but are you ready for this?" He indicated the course with a wave of the cup in his hand.

"About that," Gunny said, "I was ready to retire before because I couldn't complete the course. I can't ask my marines to do something I can't. Now, I can complete the course. The thing is, I'm not going to."

"What? Why?" Brink asked, concerned.

"Because I can't ask my marines to do something I can't," Gunny explained.

"Ok, now I'm lost. You're going to have to spell it out for me." Brink said, shaking his head.

"Everyone that runs this course hopes to set the record," Gunny explained. "Hell, I wanted to every time I ran it. My score was normally in the top ten and I wanted the record for myself. Walk with me, Sir." He walked past the first two obstacles to the first wall.

"If I run the course, you're going to record the time in that slate," Gunny continued. "When I finish, I'll hold the record time by a long shot. I can't ask my marines to chase that time. I couldn't catch it before my injury, when I wasn't servo-assisted with bionic legs. I can't ask them to."

"Now, I understand," the captain said. "What I don't understand is why you have us out here this early after only three hours of sleep if you knew you weren't going to run the course." He took another sip of his cooling coffee.

"I'm not going to run the Beast, but I am going to tackle this one obstacle," Gunny said indicating the wall in front of him.

Gunny ignored the rope, and with seemingly no exertion, jumped and grabbed the top of the thirteen-foot wall, swung his legs over, and from a sitting position dropped down. Brink, standing off to the side of it, saw everything. He tossed his slate into the air over his shoulder. "Definitely don't need this for you," he laughed. "Get off my course before you embarrass it. The last thing I need is a Tamed Beast."

* * * * *

Kevin Steverson Bio

Kevin Steverson is a retired veteran of the U.S. Army. He is a published songwriter as well as an author. He lives in the northeast Georgia foothills where he continues to refuse to shave ever again. Trim…maybe. Shave…never! When he is not on the road as a Tour Manager he can be found at home writing in one fashion or another.

\# \# \# \# \#

Tank

by J.F. Holmes

"Are you even human anymore?" she asked me. Brave, even with my gun pointed at her face.

"Honestly, I don't know," I answered. Apparently, I took too long thinking about it, because her kick caught my titanium ribs and *dented* them, despite my skin hardening around the blow. The soft vital organs behind the ribcage knew they were human enough, and pain rocketed through my body as I fired. The bullet headed for her face, but her face wasn't where it was supposed be. *Damn, she was fast.* Her second kick swept my legs out from under me, and I fell like the tank that I was. Hard.

As I lay on the ground, waiting for the pain override to kick in, she stomped on the gun and casually crushed it. I expected her other foot to come down on my vulnerable throat, but she just leaned down and smiled. It was a beautiful, bitter smile.

"I don't know if I am, either," she whispered and was gone.

I sat up, feeling the pain but not caring. O'Brian poked his pistol around the corner, scanning through his HUD. Seeing that the coast was clear, he stepped around and knelt by me as I breathed in and out deeply.

"You OK?" he asked worriedly, trying to watch everywhere at once while dealing with the information overload, a common issue for beat cops nowadays. The biometrics piped from HQ would have told him if I was seriously injured, as in, *penetrating wound*, but he still gave a shit, anyway.

"Yeah, just give me a minute. Gyros ain't as steady as they used to be." That was a 'borg joke; I didn't actually have gyros, but five years of combat left me feeling like an old man sometimes.

"Well," he said, grunting with the effort to help me up, "getting blowed up will do that to a guy. Ask me how I know."

"How do you know?" I said, groaning as I got to my feet.

He smacked my head. "Wiseguy. You got jokes. Now what do we do about Wonder Woman?"

I linked to his helmet, and, while facial recognition software burned through a search of the five hundred million people living in America, uploaded an incident report to the NYPD Special Services D-base. "We, Officer O'Brian, don't do shit. *I* go get her."

"Uh-uh. We're a team, you're my partner, and *we* go get her."

"Shit!" I groaned as her name and a face flashed up in my sight. She was a frigging scout—I knew it—though there was a big red CLASSIFIED and APPREHEND stamped across her Department of Defense official picture. Filled out the khakis pretty good, though, if you ask me. A severe Slavic face, high cheekbones, sergeant's stripes, and crossed rifles. Infantry. Could have been a model, and 'borgs made rank *fast*. Like O'Brian said, ask me how I know.

Sergeant First Class (R) Valentina Kruchenova, Date of Birth, 2021.06.13, entered service U.S. Army through Brooklyn MEPS on 2039.06.14, entry MOS 11B, end service 11B4G. Departed Service

2047.09.06. Full military disability pension. Her combat record was classified, but I did a DNA link and proved my identity, and the list dropped down.

Two tours with 2nd BN, 75th Ranger Regiment, including The Big Jump into Pretoria. Operation Blue Snake had been some *bad shit.* White farmers were being murdered wholesale as the country tore itself apart, and Blue Snake had been a clusterfuck from word go. Sixty percent casualties. I had been a dumb ass mechanized grunt at Fort Stewart when that happened, so I missed out.

After surviving that, she was recruited into Special Forces, but washed out. The cited reason was "not mentally qualified" which I read as "not a team player." That was when they were trying to rebuild Army SF after the endless War on Terror. You have to be both physically and mentally good to go, and the new SF had a 90% washout rate.

"What the hell are you whistling about?" said O'Brian. "Lemme see."

"No way, buddy, I'm just getting to the classified stuff, and Leavenworth is really cold in the winter. You don't want to see this." He made a coughing sound that sounded suspiciously like he was saying "bullshit" but stopped pestering me. Good partners were like that.

Next entry in her record was 'transfer to TRADOC, drill sergeant.' Speaking of bullshit, that was a common enough cover story for The Project. It had been a joke to those of us on the inside. I had been an "equipment tester" at the Army Research Lab in Massachusetts. Yeah, she was a scout. Loner, fast, augmented VR in her head, heightened senses, burner metabolism, and trained to hell and back in hand to hand.

"Fuck me," I muttered. She was going to be tough to catch.

"Only if you buy me dinner first," said O'Brian.

I ignored that; I had already bought him dinner plenty of times, and he never put out. Not that I was interested, too many Y chromosomes for me. I preferred mine with natural XX, like Miss Valentina here.

The rest of her record was more bullshit, piled higher and deeper, but each 'transfer' corresponded with an Operation I knew about. The hacker strike in Russia. Operation Wintermute, disabling the Chinese sub pens in the Spratly War. It had been a busy couple of years for both of us. Five years of running and gunning, until Congress shut us down.

"Hey, Tony? Earth to Tony."

I tuned back in; O'Brian was holding up one finger and pointing to the side of his helmet. Unlike me, he didn't have an internal visual display, just his HUD. "Commander is on the line, wants to know what's going on. Wants a visual."

I gave it to him. Zooming in on the three bodies sprawled out against the wall. I *thought* they were Caucasian, but it was hard to tell. Their faces had literally been smashed in, with the same kick that had dented my ribs. From their clothes, though, I guessed low level Russian mobsters. Muscle. I heard Captain Hernandez curse under his breath; he must have figured the same thing. Then he said, *"Last thing we need, another frigging gang war."*

"Yeah, and we've got other problems. She's a 'borg, like me. Well, not like me, she was a scout."

"And you were a tank, Corelli. You're the only 'borg, I've got right now, so go catch her while I give the Russians holy hell." Click. Not even a goodbye. Grumpy bastard, but if I had his job, I would be too.

"You drive, I gotta eat. Let's grab pizza from Enzo's."

O'Brian smirked and said, "You're a cop now, not a soldier. We're going to Bella Napoli for donuts. Like real cops."

* * *

"**10**-*13-UNCLE, 10-13-UNCLE, CORNER OF BROADWAY AND FORTY SEC-OND. SPECIAL UNIT ADAM NINER FIVE RESPOND.*" Uniformed officer in need of assistance. Could be anything, but they wanted us there. I knew what that meant.

We both said 'shit' at the same time, and I cued my mic. "Adam Niner Five, responding." Coffee cups were put down and donuts crammed into mouths, O'Brian stepped on the gas, and we started enough lights to give an epileptic a fit. I told him to kill them when we got within two blocks.

Flipping over to an internal com frequency, I listened to the report coming in over the net. "That's our girl," I said to O'Brian, but he was busy yelling at pedestrians to get out of the way. One gave him the finger; my partner rolled down the window and hit him with a pepper gun. The man cursed him in Swahili but got out of the way. Three blocks later, we were diverted. "*ADAM NINER FIVE, RE-POSITION FOR INTERCEPT*" and an icon started to flash in the map in each of our displays.

I had to admit, I felt damn human right then, as we went down Broadway, no lights on, Googazon cars being automatically directed out of the way. It was a thrill and always would be, almost as good as combat. One didn't move fast enough, and the massive Ford Thunder SUV clipped the bumper, sending plastic and ceramic flying, probably waking the driver. It careened onto its side, and O'Brian yelled "SORRY! BILL THE MAYOR!" as we blew past. He took a corner on two wheels, jumping the curb and wrecking a hot dog stand, splashing dirty dog water all over the hood.

"You're cleaning that up," I said to my partner as the wipers swished across the windshield.

O'Brian merely laughed and drove faster. "My family has been cleaning the City's shit up for two centuries, you stupid wop. Mostly you wise guys."

"Like an O'Brian ever made Detective."

"Like a Corelli ever lived to make it to Don!"

He was a good partner who took my oddities in stride. We worked well together, though the older cop knew to get out of the way when I went from Tony to The Tank. Like now, as a DNA sniffer screamed, and I saw Kruchenova out of the corner of my eye. I clicked to target follow, opened the door, and bailed out at fifty miles per hour.

As each part of my body hit the pavement, carbon nanofibers in my skin cells went rigid, forming a hard surface to protect the flesh underneath. I guess you could call it a combat roll, but I didn't come up firing. Instead, I stayed tucked and hit her just as she turned to run, sending her sprawling. Before the scout could recover, my iron hand locked around her ankle, and I lifted her into the air. I stood close to seven feet after my enhancements and could hold the small woman high enough that her hands flailed at open air.

"Valentina Kruchenova, you are under arrest. You have the right to—" and a shitload of electricity shot through my body. I fell over, my implants momentarily short circuited, right eye blinded, wires trailing from my mouth, one of the few vulnerable places for the taser prongs to pierce my skin.

"I don't think so, Tank!" she laughed, and this time she kicked me in the balls. Those were, fortunately or unfortunately, still human. Just a slight tap, still disabling, but I knew she could have smashed them to paste. If I had been down before, I was out, now.

"That...was a...dirty...move." I grunted and tried to move protesting muscles and joints to cover my groin. She laughed, a melodious laugh, and ran as O'Brian fired his pistol at her. I honestly don't think he was aiming too hard, though.

"You know," said my partner, kneeling down into my field of view, "I think she likes you. Really, I do. That's the second time she didn't kill you. I heard that in Italian families, that means love."

"Shut. The. Fuck. Up!" I managed to wheeze.

"*Adam Niner Five, Command, send update!*" Hernandez called. O'Brian answered.

"Dispatch, Corelli has been momentarily neutralized, and you don't pay me enough money to chase a 'borg."

There was a long moment while it seemed that we could actually hear Captain Hernandez cursing from all the way over at HQ on Randal's Island without a radio. Then he came back on, "*Adam Niner Five, from Command. Continue pursuit when able.*"

"I think he's mad. No, really. He was cursing in Spanish; I could hear it."

* * *

"So, where to next, partner?" O'Brian was driving a little more sedately now, only occasionally flashing his lights. "Take you over to Bellevue? Get you checked out?"

"I'm fine," I grunted. Truth was, I felt like complete shit, both physically and mentally. I'd had worse, like that time I caught part of an RPG in Venezuela, but this was an all-over body pain, like the worst charlie horse imaginable. I could barely move.

Mentally, I was having a tough time. I actually kind of sympathized with Kruchenova, in a way. With the war over and our program shut down, what were we 'borgs supposed to do? I had glimpsed my own file once, and a line at the top had caught my eye. Instead of being hired for a job, I had in reality been transferred from DOD to the Defense Reutilization Management Office. From DRMO, I had been transferred to DHS, and then to NYPD, as "surplus military equipment suitable for civilian law enforcement use." They tracked my transfers like I was hardware, not a person, and if that wasn't a big enough mind fuck, I didn't know what was. Normally, I kept it at bay, and enjoyed the work I did for the Special Services, but today it was really getting to me. Her question, *"Are you still human anymore?"* echoed in my brain. Was I?

"Hey Tim," I said, as we waited on the approach to the bridge. Speed wasn't necessary; she could have run to Brooklyn before our car could drive there.

"Yeah? Broad bugging you?"

"Well, she asked me if I'm even human anymore."

He seemed to think about it for a minute, waiting for the driverless mess to sort itself out. Then he said, "You still have a dick, right?"

"I do."

"Does it work?"

"Want to see?"

He glanced over at me with a smile, but then said, "NO. My point is, if you got a dick, and it works, you're human. Maybe catch this broad and put it in her, if she wants, and you have the ultimate answer."

"Life is very simple for you, isn't it?"

"Tony, my boy, the older you get, the simpler it gets."

I banged my hand on the dashboard out of frustration with the traffic, and at what was bugging me. Unbuckling my belt, I got out and walked up to where two aging hipsters were standing with their VR glasses on, trying to talk to a NYPD traffic bot. I shoved them out of the way and picked up the closest car. I tipped it on its side, then rolled it over like an egg. Then the next, and the next, making a lane for us. O'Brian leaned out the window and clapped as he steadily drove forward. As I climbed back into the Ford, he said, "Now THAT ain't human!"

"Not helping, Tim. Just drive. Take me over the bridge. We gotta go to her home turf; she knows the heat is on."

* * *

B rooklyn was, is, and always will be, Brooklyn.

My ancestors had started in the Lower East Side, fighting the Chinese south of Canal Street. When they had enough economic clout to buy townhomes in Brooklyn, they made the move rather than walk-up cold-water railroad flats. After that, Long Island and a small house in the suburbs, in towns with the names of vanished Indian tribes. Each successive wave of immigrants had followed them, and Brooklyn had become a patchwork of ethnic enclaves. When the Soviet Union fell, many ethnic Russians had fled the chaos to the Brighton Beach area, muscling out what was left of the Italians. I recited my history lesson out loud, as I had often done killing time in the army.

"Why are you telling me all this crap?" asked O'Brian as we crossed under the timeless arches of the Brooklyn Bridge. "Like us Irish give a shit, we just toss your asses in jail. We're the good guys."

"Oh yeah, well then what's a paddy wagon named for?"

"So, we like to drink, big deal!" he shot back.

I liked teasing him; he was a good partner. "What about the Westies?" I asked, referring to a particularly violent gang of Irishmen who terrorized the Lower West Side way back in the eighties.

"Everybody's got some fuckups in the family; you know that. Kinda like that cousin you hide in the closet. But again," he said, dodging through driverless cars onto the Belt Parkway. There were faster ways to get to Brighton Beach, but we both loved the view. "But again, why are you babbling about history?"

"Because I like to understand the situation I'm getting into. The territory. The culture," I told him. I had actually been reciting the history of the borough out loud.

He laughed and said, "The only thing you need to understand about the Russkies over there is that they'll shove an AK up your ass sideways as soon as talk to you."

"That's impossible; all firearms are illegal within the city and state of New York," I said flatly. That made us both crack up laughing. If the apocalypse ever DID happen, I'm fairly sure the Russians in Brighton, the Hasidic Jews in Williamsburg, hell, even the Dominicans in Washington Heights, would be able to field everything up to and including T-90 tanks and attack helicopters. Of course, they would use them on each other, mostly. It made the job interesting.

"Regardless, I just want to talk to them. Who is the main guy running shit over there now?" I didn't wait for his answer; O'Brian was a beat cop from Manhattan South. He could tell me which socialite was going to go to jail tomorrow, or if the Triads were set to go to war anytime soon, but Brooklyn was on another planet for all he knew about it.

"Says here," I said, accessing the Special Services Intelligence files on my HUD, "it's actually a Serb. Immigrant, former Serbian army Special Forces, name of Sasha Zivcovic."

"Gotta be pretty badass to make his way to the top of the Russian mob as a Serb," said O'Brian. I knew what he meant, but often the Serbs and Russians played that "all Slavs together" nationalistic bullshit. In private, though, knives came out.

"Well, we just want to talk to him. Talking is always better than shooting. Pretty sure the captain wants us to avoid a bloody mess."

My partner laughed again and said something about "political hack, naïve fucktard" under his breath. I wasn't sure if he was talking about Captain Hernandez or me. Probably both. Neither of us said much else, and I looked out over the bay. The Statue of Liberty was still encased in scaffolding, being repaired after anti-immigrants had blown off her arm. It was a wonder that the United States was still united, after all the bullshit of the last few decades. I supposed, though, that it looked that way from every part of our history.

He turned down the street that led to Zivcovic's 'hotel.' I'd never been there before, but I was sure the five NYPD cop cars parked out front, and the dozen or so officers in tac gear, wasn't an everyday thing. O'Brian flashed the lights, and pulled up next to a detective in plain clothes, his badge hanging around his neck as he sheltered behind a car. He rolled down the bulletproof window about five millimeters and said, "Hey, Costas, what's going on?"

"World War Five for all I know, though it's been quiet for the last five minutes." Then he went back to talking into his throat mike.

We looked at each other, and I blipped the Special Services freq. "Hey, Captain, this is Niner-Five, we're outside a Russian mobster's..." and O'Brian mouthed 'Serb' with air quotes, "...uh, a Mafiya HQ here at Brighton Beach, chasing down a lead on our target. There's some kind of shit going down, the Mobile Tactical Unit is holding a perimeter around the building."

"So, do your fucking job! I gotta meet with the mayor in two minutes. Wait, Russian? Zivcovic's place?"

"He's a Serb, not a Russ—," I started to tell him, but was cut off by a stream of Spanish curses. I waited him out but did hear the words *"putas"* and *"fucking organized crime unit jerk offs"* several times.

"OK," he finally said, *"enough of this interdepartmental bullshit. Go in there and figure out what the fuck is going on, on my authority."* Click.

I let out a whistle and stepped out of the car. O'Brian had heard the whole thing, and he started to get out too, but I waved him back. "I got this, let me do a recon first."

Detective Costas, who I guessed was from the aforementioned Organized Crime Task Force, just pointed at the front door and made a "be my guest" gesture. Great.

* * *

Correction: what was *left* of the front door. It had been shattered inwards, like someone had fired a breeching round into the heavy deadbolts. *Or kicked it with an augmented foot*, I thought. I don't know how she beat us there, probably ran the entire way while we sat in traffic. The door lay tilted on its hinges, and a body was crumpled on the floor behind it. An older Saiga Taktika shotgun lay ten feet away, and there was a single expended shell on the floor. I picked it up, pulled the drum magazine, racked the bolt, and then reloaded it. Being a tank was all well and good, but a shotgun beat the hell out of my Glock, and I wasn't going to hold back against these guys. If it came to it.

The foyer area had a set of glass doors with gold letter "Z"s etched into them. You know, I always thought my Italian family was bad enough, with plastic on the couches and gold horns hanging from our rear-view mirrors, but these Russian guys took the cake. The dead guy in front of me had five thick gold chains around his broken neck, and the hallway had gold filigree *everywhere*. Frigging showoffs.

In front of the glass doors, a young woman—a girl really—cowered, face stained with tears and running mascara, making her look like a raccoon. She was dressed like a hooker—micro skirt, pushup bra, the works—but couldn't have been more then sixteen under all that face paint. I flashed my badge, pointed to the door, and said into my mike, "One female civilian coming out."

"*Roger, single female,*" came back an unknown voice, and I assumed a precinct captain had shown up to take over the scene. He knew better than to tell me what to do. The girl ran past me like her ass was on fire. *Good.* I hoped she learned a lesson and went back to Russia or Long Island or wherever she had run away from.

Since the glass doors were closed, I headed up the stairs. I know, I should have cleared the entire ground floor, but time was of the essence. If there were wounded, they needed to get treated. Plus, I had an idea that my target was already gone since the gunfire had stopped, and the big boys usually lived at the top. Thankfully, the steps were marble and held my weight without creaking. One step at a time, shotgun raised, steady sight picture, rock solid. *I had become "The Tank," I could take fire and give it out at the same time. Fear me,* I chanted, like all my platoon mates had. It was to cover our own fear.

Another man lay at the third-floor landing. His face had been kicked into his brain. I know it's an old Hollywood cliché and basically bullshit for an ordinary person, nose driven into the brain, but this time, it was his entire face. A Sig-Sauer MPX-K, one of those stubby submachine guns, was in his hand, empty mag on the floor and new one clutched in his dead fist. Bullet holes stitched the wall, the last through a shattered window. She'd been moving too fast for him to track. I'd seen that a lot—tanks ate bullets, scouts outran them. I think, all in all, I'd rather have been a scout. Getting shot still hurt, even if they didn't penetrate.

I kept the shotgun up, but it turned out I didn't need it. The remnants of the Quick Reaction Force were sprawled on the fifth floor, three guys in tac vests and body armor, loaded for bear. I saw the damage before I saw them. The entire landing was chewed to shit, holes blown in the walls, shattered marble underfoot. I stepped over a dented, expended RPG that hadn't had time and distance to fuse after launch. They would have been better off using one with a frag warhead instead of antitank, but either way, it was too small a space and wherever it'd hit, it just bounced. The backblast would have been hell; I was surprised the building wasn't on fire. All that marble and brick, I guess.

One man was still alive. His legs were smashed to goo, and both hands crushed. That was probably out of spite, the hands. He was lying there, grunting in pain, biting back a scream. Tough bastard; I'll give him that.

"Which way?" I asked and got no response. "*Kakim Obrazom?*" I didn't know if he was Russian or Serb, but close enough for government work. He weakly pointed his chin up the stairs, and passed out. Or died. I never did find out and didn't care. Play games with the big boys, you take the losses as well as the wins.

At the top of the stairs was a short hallway that lead to an ornate wooden door. It too had been kicked open, but had swung back on heavy hinges, jamming shut. I stepped forward, flipping on my millimeter radar to see if anyone was behind it. One human figure, far end of the room slightly moving. Two more, one on each side of the doorway, carrying heavy metal. Could be more, though. In combat, I had learned to trust systems only so far.

Screw it, I could take anything smaller than an RPG. I slung the shotgun across my back, drew my Glock in case I had to be selective of who I killed, and started to run. The good thing about being a tank is that, well, I might not have speed, but I sure as hell have mass and momentum. The door was thick, but it shattered like a block of ice being hit by a sledge hammer.

I spun a full 360 as I came through, my pistol firing twice, then twice more, slaved to the targeting reticle in my right eye. Rounds bounced off me, and the second shooter was actually killed by the first, hammered backward even as my shots hit him in the face. As I came back around, the bastard on the far side of the room fired.

The first round hit me in my side, and I grunted in surprise at the pain, like an electric needle zipping under my skin. The second caught my forearm, probably glancing off the titanium infused bones, coming out and then burying itself in my deltoid. Fucker had a Barrett rail gun with sabots; that shit was supposed to only be on the DARPA research shelves. This might get me killed, but I was committed and had been wounded before. Lowering my shoulder, I crashed into the desk and shoved it up against the man crouched behind it. With a yell, he dropped the rail gun, useless in close quarters, drew some sort of knife, stepped in and then danced way from me. His two swings had hit me, one across the arm and the other across my chin, close to my neck, and I dripped blood on the ground. That knife had some kind of mono-molecular edge that could get through my skin and cut my throat. Stepping back, I lowered the Glock, rock steady, targeting crosshairs locked on his face, my arms slaved to the aim point.

"Sasha Zivcovic, you are under arrest. You have the right to remain silent."

"Ya, ya, whatever. I'll be out of jail in twenty-four hours, Tank," he taunted. "Then I will call a man with another gun like that," as he gestured to the bent and broken plastic and ceramic, "and he will shoot you dead from a thousand meters."

"Where's the girl?" I asked. He was right, I knew. He would be out of jail, and I'd be dead, but twenty-four hours was a long time.

The mobster shrugged, a fatalistic gesture. "You might try the ocean. She loved it there as a child, goes there to think."

"Child?" I asked, and a light went off in my mind. "Your daughter?"

"Yes. She is mad at me that I make her join army and become like she is. Dutiful, she did this, but now she is a no one, not a human anymore. Like you. Both fucking machines."

"I'm more human than you, scumbag. Pimp, drug dealer, thug. I've read your file. How many have you killed on your way to power?"

His gaze was hard, a tough man in a tough world, who thought he had the answers. "I don't remember, after the first one. But I did it for me and my family, not some fat politician sitting in office thousands of kilometers away. What was it for you, *Tank*, that made you become killing machine? That made you give up, how you say, being human?"

"Why did she come here?" I ignored the implications in his question, about why I did what I did. I didn't know myself anymore.

"Why did you push her?" He still held the knife, perhaps waiting for me to tire, but I could hold this position for days. I heard Captain Hernandez demanding a sitrep over my internal, but I ignored him.

"Because she would make a great asset to my organization. The ultimate enforcer. She came here to kill me, but I guess she didn't have the heart. I am very disappointed, not such the killer as I would have expected." He had been edging closer as we talked, trying to distract me with his talking. The hole in my arm was already sealing, but blood had dripped onto the floor, and maybe he thought he had gotten me worse than he had. The one in my side I didn't have time to think about, but my status bar was only yellow in my vision. His next slow step took me within reach of that foot-long blade.

"Do what you must," he said, and for a brief instant, I saw the pain of a father who had lost a child in his eyes. Then he lunged, fast.

I shot him.

* * *

"Jesus, Mary, and Joseph!" said O'Brian as I sat down on the bumper of an EMS truck, waving the technician away. I would be OK; my systems were repairing my body as we spoke. I just needed time, and a shitload of food. He knew this and handed me the bag of donuts. I mashed them all together and shoved them in my mouth, almost inhaling them. My partner was always amazed when I did this, expecting me to choke to death.

"No gag reflex," I said, swallowing again.

"Hey, can I set you up with my gay cousin? He'd love you." It was an old joke between us, but in the guy code, it helped to hide concern. It was his way of letting me know he was worried.

"No, thanks. Can I bang your sainted sister?" I gave back to him as I licked the bag.

"She's pregnant again. Go for it."

I took a deep breath and stood up, looking at the holes in my uniform. The one in my arm matched the one in my side, which had gratefully just been a score that glanced off my rib and went back out. Hurt like a bitch though. The one in my chest worked its way out and fell onto the sidewalk. That gun, whatever it had been, would have drilled me if he managed to hit me center mass. The knife wounds stung, but they hadn't been deep, just a surprise.

"Let me ask you a question," said O'Brian, and I knew what was coming. He wasn't stupid; he'd had been a cop a long time. "I know that when we catch this girl, she's going down for at least three murders. Why would she shoot the bossman, though? Everything else was hand or foot strikes." I had told him that Zivcovic was dead, gunshot to the face. I hadn't lied, really.

It was his way of telling me that he thought I had fucked up. He knew I had popped Zivcovic but didn't agree with it. In his heart, my partner was a lawman. In mine, I was a soldier. Killing Zivcovic had been a tactical decision, and it could be argued that he would have killed me first, but the courts would keel haul me. Frigging New York City liberals. I had heard the Special Branch Captain yelling at me through my internal coms for about five minutes now, demanding updates. Screw him.

"I dunno, she probably has some serious dad—," I started to say, then stopped, and lamely finished, "serious issues." I don't know why I didn't tell him about their relationship. I accessed the internal storage chip in my head, ran a military subroutine that played static over the hard drive recording, and piped the same virus back to the dBase at Special Branch. Might get caught, might not, but I think the captain would just write it off. It's not like a cop had never deleted bodycam footage before.

O'Brian shot me a look, guessing what I was doing, and just shook his head. "So where to now?" he asked, standing up. I tried to and sat back down. I needed time for the calories to catch up with my burning metabolism.

"Gimme a minute, Tim. Can you deal with Hernandez?" He nodded and turned away, making a report to the captain.

For my part, I sat and thought while my head cleared, running over the whole thing in my mind. She could have killed me, twice. Kicks that would crush a normal skull were strong enough to jelly my brains, regardless of how reinforced the bone was. All the dead Mafiya goons could be written off as combat, where bad shit just happened. After all, you have to get to your objective alive, or there was no point, and she probably had as little regard for the men who worked for her father as I did.

Which left, what? When we first started, I thought she was a maniac killer. One of my own, gone bad like a rabid dog. The veteran who snaps was a common enough trope, and not really true, but it felt like there was more to this than that. I had to tell her, somehow, that her father was dead. Maybe then she could find some peace and stop. After that, well, we would see. I started formulating a plan in my mind.

"Coney Island," I said to my partner, who looked over, nodded, and signed out of the conversation in the middle of a loud ass chewing.

He grimaced, and said, "Looks like I'm gonna be working traffic on the Triborough bridge until I retire. This better be worth it, Tony. Why Coney Island?"

"Something her dad said, just before he died." I took a deep breath, and said, "I'm going to bring her in," and was met by an incredulous stare over the roof of the car.

"You gotta be joking me. She almost killed you, like twice, and wasted the shit out of those guys there. I was only kidding!"

I shook my head and said, "I think I know what makes her tick. She's angry, sure as shit like I was, and she doesn't have a home. You know, like you guys gave me." He just shook his head and climbed in. I didn't buckle up, since I didn't know if I would have to bail again.

* * *

It was dark, or as dark as it ever got in the City. We sat in the parking lot of a White Castle, eating sliders and waiting. We both figured that she would wait until dark to come out, keeping the net from grabbing her mug for an ID.

"You know," I said, "it was easier in the old days." My mind kept going back to how long it took Zivcovic to admit he was dead. The round had entered his throat, a perfect kill shot just under his chin, just as he started to dart forward and stab. His spinal cord must have been cut instantly, but the look of hate and despair in his eyes bored into me.

"Whadda ya mean?" O'Brian asked, dipping fries into his milkshake and cramming them into his mouth.

"Well, like a hundred years ago. My ancestors took care of their own business, and yours could break some heads to keep the peace."

"You read too many books, Tony. Sure, it worked, but it wasn't the law, you know? It was just tribal bullshit. Now here's me, and here's you. We're New Yorkers, nothing more or less, and we do our job to keep the world moving. Step outside of the City, and we're outsiders, you know?"

"So, different tribes now. I see your point," I said. "I lost my tribe when I got out of the army, left the unit." Maybe it was something that might make sense in regard to Kruchenova. Maybe she was as lost as I had been, and I wondered what she had been doing for the last two years.

"Yep, you're an NYPD tribesman now." O'Brian leaned over and punched me in the arm, then made a great show of waving his hand and muttering, "OW!"

"There she is!" I said, catching a glimpse of a slim figure moving down the street, wearing the same hoodie as before. She kept to the shadows, but my enhanced vision easily picked her out. There was no mistaking that feline movement, either. Her scout enhancements had also made her, in addition to more than human—or less than—more of a woman, too, in the way she moved. I liked it.

O'Brian keyed on the movement too. Being a cop for twenty years taught you a lot about urban combat, whatever he wanted to call it. He looked over to me, and I held up a hand with a wait gesture. "You sure?" he said, and I nodded.

"If she comes back out alone, just let fly with that scattergun and call for all the backup you can get." There was a Special Services Tactical Team, run by a buddy of mine, a block away, and they probably had eyes on her too. No one, enhanced or not, can take a .50 caliber AP round to the head and walk away, and she wasn't THAT fast.

We had taken a chance that she would go to Coney Island, but it really was the nearest beach, and if she had grown up here, well, people do what they know. Not much of a beach, but the pier would be the place; the boardwalks had all been wrecked by Hurricane John five years ago and had never been fixed. It was the closest thing to actually being out on the ocean there was. Waiting here had been a slim chance, but it had worked. With her main plan shot, if she even had a plan, Kruchenova, or Zivcovic, or whatever her name was, would need to think and regroup, and what better place to think? Those of us who had grown up near the ocean, even in the boroughs of the City; it never left us. Best place, the beach at night, and she needed that time.

I waited until she had disappeared around a corner and stepped out of the car. In my hand was a barometric area denial weapon, something we just called a 'thud,' after the sound it made. It was basically a bean-bag gun, but the "bag" in this case was a circle of air, compressed almost to a solid, expanding out to cover a ten-foot diameter circle at twenty feet. It was non-lethal, in theory. At ten meters, optimal for crowd control, it was like getting swatted to the ground with a giant, solid pillow. Set that sucker off within a few feet, though, and it was like getting punched with a battering ram. In my left was another toy I had borrowed off the Tac guys, called a T-whip. Like a taser, is sent a jolt of energy through your body, but instead of firing it, it really was an actual whip, with contacts along ten feet of it, and I was trained to use it. I bet that I could move it in enough of an arc that I'd catch her, while a taser might miss, and once wrapped in it, the thing didn't let go.

I swung wide of the corner she had disappeared around, ducking down one street over and flying a microdrone a block ahead. It was clear; though a scout could mask their body heat, I had it set to pick up the electrical rhythm of heartbeats. It would have to get within a hundred feet of her, and was no good through walls, but I was sure she was out on the street. Or I hoped she was, or else there was no point. Each person that registered showed up on my screen, overlaid with the visual picture. I finally picked her up, a hundred meters ahead, and moving slowly though a scattering of people. The height parameters and body mass matched my AI evenly. The weather had turned nasty—which was good—less civilians around and probably not anyone close to the beach. As I expected, she headed toward the pier, and I followed at a distance. "You watching this, partner?" I asked, and O'Brian came back with "*10-4, good buddy.*" Civilians, geez.

When I first ran into her, her head had been exposed, but this time the hood was pulled up. A tactical mistake on her part, to cover over her ears and dull her hearing. She stood, fifty meters away, back to me, leaning up on a rail that had been set up to block access to the wrecked part of the pier. The far end, what used to stick out into the ocean, was a mass of rotting pilings and broken timbers. Still, though, where she was standing was solid and a good ten feet above the Atlantic breakers as they rolled in. I stepped from the street and onto the pier, flashing my badge to a couple that stood there watching the waves, making a little shooing motion. Typical New Yorkers, minding no one's business. They didn't even hesitate.

Neither did I. When I got within ten feet, the waves crashing and concealing my approach, I said nothing. Just hit her with the whip around her legs, trying to immobilize her before that lighting speed kicked in. The hundreds of micro needles penetrated through her jeans and delivered 0.75 microcoulombs of electricity to the body. She went rigid as a board and collapsed sideways, cracking her head on the rail. Shit, I didn't mean that to happen, but what followed was even worse. Long blonde hair spilled out of the hood, and Kruchenova wore hers short and black, in a soldier's cut.

Both feet hit me in the left shoulder. I had turned and hunched my back against it, because I knew that attack would be instantaneous, and I caught a blurred figure flipping up from under the deck of the pier. Rolling with the hit, I continued the motion and let fly with a backhand that caught her a glancing blow on the hip. The scout flew ten feet through the air and tripped over the decoy woman, sprawling flat. I may not be fast, but when I hit something, I hit HARD, and she didn't have the protection I did. Still, my left shoulder howled with pain, the joint damaged. My right hand dipped and came up with the Thud. She started to say something, and no fucking around, I fired.

Kruchenova leapt straight up in the air, the bottom of the air slug catching her feet and flipping her head over heels. She landed with a crunch directly on her face, and I dove on her with my full weight. The air went out of her in a whoof of exhalation, and my arms snaked under her shoulders and behind her neck, pinning her face to the tar-stained boards. When you get held by a tank, you get held, no shit.

"ENOUGH!" I yelled in her ear. With my augmentations, I weighed almost four hundred pounds, and she couldn't have been pushing one thirty, even if most of it was enhanced muscle. I wrapped my legs around her waist in a scissor as she struggled, and slowly started to squeeze. Her bones were tougher than a normal human, but nothing compared to mine, and I could imagine the pain on her internal organs, which were wholly original.

"ENOUGH!" I yelled again and started to force her head downward. A little more, and I could snap her neck. She was crying now, and still struggling.

"DO IT! JUST FUCKING KILL ME! I AM IN HELL!" Tears were flowing down her face, onto my arms, and I felt great wracking sobs run through her body.

I didn't let up the pressure, because this was one sneaky broad, but I whispered in her ear. "Your father is dead. Come in from the cold. Join me. Be a cop. Be human again."

"Fuck you, monster," she spat. "We're both going to hell." She went limp in my arms, then tried to headbutt me. I pinched my arms together and choked her out. Laying her on the boardwalk, I slipped cuffs on her wrists and ankles, then turned to check on the other woman.

* * *

"Can you shut her up?" asked O'Brian. Our prisoner had been steadily cursing us all the way across Brooklyn, and I almost did regret not taping her mouth.

"No, I need to talk to her." I slid the partition back and looked at her. Her blue eyes gazed back at me. She really was stunningly beautiful, except for a vicious burn scar across her cheek.

"I want you to listen to me, Valentina. I'm proposing a deal. You come work with us at Special Services, and everything you did gets buried."

O'Brian started to protest, but I just held up my hand, not looking away from her. On her face was such a sense of loss, and a haunting hollowness that I knew all too well. The things we had done in the wars…

"Listen, I know you. I *am* you. I'm a tank, you're a scout, but we're both 'borgs. There are good people here in the City, decent people, and we can protect them from the guys like your father."

At the mention of him, she closed her eyes. "Did he suffer?" she asked.

"No, but he died fighting. Almost got me."

Tears rolled down her face, and she whispered, "I loved him, you know. Even as fucked up as he was."

"I know. I think he knew it too. Sometimes life makes us into people that are trapped by the choices they make. Like us, us 'borg. But I'm offering you a chance."

She said nothing for a long moment, then quietly said, "I don't want to kill anymore. Do you understand me? God, I am so tired." Tears were flowing down her face, her laughter gone.

I reached through the partition and touched her face. "Valentina, listen to me. Can you feel that? I can. Your skin is warm, and your tears are wet. You asked me if we're human. Machines don't cry, don't feel pain, or loss. We do."

She lifted her head and gazed back at me, eyes so blue they looked almost white, and smiled weakly. "Is your partner always such a sappy shithead, Officer?"

"Tim O'Brian, Ms. Kruchenova, but you can call me Tim. And yes, he is generally full of shit."

She did laugh then, and it was beautiful, even with the blood splattered across her face. "You know, my father originally wanted me to infiltrate the NYPD and work for him that way. I joined the army to get far away from him, but he still pulled my strings like a goddamned puppet. Yet here I am, back in the City. I would look good in blue, don't you think?"

She would, too. "Captain Hernandez is a hardass, but fair. If he can use you, and you're loyal to him, he'll go to the ends of the Earth for you."

"And the scum I killed? What about them?"

I looked at O'Brian, and he stared back. "I didn't see nothing, Tony. Saw you get your ass kicked by a little girl, but that's about it."

Turning back to her, I saw the desperate hope in her eyes. "Listen, Valentina. It's not like the Unit, it's different. We have lives, and hopes, and we do good things. You *are* human, like I am."

She said nothing for a minute, and I thought about the wreck of her life. Then she laughed. It was a beautiful, human laugh. "OK, I will take you up on your offer, Tank. You can clear things with the army?"

"Probably. The Special Services has to deal with the DoD a lot and has a good relationship with them."

* * *

We were headed up FDR drive when they caught up to us. I don't know who they were, exactly, since I've been out for more than two years, but when I called it in to Captain Hernandez, he just told us to cooperate.

"Captain," I said, as the four SUV's boxed us in, "what is this shit?

"Just play nice, Tank. They're Feds, is all I know. Military, from the look. Be care—" Then the carrier wave went dead, and my data signal disappeared. Jammed. O'Brian looked at me, and I shook my head. He needed to stay out of this. Through the window, I saw four guys get out of the front two vehicles, big panel vans. Further down the road, all the driverless cars had disappeared, and I suspected that it was the same behind me. Googazon was deep in bed with the Feds, and pretty much did whatever they asked.

The sides dropped down on both the vans, just enough to show two 20mm autocannon, angled to catch the squad car in a cross fire. A half a dozen troopers in full body armor, two up-armored, and two guys in business suits. I was more scared of the suits than all the hardware pointing at me. My headset crackled to life. *"Officer O'Brian, step out of the car, please."*

"Not your fight, partner. They'll let you walk."

He looked at me, then back at Kruchenova. "Dinner, my house, Friday night. Lisa has another girl she wants him to meet, but I think Tony has the hots for you."

I laughed. "I'd rather fight these guys, honestly, than deal with another one of your wife's 'blind dates.'"

"Meatloaf. Come on!"

I sighed. "OK, but tell her I'm bringing a friend. Get outta here." He saluted me and slid out the door. I took a deep breath and watched him walk past the Feds. They ignored him, never changing their aim.

"Master Sergeant Corelli, please remove Sergeant First Class Kruchenova from the back seat and lay her on the ground." Yep, it was the Army. Fuck them.

I looked back at her, sitting up now in the back seat. "Go," she said, with resignation in her voice. "Maybe I'll see you after they let me out of Leavenworth. You're a good man, Tank." She smiled, and it was dazzling. I reached back and touched her face one more time, human contact for both of us. Then I opened the door.

I stepped out and held up my hands. "Listen," I said, as loud as I could. "I've made a life here, she can too. Let her be a cop."

The suits walked toward me, one white guy and one black guy, of course. Probably program managers from Weyland Corp, the contractors who had turned us into 'borgs. I lowered my arms and stepped aside; I was taking no chances with these guys. Suits scared me more than guns. White Corporate was tapping on a device on his wrist, and the order came out. *"Subject confirmed, carry out protocol."* Black Corporate raised a pistol that I knew for sure would go through the armored windows like that railgun had gone through my arm and put his hand on the squad car door. "Sergeant Kruchenova, you're to come with us."

I saw the 20mm swing from their crossfire positions and line up on the squad car. She squirmed through the window between the front and back, cuffs falling off. The key that I had dropped through stood out from the metal like an engagement ring. In a flash of augmented speed, she was out the far door and running. I swear I saw her legs blur.

They tried to track her with their fire, the cannon hammering away. As I suspected, the Tac guys opened up on me, but I squinted my eyes and shrugged off the 6mm rounds like they were sleet as I stood and watched. Both the suits were torn to shreds; I guess corporate loyalty only went so far. The cannons chewed their way through a concrete support, trying to catch her, and the scout stood behind it, looking at me and smiling. She held up three fingers, then put her hand to her head in a classic telephone gesture. I dialed in, heard her say, "*See you at dinner, Tank!*" over our internal combat frequency, then she turned, gave them both fingers, and shot into the air with the grace of an Olympic gymnast. Sergeant First Class Valentina Kruchenova, ne Zivcovic, disappeared into the river with hardly a splash, and I clapped my hands together. Bravo. Fucking Bra-vo.

It got really quiet, really fast. The loudest thing there was my smile. The 20mm cannons slowly turned toward me, and I got ready to charge. Tank or not, those would surely eat me for lunch. Sirens were starting to get closer; the feds might think they're hot shit, but you don't go throwing heavy artillery around in *my* city without starting up a shit storm. The cannons swiveled down, and the panels closed, while the tactical unit guys safed their weapons and got back in. As they packed up their vans, one of them shouted to me, "Be a good boy, Master Sergeant Corelli. We'll be watching you!"

"That's Officer Corelli, of the NYPD!" I shouted back. "Come back to my city, and I'll have you arrested!" Human indeed, and the memory of ice blue eyes and a beautiful smile stayed in my mind. Dinner was going to be...interesting.

* * * * *

J.F. Holmes Bio

J.F. Holmes is a retired Army Senior NCO and Iraq War veteran. He is the owner and editor of Cannon Publishing, and has 17 books of his own published. Two were 2017 Dragon Awards Finalists. Find him at www.amazon.com/author/jfholmes.

# # # # #

Cradle and All
by Quincy J. Allen

Part 1

Rock-a-bye baby, in the tree tops
When the wind blows the cradle will rock
If the bough breaks, the cradle will fall
And mother will catch you, cradle and all

* * *

Doctor Maria Magdelain Fujimoto didn't know how she could save them, and it was killing her. She wouldn't let Paragon Savage Genetics turn the Gen3s into slaves like the others.

She stared at the thirty rows of maturation chambers lining the south side of Lab 4, deep within the bowels of PSG headquarters. *Her* lab, for all intents and purposes. It was dimly lit, with the sterile, white walls a pale backdrop to what she'd always considered a work of art. Each chamber was illuminated by a potent overhead spotlight that highlighted a gurgling cocktail of blue amniotic fluid designed to promote the rapid growth of mammalian tissue. Each chamber looked like a living sapphire, with swirls of bubbles rising to the top.

It was the humanoid shadow within, however, that was the true gem. The genies, as most people called them, looked almost like shadowy mermaids in deep blue water, dancing in syncopation with one another. The auto-programmed motions built musculature, increased flexibility, and hardwired each subject's motor-neurons so they could emerge from the chambers capable of virtually any physical task required.

But they would also be slaves.

A complex web of emotions clutched at her heart—love, fear, powerlessness—and all three vied for supremacy within her. They were *her* creations, and she'd sold her soul to the devil to bring them into existence. She just couldn't figure out how to break their chains of bondage, and it weighed on her. She'd planted seeds all along the way, since before she created them, but she'd been waiting for something—a catalyst—that would give her the opportunity she needed.

"How is Selina?" Maria asked, glancing at Altra.

The slim, distinctly feminine robot, whose white outer casing gleamed like alabaster in the dim light, turned its head toward Maria as it strode after her with a soft, precise clicking of silicon on tile. ALTRA, or Artificial Lab Technician, Researcher, and Assistant, wasn't intelligent in any Asimovian sense of the word. It was, however, an exceedingly functional example of humanoid robotics, capable of executing a wide array of both routine and complex tasks.

"Subject G3FØØ is in her maturation chamber in Lab 1, absorbing the infiltration and assassination skills Mr. Sakai ordered. She should be out next week." Maria had always found it amusing that Altra never referred to them by the names she had given them.

"I don't suppose he communicated why he made the request, did he?" Maria asked. She knew the answer, but she liked teasing her assistant.

"Of course not, Doctor. Mister Sakai does not confide in me. I have concluded that he does not care for robots."

Maria was surprised by Altra's conclusion. "I suspect it is *me* he does not care for, Altra," Maria said. "Don't take it personally."

Altra stared at Maria with the glowing, green sensor orbs that served for her eyes. "Noted, Doctor," she said. "But I am incapable of taking anything personally, as I am not a person."

"Sometimes I wonder," Maria said under her breath, and then she sighed. She was concerned about what Sakai might have in mind for the prototype of the Gen3s. She was accustomed to him keeping secrets, but he'd never requested that one of her children be modified before. She shook her head and then stared down at the readouts on the console in front of her. She'd already checked half of the consoles dedicated to the maturation chambers. There was one console for each row of chambers, and they served two distinct purposes. The first was as a biometric data monitor as it sustained the subjects with a complex mixture of nutrients, growth hormones, and pharmaceuticals that allowed for hyper-accelerated development. The second was to perform the indoctrination process, which did much more than provide them with motor control. Combined with the basic mobility programming, the subjects would come out of the chambers with virtually any skill set PSG required.

Every Gen3 would receive a spectrum of hand-to-hand and weapons-based combat disciplines. They would also learn the operation of vehicles, from automobiles and grav-cars to interface craft and starships. Security, anti-terrorism, and assassination skill sets were also on PSG's menu of available options.

PSG was preparing to corner the market on selling private armies of genetically modified soldiers, for Maria's children were the most advanced and capable genies to have been bred. They were stronger, smarter, and faster than not only any human, but any genie bred outside the walls of PSG—as Marketing proudly stated.

A soft chime from the elevators at the far end of the lab drew her attention. The doors opened, and Maria was surprised to see Richard Cabrillo step out. He had the dark hair and slim features of the inhabitants of Montoya III, descendants of Colombian forbearers who had settled the capital world of the Republic of Escobar.

"Good morning, Richard," Maria called across the lab, a bit confused. He was her immediate subordinate, and a man she found at least mildly distasteful. He did not normally come down to the labs, especially not before lunch. She had inherited him when she first took the job with PSG. He was a competent geneticist, but nowhere near Maria's league. She'd always found him to be only mildly intelligent, but he made up for it by being well-suited to dealing with the sales department and all outward-facing interactions with clients and the military. She tolerated him, because he was a buffer between herself and the outside world. She had always suspected he resented her being given the job of Senior Researcher, but she'd never been entirely certain. "What can I do for you?" she asked as he walked up.

"I was hoping to get an update on where things are down here," he said with an almost sincere smile.

"I was just doing a check on the Gen3s," Maria said a bit impatiently. "Is this something that can wait until later?"

"Julio asked me about where we were at with the new batch, and you know how he gets," Richard said. He almost sounded apologetic.

Maria sighed. "Altra, would you give him a status report?" she asked, glancing at her assistant. Without waiting for an answer from either of them, she moved to the next console in line.

"Of course, Doctor Fujimoto," Altra said, its head turning around completely to face Richard as her body walked forward to maintain a consistent distance from Maria. "The Rhinocerotidae,

Canis, and Panthera subjects of the Gen3s are in nominal condition. We will be initiating the educational procedures tomorrow. As you can see," she added motioning with her slender arm toward the chambers, "Since inception, only nineteen percent were lost to still-births and genetic anomalies, a twenty percent improvement over the Gen2s now being trained by the military. As of this morning, the Gen3s are ready to begin the indoctrination process, and I have up-dated the consoles with the new training protocols devised by Doc-tor Fujimoto."

"Very good," Maria said. "Thank you, Altra."

"Of course, Doctor Fujimoto," it replied.

Maria glanced at Richard with an *are you satisfied?* look on her face and then returned to the console.

"You'll be happy to know there hasn't been any more fallout from the two escapees a couple weeks ago," Richard said, obviously trying to make conversation. "And we finally got the report on what happened from that general."

"Did you?" Maria asked. She didn't look up from the console, but she did want to know the official story. "What did it say?"

"Well, basically, we're treating it as a successful implementation of the Methionine Protocols, but that's more spin than reality, if you ask me. Apparently, it was subjects G1C34 and G1F17 who escaped a small military installation on the other side of the city. They were shot multiple times during the escape and, apparently, fell into the *Sagrado del Corazon* river. The major involved said that he saw several of those big reptiles in the river where they went in and assumed both subjects were eaten. Neither of their bodies were discovered. We assured him that, even if they survived, the Methionine Protocol would have stopped their life functions within a matter of three to four days without the enzymatic injections, so we're in the clear." She felt Richard peering at her. "It's a good thing we have the protocol in place with all three generations. They're a safety net for both PSG and our clients. Wouldn't you agree?" he asked.

"Absolutely," Maria replied flatly, her eyes firmly focused on the screen. She was doing her best to show no emotion.

"The PSG board approved my idea to provide the military with a canine and feline replacement from the Gen3 pool at no additional cost, once they were ready, of course."

"I'm sure they were very happy with the free upgrade," Maria replied. She made an adjustment to the console and moved to the next one. And then she stopped, stood up straight, and looked at him like she would an anomalous piece of data.

"Do you ever struggle with the moral implications of what we're doing?" she asked. "That we're creating slaves?"

Richard got a hurt expression on his face and tsked. "Slave is such an *ugly* word. I'm surprised to hear it coming from you," he added, "considering you created them."

"A means to an end," Maria said, trying to look bored, but his answer troubled her deeply. She let out a heavy sigh and turned from him, heading toward her office. Altra followed, while Richard kept pace not far behind. Maria entered her office, crossed the gulf between the door and her massive, maple wood desk, and sat down in a large, leather office chair. Two large monitors occupied the left-hand side, and a wafer-thin keyboard lay directly in front of the chair.

Her office was a complex contrast to the stark, dimly lit lab outside. Bright, warm lighting filled the space as well as a flawless sense of Feng Shui. Three low-backed chairs sat across the desk from hers. There was a low couch and divan in one corner, several tall potted trees in another, and the wall across from the desk held a five-hundred-gallon salt-water tank full of indigenous corals and sea life. A wide, wall-mounted waterfall filled the room with a subtle gurgling noise reminiscent of the maturation chambers.

Richard took up a position directly in front of her and did not sit down.

Maria raised an eyebrow. Was he playing with her? What was he in the lab for? And his answer was eating at her.

"I just don't see how you can be so dispassionate," Maria said, and she couldn't keep the slight edge of accusation out of her voice. "Yes, I did create them, but they're still sentient. It has to make you stop and consider the implications at least once in a while."

"Does it?" he replied dryly.

"I would certainly hope so," she said.

"You know me, Maria." He gave her a Cheshire grin. "I'm all about the bottom line. As long as nobody goes to jail for what we're doing, I'll leave moral philosophy to the eggheads at the university." His eyes shifted from her to the gray stone waterfall behind her. Like a large piece of art, it was textured with vertical lines across its entire surface. "I was wondering, does that thing come off easily, or is it built into the wall?"

Maria was startled by the change of subject. She turned and looked at the waterfall. What was he up to?

"It's anchored, but it can be removed," she replied, turning back to him. "Why?"

"Oh, no reason. I was just curious." He looked at his watch and gave her an almost expectant look. "So, the plan is to fire up the indoctrination processes tomorrow?"

She frowned. "Yes," she replied slowly. "I'll be coming in early to initiate the protocols myself."

"Will you?" he asked. The smile remained. "And you don't expect any issues with the new batch of educational programs?"

"No," she replied. He was definitely up to something. He rarely took such direct interest in what happened in the lab.

Maria's comm implant buzzed in her ear, and the internal display projected onto her retina indicated it was a call from Julio Sakai, the CEO of PSG. She reached up and pressed the actuator behind her ear.

"This is Doctor Fujimoto," she said.

"Good morning, Doctor," Sakai said. His tone was stony, almost curt. "I need you to come up to my office, if you please."

Maria's insides churned. Julio rarely called her up, and their interactions were usually limited to her formal presentations or updates on the project to the executive team.

"Of course, Julio," she said. "I'll be right up."

Julio ended the call without another word, and Richard wore a knowing smile that he tried and failed to hide.

She was suddenly fearful that, somehow, they had discovered one of the seeds she'd planted.

She rose out of her chair, keeping her face impassive, and said, "Would you excuse me, Richard?"

"Of course," he replied easily. "I wonder what Julio wants…that's a bit out of the ordinary, him calling you up."

"It is." She tried to remain calm. "I'm sure he just wants an update on the Gen3s."

"That must be it," Richard said.

Maria walked past him, expecting him to follow her, but he just stood there watching her walk out.

When she reached the door, his voice called out from behind her.

"You know, Maria," he said slowly. "I've always liked your office."

Maria paused, and her mouth went dry. Without turning back, she quickly walked out into the lab and to the elevator.

* * *

"Are you out of your goddamn mind?" Julio shouted.

Maria stood in his cavernous office. It had two full walls of floor-to-ceiling glass looking out on the city on one side and the rolling mountains on the another. The wide *Sagrado del Corazon* river ran along one side of the city, flowing from the high country. Julio's office was the epitome of opulence. It looked almost like a penthouse suite at a five-star hotel, with the most expensive furniture and fixtures to be had in *La Republica del Escobar*, a multi-world "republic" owned outright by Presidenté-for-life, Pablo Ramirez Vasquez.

Maria stood there, stunned. She'd merely walked in, said good morning, and then got broad-sided by the question. Her mind raced. *Did he know? If so, how much?* There were no police present, so it was unlikely he knew everything, and the two PSG rhino guards had remained outside when the door closed. Julio had requested them as a permanent fixture several weeks earlier after rioting had cropped up across Montoya III and the other three worlds of the Republic.

Play it cool, she thought.

"I'm sorry?" she said, sounding confused. "I don't know what you mean."

Julio took a deep breath and let it out as almost a hiss. He narrowed his eyes and glared at her.

"I said," he started in a low and menacing tone, "are you out of your god damn mind....? Those things can process methionine on their own."

"What are you talking about?" Maria asked. She knew exactly what he meant, but she needed to play dumb for as long as she could. Everything rested on him not finding out the whole truth, or she would go to jail and her children would be lost.

"Don't try to deny it," he growled. "The Gen3s do not have the Methionine Protocol in their DNA."

"That's ridiculous," she said, sounding hurt and confused. "I showed you the markers months ago. I can show them to you right now," she added defensively.

"Don't insult my intelligence, Maria," Julio said, holding up his hand. "Richard ran a full battery of tests on the Gen3s over the weekend. He glared at her. "Every single one came up negative, save for a ghost gene that mimicked the Protocol. He reported his findings to me this morning." He leaned forward in his chair. "Right now, only the three of us know, but if you keep denying it, I'll call for a formal inquiry, the executive board will hire an outside agency to audit the entire program, and you will go to jail."

Maria backed down. She couldn't go to prison. Not yet.

Julio leaned back in his chair and folded his hands in front of him.

"Why did we initiate the Methionine Protocol?" he asked suddenly.

"Control," she said, giving the obvious answer. It was the one truth that had haunted her from the very first time PSG asked her to design the Protocol. Maria had been forced to modify a gene that would make all PSG genies dependent upon an injected enzyme so they could produce methionine. Without the daily injection, they died.

"And you helped write that protocol?" he asked, knowing the answer.

"Yes, I did," she said. A pang of shame ran through her like a shot. "But if you recall, I wanted to make the protocol a punishment, not hardwire it into their genes from birth."

"I do. I also recall that your suggestion was rejected by the board because of the undue risk to PSG, our clientele, and the populace at large." He covered his mouth with his fingers, his elbow resting on the arm of his chair, and stared at her, a pained expression on his face. "I thought we'd settled this long ago," he added, half under his breath. He took a deep breath and sat up straight. "How did you do it? I know they were *created* with the Methionine Protocol."

She had to be very careful now. She needed to give him just enough to be plausible without inviting further scrutiny of her methods...or her motives.

Her shoulders slumped in guilt, and she closed her eyes for a moment. Finally, she said, "Before the second trimester, I inserted a retro-virus into them that rewrote the gene."

He looked surprised. "You can rewrite the genetic code after inception? I thought that was impossible."

What will he believe?

"Only if it's early enough in their development," she said. "Anything introduced after that leads to system failure or genetic mutation that then leads to death or worse." She kept her face calm. He *had* to believe that part.

He shook his head. "This company is not prepared to run the risk of having rogue...*animals* out there killing people. The lawsuits alone would wipe us out, never mind the bad press. Those two that escaped are *precisely* why the Protocol was initiated, and you know it." He shook his head. "I'm sorry, but I don't have a choice here. For allowing genies to be created without the Methionine Protocol, you are hereby terminated, effective immediately. I must remind you that you signed both a Non-Disclosure Agreement and a Non-Compete. If I discover you have taken up genetic research anywhere in the Republic, or otherwise exposed trade secrets that would be necessary in such a pursuit, I will make certain you are crucified with a lawsuit that will have you so far in debt you'll spend the rest of your life as an indentured miner in the asteroid belt."

"You can't be serious!" Maria shouted. "Genetic research is my life!" she cried.

"I'm sorry, Maria. You've done wonders for this company, but I don't have a choice. I'm doing you a favor here and covering my own ass. If the board finds out that you'd deliberately sabotaged the Protocol, they'd want you thrown in jail for reckless endangerment and I would be terminated for gross negligence. As it is, I'll have to sell them a line of bullshit that it was all an accident, resulting in your termination. Don't push me," he warned, "or it will get much worse for you. And remember that Richard knows about this too. Your freedom rests in *his* hands as well as mine."

Maria stood there, a defeated look upon her face.

"Alright," she said, finally. "I'll go quietly." She met his eyes, a worried expression on her face. "What about my children?"

Julio sighed wearily. "The entire lot of Gen3s will have to be euthanized because of you," he said flatly.

"What!" she screamed, horrified. "You can't just kill them!" She felt tears welling in her eyes.

"Maria," he said quietly. "You know the board will demand it." He placed his hands on the desk. "It's out of my hands." He moved his left hand under his desk as his eyes shifted to the door. The door opened and both rhino guards came marching in. She knew them by name as well as designation but said nothing. They were massive, nearly seven feet tall and weighing over six hundred pounds, with gray skin and mostly humanoid features. Their skulls were elongated, with deep, black eyes, wide nostrils, and a snubbed version of a horn protruding a few inches from the tips of their snouts. Their shoulders were impossibly wide. They had thick limbs, and their hands ended in three nearly human fingers with wide nails. "Please escort Doctor Fujimoto out of the building. She is not to be allowed back in under any circumstances."

"*Please*, Julio," she begged. "At least put them in cryo-storage. The facilities on level eight can house them. I'll work on my own time…at home…come up with a way revise their DNA and re-instantiate the protocol. You've seen my lab. You know I have the resources to at least try. I've already been working on some genetic designs that might make it possible…. I'll give PSG all the code and the rights to them as well. *Please….*"

Julio sighed again and shook his head.

"At least save the prototype," she pleaded. "She has the Methionine Protocol. I swear!"

Julio's eyes met hers, and there was a hint of kindness.

"I'll have Cabrillo confirm it. If she does, then she'll live. The rest must be euthanized, though. No exceptions."

Maria's shoulders slumped. She was helpless to save them. She felt a large hand wrap gently around her left arm. She looked up into the black eyes of one of her children, and she could see a glimmer of sadness there.

She locked eyes with Julio one last time. "You don't need to kill them," she said. "Just give me a chance."

Julio nodded to the guards, a grim expression on his face. "Your personal belongings will be sent to you tomorrow," he said.

In a flash, she realized she'd run out of time. *So it begins*, she thought. She let the concern for her children fuel the determination she now felt for moving forward with her plans.

The rhino pulled gently on her arm as the other led the way out of the office. They passed by Julio's executive assistant, and the young lady refused to even meet Maria's eyes. As they walked toward the elevator, Maria pressed the comm actuator and selected a number from the display.

"Altra here," the robot said on the other end.

"Will you meet me out in front of the building. Immediately, please."

"Yes, Doctor Fujimoto."

"And initiate the file Seed Seventeen in my personal library."

"Yes, Doctor Fujimoto."

Maria cut the link, a grim look on her face.

She and the rhinos rode the elevator in silence. It was a long way down, and several company employees got on and off as they went down. She knew some of them and even nodded her head when they saw her. Every single one looked at the rhinos with concern and worry, but she offered no explanation, and none of them asked. When the doors opened on the first floor, the rhinos marched her out into the lobby, through the soaring, jungle-like atrium, and out through the main doors to the street.

Just outside, Altra stood, waiting like an alabaster statue in the middle of an ancient Greek courtyard.

One of the rhinos immediately turned and marched back into the building without even looking at Maria, but the other, the one who had taken her arm, stood beside her with what had to be a pained expression on his thick, gray features.

"I'm sorry, Momma," he said in a low, rumbling voice. "We have to do what we're told," he added.

Her heart broke. She knew the truth of his words better than he did. She'd designed him that way. "It's alright, Toku," she said, placing her hand on his chest. "I understand. I don't blame you. *Survive*, baby," she added, meaning it. She wanted them all to survive, but now she had to advance her timetable and take risks that might get more of them—and her—killed.

* * *

Part 2

Maria landed her air car on the roof of the warehouse she'd called home for years. The gray, polysteel building, almost completely windowless, sat on the edge of the industrial sector, right on the banks of the *Sagrado del Corazon*. It had been a storage facility for textiles before she'd bought it and had it heavily remodeled. It now served as both a lavish home and her own private research facility, save on a far smaller scale than her lab at PSG.

She and Altra exited the vehicle and entered the elevator on the roof, quickly descending into her home.

The doors opened on the second floor, and as they stepped out, two tall, lithe humanoids covered in fur greeted her. They were clothed in simple shorts and collarless shirts of gray, and their roughly human feet were bare. The first humanoid was a feline female, with smooth black fur, fiery yellow eyes, and just the hint of canines projecting from her slightly pointed snout. Her head was clearly that of a cat, but her body was as humanoid as Maria's, her fingers and thumb, while shorter than a humans', looked nimble, although they ended in severe, retractable claws. The second humanoid had a pelt of short hair with dark brown and black brindle patterning. His head had an elongated snout, a black nose, and orange eyes that glinted with intelligence.

"Carmen," Maria said, nodding to the feline. "Angel," she added with a smile for the canine. The two had been given the designations G1C34 and G1F17 when they were created. When they'd escaped from the military installation, they made their way to Maria, who nursed them both back to health. She'd also given them their daily injections to subvert the Methionine Protocol. "We have work to do," she said simply as she rushed past. "Follow me."

* * *

Maria sat before a bank of monitors arrayed in two rows above her desk on the third floor of the warehouse. There was another workstation across the room, and the rest of the space was occupied by an assortment of medical equipment, a gurney, and a wall of cabinetry that made a corner of the warehouse look like a cross between a laboratory and an operating room.

Altra stood off to her right, motionless, while the genies stood behind her, watching what she was doing.

She pulled up an interface on the computer for remote-accessing PSG's internal network.

"You ran Seed Seventeen before you left?" she asked Altra.

Altra turned to face her. "Of course, Doctor Fujimoto," she replied.

"Good, then this should work."

She entered a set of credentials, and the screen changed to the PSG corporate UI. She navigated through the system, flicking past one screen after another, until she found what she wanted.

"Is that the internal PSG network?" Angel asked in a low, growling voice.

"Yes," Maria said without taking her eyes away from the screen. "It is."

"How were you able to gain access?" he asked. "Wouldn't they would have disabled your access immediately?"

"I can rewrite DNA in my sleep, Angel," Maria said with a good deal of pride. "There isn't a software language in existence that isn't child's play to me. The command I had Altra run before she left created an administrative user on their network. Now I have full access to more of their systems than Julio does." She turned and looked at Altra. "Hacking software is a lot easier than even just changing an organism's skin color predictively." She looked at him. "Where do you think you got that brindle pattern?" she asked. "I created Seed Seventeen months ago for just this situation." She turned back to the screen. "Julio has no idea who he is dealing with."

A few more keystrokes and screens found her looking at an email interface. She read through a dozen subjects quickly before stopping at one and opening it.

A wicked smile crossed her lips, and she reread the very brief email, a surge of joy flushing her cheeks. "He isn't going to euthanize them," she said, mostly to herself.

"Who?" Angel asked.

"Julio. He said he was going to euthanize the Gen3s. I begged him to freeze them, just to buy us time, but he *said* he was going to terminate them. This email is an order for Richard Cabrillo to let them receive their indoctrination and freeze them before they are awakened." She turned to the genies. "We have time," she said urgently.

"What's happened?" Angel asked.

Maria told them about being fired and why.

"So," Carmen said, in her quiet, almost mewling voice, "what do we do now?"

Maria met the eyes of Carmen and Angel. "We do whatever we must to save as many as we can." She glanced at Altra. "Which reminds me..." she said, "Altra, please come here and expose your data port."

The robot stepped up, turned to the side slightly, and a small compartment opened up on her right thigh, exposing an empty space with a line of ports recessed into the back.

Maria pulled a narrow optical cable from the back of her desk and plugged it into one of Altra's ports. Switching to another screen, she pulled up another interface for Altra's command program where she'd made modifications months earlier. "I'm about to upload a massive amount of data, Altra," she said. "It will include some new skills as well as the full body of my research and all the technical specifications. It is vital that you protect this data at all costs."

"I understand, Doctor Fujimoto," Altra replied.

Maria turned back to the terminal, activated the upload, and watched a series of protocol titles flash by, including combat, vehicle and starship piloting, farming, engineering, and a litany of others. "You are the key to their future," she said, turning back to the terminal.

She began scanning Julio's emails again, looking for something—*anything*—that might be of use, but there was nothing. *At least the Gen3s are safe...for the time being.* "And now for the next part," she said, turning to the genies who stood anxiously behind her.

"*Atlantis Dolos Leto*," she said slowly, staring into their eyes.

Both genies shuddered slightly and blinked several times. They both got curious expressions on their furred faces as—Maria hoped—a series of memories opened up to them.

"Were either of you able to create a back door?" she asked hopefully. Everything now rested on the chance that one of them had been in the right place at the right time. She knew that both of them had been assigned to a Black Ops unit working for Presidenté Vasquez.

Carmine shook his head, but Angel smiled and nodded. "I did," she said. "They had me working with a team in counter-intelligence."

"How did you do that?" Angel asked after a moment. "I remember doing things...secretly...and I only just now can recall having done them."

Maria smiled. "It's one of the seeds I planted. I've been planning this since before I joined PSG," she said. "When I began the research into this project, I knew that humanity would want to keep you as slaves. I don't intend to let that happen, but I had to make a deal with the devil for the resources I needed. I wrote the primary indoctrination process, and I built into all of them a ghost program. Essentially, it turned all of you into sleeper agents. Until the code phrase was spoken to you, you would have no recollection of anything." She turned to Carmen. "So, do you think you can get into the military network?"

Carmen's smile was predatory. "I know I can," she said.

"Then I want you to start monitoring military operations and communications. Focus on a military installation in *La Junta* called *Escuela de Guerra*," she said. "You can use that terminal over there," she added, pointing to a desk and terminal across the lab. "And look for a newly built starship—military or commercial, I don't care which—that is slated for launch," she added. She looked at her children, her eyes full of determination. "We'll get through this," she said. "The timetable has been accelerated. Instead of years, it's looking like weeks, maybe even days, but I think I've planned for just about everything. Will you help me save them?"

They both nodded. "Momma, we will do anything to save our brothers and sisters."

"Good," Maria said. "We're just getting started."

* * *

24 Hours Later

Maria leaned over the micro manipulator, redesigning a retro-virus that would serve her purposes. She'd laid the groundwork for the little beastie but had set the work aside with the intention of getting to it later. Her plans now required it to work, work the first time, and not kill the subject when it was finished. Altra stood nearby, ever willing to perform whatever task Maria gave it. Carmen had left her terminal once for a quick cat-nap, and Angel did what he could to assist her in brainstorming areas to search within the military network.

The government news station played in the background while they worked so Maria could keep track of events unfolding within in the city, and it sounded like they were drawing closer and closer to a civil war.

"Today, Unified Public Liberation Force rebels blew up a new Citizen Identification and Authorization center. The Citizen Identification Bill, or CIB, was signed into law last week by Presidenté Vasquez. It required all citizens to register their DNA with the government and carry a new, encrypted ID card with them at all times that would include this data. It is believed the CIB was the motivation for the attack. Two dozen administrators, forty-three Republican Guard soldiers, and nearly a hundred civilians were killed in the explosion. In response to growing unrest across all four worlds of the Republic, Presidenté Vasquez has announced he is bringing twenty-four corvette-class warships and a dozen troop transports out of mothball to expand the government's defensive capabilities. He had undertaken these steps as both as a security measure to protect the people as well as to ensure that external governments do not take advantage of the growing turmoil. Admiral Cortez acknowledged that it might take several weeks to gather enough personnel to man all of the vessels.... In other news, there have been skirmishes near and inside several remote cities on Montoya III, with dozens of civilians getting caught in the crossfire between the Republican Guard and forces of the UPLF. Presidenté Vasquez has vowed to take any and all steps necessary to eradicate the UPLF and return peace and tranquility to the capital world of the Escobar Republic."

"It's getting bad out there," Angel said, placing a cup of tea on the table beside Maria's micro-manipulator.

"All the more reason for us to move as quickly as possible," she said, without pulling her eyes away from the oculars of the manipulator. She made another alteration to a protein chain and waited for the structure to settle into place. When it held together, she lifted her head and rubbed her eyes. "There," she said tiredly. "I think that should do it."

"What are you working on?" Angel asked, scratching behind his ear.

"Something special for you and the other children," she said with a wink. "I need to let it multiply overnight to ensure it's viable. I know the base coding is correct, but I won't know if it's stable until tomorrow morning." She hit a button, and the sample she'd been working on slid out of the manipulator and into the incubator next to it.

Her comm buzzed in her ear, and the internal display showed that it was a restricted number. She pressed the actuator.

"Hello?" she asked, expecting some sort of sales call.

"Doctor Maria Magdelain Fujimoto?" a man's deep voice asked.

"Yes."

"My name is Mario Acevedo. I am the senior aide to Presidenté Vasquez. He would like you to take a meeting with him tomorrow morning at ten A.M."

"Excuse me?" she asked, stunned. "Are you sure you have—"

"Yes, Doctor. My staff is incapable of making such a mistake. Presidenté Vasquez has insisted he meet with you. A car will be arriving at your location tomorrow at precisely nine-forty-five. Please be ready. No one may come with you. You will be searched for any sort of recording device, and your comm unit will be disabled while in his presence. I must insist that you tell no one about this meeting. Am I understood?"

"Yes," she said. "Perfectly."

"Thank you, Doctor, and good day."

He severed the link.

"Are you alright?" Angel asked. "You look pale."

Maria took a deep breath. Her mind raced, and a tremor of fear worked its way into her thoughts. It was no secret that Presidenté Vasquez was a dictator who ruled the Republic of Escobar through political leverage, blackmail, extortion, and murder. *What could possibly have placed her on his radar?* She looked up at Angel and got a sinking feeling. There could be only one reason. Her eyes darted back and forth as she contemplated possibilities if her guess was right.

"I'm fine," she finally said. "Listen. I need you and Carmen to redouble your efforts. Gather as much information about that base as you can. I want blueprints, duty rosters, schedules, personnel reports. And start formulating a plan on how you would break out of it if you had a hundred and eighty troops." The news report echoed at the back of her mind. The mothballed corvettes.... She looked at Carmen. "And see what kind of interface transport lifts from that base."

Angel's eyes went wide. "You don't mean—"

"Yes," she said flatly. "Assume both armed and unarmed scenarios," she added. "At this point, I don't think there will be any other way."

"Yes, Momma," Angel said.

Maria looked over to where Carmen sat, staring back at her. "We're running out of time, and there may be no other way than to fight our way out," she said.

Carmen nodded; her eyes stony.

"I need you both to leave me alone until tomorrow. I have a great deal of planning to do, and I can't afford any distractions. And can you turn off that broadcast?" she asked. "I think I've heard enough."

Carmen reached over and hit a button on the monitor, turning it off.

Without another word, Maria moved over to her terminal and pulled up the PSG link. She had to plant more seeds.

* * *

Maria checked the time on her internal clock to find that it was nine-twenty-seven. Closing the backdoor access into PSG, she rose to her feet and moved over to the incubator to check the status of the retro-virus. The green status lights across the panel showed that not only had the structure held, but it had multiplied to a point where she could use it. She punched in several commands on the incubator, waited a minute, and then watched a small drawer slide out of the bottom of the unit. Two small syringes lay in the tray, full of a clear fluid.

She turned to where Carmen and Angel hovered over the terminal.

"Would both of you come here?" she asked. The genies rose to their feet and strode over as gracefully as the predatory animals they were. Maria had to smile. They truly were magnificent. More than she'd ever dreamed possible. "Do you trust me?" she asked.

They both nodded. "Implicitly," Carmen said.

"I need an insurance policy...in case this meeting goes badly," she added grimly.

"What do you mean?" Angel asked. He looked worried.

Maria ignored the question. She didn't have enough time to explain.

"I've created a retro-virus that *should* rewrite the gene affecting your ability to manufacture methionine. If it works, you will no longer be dependent upon the injections, but I've never tested it, and I don't know if there will be any side effects. I need one of you to act as the initial test subject, and if there are no ill effects within the first twelve hours, then it should at least be safe for the other."

"I volunteer," Angel said immediately. "Carmen has all the skills necessary to continue gathering data on the installation without me. We've found a good deal already, but we're not finished. I am the logical choice," he added.

"You need to know that there is a possibility that this could kill you. If there are errors in replication, it could cause a total system failure."

"I understand, Momma," he replied. "But you said it yourself. We're running out of time."

She nodded. "Then give me your arm," she said. She grabbed a bottle of alcohol with a swab and cleaned an area on the upper portion of his right arm. Grabbing one of the syringes, she quickly injected him and rose to her feet. "If all goes well, I'll be back soon. If you don't hear from me by the end of the day, assume the worst and proceed as best as you can."

"Yes, Momma," they both said, worried looks on their faces.

"Altra," she said, turning to the robot.

"Yes, Doctor Fujimoto?"

"I need you to make several liters of the serum in the incubator."

"Of course," Altra said, immediately moving toward the unit.

Maria smiled, feeling affection for what she knew was merely a walking computer. "I'll see you soon, Altra," she said to the robot standing nearby.

"Yes, Doctor," Altra replied. "Safe travels," she added automatically.

With a wry smile, Maria strode to the elevator, stepped in, and hit the button for the roof. She checked the time again to see that it was nine-thirty-six. She took a deep breath and let it out slowly. She couldn't help wondering if she would ever see them again.

When the doors opened, a long, black, executive air car sat waiting for her. A rear door opened, and an officer of the Republican Guard stepped out, holding it open for her. He was slim, dark-haired, and had a nearly lifeless expression on his face that seemed to hide a sneer.

As Maria approached, he stepped aside and motioned for her to get in. "Please get inside," he said. She could see now that he was a captain, and there was no "please" in his tone. It was an order.

She did as instructed and found another officer, also a captain, sitting in the forward seats. His face was as lifeless as the first one. He nodded once as the other captain got inside and closed the door, and then he held out a device, running it over her body. Looking at the readout, he pressed a button on the armrest, leaned over, and said, "We're clear."

Without another word from either of them, the car lifted off and accelerated hard toward the Presidential Retreat.

* * *

Part 3

The car landed on the roof, and both captains escorted Maria into an elevator that went down an unknown number of floors. They didn't have to touch any buttons, because there weren't any. The doors opened on a wide hallway, with a half-dozen doors on either side, as well as small tables, mirrors, and chandeliers running down its entire length. One of the captains motioned for her to proceed, and they marched her down the hallway. She felt like she was being led to an execution, but there would be little point in them killing her in the palace. She'd made it that far, so she assumed she was going to meet the Presidenté and not an untimely demise.

Maria could not believe the opulence of the Presidential Retreat. Everything was gold, marble, and crystal, with some of the most exquisite furniture she had ever seen. When they exited the hallway, she found herself in a grand room, with tables on either side, covered with what could only be described as a banquet. Grand staircases flanked both sides, and the captains guided her up the right-hand side to a wide landing and a pair of large double doors. Through them, she recognized the Presidential Office from official broadcasts. The view outside was of the Capital Gardens and the city beyond. There were two full sets of couches and chairs facing wide fireplaces on either side of the room. Each conversation pit was designed to allow for separate conversations. Straight ahead was the largest desk Maria had ever seen.

In front of the desk, and turned in his seat to face her, was a Republican Guard general that looked familiar. He was middle-aged, in excellent physical condition, and had salt and pepper coloring running through his goatee and close-cropped hair. He had stern eyes that seemed to take Maria in like a wolf evaluating an injured animal. He stood as Maria passed through the doorway, and both captains took up positions just inside the room.

Behind the desk sat the heavy-set but still handsome Presidenté Pablo Ramirez Vasquez. He wore a perfectly fitted, dark gray suit with a sapphire blue tie. His dark hair was cut short, almost in a military fashion, and both hands had large, gold pinky rings that glinted as he rose to greet her.

"Good morning, Doctor Fujimoto," Vasquez said, smiling a perfect politician's smile. "You know me of course. Permit me to introduce General Valdez," he added motioning toward the general. Maria realized who the man was. He was commander of the entire Republican Guard and the President's Chief of Staff. "Please," Vasquez continued, "have a seat. I don't have much time, and I am in desperate need of your help."

She raised an eyebrow. She may have been right about what he wanted from her. "Good morning to you both," she said, nodding to each of them. She quickly took the seat beside the general and looked at the president expectantly.

"I apologize for the short notice," he said, "and I hope my staff did not make you feel too unsettled. I have trained them to be direct and to respond to my requests quickly," he added with a confident smile.

"No need to apologize, Mister President," she said. "They were perfectly agreeable, and it is a sincere pleasure to meet you."

"I'm sure," he replied. "But enough pleasantries. As I said, I have a busy day ahead of me."

"What is it I can do for you, Mister President?" she asked.

He leaned back in his chair and looked at her for a moment. "It is my understanding that you are no longer with Paragon Savage Genetics. Can I assume you find yourself in search of new opportunities?"

Maria tried and succeeded not to smile. She kept her features calm and impassive. "Indeed I am," she answered truthfully.

"Excellent," Vasquez said. "Then I believe I can offer you the greatest opportunity you could imagine," he said enthusiastically. "An opportunity to continue your work, unfettered by corporate policy, and with virtually unlimited resources. Carta blanca, in fact, so long as I get what I want." The smile he gave her was more unsettling than the grim countenance of the General. "I would like you to continue the work you were doing for PSG, but for me. *Exclusively.*" He leaned forward, a hungry look upon his face. "Would that interest you?"

I guessed right, Maria thought, but she feigned surprise at the suggestion.

"I believe it would, Mister President," she said. "I want nothing more than to continue my work, and to be honest, I had no idea how I was going to proceed without PSG."

"Indeed. Your line of work requires a very significant level of resources, resources I am more than capable of providing." He eyed her, searching her face for something. "To put it simply, I want a genie *army* capable of wiping out the insurgents who have made life so difficult for my citizens." He raised an eyebrow. "Am I correct in assuming that was what PSG intended to provide to any paying customer that came through the door?"

"That's correct," Mister President," she replied.

"I've been informed that the second generation of your creations have been highly successful in war games against my Republican troops. I must admit, I am impressed. To that end, I will require more of them...much more...but I would have to add some additional constraints."

Maria eyed him warily. "What might those be?" she asked.

"It's very simple. The Methionine Protocol must be implemented without fail or exception. I can assure you, if that condition weren't met, you would suffer far worse than being fired." He smiled, but there was deadly menace in his eyes. "Furthermore, I would require that all subjects be made utterly loyal me and me alone. I am correct in my understanding that such a thing is possible, yes?" he asked.

"Yes, Mister President. It is already part of the process."

"And what of the two escapees?" he asked suspiciously.

"As a result of that situation, we implemented a more stringent process that insured there would be no further anomalous behavior."

"Good!" he said.

"I must add that because we are dealing with living organisms, I cannot guarantee with absolute certainty that there would never be another anomaly, but I can assure you that what we implemented raised the bar significantly. They would be more loyal than any normal person is capable of."

Vasquez cast a sidelong glance at the general and a smile played about his lips.

"Excellent," he said, turning his eyes back to her. "Furthermore, I want a virus, or toxin, something that could be released that would kill them but not full-blooded humans. Would that be a problem?"

Maria was not surprised.

"Not at all, Mister President. In fact, PSG had required such a virus at the beginning of the program. It kills within a minute or two, disrupting biological functions once it hits the lung tissue. I developed it as we were creating the first generation. There are even stores of the serum at PSG that could be dispersed via any airborne delivery system."

"You are certainly full of good news," Vasquez said. "And I am delighted you are as receptive to the idea. But let me sweeten the pot." He said. "As I mentioned, I would give you, essentially, *carta blanca*. Additionally, I have at my disposal a...recently unmanned orbital research station that would suit your needs. You would have access to a personal shuttle that is ready for delivery, and a pilot could be made available to you."

"No, Mister President," she replied, trying to remain calm. "I have an assistant that is fully capable of piloting orbital craft." She could not believe what she was hearing. As she sat there, she started working through possibilities.

"As you wish," he replied. "The station is already equipped with most of what you need. It already has one hundred of your first-generation maturation chambers and consoles installed. And there are another four hundred of them awaiting you in a cargo bay aboard the station." He smiled wickedly as Maria got a shocked look on her face. The specifications for the chambers were one of PSGs most closely guarded secrets. "I have people everywhere," Vasquez said. "One of my agents was able to get those specifications and the software near the end of the Gen1 stage."

"I don't see how I could refuse you, Mister President," Maria said, suddenly appalled at the resources such a man had at his disposal. She never imagined that something like what he was suggesting was even possible. He would be an even worse devil to deal with than PSG, but she had her own plans, and he was offering much of what she needed to achieve them.

"It would be foolish to refuse me, Doctor Fujimoto. As the general here can attest, I am very accustomed to getting exactly what I want. And in this case, it is my way or the highway. Besides, where else could you possibly find such an opportunity?"

"I have no doubt I couldn't," she replied. "I'll need a week or two of preparation for such a large undertaking, and I would like to begin the process of seeking appropriate staff before I go to the station."

"I expected as much," he said. "I don't have a problem with that. As impatient as I can be, I'm not an unreasonable man."

"Thank you," she said. "Then I can see only one problem."

"Oh?" Vasquez replied, raising a surprised eyebrow. "And what might that be?"

"PSG holds an NDA and Non-Compete over my head, and the CEO made it clear upon my departure that he would have me arrested if I undertook genetics work again. It would be a very public matter, I'm afraid."

The smile on Vasquez's face sent a chill up Maria's spine.

"You needn't worry about him," he said simply. "I've already seen to that." He rose out of his chair and held out his hand. "So, Doctor Fujimoto, do we have an agreement?"

She stood quickly, stepping up to the desk, and the general rose as well.

"I believe we do," she said, and shook his hand. "Can you have the shuttle delivered to my home? Assuming it isn't too large to land on the roof."

"Oh, no," Vasquez said. "It's not much larger than a cargo van, so it should be fine. You will schedule regular meetings here in my office, to keep me up to date on your progress. Once a week should suffice."

"As you wish, Mister President," she replied.

"Then I'm afraid I must say goodbye, Doctor Fujimoto, and thank you for being so accommodating."

"The pleasure was mine, Mister President." She turned to find both captains standing just behind her chair. She walked out between them. They fell in step behind her as she walked out, and the General took up the rear.

"Oh, and Doctor?" Vasquez called out.

Maria paused and turned in the doorway.

"I can't emphasize enough how important it is that you understand, *any* betrayal will have the direst of consequences." He fixed his eyes upon her, and there was no humor left in the man. His face was as cold and menacing as any she could imagine.

"I understand, Mister President," she replied.

"Good day," he said, as he sat down and waved his hand dismissively.

She felt a firm hand on her arm and was guided out. Both captains and the general escorted her out of the palace and up to the roof where the same car sat waiting.

As they approached it, the general pulled on her arm and turned her to face him. She met his gaze, and he stared at her for several moments with narrowed, calculating eyes.

"I don't like you...or the work you do," he said evenly. "In fact, I believe that genies and the people who create them are the greatest threat to the Republic since it was established." Maria felt a chill.

"For now, the Presidenté has a use for you, so my hands are tied…but that may not always be the case," he added, and there was a profound menace to his words. "I'll be keeping my eye on you, Doctor," he added.

Nodding once to the captains beside her, he turned and marched away.

One of the captains opened the door and got in. The other motioned for her to follow, and she did so. Both captains sat across from her, their features stony and menacing. The car lifted off, and as it carried her home, she could only think that she had even less time than she thought. And now the general would be watching.

* * *

When the car landed and she got out, she saw the shuttle the Presidenté had spoken of was already sitting on the roof. It was a small, military interface shuttle, designed for atmospheric and orbital space flight. The Presidenté had made good on his first promise, and as Maria stared at it, a plan started to form.

She would have to move quickly. She called up the elevator, stepped inside, and hit the button for the lab level. When she stepped out of the elevator, she found Carmen at the terminal and Angel behind her with a blanket over his shoulders. He was shivering slightly, and the news was again playing in the background. They both turned, and their faces showed relief at the sight of her.

"Momma!" Carmen said, rising. "You're alright.".

Maria nodded. "How are you doing, Angel?"

He smiled weakly. "I think I'm okay. A little feverish, perhaps, but that's all."

"That's to be expected. Let me know if it gets worse."

He nodded.

"Julio Sakai is dead," Carmen said, pointing at the news station playing on the monitor. "His air car went down in the jungle as he was flying home." Both genies looked at Maria expectantly.

Maria shook her head, but she wasn't surprised. "The Presidenté doesn't waste time, does he?"

"You knew?" Carmen asked.

"It came up during our conversation this morning," he replied.

"Are you going to tell us what happened with him?" Angel asked. There was strange insistence to his question.

"In a nutshell," Maria said, "he wants me to start up the program, using his resources to create an army of genies loyal only to him."

Their eyes went wide, and then they looked at each other with worried expressions.

"They're going to kill him," Carmen said.

"What?" Maria asked, stunned.

"They're going to kill El Presidenté..." Carmen clarified. "Our old team...they've been tasked with neutralizing Omega Deuce...it was our internal designation for the President."

"Omega Deuce?" Maria asked, confused.

Angel got a mischievous smile. "It means 'big shit,'" he said, chuckling.

Maria didn't get the joke. All she could do was stand there, over-whelmed at everything that was slamming into her. She took a deep breath and considered the implications. Like pieces in a puzzle, things started falling into place, and as they did, the general's parting words echoed in her thoughts. She understood it now.

"When?" she asked, looking at the genies. "When are they going to kill him?"

"Two days," Angel added.

"That means we're next," Maria said. "*All* of us." The plan she'd been formulating resolved quickly in her mind. *Could it be done in two days?*

"There's some good news," Carmen said.

"I could use a little of that," Maria replied.

"We have a plan for getting the Gen2s out of Escuela de Guerra, and there are already several troop transports assigned to the base."

Maria breathed a sigh of relief. "That just leaves a few other small details…" she said wearily. Like winning a battle against hardened Republican Guard troops and getting nearly three hundred Gen3s out of their maturation chambers and loaded onto a troop transport on the other side of the city.

"Were you able to find a ship?" Maria asked. Everything else was merely details, planning, and execution. Between herself and Angel, they had access to resources at both PSG and within the military, which would cover a lot of ground. But without a starship, they were dead in the water.

Carmen and Angel *both* smiled at her question.

"Then let's put this all together," she said. "Tomorrow night we rescue your brothers and sisters."

* * *

Part 4

Altra sat at the controls of the shuttle as they entered the airspace of Escuela de Guerra. The sun was setting over the mountains, and a cloud-darkened storm front promised rain in the near future. Maria sat next to her, wearing her most expensive suit as she monitored the comms. Carmen and Angel sat behind them, wearing their custom-issued matte-black combat armor. They'd had to wash the blood off, and there were still a few bullet holes in the back, but they would pass anything but a close inspection. They both carried standard issue 4mm Tamaki assault rifles that fired magnetically-accelerated, high-density rounds with little more than a whisper of air. They wore combat vibroknives in breakaway scabbards over their left breasts, and Angel had a 3mm Ramirez y Rodrigo "Ram-Rod" pistol strapped to his left thigh.

Maria checked the time. It was eleven-thirty P.M., and the clock was ticking.

They'd planned everything and put the various pieces into motion over the past thirty-six hours. Once they got inside the base, things would happen very quickly...and if anything went wrong, they would get very, *very* bloody. Maria felt her conscience well up inside her. For years, she'd felt guilty about what she'd done to the genies. She'd made her children slaves, although she wasn't alone. Humanity was pursuing genetic engineering like hers all over. She'd just been better at it. And now, what they were about to undertake would cost lives. She thought back to the day she agreed to work for PSG. From that moment on, she'd been able to put off the decision between endless slavery for her creations or wanton murder on a large scale for those who would enslave them.

When the decision was finally forced upon her, she chose her family.

"Echo Bravo Seven Niner," a woman's stern voice called over the comm. "This is flight control at Escuela de Guerra. You are about to enter restricted airspace. State your business or turn around immediately. Over."

"Flight control," Maria said. "This is Echo Bravo Seven Niner carrying an inspection team from PSG. We have been ordered to review the health and condition of the Gen2s in preparation for an evac. There should be an authorization listed for us, and we are requesting clearance to land and disembark. Over."

"Roger that, Echo Bravo Seven Niner. Stand by. Over." The comm went quiet for a few heartbeats. "Echo Bravo Seven Niner, clearance to land has been approved. Turn to one-eight-four and make your approach. Note that any deviation could result in you being fired upon. Over."

"*Understood, control*," Maria replied. "*Making our approach now. Over.*" She cut the comm and turned toward the genies. "I wish it didn't have to be like this," she said. "Sometimes I wonder if I ever should have..." she shook her head and closed her eyes, trying to say something that had been eating at her since the first Gen1 was conceived. She was suddenly wracked with guilt. "I'm sorry," she said suddenly. It was first time those words had ever crossed her lips for the guilt she'd felt from the very first day.

"Momma," Angel said slowly, placing her hand on Maria's shoulder. "You gave us life. You made us smart and strong. And here you are now, risking your life to free us."

Maria opened her eyes to see both genies looking at her with compassion in their eyes.

"No apologies," Angel added.

Maria took a deep breath and let it out slowly. Nodding, she smiled weakly. "Alright," she said.

"We're coming in for our landing now," Altra said, the youthful, childlike voice incongruous with the fact that she was piloting a military shuttle. "Please ensure your safety belts remain fastened until the shuttle comes to a complete stop," she added.

The shuttle descended quickly, dropping into the shadow of the mountains as it came in at a steep angle as Alta reduced their speed dramatically. The wide tarmac came into view, illuminated by bright floodlights surrounding the entire area, where three large troop transports and a half-dozen shuttles identical to Maria's squatted in the growing darkness.

"Time for you to get out of sight," Maria said over her shoulder.

Both genies rose out of their seats, moved to the back of cockpit, and slipped through the rear hatch into a personnel bay big enough for eight troopers. They closed the hatch behind them just as Altra came in over the landing pad and dropped with a whine of repulsors. The wheels rotated out from under the airframe and the shuttle settled onto them with a hiss of hydraulics. The shuttle rolled forward and moved into a parking position beside the row of shuttles that were already there. When it was in position, Altra cut the engine and powered the shuttle down as if it had been piloting them from the day it came off the assembly line.

Looking out through the windscreen, Maria saw three Republican Guard soldiers marching with purpose across the tarmac straight for the shuttle. The first appeared to be an officer, while the two flankers were regular soldiers with rifles slung over their shoulders and their sidearms holstered. Maria took a deep breath to calm her nerves.

"Come on, Altra," Maria said. "It's time." She rose out of her seat, moved to the back of the cockpit, and opened the side hatch. She walked down the steps and started toward the approaching soldiers as Altra clicked down behind her.

With Altra walking only a step behind and to her right, Maria closed the distance with the soldiers, who she could now see had grim expressions on their faces. All three of them reminded her of the General Valdez's captains. Lifeless, humorless, and grim.

The soldiers came to a stop in front of her, with the officer in front and two troopers off to either side.

"Good evening," Maria said, "I'm here for—"

The troopers pulled their pistols and leveled them both at Maria.

"Save it, miss," the officer said. "You're under arrest for treason."

Maria got a surprised and fearful look on her face. "What are you—?"

"Enough!" the officer barked. Glancing over his shoulder, he said, "Search it."

The trooper on his right holstered his pistol, unslung his rifle, and jogged over to the shuttle. Maria looked over her shoulder as the trooper cautiously stepped up into the cockpit. The officer, a lieutenant, stepped forward and patted Maria down, searching for weapons.

"I'm unarmed," Maria said.

"We don't take chances, miss," the lieutenant said, searching her thoroughly.

As he stepped away again, Maria heard boots coming up behind her.

"It's empty," he said. "Nothing in the cockpit or the deployment bay," he added as he slung his rifle again. He drew his pistol and aimed it at Maria.

"Don't worry about it," the lieutenant said. "There was just supposed to be the two of them." The lieutenant turned back to Maria. "Follow me. Any attempt to escape will be met with deadly force. This is the only warning you will receive."

He turned on his heel and began marching away. Maria and Altra followed, with the troopers close behind. Maria did everything she could to keep the panic off her face. She needed to remain calm, or they'd kill her instantly.

The lieutenant led them off the tarmac and past a control tower where two guards stood watch outside a pair of double doors. Beyond that were several administrative buildings and a row of five barracks, one of which had a pair of armed guards standing outside it. Off to the other side of the large compound was a long building Maria guessed was a mess hall, and a short distance from that stood a thick, armored-looking building with a chain-link fence around it topped with concertina wire. A pair of guards stood outside it, rifles slung.

As Maria cleared the last barracks, she spotted a small, isolated building further back from the main street they'd been walking down. It looked to be about the size of a large house, and there was a single light over the outer door at the top of a small set of steps. All the windows of the building were barred and appeared to have the shades drawn, with pale light shining through them. A pair of guards stood watch at the base of the steps, rifles over their shoulders.

The lieutenant ahead of Maria marched straight up to it. The guards saluted as the lieutenant approached. He returned the salute and then walked past, straight up the stairs. He opened the door and walked inside, holding it open for Maria and Altra. They entered a small office space with desks and filing cabinets on either side, and the lieutenant walked down a hallway running down the middle of the building with a door on either side. He strode up to the one on the right, opened it and motioned for her and Altra to go inside.

"Wait here," he ordered. "Sit in the far chair. There is someone coming to see you shortly."

As she entered, she found a small table and a small, folding chair on either side. She did as she was told, taking her seat on the far side, and Altra remained standing, staring into space like a statue. There was the sound of a lock turning.

Maria waited for about twenty minutes, and then heard voices in the main room.

There were footsteps outside the door. The lock turned, and the door opened.

She recognized the first captain immediately, then the familiar, grim face of the second of General Valdez's aides appeared. Both of them now wore sidearms. A moment later, they were followed by General Valdez, himself. The general took up the seat across from Maria and sat there for at least a full minute, as if he were examining a piece of art.

Finally, he took a deep breath and let it out slowly.

"What did you hope to accomplish?" the general asked. "Did you really think the two of you could somehow free those wretched genies from the barracks without someone reporting it? There's an entire company stationed here," he said. "I was under the impression you were an intelligent woman," he added, shaking his head. "This," he motioned to the room, "this doesn't look like any sort of plan at all." He gave her a condescending smile. "Hope is not a strategy, Doctor Fujimoto," he added.

"You're right," she said, "it's not. But my plan doesn't rely upon hope. It relies upon human nature," she said, and she let a slim smile cross her face.

"What makes you think you're getting out of here alive?" He frowned. "You were dead the second you got out of that shuttle."

"I'm sure it looks that way from where you're sitting," she said. "The truth is, I expected you," she smiled.

The general frowned, and the lights went out for a second. A few seconds later, an emergency light above the door glowed a pale blue. There was a shout from outside the door and a muffled yelp of pain. The two captains exchanged nervous looks.

"What makes *you* think you're getting out of here alive?" Maria asked, and the smile on her face was suddenly more menacing than the President's had been.

Both captains suddenly looked terrified and reached for their sidearms, but it was already too late.

Altra's mechanical reflexes were faster, and her new software was more than up to the task. The hatch on her leg popped open and her right arm darted to where another Ram-Rod pistol had been sequestered. Before the captains could pull their pistols from their holsters, Altra's Ram-Rod made a static-hiss, almost like a whisper, and the hyper-accelerated round splashed the back wall with the first captain's blood and brains. He started to topple. The second captain's pistol cleared the holster just as his brains decorated the back wall. Their bodies hit the floor on either side of the general only a half-second apart.

The general sat there, a stunned, terrified expression on his face.

"I'm taking my children, General," Maria said calmly. "With both you and El Presidenté gone, your troops will be more worried about filling the power vacuum and killing each other than they will be hunting down a group of genies who are no longer on Montoya III." She glanced at the robot. "Altra?" she asked, cocking her head to the side thoughtfully.

"Yes, Doctor Fujimoto?"

"Kill him," Maria said.

There was a static-hiss, and a neat hole appeared in the center of the general's head, splashing the wall with crimson, and he toppled forward, his face slamming into the table. A pool of blood started spreading across the table.

The door to the room exploded inward as a tall rhino in black combat armor crashed through it, hit the floor, and rolled to the side as two tabby felines, also in combat armor, appeared in the doorway with assault rifles leveled.

Maria smiled.

"It's good to see you," she said, a smile spreading across her face. She recognized three of the Gen2s she'd raised to maturity. The rhino was Dolan, and the two felines were Isabella and Valeria. Maria rose out of her seat and moved toward the door. "Carmen and Angel got to you?" she asked.

All three genies nodded. They had comm-sets in their ears and mics over their throats.

Isabella stepped forward. She wore captain's bars on her collar but no other insignia, and one of her hands was bloody. "They used a sleeper code, and apparently they've all been busy here for weeks while we slept." She smiled. "Everyone is *awake* now, Momma."

"Good," Maria said. "We're almost there," she added.

Valeria, a sliver lieutenant's bar on her collar, bent down and picked up both of the pistols that had fallen. She checked the chamber of one, ensuring it was ready to go, and handed it to Maria. Maria wasn't all that familiar with firearms, but she knew which end to point at an enemy. As Maria took the pistol, she saw that Valeria had blood on one of her hands as well. The blood had gotten onto the grip of the pistol, and there was now blood on her hand as well.

"Just aim and pull the trigger," Valeria said in a lower but similarly mewling voice as Carmen's. Valeria checked the other pistol and slipped it into her empty holster, securing it.

"All of our weapons are in the armory," Dolan said in a deep voice, "but the felines are going through the barracks, slitting throats and policing up any rifles and pistols they find." He had three gray chevrons on each forearm, indicating he was a sergeant. "The canines are out on the perimeter, hunting down the sentries."

"Angel told us what you wanted to do, and thanks to what we had all done as sleepers," Isabella said, "we pretty much own this base, all the way up to the airfield. The power has been cut, and the generators disabled. The comms are down, the tower is ours, and the barracks are being cleaned out. We'll be hitting the armory shortly. There's part of a platoon holed up there, but it shouldn't be too much trouble. We have all the codes, and the humans are no match for us."

"Kill them all," Maria said, and a pang of both guilt and remorse hammered into her heart. She looked at the blood on her hand, realizing what was going on around her. "We need to buy a few more hours," she added, "and I won't take the chances that any of these soldiers might get a message out." She was committed now, and although every single drop of spilled blood was on her hands, if there was one thing she knew for certain, it was that her children would never be free without the sacrifice. "I need to get back to the shuttle," she said.

Isabella placed a finger on her comm-set. "Kolos, we're coming out. Is the area secure?" there was a brief pause, and she nodded once. "Follow me," she said, hefting the rifle. She turned on her heel and walked out of the room and down the hall.

Maria followed, and when she got to the main room, she found the lieutenant and both troopers lying on the floor. The troopers had three bloody holes in each of their chests, visible because they lay face-up on the floor. The lieutenant's throat had been torn out where he sat, leaning back in a chair at one of the desks, his lifeless eyes staring up at the ceiling.

Maria exited the building to find both guards crumpled on the ground. Their throats had been torn out, and wide pools of blood had spread across the concrete where they had been standing only thirty minutes earlier. A dozen genies in black combat armor stood a few meters away from the steps. There were four unarmed felines and six rhinos, as well as two canines armed with pistols.

They all turned and nodded to her, then returned their gazes out into the compound.

A muffled explosion echoed across the compound from the beyond the chain-link fence. She saw a dozen shadowy figures, feline, canine, and rhino, disappear through a set of double doors, and then there was a series of distant shouts and screams.

Maria took a slow breath, knowing more were dying, then strode down the stairs and walked through the group of genies. Altra walked behind her a few steps, and both Isabella and Valeria stood off to the side, their eyes scanning the compound with their rifles held at the ready. Dolan took up the rear, and as they passed the other genies, the group of twelve dropped in behind then in a wide line, each one scanning for any sign of trouble.

By the time Maria reached the barracks, she saw movement over at the armory as nine genies walked out of it. All of them were armed now, holding assault rifles. Two of them were leaning heavily on a compatriot, while three others held hands over different parts of their bodies. They'd obviously been wounded, but the armory had been taken.

Isabella put her hand to her ear. "Copy that," she said. "All units in the compound…be advised that the armory is open. Get there as soon as your objectives have been accomplished. Equip yourselves and carry out any and all weapons and munitions you can. Meet up at the control tower as soon as possible."

"The compound is secure, Momma," Isabella said. "All that's left are the outliers, and the canines are mopping them up right now."

"Excellent," Maria said as she turned the corner of the first barracks. A hundred genies in their black combat armor were walking down the middle of the street in a loose group. Dozens more were walking out of four of the five barracks. The guards who had stood outside the last barracks were on the ground, dead, and the two guards outside the control tower were also lying on the ground motionless. "Have the canines sniff out any survivors. Search the entire base, but don't take more than two hours."

"Understood."

Every single genie present looked at her with kind eyes.

She smiled, nodding to them as she walked by, but there wasn't time for words. That would come later, if everything went according to plan. She had one last task to perform. With the genies in tow,

Maria walked out across the tarmac to where Angel and Carmen waited.

"You have them," Maria asked.

Angel held out two large suitcases. "It's all here," he added with a smile.

"Good," Maria said. "I want both of you to give them all the serum before you lift off." Maria breathed a sigh of relief. The suitcases were full of 200 syringes, each loaded with the retro-virus she'd created. The Gen2s would be free of the Methionine Protocol. "You have a team for the *Cortez?*" she asked.

Angel nodded. "Isabella will be leading it with Valerian and Dolan, with a full squad going along to handle the skeleton crew. We sent the orders and got confirmation only a few minutes ago." She added. "When we pull out, the shipyard will think we're taking it for a training cruise."

"Very good," Maria said. "We'll meet you at the rendezvous location as soon as we can. If you don't hear from us by four A.M., you pull for deep space just like we planned."

"I wish we were going with you," Carmen said. "It could be dangerous."

"You can't be seen there," Maria said. "As long as the populace has no reason to believe genies did what we're doing, there won't be an outcry for their extermination. You know we can't take all of them with us."

Carmen nodded and then stepped forward, wrapping her arms around Maria. "Thank you, momma," she said. "We all owe you our lives."

Maria hugged her back fiercely, then she let her go. "Just make sure the transport is waiting for us," she said. "I'll see you soon," she added. "Come on, Altra," she said, then she walked past and got into the shuttle.

* * *

Part 5

Altra set the shuttle down on the roof of PSG, and they both got out, Altra carrying a small briefcase in one hand. It was a short walk to the executive elevator, and when they approached, Maria entered the pass code she had created. A moment later, the doors opened and the two of them got in. As the doors closed, a voice came in over the speaker in the ceiling.

"Hello, momma," Toku said in his low, grumbling voice.

Maria looked up at the camera in a corner of the ceiling. "Hello, Toku," she said. "The security recordings are off?"

"Yes, Momma," he said. "All the way down to Lab 4. I did like you asked. I created substitute recordings, and I'll install them as soon as you leave, using the credentials you gave me."

"I thought we agreed you were coming with us," she said, suddenly concerned.

"We did," he said, "but I was thinking that if any of us here at PSG disappeared, they'd know we were involved." He sighed. "It will be better if I'm here to tell them there was never anything on the video. That way, the others will be safe."

Maria closed her eyes and fought back the sudden urge to weep. "I understand, Toku." Looking up at the camera, she smiled. "I'm very proud of you," she said.

"I know, Momma. You were always proud of all of us." There was pause. "There's one thing," he said, worriedly.

"What's wrong?" Maria asked, suddenly afraid.

"Selina's gone, and I don't know where," he said. "I'm sorry."

Maria's heart sank. One more of her children lost. "Dammit," she muttered. "It's alright," she said, looking up at the camera. "There's nothing we can do about that. Hopefully, she'll be safe."

"I'll do what I can, if she comes back," Toku said.

"Thank you," she said. "I'm going to leave something in her room. It's for all of you. There are instructions inside. Just make sure nobody else finds it."

"I promise, Momma," he said.

The elevator dinged, and the doors opened.

"Thank you, Toku," she said.

"Anything for the family," he said, and the comm went dead.

Maria sighed and stepped out of the elevator into the main aisle of Lab 4. It looked exactly as she had left it, save for the fact that the shadows inside the maturation chambers were now motionless. Asleep. As she stared at the chambers, something occurred to her…about what El Presidenté had offered her.

She walked down the aisle, inspecting each console to make sure all systems were nominal. When she reached the middle, she heard a motion behind her.

"Maria?" a frightened man's voice called out.

Maria spun, pulling the pistol from her waistband. She leveled it at Richard Cabrillo, standing in her office doorway.

His eyes went wide.

"Don't move," Maria said, approaching him slowly. Altra kept pace, her feet clicking across the tile. "What are you doing here?" she asked.

"I guess you've come to finish the job?" he asked, terrified.

Maria cocked her head to the side. "What are you talking about."

"You had Julio killed, out of revenge, and now you want to kill me," he said, backing up.

Maria chuckled. "I didn't have Julio killed. El Presidenté did that. Although, I have to admit, I didn't lose any sleep over it when I found out." She eyed him. "Where is Selina?"

Richard looked surprised. "Julio had her sent away for training somewhere."

"Why?"

"He planned on keeping her for himself…as a body guard. She's not due back for weeks."

Maria's heart broke. There was no way they could stay for her. She realized that all of it was Richard's fault. His ambition had set the wheels in motion. Her heart went cold, and apparently, her eyes did too, because Richard got an even more terrified look in his face.

"Please—" he started.

She raised the pistol and pulled the trigger three times. Crimson blossomed on his chest and he staggered backward, falling to the floor. She looked around her office, and back at Richard's body. She was amazed at how easy it had been to kill him.

Slipping the pistol into her waistband again, she walked out of her office and turned left toward the end of the aisle. She opened the door there, revealing a long hallway lined with doors on either side. Stepping up to the first one on the right, she opened it and stepped into a small dorm room of sorts, with a small desk, chair, and a single bed.

"Altra, slide…*that* under the bed," she said, gesturing at her dead former colleague.

"Yes, Doctor Fujimoto," Altra replied, and did as she instructed.

Maria went to the desk and pulled out a pen and a piece of paper, writing a quick note.

Selina, find Toku. He has something for you. I wish you could have come with us, but there just wasn't time. I will always regret having to leave without you. Please forgive me. Please survive. Love, Momma.

She stepped up to the bed and slid the note between the blanket and pillow, where only Selina would find it.

"Come on, Altra, let's wake them up and get out of here," she said.

"Yes, Doctor Fujimoto."

* * *

Five private busses rolled down the nearly empty highway, having left the city twenty miles behind them. Maria sat in the front seat as Altra drove the first bus. She looked over her shoulder at the faces of sixty-five of her children. Feline, canine, and rhino all looked up at her with a mix of fear and wonder.

Maria had awakened them as quickly as possible, told them they were escaping, and marched them up the stairwell to the lowest level of the parking garage where busses she'd charted through PSG sat waiting for them.

Altra guided the bus onto a narrow side road bordered by thick trees and continued on for another four miles until they came to a wide swath of farmland that opened up for miles. Not far ahead, squatting in the middle of a green field, sat the interface troop transport. Altra pulled off the road, and they bounced over the rows of plowed soil, coming to a stop forty meters from the transport.

In the darkness, just outside the open loading ramp at the back of the transport, stood Carmen and Angel, illuminated by the bay loading lights.

Maria led her children to the rear of the lander and heard low growls, muttering, and mewling behind her.

"Did they get it?" Maria called out.

"In orbit. It is no ship of the line," Angel replied with a smile, "but for a mothballed assault ship, it will do."

"It all went like clockwork," Carmen added.

"Excellent," Maria said. "Once we're aboard, we'll assign duties and set course for Montoya Four-Gamma. We have four hundred maturation chambers, and the consoles to support them ready to go. Vasquez will be dead by the time we're gone, if he isn't already."

Carmen and Angel smiled.

"I'll get right on it," Angel said, turning and walking into the transport.

"What happens now?" Isabella asked from behind her.

"There's a ship up there, waiting for us. With it, we're going to steal some equipment, and we're leaving this system as quickly as we can." She looked into his eyes, then looked out at the ocean of furred faces looking to her with hope in their eyes. "It's time to find you all a home."

* * * * *

Quincy J. Allen Bio

Quincy J. Allen is a cross-genre writer with numerous short story publications and a growing list of novels. His first short story collection *Out Through the Attic*, came out in 2014 from 7DS Books, and its sequel was released in 2019. His most recent short story, "Sons of the Father," appeared in Larry Correia's *Monster Hunter: Files* from Baen, published in October of 2017.

Chemical Burn, his first novel in the sci-fi detective noir series Endgame, was a finalist in RMFW's Colorado Gold Contest in 2011, and the latest installment of the Blood War Chronicles, *Blood Oath,* is book 3 in an epic fantasy series featuring a clockwork gunslinger in the Old West. His first media tie-in novel, *Colt the Outlander: Shadow of Ruin,* set in the Aradio brothers' Colt the Outlander universe, debuted at San Diego Comic Con in July, 2018. It's a post-apocalyptic sci-fi adventure with bounty hunters, feline assassins, and killer machines of alien origin. He is currently working with Kevin Ikenberry and Mark Alan Edelheit on new novels, as well as continuing books in his own series.

He is a writer, publisher, and editor who works out of his home in Charlotte, North Carolina with the woman of his dreams, the best dog ever, and a cat that is either an angel or the devil incarnate.

# # # # #

Do or Die

by Jamie Ibson

"**M**icah Carillon, you have been convicted of murder, piracy, slavery, and petty theft. You have been sentenced to death for your crimes, and by the power invested in me by Her Royal Highness, Queen Suzanne of Windsor, I hereby carry out said execution forthwith, etcetera, etcetera."

"*Miff iff oolhüt,*" the condemned protested, and received a cuff to the back of his helmet for his protestations that had him seeing stars again. He'd been gagged after spitting in one of the bastard's titanium faces.

"Moments like these remind me of an ancient saying. *You can't control who comes into your life, but you can always choose what airlock to throw them out of.* As it happens, we stand here today *in* one such airlock. You're an inhuman savage, Carillon, and it is my distinct pleasure to put you down." The leader of the cyborgs closed Carillon's cracked polymer visor, and mashed a transponder onto it with sealing putty.

There were three of them in the airlock. The two troops in stylized ancient Greek armor, complete with Trojan helmets, were tethered to the deck. Micah Carillon, murderer, pirate, slaver and thief, was decidedly *not*. His suit went tight as air was evacuated, and then the door opened, bathing them in blinding sunlight and radiant heat. The ship's screens filtered out the many harmful rays Parker-Barrow's sun put out, but when one was close enough to a sun to deploy a fuel scoop, it was dangerous to be out of doors.

Carillon writhed and struggled, but he was on his knees, his hands and ankles poly-cuffed and bound to each other. His shipsuit would have protected him from mere vacuum, but it couldn't handle the heat at a mere hundred fifty light seconds and sweat dripped into his eyes, burning. A brutal kick from behind sent him tumbling forward, away from the ship. His rib cracked from the impact, and he watched, helpless, as the airlock hatch to *his* ship, the Free Mercenary Ship *Reprisal*, closed with him on the wrong side.

* * *

Forty three seconds passed before the transponder on Carillon's visor confirmed his vitals had ceased, overwhelmed by the brutal heat of the danger-close sun. Fifty-one more seconds passed before the vac suit spontaneously ignited, and another thirty seconds passed before the transponder ceased transmitting.

Having confirmed Carillon was now nothing but carbon and ash, Bellerophon returned to the interior of the reclaimed ship. There was work to be done.

* * *

"Ahoy, *Pandora's Hope*,"

"*Ahoy,* Reprisal," Captain Mick Mitchell replied. "*All goes well?*"

"The primary business is concluded and recorded for the courts, and we have better than thirty innocents to transfer over. We will remain aboard with our prisoners to avoid any mischief, but Daedalus assures me this heap can keep pace with *Hope*, despite its appearances. If you and Kari would join us, I think our new guests in the hold want to see a friendly *female* face, rather than these ugly mugs."

"You mean your cyborg death's head doesn't win hearts and minds? I'm shocked, Roph, positively shocked. I'm sending Daedalus the intercept now, we'll meet you above Parker-Barrow Three."

"See you soon," Bellerophon replied. Mitchell was right, of course. Long ago, when he'd swapped his failing, crippled meat body for this synthetic one, he'd gotten one of the scarier looking visages they had. It made sense at the time, since the Lakonia Project was a military one, and any psychological advantage was a good one. But there were times when he didn't want to look utterly terrifying, which generally meant having to hide behind a blank-faced helmet.

"Course set," Daedalus confirmed from the pilot's station. "Our passengers might wish to know they've been rescued, boss."

"I'll take care of that now," Bellerophon replied, and used the comms desk to open a channel to the inner hold of *Reprisal*.

"Attention, passengers, this is Commander Bellerophon of Myrmidons Incorporated, a contractor group operating under writ from Windsor Court. We have seized this vessel from the slavers who captured you, and their captain, one Micah Carillon, has been executed under Queen Suzanne's own authority. Please remain calm, we will be rendezvousing with our partner ship, *Pandora's Hope*, in approximately four standard hours. You will find the accommodations rather more pleasant there, if perhaps a tad crowded. We are currently six jumps and a hundred light years or so from the Windsor cluster, so it will be a little less than three weeks before we can get you home. Please make any injuries or illnesses known to *Hope*'s crew so they can be treated, and then help yourself to a meal. Bellerophon, out."

* * *

"Why do we do this honor guard bullshit again?" Kratos whispered to Artemis.

"Because the kids need to know there are good guys too. Now shut up and fake it," she whispered back.

"Myrmidons, hah-ten, CHUN!" Captain Mitchell ordered, and the eight cyborgs came to attention with crisp, mechanical precision. They towered over the unaugmented humans, their average height being close to two hundred centimeters. *Hope's* pilot, Kari Castell, escorted the first woman down the line of armored hoplites, still as statues. The woman had a young boy perched on one hip, and the child's eyes went wide as he took in their armored plate, finned helmets, and obviously extensive mechanical parts. The child tugged at the woman's sleeve and whispered in her ear.

"I don't know, Eric, why don't you ask him?" she answered and let the boy down. He timidly approached Kratos, and stared up at the Myrmidon's armored form.

"Sir? Is it true you chopped off your *whole body*?"

"*What the hell?*" Kratos subvocalized on his internal circuit, inaudible to everyone but the cyborgs.

"Answer him, you ass," Artemis replied. *"And take a knee, while you're at it."*

Kratos stood still for a moment, and then did as bidden and knelt before the boy, putting them face to face.

"Kind of," he answered. "My…the body I was born with is long gone. My brain and spine are still in here though," he said, rapping on his helmet with an armored hand.

"Why?" the boy asked.

"Why…?" Kratos repeated stupidly. *"This is why I hate kids,"* he grumbled inaudibly and Artemis might have let her form slip a tad as she suppressed a giggle.

"Why did you chop your body off? Didn't it hurt?"

"Oh. Because I was dying," he replied, blunt and direct. "I was born with a disease called cystic fibrosis, and a *really* awful case of it. All of the bits in my body that were keeping me alive were failing, and I was going to be dead before I was twenty standard. Same for all of us, we were all dying, and now we're better."

"Thank you," Eric said in a quiet voice, and wrapped his arms around Kratos' neck.

"For…what?" Kratos stammered. It was, to be precise, the *second* time he'd ever been hugged in his twenty-five years as a cyborg.

"If you hadn't chopped your body off, you wouldn't have been here to save us!" Eric beamed. "I'm sorry you were dying, but this new you is *awesome.*"

"Thanks, kid," Kratos replied. "How about you go get aboard ship so we can get you home, huh?"

"Mmkay," Eric nodded and took the woman's hand, and she led the boy down the passageway to *Pandora's Hope.*

"Dawww," Artemis teased over the circuit. *"You have a* fan!"

"Let's just get this over with," Kratos replied. "I hate kids. Mostly. I concede young master Eric seems pretty alright."

* * *

"Once again, I can't thank you enough Mister, I mean, *Commander* Bellerophon. It is contractors like yourself that truly does your guild credit," Sterling North, the Duke of Rideau gushed, shaking Bellerophon's hand with both of his.

"Thank you, your Grace," the Myrmidon commander replied. He gestured broadly to the soiree the duke had thrown in his team's honor. "This is all a bit much; none of my team are really "tuxes and ties" types. The Hellenic Augmented and Robot Defense Corps occasionally hosted Regimental Dinners, with allowances for cyborgs in dress uniform. We'd get a really nice buff job on our armor plates and would pin our medals on with magnets, but that was it."

"I had been meaning to ask about that, Commander, as I never got your full story. I met with each of the survivors upon their return, and one young lad said something about your troops being ill?"

"Not any more, of course," Bellerophon nodded. "But yes, we were all dying, once upon a time. Medicine nowadays is basically divided up now into 'fending off foreign viruses or bacteria,' and 'failing body parts.' The former keeps us hopping, what with xenovirii and exotic conditions. Failing body parts, unless it's the brain, we've got beat. In my case, I had Duchenne's muscular dystrophy. Had I not swapped out my meat body for this one, I would have been dead and gone thirty years ago. The Lakonia Program made it possible."

"What is the Lakonia Program, precisely?" The duke finished his rye, and motioned to a server for another. "I imagine some details are secret, but there must be some public knowledge, or no one would sign up?"

"In Ancient Greece, the Spartans threw imperfect babies from the cliffs to be dashed to death on the rocks below, or eaten by predators, or what have you. It was a harsh time, and the Spartans were a harsh people. Spartan men were raised to be some of the toughest soldiers in all of ancient Greece. The Hellenic Cluster's Lakonia Program subverts that, somewhat, by helping those imperfect babies *become* some of the toughest soldiers we have. My failing body was gradually replaced over the years I attended the Hellenic Military Academy. Kratos, who told the boy about being 'ill,' had cystic fibrosis. My second in command, Daedalus, had Guillan-Barre Syndrome. Everyone on my team had something serious; everyone was dying of *something*. You have to be facing death square in the face to be willing to undergo full conversion; nobody in their right minds wants to be...*this*." Bellerophon gestured to his death's head face and synthetic body. "We bought our new bodies and a new future by serving our government for twenty years in the HARD Corps, or whatever their local equivalent was. Thor is a 'Forgeborn,' from Asgaard. Ryu is from Kagoshima's *Masamune* program. Janus is from Palermo, and Nephilim is from New Tsiyyon. Now, I'm the majority shareholder of Myrmidons, Inc: a consultancy corporation engaged in high-risk problem solving, troubleshooting, and holder of several Writs of Marque. My hoplites all hold shares in the Corp, and we've shared a lengthy partnership with *Pandora's Hope,* one of the fastest corvettes you'll care to hire. You'll note it took us barely eighteen days to get here all the way from Parker-Barrow."

The duke laughed. "No doubt my citizens appreciate your speed and customer service, I know Her Majesty and I do. A trip like that in *HMRS Toronto* would have taken five weeks, minimum, more likely six." A well-dressed man in his fifties or sixties, with steel-grey hair and an extensive body-sculpt joined them. "Have you met Mister Lauzon? He's a vice president with Apex Energy, handles procurement contracts and such."

"Sir," Bellerophon said, shaking the newcomer's hand.

"Congratulations, Commander," Lauzon said, and the duke bowed out of the conversation and drifted into another. "That was a dynamic situation, and your team handled it professionally. Everyone is pleased to be rid of Carillon and his gang. Could I perhaps get your comm info? It is always in a Corp's best interests to have a team of heavy hitters on speed-dial."

"Certainly. Now that we're off contract, we're looking for work again. Anything in mind?"

"Perhaps," Lauzon hedged, looking thoughtful.

* * *

"Hey, Boss, there's some Johnson here, says he's got a contract for us," Daedalus sent over the internal comm. "It's *time sensitive*," he added, the finger-quotes audible in his tone.

"I was just searching the hub for a job. Search 'em, and bring 'em up," Bellerophon replied.

The soiree had gone late, as they tended to, and he'd woken early, as he tended to. No amount of cybernetic conversion could change the brains' need for sleep, although 'plants could reduce it. Nor did he suffer any kind of a hangover, despite putting away several glasses of Ridian rye whiskey the night before. He had subroutines to dial up his synthetic liver's function and was able to filter out all the alcohol in his 'blood' without needing to worry about awkward things like hangovers.

The door chimed, and Bellerophon's second-in-command escorted a suit into their ready room.

"A mutual friend mentioned some unusually competent contractors were in town," the suit said, with a thick New Rhodesian accent. "I have a time-sensitive window of opportunity for a fast-moving, hard-hitting team of professionals."

"It's nice to hear our qualifications summed up so well," Bellerophon replied. "What's the job?"

"Two-fold. As you may or may not be aware, *El Republica del Escobar* is undergoing a bit of a crisis. Seems El Presidenté was holding the entire system together through a network of bribes, blackmail, contracts, and coercion. He got whacked about the same time you were rescuing all those poor lost waifs out in the UST, and the entire Escobaran cluster began tearing itself apart an hour later."

"What's the job?" Daedalus interrupted. "We can get the cultural sensitivity brief on the way."

"As I said, two-fold. One, Escobar was a valued client, but their money isn't worth Jötunn shite anymore, and Paragon Savage just made a fatal mistake." Johnson swiped a command on his wrist tablet, and a holo of Montoya III, one of Escobar's planets, illuminated the air in front of them. "They have a major facility in Montoya's capital, and *had* been in Presidenté Vasquez' pocket. With him gone, their...arrangement, is gone too. They've just pulled a significant chunk of their genies out and left the facility dramatically under-staffed, security-wise. Get in, plug in. I have a Hydra worm that will sort, prioritize, and extract as much data as it can in whatever time you can buy."

"What kind of genies?" Bellerophon asked.

"Paragon Savage is an Alpha tier gene-mod MegaCorp," the suit replied. "Their top tier operatives are baseline human with wolf, cat or rhino mixed in. The rhinos are living tanks, their skin can stop gauss rounds. Cats tend to be assassins and agents, the wolves..." Johnson trailed off, swallowed hard, and regained his composure, "Intelligent, rational, pack-based werewolves in custom power armor doesn't really do them justice. Paragon used to be strictly research. Now they have an entire "Direct Action" division and they're making *bank*. Living or dead samples are a bonus."

"That's a little grim," Bellerophon replied, "I don't mind bringing home gene samples from dead combatants but we won't kidnap someone to turn them into a lab rat, werewolf or not."

"Johnson" blinked. "Killing is fine, but capture is not?"

"There are fates worse than death. I'm quite sure our mutual friend briefed you on our last job—recall what happened to Mister Carillon, and more importantly, *why*. What else?"

"There are some friendlies caught in a cleft stick. Apex Energies' people would appreciate a ride home, but we—*they*, don't want rivals to raid *their* facilities. So you'll need to scrub the lab and servers, and then demo the building before you extract. Ridian security staff need a ride home as well—they're co-located with Apex Energies and there's no way a Ridian frigate could enter the system now, so there is a quiet bonus on the side for them. The Escobaran government is heavily backing contractors, which gives you some leverage to get in where govs cannot."

"Not asking much, are you? Raid PSG, fight off their commando werewolves, collect samples, evacuate AE's people, evacuate the Ridians, and demo the AE building, all from a system in the midst of a civil war," Daedalus summed up. "Is the juice worth the squeeze?"

"I believe this fee should cover your transportation to and from, and adequately address your expertise and the risk involved," Johnson said, and flashed an eight-digit sum on his tablet. "Half for the PSG raid, half for extraction of AE's personnel. Ten percent bonuses for each additional objective—the samples, the Ridians, and destruction of AE's facility."

"Make it...*twenty* percent, and you've got a deal," Bellerophon said. "Send Duke North the bill."

* * *

"It occurs to me the potential for chaos and disaster is rather high on a contract such as this," Thunderpaws said thoughtfully, and smiles broke out around the ops center on board *Pandora's Hope*. Thunderpaws had a gift for understatement, which fit his tiny frame well. The mogwai were aliens from beyond the Windsor cluster, but the two xenos on board could not be more dissimilar. Silver, the ship's loadmaster, was a xeno from beyond the Yggdrasil cluster. Jötunn were massive, thick-hided, xenos with a reputation for alcoholism and fist-fighting. Thunderpaws, however, was a mogwai. They were the first alien race humanity met when it left the Sol system, and the origin of the aliens' name was shrouded in history. He was short, barely eighty centimeters tall, nimble, and fiendishly clever; he was a share-holding member of the crew, unlike Silver, and served as their science officer. He had broad birch-leaf-shaped pointy ears, large expressive eyes, and fine fur covered his body from head to toe. Their fur patterns varied with the individual as much as domestic housecats, and Thunderpaws' own fur was snow-white with wide patches of dark brown.

"Humans are inherently chaotic, and residents of the *Republica del Escobar* even more so. Montoya holds eight of the ten standard markers for a failing colony, and Marquez is in open rebellion as they have, as you humans say, 'seen the writing on the wall.' Unconfirmed reports indicate that El Presidenté's Republican Guard, having failed in their primary duty to protect Presidenté Vasquez, has been putting down rioting with not just lethal force but *excessive* lethal force. Bipedal warbots armed with high energy and mass driver weaponry have deployed against civilians armed with little better than rocks and homemade incendiaries. *Los Jaguares Negros* are suspected in several assassinations against the rebellion's leadership, and any journalist who voice their suspicious out loud. Civilian casualties are, at minimum, in the six-digits."

"You'd think the Ridiots would have known to cut bait before it got this bad, *eh?*" Kratos mused.

"A study of human history would show they, culturally, have a multi-century long history of blindly hoping all would work out for the best, and then blaming their political leadership for failing to take decisive action when it was clearly necessary," Thunderpaws replied. "Excessively optimistic, polite to a fault—barring ice hockey of course—strong social net but weak military, unwilling to—"

"It was sarcasm, Thunderpaws," Mitchell cut him off. Thunderpaws stopped mid-phrase, stroked his white-furred chin for a moment, and widened his already overlarge eyes.

"Ah. Yes, I see. Your linguistic subtleties occasionally escape my notice," he said in a detached tone. "I have not yet mastered 'sarcasm.'"

"And we'll all be in a hurt locker when you do," Aubyn "Ben" Faolain said with a grin, eliciting a chuckle from around the conference table. The human smiles were Thunderpaws' cue to smile along with them, but the atmosphere at the table dropped ten degrees when his needle-sharp incisors and canines were bared. The xenos were furry and cute, but their nature as obligate carnivores made for fierce smiles.

Bellerophon resumed his briefing. "Chaos, panic, and disorder will absolutely be the name of the game on the ground, but that's why they pay us the megacreds. Hitting Paragon Savage will be a standard corporate raid, one each. I don't mind clipping ears if we get into a firefight, but under no circumstances are we kidnapping a genie for AE's mad scientists to enslave and torture, fuck that noise. Not even for three million."

"Three million yen? For a seven-system run headlong into a civil war to rescue some Darwin candidates who couldn't see their way out the door?" Kratos interjected. "What the hell, over?"

"That's the *bonus*," Bellerophon calmly replied. "Total vig is fifteen million, with three additional objectives worth three million per. Genetic samples, extracting the Ridians, and demoing the Apex megascrape means fifteen becomes *twenty-four* million. The crew of the *Pandora* get their standard one quarter cut, plus combat bonuses, if any. After the Corp gets its percent, we divide the rest."

Kratos did the math in his head. After Myrmidons Inc and *Pandora's Hope* took its slice, the payment was divided out on a share-by-share basis. He'd invested heavily in the Corp, despite being junior,

182 | IBSON & KENNEDY

and "owned" ten percent of the shares in the company and was therefore owed ten percent of what was left. ¥1,440,000 was a helluva payday for one nights' work, even given the travel time and the risk. Bellerophon owned three times as much, but then again, he'd founded Myrmidons Inc and heavily reinvested in the Corp with his own take too. Part of what made Myrmidons Inc so desirable was their partnership with *Pandora's Hope*, which could scream across vast interstellar gulfs at omega band speeds, the fastest blue-shift tech was currently capable of. And *that* was what earned the *Pandora's Hope* crew twenty-five percent of the Myrmidons' gross contract fees.

"Well in that case, the juice is *definitely* worth the squeeze," Kratos opined. "How many friendlies, how many tangos? Do I pack more demo or more ammo?"

"The Ridians have one light squad from the Queen's First Lancers in powered Coyote armor, so they ought to be solid in a fight, and Apex Energies has moderately well-equipped security forces as well," Bellerophon continued. "Modern environmental hard armor, and they of course issue their staff their own brand of carbines and sidearms. PITAs likely outnumber us a couple thousand to one. *Pegasus* can't lift everyone at once, so if at all possible, we secure the ground level while *Pegasus* lifts the first wave from the roof. There should be twenty civilians and the AE light security troops; they can go first. We'll return with Charlie and the Lancers second, and if we have to blow their armor in place, so be it. Gents, that means BRUTE armor, power packs and energy weapons. Ladies, bring your ANGEL gear. Silver and Ben will handle the evacuees on *Hope* and get them stashed away while we're still dirtside."

* * *

The trip to Montoya was tedious, even though *Pandora's Hope* was as fast or faster than any ship one cared to name. Smaller ships with larger power plants could reach exponentially higher FTL speeds, meaning they were the modern equivalent of Ye Olde Ocean-Going-Hydrofoils, compared to frigates and cruisers that once sailed Earth's seas using *diesel* and *propellers*. They were still traversing nine systems, though, and it took just over four weeks to travel more than a hundred sixty light years.

Every time they dropped out of blue-shift in a new system, the NavBeacons relaying the latest news made the situation on Montoya sound worse and worse.

* * *

"Dropping out of omega band in four, three, two..." Castell warned, and then Montoya's sun filled the viewscreen. The usual NavBeacon data began scrolling across the viewscreen, when Thunderpaws spoke.

"Heavy cruiser *Bogota,* already hailing us," he said. "They're ten minutes out and slowing. Deceleration profile suggests...omicron band, about all most Heavies can handle. They'll overshoot somewhat, but the *Cordoba* and *Nariño* are cutter escorts and they're already slowing at two hundred thirty standard gravities."

"What do they—" Mitchell started to ask, but Thunderpaws interrupted, continuing his update.

"Flash update from NavBeacons, Montoya system is under martial law and unauthorized entry will be met with lethal force. *Bogota* has sent a track, and requires we not deviate as they maneuver to intercept."

"Seems the system has collapsed even faster than we anticipated. Follow their directions," she ordered, then activated her comm. "Roph, get up here. Our plan may have just contacted the enemy early."

Castell set the direction and speed the *Bogota* ordered, and accelerated to match, making sure to keep their top acceleration at 144 gravities, the top acceleration rating for the *upsilon* band in real space. It never paid to give away tactical data when one could help it. Minutes passed as the heavy cruiser and its gunboats settled into an ominous overwatch position to their stern and flanks.

"We are now close enough for live video comms without significant delay," Thunderpaws announced. "They are hailing us."

"Onscreen," Mitchell nodded. A handsome, darkly tanned man with an aquiline nose, close-cropped salt-and-pepper hair at his temples, and white naval beret filled the screen.

"*Buenas dias,* Pandora's Hope, *soy el Capitán Ernesto Guerrero,*" the man said.

"And I am Captain Mick Mitchell, of the Free Mercenary Ship *Pandora's Hope*, with business on Montoya Three. We request safe entry into the system on an evacuation and extraction contract."

"*You may have noticed, Captain Mitchell, that Montoya is not stable at the moment,*" Guerrero replied. "*Who, precisely, are you evacuating?*"

"My contract includes a non-disclosure agreement above and beyond the usual discretion afforded contracts," Mitchell said. "Sending you the redacted copy now. All I can tell you without breaching contract is they are neither Escobaran citizens nor are they belligerents in your current troubles. Standing contractor law.

"*Yes, yes, I know all about your 'contractor law,' Captain Mitchell,*" Guerrero snarled. The shift in his demeanor was abrupt, as though

Mitchell had struck some nerve. "*I do not think it is so relevant when the planet itself is in rebellion, and the only law that exists is that which the Escobaran government will enforce. Why should I not simply vaporize your ship and be done with you?*"

"Because you like being a captain in the Republic's Armada," Mitchell answered evenly. "You and I both know Escobar uses contractors *extensively,* and I guarantee your boss would be asking some very pointed questions about how they managed to put an idiot of your subcaliber, who doesn't understand contractor law, in charge of a cruiser like the *Bogota.*"

The Escobaran ship captain's face contorted with rage, and, as he lit into another rant, Mitchell muted him. Kari Castel at the pilot's controls fought to control a smirk as the man raged silently at them, and Mitchell continued.

"For the record, contractor law states that if you, as a government actor, *unlawfully* interfere in *lawful* contractor business, every contract your government holds with *any* registered contractor comes due in full. The yen held in escrow transfer, *every* contractor backstopping your forces on Montoya Three walks off the job with a fat payday, and it would be *your* fault. You will have blasted one minor corvette, no threat to any ship of the Armada, and in doing so you will have compromised the safety and security of the *entire* Republic. Every garrison contract walks. Every security post, walks. Every direct-action group not currently in a firefight, *walks.* This isn't my first rodeo, Captain Guerrero, and if you think *Hope* isn't loaded with a post-mortem drone or three, you're some special kind of stupid."

She let the angry face on the other side of the view screen rant for a few more seconds, and when he appeared to pause for breath, she unmuted him.

"Are we done here?"

Guerrero stabbed a button, and the screen winked out.

"*Bogota, Cordoba,* and *Nariño* are accelerating away," Thunderpaws advised a moment later. "They've transmitted a security certificate, valid for 168 standard hours, with a warning to be gone by then or face seizure on suspicion of espionage."

"Better than nothing," Mitchell replied. "Kari, no screwing around, get us to Montoya Three."

"Course laid in. I don't trust those bastards, so I'm going to pretend we're slower than we are. At upsilon band Gs, we'll be there in a little more than seven hours,"

"I'll tell Bellerophon to get his party dress on," Faolain declared as he stood to go aft. "And then I'll warm up *Pegasus.*"

* * *

"Been a while since you went in heavy," Faolain observed. The Myrmidon's armory was buzzing as each of the cyborgs armored up in their Hoplite BRUTE armor. The Ballistic/Reflective Urban Tactical Exo was Ares Interstellar's top cyborg armor go-to for close work, as it was just as effective against kinetic rounds as it was against energy weapons. Working in pairs, they checked and double-checked each plate as sabatons, greaves, pteryges, cuirass, pauldrons, and vambraces were bolted to calves, thighs, torso, chest and arms. It more than doubled their mass and slowed them down somewhat, but the BRUTE armor would render their limbs and systems nearly invulnerable to small arms. Nobody liked an escort mission, but being able to soak up incoming fire could mean the difference between a successful payday and catastrophic failure.

"Carillon was scum," Kratos replied as he bolted Janus's second vambrace on. "If he hadn't had those hostages, we could have taken him and his gang naked and unarmed."

"Some days I feel like we're the galaxy's garbage men," Janus complained. "But then I remind myself we're *very well paid* garbage men, and I don't mind so much."

Each plate shone in the Myrmidon's preferred burnished bronze, which reflected the electric-blue hoplon shield that winked into existence on Janus' forearm. Testing complete, he put the shield away, donned his load-bearing harness, camo cloak, holstered his gauss pistol, slung his ion carbine, and sheathed his blade.

Nephilim tested her ANGEL armor, which let her bounce all over the hold in a series of controlled, gravity-defying leaps. Her cybernetic legs were already tremendously powerful, able to leg-press more than a thousand kilos, and her ability to jump was magnified. The Advanced Null-Grav Exo; Light was one of Ares Interstellar's newest products, it hadn't been available when she'd been in New Tsiyyon's Shayetet 21. It didn't precisely *nullify* gravity, but it did reduce it by ninety percent for the wearer, in ten-second bursts. It allowed both of the team snipers to leap tall buildings in a single bound, glide on their wingsuits for short distances, and dramatically improved their climbing grapnel's performance. Neph bounded across the hold from wall to ceiling to wall with the lithe balance of an Olympic gymnast, and tucked her legs under her when the ANGEL effect cut out at the expected time.

Their armor fitted, Kratos and Thor turned their attention to their demolition kits, prepping tubes and blocks of D-8 for rapid deployment. Kratos considered it a point of pride that he had never failed to cut through an operational Gordian Knot with sufficient application of enough Deton-8 plastique.

One by one, as each of the Myrmidons finished their preparations, they locked their Trojan-style helmets on. The "horsehair" plumes were actually a fine mesh of sensor strands that detected sound, energy, and radiation. The energy shields that rendered them faceless behind the cheek plates and nosepiece further improved the protection offered to their most vulnerable part—their brain—against incoming fire. Finally ready for battle, the Myrmidons boarded *Pegasus* and strapped in.

* * *

"This is...peculiar," Thunderpaws murmured from his station. "The sole craft in orbit above Montoya III is the *FMS Kiberskiy Medved*, a Ship-Corp from Putinskaya Zvezda. The ship crew and troops on board are a single Corp, not the partnership like we enjoy with the Myrmidons. The CEO and crew are wanted in the United States of Texas on multiple charges of murder and wanton destruction. There are *no* Escobaran ships in orbit, which is highly unusual, especially for a planet in crisis."

* * *

Pegasus released from the belly of *Pandora's Hope* and began its descent. The interface ship shuddered as atmosphere superheated its exterior until it broke through the hundred kilometer Karman line that marked the change from space to atmosphere. As the air grew more dense, *Pegasus'* aerodynamics took over until the ship's gravity drive cut out and turbo fans took over.

"Fifty klicks from Magdalena," Faolain updated. "We'll be on the ground in twenty minutes. There's the port authority escort now." He tapped a display. A pair of variable-wing interceptors had pulled in behind *Pegasus* and taken a five-and-seven o'clock escort position, much like the *Bogota*'s cutters had. He followed the AR guidance rings down until he reached the designated pad, and set the interface craft down on landing jacks.

* * *

The squad of security goons waiting for them wore *Prioridad Una Seguridad* uniforms and had subguns slung over their shoulders. They had two ground cars with spotlights focused on the ramp as it lowered, and they stayed in the shadows, not realizing the Myrmidons could see them easily in the nighttime darkness with their filtered optics. The senior NCO stepped forward and held out a hand.

"*Identificación, por favor,*" he demanded, and Faolain turned over his tablet. The holo of the security certificate the *Bogota* had transmitted was already lit, and "Sergeant Lopez" examined it, the attached ID clearances, the attached weapons clearances, and their bonded contractor status. One of the many compromises interstellar governments made to secure the assistance of contractors and ship-corps, they would be permitted to carry personal arms, up to a certain level as they went about their business, with the understanding that they would be legally liable for any illegal activity. Much of what they did *was* illegal, of course, which just meant some of the best contractors were the ones who knew how to get away with it. The Myrmidons

190 | IBSON & KENNEDY

knew it, the Priority One Security contractors knew it, and the Gov knew it.

Ten security troopers fanned out, checking the identification of each cyborg and matching it to the certificate, while Lopez looked up into the hold of *Pegasus*. He eyed the nose of their preferred ground transport, visible inside, and frowned.

"*Stay out of trouble,*" he said, still in Spanish. "*We have enough as it is.*"

The Myrmidon's chosen ground vehicle was a M.A.T.T. from Titanium Allies. The Multipurpose Armored Tactical Transport rolled down the ramp, and Janus activated its passive defensive systems. The Combat Command & Control Carrier, nicknamed "Charlie," or "Charlie Four," had variable-surface skin camouflage, and rippled as it adopted a mottled brown and grey to better blend in with the urban terrain. The Myrmidons got on board, and Janus headed for the exit.

Four swing-arms mounted eight drive wheels, giving Charlie unprecedented maneuverability. Each pair could pivot and rotate independently, allowing the carrier to drive like a standard ground car, jink left and right, even rotate in place. With the swingarms out and extended, Charlie could level itself climbing or moving across a slope, depress the nose and lift the stern to get a better angle on targets above or below them, roll clear over debris, and then retract them and punch it for high-speed travel on normal roads. It was an invaluable tool for urban operations, and being able to nimbly pop out from cover while keeping its thickest armor oriented toward the enemy had saved lives. The turret on the aft deck mounted a 14 cm gauss cannon that fired armor-piercing fin-stabilized discarding sabot rounds at more than four thousand meters per second, a light chainblaster for engaging infantry, and a six-pack of SAMs in case of hostile air. Charlie was fast, nimble, and packed a punch, much like the Myrmidons.

"Charlie is clear and rolling," Bellerophon said. "Dustoff, but don't go too far." Ryu passed him a tablet with news feeds scrolling past even as he gave orders. "Sounds like the rioting has escalated into an all-out uprising, we don't want to get bogged down in this shit show. Paragon Savage is only twenty-two klicks, six freeway exits from here. We'll see what we see en route."

* * *

J anus maneuvered Charlie out the gate and pulled onto the main freeway, while Daedalus manned the turret, and Ryu kept a watch on the news feeds. Drones whirred by overhead, following the designated air corridors, delivering packages from the Orinoco warehouses maintained by the port, and returning to pick up more.

"Boss? I'm getting some…interesting news updates," Ryu said, sounding nervous. "Something is going on. Downtown, there was a full scale, no shit, drag out fight between the cops and "La Gente," but now they're talking, something something, mass-casualty event, live feeds are showing—*nanite kotoda…*" he cursed in Japanese, "dozens, no, *hundreds* of people down."

"Show me."

Ryu slugged him one of the feeds he'd been monitoring. A live selfie feed showed an entire intersection strewn with bodies, urban grey powered suits standing fifty meters distant, illuminating the intersection with spotlights and drones above. A few of the suits seemed stunned, another was panicking and gesturing to the troop leader. Few, if any, of the prone Escobarans appeared injured; it was like several hundred people had just laid down for a nap in the middle of a teargas-hazed road.

Men, women, teenagers, and children littered the streets. A few looked like they'd come armored with homemade sports equipment and disposable breathing filters, but the vast majority were wearing little more than normal clothes. The camera focused on one teenage boy, laying across the legs of an older woman, as he coughed, vomited explosively, and then began coughing and choking on the vomitus. The account broadcasting, *ChicaNorte69*, reversed her camera to pick up her face. Her breath came in ragged gasps, distorted by some kind of respirator, and she staggered and tripped. The comm broadcasting the footage fell face up, on another prone body judging from the angle. The suits in the distance retreated toward the scraper and out of view of the camera, leaving the entire intersection very still under the watchful eye of the spotlight drones.

"This just got *bad*," Ryu pronounced, "but I've got *nothing* on sensors. Onboard NBC systems are negative, radiological is normal background average, and any kind of nerve gas or weaponized bio agent would have my threat indicators lighting up like the *Omagari* festival. I've got *nothing*."

"Mission continues," Bellerophon replied. "I agree it looks like some kind of chem weapon. We hit Paragon Savage first, then we reassess. Anything else is secondary."

"Easier schemed than done, Roph," Ryu argued, and he scrolled back the livestream to before the broadcaster fell over and paused the feed. The scraper beyond the scattered bodies bore the stylized Æ of Apex Energy.

"Those suits must have been the Ridians," Bellerophon said, "re-assessment complete. They're alive: the contract continues."

* * *

Three kilometers further down the freeway, a Mitsuyota ground car ahead of them edged closer to the shoulder, until the onboard driver assist nudged it back into its lane. The gentle pressure the unconscious driver applied to the steering wheel overcame the VI assist, and the car collided headlong into several barrels filled with safety foam. The safety foam, compressed in an airtight barrel, exploded outwards, cushioning the impact and reducing the severity of any injury to those in the vehicle. Janus had noted the vehicle drifting, and had backed off well in advance. He brought Charlie to a halt just short of the wreck, and dropped the ramp.

Kratos was first out, carbine at the high port. He and Ryu moved quickly but cautiously, stepping over the gooey impact foam, and pulled the driver's door open. The driver, a young woman with glossy black hair and deeply tanned skin, was caked with foam and had vomited over the interior of the car. She wasn't moving. He slipped a monitor patch from his harness onto the side of her neck and frowned when it came back *null*. He reset the patch, reapplied, then shook his head.

"No vitals, boss," he updated and moved to the back seat. He applied another patch to the rear passenger, a boy, maybe thirteen standard, also limp and lifeless. "There's a kid in the back. He's flat too. *Still* nothing on sensors, no sarin IX, no VX, nothing."

"Neph, can you scan a sample?"

"I'll need to take some blood, but yes, I can run tests in Charlie's medical suite. I concur, there's nothing radioactive, and air is clear for known chem weapons." She leaned down to examine the female driver, and gently slipped an eyelid open. Her pupil was dilated, almost entirely hiding the colored iris.

"This isn't nerve agent. If it was, her eyes would be pinpricks."

"Take your samples, Neph," Bellerophon instructed. "Then we carry on. The first thing we do when we're back aboard *Hope* is archive our own recorders, everything we've seen, everything we've touched. If this *is* some new mass destruction weapon, we don't wanna wear it."

* * *

The freeway ahead was littered with yet more wrecks, and curved around a long bend until the claws-and-teeth logo of Paragon Savage Genetics glowed above the shorter scrapers. The facility itself was an enormous pyramidal arcology that sprawled over nearly four square kilometers. The exterior frame was illuminated by spotlights at ground level, showing off soaring arcs of carbon fiber buttresses supporting dense green jungle foliage.

"I'm reluctant to just roll up," Janus opined, "but that might be the simplest thing. I've got nobody moving, nothing on thermal, no security, nothing. Everything inside seems to be functioning just fine—and, correction—I've got armed security staff, prone, out front."

"We dismount here, approach on foot, and set Charlie roving once we've cleared the area. We just have to hope our VIPs at AE aren't affected, either they're alright or they're not. I strongly doubt that was them in the Coyote suits."

"Baldur's blood, Commander, that's pretty fucking cold," Thor cursed. "They leave a conscience in there when they swapped out your heart?"

"Stow it," Daedalus replied for the team leader, glaring at the Asgardian. "This ain't our fight, whatever happened here. Security would be so much meat if they'd been alive to defend this place if we hit it, so the fact they're dead doesn't change much."

Nephilim checked the prone security guard. He was enormous, even taller than the Myrmidons and broad across the shoulders, like an ox. She heaved him over onto his back, revealing a leathery grey skin and misshapen face.

"Genie, rhino," she identified. "He's dead, still warm, like the rest of 'em."

"How long till your toxicology tests are done?" Bellerophon asked, looking the body over.

"Hour, maybe less," she replied. She used a small medical scalpel to slice off a corner of the rhino-genie's ear, and tucked it into a sample pouch. "Let's keep moving."

* * *

The team steadily advanced under the protective aegis of Charlie, above and behind them on the roadway exit ramp. They stacked, and when Kratos got the squeeze on his shoulder, he took two steps out, clearing the entryway and moving inside and left, sweeping for targets. The carbon-fiber frame atrium was twenty storeys high, a triple-canopy faux-jungle open to the humid Montoyan air, angled to match the outside pyramid shape of the arcology. High-intensity illumination from outside gave an ethereal feel to the interior as thin shafts of light pierced the jungle veil and glinted off banks of mist that shrouded the upper structure. The entire atrium remained open to the elements, with trees, ferns, and looping vines hiding the structure behind, like a nature center at a zoo. Small kiosks and infotainment displays deliberately made to look ancient were tucked among the leafy green branches.

Another dead security officer lay in front of the welcome kiosk, his radio just beyond an outstretched hand. This one looked far more like a werewolf than the dead man outside had looked like a rhinoceros. Tall, lean, broad shoulders and narrow waist, exaggerated biceps, forearms, hands and claws. The head was completely furred, pointed canine ears mounted high on the head, not on the side of the skull like a human's. If he didn't know better, Kratos would have guessed the wolfman was another species altogether.

The uniform the dead officer wore was obviously custom tailored to his own unique size and shape, with a strong but light non-Newtonian breastplate, pauldrons, and greaves. He wore a sergeant's chevrons on his collar and a thick power cord connected his Nano-Tempest™ ion blaster to a twenty-five kilo powerpack on his back. Kratos was impressed—ion blasters tended to be cyborg, crew-served or vehicle-mounted weapons, due to the energy-pack requirements. That this wolfman was patrolling with the same blaster on his back as Kratos was spoke volumes about the wolfman's strength and vitality. Kratos grimaced as he collected an eartip from the deceased security officer, and muttered "*a million four, a million four*" as he stashed the sample on his harness.

"Search in pairs," Bellerophon ordered, and Kratos moved down the concourse with Ryu watching his flank. He found four more wolf genie bodies and two "infotainment" animal pens. One pen held a pack of Terran wolves, dead, and another had a leopard, dead.

"This whole city is a fucking crime scene," Kratos complained. The informational kiosks were on a quiet loop, explaining how the mad scientists at PSG had found a way to introduce non-human mammal DNA to their volunteers, 'gifting' them with that which evolution had not. The last, largest pen had three rhinoceros, but unlike everything else, they were unconscious, or sleeping. They were the first living beings they'd seen since clearing customs.

"What the fuck happened here, boss?" Kratos wondered over their internal circuit.

"I don't know, and I don't care to know. I need you to blow the door, we need access to a higher-tier network hub than these little infotainment displays. We're going in."

* * *

"I t's about time they started figuring this "genetic manipulation" shit out, huh?" Kratos opined. "Maybe if these Paragon guys had gotten started on their genetic work, say, a century or two ago, none of us would be 'borgs.'" He'd blown open two barely reinforced doors, and had just *kicked* open the third, to get into a secure section of the arcology. He wondered idly if Paragon Savage Genetics had pinned their security strategy on "hope no one hits us," which didn't seem like much of a strategy at all.

"I'm not real keen on messing with genetic coding," Daedalus disagreed, from behind the security feed display. He pointed to the menagerie of animals kept on site as a source of DNA for PSG's mods. "Look at these mods they're doing. Genetically, they're ninety-

198 | IBSON & KENNEDY

eight percent human. But the two percent they're fucking with, twists them until they're anything but."

"That's what I'm saying!" Kratos retorted. "I would rather be ninety-eight percent human, and two percent badass werewolf, than ninety-eight percent titanium alloy and two percent brain. For one thing, genies get *laid*. Artemis, seriously, back me up here, tell me you wouldn't rather be a cat woman. *Me-oww!*"

Artemis shook her head. "How many times have you had a limb blown off, only to fab a replacement in the field and get back to work?" she argued. "Meat is all well and good, but healing from injury is a pain in the ass and some injuries just don't get better without synthetic parts. I'd choose synthetic every day and twice on weekends. Besides, VR stim works just fine for me, and that's all you need to know about that, thank you very much."

"*Sababa!* Download's done," Nephilim announced. The drive their employer provided had scoured the PSG network for three long minutes before dumping huge volumes of data onto the multi-petabyte drive. They hadn't gotten the entire database, but the drive's worms had known what kind of data to look for, and had prioritized what to download. The internal firewall hadn't stood a chance; it was far more vulnerable to physical intrusion than hacking via the local 'net. "If you *shovav* are done kibitzing instead of standing sentry, we can bounce."

"I've got another movement alarm, one floor up," Daedalus said, looking up from the terminal. He ran the footage back, and caught a shifting shadow on the edge of the camera.

"Hit the stack, Jack," Kratos urged. "Whatever that was is the only other living thing here beyond us and the rhinos. They're too late."

"Bringing Charlie around," Janus advised, and activated a macro he'd established while they waited for the worm to pillage the database. They exited the arcology and met their M.A.T.T. at the atrium gate, ramp lowered.

Kratos paused at the ramp to scan the environment behind them as the remaining cyborgs mounted up. As sensitive as the sensor hairs on his helmet were, the human brain was wired to perceive movement as a primary threat indicator, and his helmet reduced his peripheral vision somewhat. He was therefore surprised when a heavy impact from *above* knocked him prone onto his back. A long, lean female figure crouched over him with a knee on his ribcage and a hand at his throat. Her other hand controlled his elbow, shoulder and wrist, all locked out, and she crouched behind *his* hoplon e-shield as cover. She wore black, form-fitting armor that could have been a wetsuit, with a helmet, tinted visor, and rebreather.

Seven rifles swung to point at her, and she shouted "STOP!" in a harsh, rasping voice, made even stranger by the rebreather she wore. She released her grip on Kratos' arm, pulled the vibroknife she'd held to his neck away, and took a step back.

"I could haf keeled him, but I didn't," she declared in heavily accented Escobaran English. "I don' know who you are or what you want, but if you have a way out of this... *cemetario*, I beg mercy—take me with you?"

Kratos scrambled to his feet and took a step back.

"Fuck you, lady," Kratos spat, "Attack me and then beg for a ride?"

"Had I wish' you dead, you would be dead, sir," she replied evenly. "I would be as well, after your amigos open' fire, but *la muerte es no bueno* for either of us. How better to prove I mean you no harm, than to have you at my mercy and let you live? I merely ask you return the favor."

"Takes some talent to skulk up on a Myrmidon, lady," Bellerophon said, stepping out of Charlie's interior, "and you're only the second living thing we've seen. The rhinos snoozing out front don't seem to be talkative, so maybe you have some idea why everyone around here has caught a severe case of death?"

"I don' know," she replied simply. "I am a genie, an infiltrator for Paragon Savage. I was practicing insertions in our swim tank, but when I come up, my trainer, he'd collapse.' Security was responding to Rico, when the other tech collapsed too, less than a minute later. I watched, and they breathing slow, more and more, until they stopped breathing altogether. I called for help, but no one come, and when I go searching...*todos murieron*, all dead, all gone. I have nowhere to go, but PSG had food, had facilities, so I stayed put while I tried to figure out what was going on. Then I watch you arrive in your fancy tank and hoped it was rescue. Up to you, whether it is."

"Artemis, search. Thor, cover," Bellerophon ordered. "If she twitches the wrong way, we blast her. Your name?"

"My name is Selina Linares," she replied. "But my team lead called me Ocelot. I find myself very recently unemployed—you hiring?"

"Maybe," Bellerophon replied, cautiously. "Whatever happens, until we're done with the op, you're a neutral third party, at best. You want a lift to orbit or beyond, it'll cost."

"I can pay," Selina promised.

* * *

The C⁴ M.A.T.T. stalked the death-stricken streets of Magdalena, avoiding wrecked ground vehicles that choked the inner roadways and too many dead innocents to count. They'd diverted around two major riots-turned-mass graves, hundreds or thousands dead in the streets, no signs of trauma. Escobaran law enforcement, in their visored riot gear, lay dead too. A few wore gas masks, but whatever had killed them had bypassed even those. Janus took Charlie around one more corner, and Apex Energies' Escobaran headquarters came into view. The HQ was a megascraper that occupied most of the city block and soared ninety storeys into the sky.

"I've got two of those Coyote suits on post out front," Daedalus warned. "Active emissions, live pilots. Broadcasting in the clear: *"Attention Queens' First Lancers, this is Myrmidons Incorporated. Relief and extract have arrived. Stand by for Duke North's authentication,"* he sent, and uploaded a proprietary security certificate that could only have come from the Duke.

There was a delay before the heavily armored troops in front of the building responded.

"It's about goddamn time," came a gravelly response. *"I ain't no tenply, but front row seats to an apocalypse are overrated. You could be cloneleggers from New Shanghai, and I wouldn't care, bud."*

* * *

Apex Energies' vehicle park was in the basement, accessed via thorough security protocols for every person and the entire vehicle. The two Coyotes marched in, flanking Charlie, and were hosed down and blown dry. Four more of the eight foot suits of armor stood inside, empty. The Ridian OIC dispatched two of his troops to resume guard outside until matters were settled, and they came running from a ready-room already suited up.

Once past the gauntlet of cleansers, scanners and UV, *Lef*tenant "call me Wayne" Keeso dismounted from his suit. He shook hands and escorted the group to a cargo elevator that could carry their combined mass all at once.

"Well, how to sum up?" Keeso began. "Apex Energy is about the only other Ridian interest our embassy had in the area, and we'd already integrated with them, what with the riots and the unrest. Ambassador Mylette gave the order weeks ago, we lit the burn bin, and escorted her and her family here in a proper Grizzly M.A.T.T. of our own. We were charged with holding the front as the riots and attacks got worse and worse. Per the journos, anyone working for a Corp is "the enemy," and "greedy capitalists." Heavy weapons were few and far between, so there wasn't much threat to us. We had scanners running 24/7 looking for high density e-packs, microfusion cells, explosives, anything really dangerous. Had to zap one or two, but for the most part it was water cannons and retch gas."

"Then...maybe ninety minutes ago...they just started dropping. Everyone in full enviro was fine, anyone not, dropped in place. The LEOs out front died just like everyone else. Twenty minutes after that, Cyberian Bear mercs attacked us. They weren't expecting Coyotes, and we had a merry slaughter before they fucked off. I've got one damaged suit but the operator is fine. It's kinda fucked up, but...I actually preferred the rioting to the silence."

"The more and more I work this over in my brain, the more there's something nagging at the back of my skull, boss," Nephilim said. "Widespread vomiting, collapse, depression of heartrate, depression of respiration, death. It screams nerve agent, but there's no agent our filters can detect. This doesn't fit weaponized bio weapon, and nanites would have shown up on our scanners. What else is there?"

"Drugs," Ocelot interjected, and nine pairs of eyes turned to look at her, Now she was in a clean zone, she felt safe to remove her rebreather, revealing a distinctly feline face, long tawny hair with black stripes, and furred, pointed ears. "You know those Spetznaz types use all kinds of combat drugs to amp their capabilities. What if they deployed an *offensive* drug as well?"

"How do you drug an entire city all at once?" Keeso asked. "Water supply? Air bursting agent?"

Nephilim looked thoughtful for a moment. "Sure, either, both. Drugs would depend on potency, delivery method, and how quickly it's metabolized. Crop duster, drone sprayer, air bursting charge for sure, any, all. Getting the potency right wouldn't matter if the goal was a mass casualty attack, they'd just pile it on higher and deeper. I should have an answer shortly."

"Good. In the meantime, *Lef*tenant, we need to organize the extraction," Bellerophon continued. "Our briefing suggested you had a dozen civilians and another dozen AE Security? The longer we're on the ground, the sooner plans go to shit. Let's call for extract."

"Solid," Keeso agreed. "Apex's chief of security, Dan Wilson, can organize them, he's integrated well with the Embassy staff."

* * *

Hovering over a city collapsing into outright rebellion was nerve-wracking, since *Pegasus* was a big fat target, vulnerable to any asshole within a kilometer who had a laser. They'd found *some* survivors, so there were probably more. Ben Faolain carefully balanced the thrust against the crosswinds like he had one foot on a bowling ball, juggling chainsaws. One mistake could be disastrous. The ramp hinged from the rear of the lander, meaning the nose of the craft was well over the roof of the scraper. The rooftop aircar pad was far too small to land on, but made for a nice flat space to stage off of.

"Everyone's aboard and strapped in," Artemis confirmed over her comm as she hopped lightly off the ramp. *"You're good to go, Ben."*

The ramp lifted and sealed against the underbelly of *Pegasus* as Faolain drifted back from the building's edge, rotated away from the building, and accelerated away. While in VTOL mode the turbines screamed, and every movement was careful and planned. Once *Pegasus* reached a certain velocity, the turbines rotated to gulp air like a normal jet.

Vice President Lauzon, Chief Wilson, Ambassador Mylette, and their assorted hangers-on had taken instruction very well. Being trapped on a planet in full civil war was bad. Watching the city die around them had been *infinitely* worse, and adequately motivated them to move with a sense of urgency once the order was given. AE had a store of full-seal enviro suits in their lab that would keep them alive when they transitioned from the megascraper to the lifter. They'd taken basic scrub-down materials aboard, and Ben would purge *Pegasus'* cargo hold before anyone unsealed. They didn't yet know what caused the urbicide and couldn't risk contamination, either.

* * *

"Hey D—that look normal to you?" Kratos asked, pointing to a small self-shipping cargo-tainer, a meter cubed, sitting precariously near the rooftop edge. Six rotor-nacelles lined the upper edges of the 'tainer, and two sides were open to the high-altitude breeze. Daedalus shook his head, and the four contractors cautiously approached the 'tainer. It contained trace amounts of a white, crystalline substance that could have been table salt.

"No it does not," Daedalus declared. "Neph, grab a sample. Our genie may have been right."

"Myrmidons, this is Pegasus! Someone's going for missile lock, watch for countermeasures and counterbattery!"

Pegasus dove for the deck and raced down the broad city streets, ducking back below the AA site's radar coverage. The Myrmidons lost sight of their ride home, until it abruptly popped back up into view and spat plasma from a chin turret at a rooftop a klick away. It fell away again, but by then Nephilim and Artemis had found *Pegasus'* target and shouldered their full-size gauss rifles. A series of follow-up shots from the rifles ensured all the hardware on the roof was destroyed, and Daedalus opened a commlink with Faolain again.

"You're clear to boost for orbit, we'll relocate for secondary pickup," Daedalus said. "Not worth the risk to return here again."

"Roger, boosting," Faolain replied. *Pegasus* went vertical and the gravity drive kicked in, sparking blue lightning as the drive fought free of Montoya's gravitational field.

"Now, what is this mystery 'tainer?" Daedalus asked. "And what is that inside it?"

* * *

206 | IBSON & KENNEDY

"**C**arfentanil, or an analogue of it," Nephilim reported. "One of the deadliest, most underrated poisons known to man. That matches what I just got back from the test kit in Charlie—all the dead at PSG show acute opioid overdose."

"I thought that was some kind of pain-killer medicine," Kratos objected. "Poison?"

"With opioids, it's all in the dosage," Nephilim replied. "Addicts have been hooked on one form of poppy high or another for centuries, maybe even millennia. But it's a central nervous system depressant, meaning it slows the heart and respiration. Take too much, and your brain forgets to tell your lungs to inhale. Heroin is three times more potent than morphine, and fentanyl is thirty times more potent than heroin. *Carfentanil* is a hundred times more potent than vanilla fentanyl ;it is lethal at the *nano*gram level. They literally can't make it small enough that it won't kill humans. Historically, it was a 20th and 21st century veterinarian's anesthetic for massive mammals, like elephants or rhinos."

"And we're unaffected because of our systems?" Janus asked.

"Exactly. We're immune, our synthetic systems filter out anything sketchy without us even noticing. Ms. Linares was wearing her drybag suit and rebreather, keeping it out, and the Ridians were in armor," Nephilim nodded. "PSG was open to the elements, unsealed, unfiltered, *au naturel*. I seem to recall Apex Energy was invaded by a nanoswarm once upon a time, and they take their air quality very seriously. Sticking to their standard counter-nano protocols saved their lives. We didn't detect it, because it's neither fish nor fowl—our systems aren't tuned to detect recreational opiates *or* elephant tranq, and to be frank, it's a huge gaping hole in our sensor systems. Some evil motherfucker *knew* it would go undetected, and I'm a little appalled."

"Bigger picture: one, I assume there are more crates like that, elsewhere in town, and two, who in the hell set these crates of poison death up?" Keeso asked. "That crate on the roof could have held *kilograms*. A simple timed bursting charge, and they're dumping this shit *everywhere* downwind."

"Live feeds from drones suggest most of the city is affected. If so, they've just murdered a *million people*, give or take," Bellerophon said flatly. "Wars have started over far less. Some very serious people will be asking some very serious questions, and we need answers for them. We will all undergo class one decon before getting back aboard *Pandora's Hope*. I don't care if we spend the entire trip back to Rideau in *Pegasus*. If Kari, Mick, or Ben were to OD on this…" he gestured expansively, "poison, then it would be *our* fault. If the ship's crew were to go down, we would be well and truly hosed."

"*Lef*tenant, you said they got hit by those Spetznaz contractors *after* everyone started dropping. Their ship was still in orbit when we arrived," Daedalus said. "They've *gotta* be the prime suspects."

"They didn't hit AE very hard though. Is that because they're opportunists?" Artemis wondered. "Or did they think everyone would be dead? Was Apex Energy their primary target? Why kill *everyone?*"

Bellerophon shook his head. "Motivations can wait. Destroying that AA site has probably just pissed off whoever is still alive and in charge. We'll have to file a complaint with the Council once we're out of this mess. Primary objectives are complete, and we have two clipped ears for AE's geeks to study. Speaking of AE, we have a megascraper to destroy."

* * *

"*All problems can be solved with the proper application of enough Deton-8,*" Kratos whispered to himself. He'd laid in cascading EMP charges in the server rooms, and used an electromagnetic switch as the primary detonator for the incendiaries above. When the EMP scrambled the servers, it would disable the EM field holding the gate open. When the gate closed, the det cord would explode, virtually instantaneously, along its entire length. The lab had plenty of highly energetic chemicals on hand, and hydrogen lines with which they could saturate the entire lab with hydrogen gas, just by turning some spigots open wide. The overpressure protocols of the building made it even easier to turn the lab's three floors into one enormous thermobaric fuel/air bomb.

To bring the building down, he'd laid in breaching charges around the support piles in the vehicle park. The front of Apex Energy was the riot grounds, and it would be...tacky, to drop the building on the hundreds of dead out front. The reverse side of the megascraper, though, was a ground-level eight-lane freeway, a sound-absorbent barrier wall, and then broad, open park. Kratos wasn't too worried about the local squirrel-analogues' homes, and rigged the charges to drop the building in a "safe" direction. Thor was the team's other demolitions specialist, and he'd double and triple-checked all of Kratos' work from top to bottom.

Keeso's Lancers had mounted their Coyote suits again, and stood by the park-side exit, ready to roll out. Ocelot and the Myrmidons were back aboard Charlie, and Kratos followed Thor aboard. They transitioned through the scrubbers one last time, and then the Coyotes led the way into the pre-dawn morning.

"*Sensor hits,*" Keeso advised. Coyotes were, by long Ridian tradition, armored reconnaissance and had a superior sensor suite. "*Multiple, heading this way. They probably had a track on Pegasus and saw where it made pickup.*"

"Run," Bellerophon urged. The Coyotes took long strides along the parkside freeway, and Keeso knew his way through the city. Janus goosed the throttle to keep up, and pretty soon they were tearing along the lanes of the freeway, dodging wrecks at ninety kilometers an hour.

"Contacts are closing fast," Daedalus called from the gunner's station. "Looks like multiple warbots and low-flying VTOL. IFF isn't saying a thing, which is weird. Keeso, is this the government response you were expecting?"

"*Fuckin, nope,*" the armor lieutenant replied. "*On one hand, we've been waiting for hours and nada. On the other hand, Murphy does love his fuckery. No IFF at all probably means The Black Jaguars. I've seen some footage of these savages since everything went to hell, they are Bad Dudes.*"

Bellerophon studied the map with the sigs overlay. "Copy, Kratos, stand by to send the detonation signal on my mark...three, two, *now,*" he ordered. Kratos triggered his primary charge, and a kilometer behind them, the EMP grenades fried the electronic server farm.

The EM switch, sans electricity, closed and ignited the det cord. The explosive cord propagated at nine klicks a second, simultaneously igniting two dozen incendiary charges throughout the multi-storey laboratory. The hydrogen-air mix detonated, shattering equipment and fracturing the blast-resistant aliglass. The Deton-8 charges burned hot enough to ignite the very metal structure of the lab, even as the blast wave fragmented walls and floors. The guts of the lab burst outwards from the building like so many oversize fragments from a ship-sized grenade.

But that was only the beginning.

Two *more* spools of det cord ran from the lab down through the stairway to the parking garage. They branched again, fanning out to multiple shaped charges set against the columns and support structures holding up the eastern three quarters of the building. The pressures on those ground level supports were immense, given they were holding up ninety floors of corporate headquarters. There were limits to what they could do, and while the building had been designed to survive a truck bomb, it *hadn't* been built to withstand two professional combat sappers with time to scheme. The sudden loss of integrity in the laboratory and the destruction of the base supports meant Apex Energy Headquarters, Montoya III, Republica del Escobar, was doomed.

So, too, were two of the three VTOL pursuing Charlie and the Ridians. One flying shard of aliglass punched through a ZP-24 Havoc cockpit's window like a dinner-plate sized shuriken. It decapitated the pilot, whose death spasm veered the gunship into a scraper wall at top speed. Another shard bisected the trailing ZP-24's port-side fan ducts, crippling the engines instantly. The VTOL had been flying low to delay detection by the Coyote's sensors, but the low altitude meant the pilot didn't have time to recover from the sudden engine loss; the assault VTOL, belly laden with troops, barrel rolled into the ground, killing everyone aboard.

Then the three hundred meter tall building began to fall.

Several of the ZAZ-60 APCs racing to scene stomped on their brakes, not recognizing that they had time to race through. Instead, they were crushed. One driver even slewed his vehicle into a hard left turn, smashing through the sound-barrier wall in an effort to cut through the park, but failed to escape the shadow of the falling tower and was smashed to parts and paste.

Several of the heavy bipedal *Santa Muerte* warbots were able to halt their dash and backpedal, escaping the catastrophe by mere meters. One pilot managed to avoid the initial impact, but more frag blew out from the building as it impacted and a polycrete boulder the size of his torso hit the walker at several hundred meters per second. The bot was thrown over backward, badly damaged by the impact, the pilot concussed and out of the fight.

One pilot though, raced all the harder when he saw the building coming down. Capitán Hector Garcia had been fighting in bots since battle college and *knew* he had time to shoot the gap before the building came down. Speed and aggression were key, and the *Santa Muerte* suits were the finest armor *Los Jaguares Negros* had in their inventory. They could sprint at highway speeds, and Garcia redlined his throttle to get *under* the catastrophe before access to the fleeing criminals was cut off. Indicators on his control panel winked grey as the ZAZ-60s were crushed, and it enraged him all the more—*they were getting away*. Only one of the ZP-24s had avoided the explosion and falling megascraper. It flared hard and banked counter-clockwise around the falling building, passing over the dead rioters. The pilot rejoined Garcia on the far side and stayed at his six o'clock, racing between the scrapers, staying a hundred meters above and behind him.

Garcia's warbot was running at well over a hundred thirty kilometers an hour, and his sensors told him the mass-murdering scum ahead of him had left the freeway and were zig-zagging through the roads to break line of sight. He rounded a corner and caught sight of the last two stragglers in their puny Coyote armor, and tagged both with his shoulder-mounted micro-missile system. He queued six missiles to each and mashed the firing stud. A dozen missiles streaked away, their HESH warheads slamming into and penetrating the rear of the suits, spall shredding the Ridian Lancers on board. Both Coyote suits collapsed, and Garcia howled in triumph as he closed the distance.

* * *

"We just lost Dales and Johnston," Keeso shouted. "Split up, keep behind cover, we can't outrun this guy."

Janus stomped hard on the brakes and used the M.A.T.T.'s swing arms to jink sideways into a broad alley. He rotated Charlie in place, bringing his admittedly too-light-for-this armor to the fore, and popped the ramp. "DISMOUNT!" he barked, "EVERYONE OUT!"

He followed the other eight passengers down the ramp, switching from active to remote control. Ocelot followed Janus to cover where he could run the M.A.T.T. uninterrupted. Artemis and Nephilim activated their ANGEL systems and jumped for the rooftops, and the remainder formed up in the alley in a hoplon-shield wall they could use to buy Janus time.

Lt. Keeso and his three surviving Lancers also scattered. The Coyotes were a mere four meters tall compared to the *Santa Muerte*'s seven, and Keeso chose to barrel through the front wall of a restaurant to disappear into the debris. The four Coyotes were outclassed by the much larger mech and couldn't stand toe to toe with the larger, heavier warbot. They would have to hit and run to stand a chance.

"Streaming a feed now," Artemis sent over her comm, and opened a channel from her own optics for Janus. Janus spotted his target via the feed, and knew where the *Santa Muerte* was before rolling Charlie out of cover. With the cannon primed and missile rack on standby, he punched the M.A.T.T. out from the side street and fired.

The APFSDS dart roared forth at four kilometers per second, hitting with 280 *kilo*joules of force. It had been a snap shot, however, and the round impacted wide of the pilot compartment, taking the warbot in the shoulder. The Escobaran robot returned fire, stitching Charlie's front glacis with bolts of railgun fire, and then Charlie was across the intersection and out of the line of sight again.

"Keeso! Do you have anything that'll kill that thing?" Bellerophon asked over his comm.

"Hard no! We're going to have to wear it down," Keeso replied. "Go for the legs!"

"Incoming VTOL!" Nephilim advised from another perch above them. "Assault bird is dropping troops to support the warbot. I've got laser on it."

"Moving now!" their M.A.T.T. controller said, and Charlie jinked out of cover and into the street. Missiles found Nephilim's targeting laser and streaked up and away. The ZP-24 ate two, belched flame, and came apart mid-air. The troops already safe on the ground scattered as their ride came crashing down, but those still onboard died. The survivors were too busy diving for cover to notice another micro-missile swarm from the *Santa Muerte* warbot. One of Charlie's front swingarms was blown clear of the frame, crippling its mobility, and another missile severed the command link between the chainblaster and Charlie's autonomous controls.

214 | IBSON & KENNEDY

Janus ignored the damage and stabilized as best he could, bringing the gauss cannon to bear. He was too late, the turret too slow, and the warbot was already in motion. The cannon round flashed past, harmless. The *Santa Muerte* bot disappeared around another corner, and Janus stitched the building, but the gauss rounds couldn't find the warbot.

"We gotta move!" Janus shouted. Kratos hadn't been wasting time in the alley, and threw up his e-shield to protect Ocelot as he detonated a charge, blowing a passageway into the building adjacent. Janus shrugged and drew his AE gauss pistol, passing it to Ocelot with a reload. "You might need this," he said, before charging through the breach.

The interior appeared to be the back room of a custom ladies' clothier. Designer suits and dresses hung on hangars and raw material sat in piles, all thoroughly coated in plaster dust and brick from the demo charge. Kratos paid them no mind as he kicked in the door. That provoked fire from the surviving Black Jaguar troops across the street, and he threw up his e-shield again to deflect the incoming bolts. The Myrmidons kept on the move, covering each other as they moved up to the front of the store, laying down a thick base of fire. A gauss round cracked down from above, and Artemis commed, *"Their commander's down."*

Another fusillade of ion bolts crashed through the front of the store, and the textiles inside ignited, adding to chaos. Thor swore. "Medic! Arm's off! Pulling back!" he shouted, and crawled back from the window front where he'd been hit. The forearm that bore his hoplon energy shield had been blown off at the elbow, one of the BRUTE armor's few weaknesses. He dragged his damaged forearm with him deeper into the store.

"Here!" Daedalus shouted, and dropped his carbine on its sling so he could pull a cylinder from his harness. He adjusted the settings on it as Thor crawled to him, and when his teammate reached him, he clamped the cylinder over the damaged ruin of his stump, with the forearm laying just below.

"Two minutes!" Daedalus yelled to be heard over the firefight, and flashed two fingers. Thor nodded, and Daedalus crawled forward again. Inside the cylinder, lasers cut away the damaged ends of the artificial bone, synthetic nerves, and polymer muscles on both halves, restoring it to some semblance of functionality with 3D printing tech. A nanite slurry fabbed a weaker, temporary replacement for the destroyed joint, getting Thor back into the fight. It wouldn't be nearly as robust as what he'd had, but it was better than losing the limb completely.

Kratos tapped into Artemis' feed, still streaming from above, as he withdrew more Deton-8 from his harness and began shaping it into baseball-sized lumps of good news and fit each of them with a remote detonator. He found the warbot, angling for a better flanking position on the group, still out of Charlie's LOS. Losing the heaviest weapon on the field *sucked* when going up against heavy armor.

All problems can be solved with the proper application of enough Deton-8, he repeated, and then rolled out from cover to whip the spheres of plastique at the warbot. He had cocked his arm to throw, when the first ion blasts struck. They sizzled against the shield and overloaded it. Three more blasts punched through, and he stumbled. Internal diagnostics flashed yellow and red, but he ignored them, so long as he could hit what he was throwing at. The plastic explosive mashed itself into place, and then he sent the command to explode.

The five quarter-pound explosives blew as one, crippling one of the warbot's legs and damaging an arm at the shoulder. Micromissiles in its shoulder rack cooked off, adding to the damage, but the bot was still semi-mobile and returned fire with an ion blaster on a small shoulder turret. Most of the bolts went wide, but without his shield, Kratos was exposed and took another in the leg, but the BRUTE armor held. His internal systems were scrambled from the first salvo, and he dropped in place, calling for a medic.

"Standby!" Daedalus yelled. Thor's limb needed another forty seconds before the repairs would be complete.

* * *

Combat is no place for a cat-girl, Ocelot grimly reflected. *But then again, neither is this planet, any more.* The gunfire between the Ridian suits, these strange hoplite contractors, and *Los Jaguares* was hard on the ears, as her ears were far more sensitive than any ungifted human. The explosions were *particularly* painful. But when hunting, one used whatever concealment one found. She'd followed Janus through the door, and immediately hugged the floor. A heavy impact blew open a side wall from the dress-makers into the fancy restaurant next-door. She leapt through the gap headfirst and stayed low in case more bolts penetrated the walls. The dining area let her slip out the front foyer, using the faux Mediterranean columns for cover. From there, she crept between two ground cars, dashed across the narrow street, exposed to the warbot for a moment, but the pilot was distracted. She burst through the front door of a cantina that was the very *opposite* of ritzy, and surveyed the walls.

There.

She leapt onto a booth's seatback, and pressed up at the cheap ceiling tiles, which slid aside at her touch. The void above the tiles was open to the storefront next-door, and she leapt straight up, nearly three meters, to cling to the underside of the rafters. She crawled along their length by her modified, freakishly-strong fingers and toes, until she was directly above one of the security troops exchanging fire with Keeso's Coyotes.

A brief lull in the firefight was all she needed. She hooked her knees over the rafter, released her hands and hung upside-down for a moment to orient herself. Her first three targets were ducking down behind concealment, snap-firing at the Coyote power armor, and one glanced up just as she was lifting Janus' pistol. He started to react, but the gun barked, and a gauss bead took him between the eyes. The shot was lost in the cacophony of gunfire as she shifted targets, shot again, shifted, and killed the third. She released her knees from the rafters and curled mid-air to come down among two more. The three shots had been so quick, the survivors hadn't even realized their squad mates were dead, let alone located the threat. She landed in a low crouch and rose to throat-punch the *Jaguares* NCO with her claws. Blood mixed with dust and shattered plaster as she tore his throat out, and she pivoted into a low kick that staggered the next trooper. She ripped the Tavor-26 from his grip and fed him the buttstock, shattering the supposedly shatter-proof visor on his environmental helmet. He hit the floor, stunned, caught a whiff of nanogram-potent opiate, and drifted off into oblivion, never to wake.

Ocelot surveyed the damage she'd wrought, and slung the Tsiyyoni carbine over her back. Satisfied that the pressure was off the Ridians, she leapt *back* to the ceiling's rafters and disappeared before the warbot pilot could notice his surviving infantry support was KIA.

* * *

*N*othing's *gonna kill that thing but a shaped charge,* Kratos thought to himself. *Do or die time.*

The warbot's missile rack was gone, and the pilot's attention was on the Ridian armor. Kratos cursed and pulled one of his last shaped penetrator charges from his harness. He vaulted out of the storefront and dashed across the street, angling right, but the warbot caught the movement. The chainblaster was mounted in the warbot's right shoulder and swiveled to track. Bolts of energy struck the pavement behind Kratos as he ran, but he cut the angle and the bot couldn't keep up. He leapt on the stricken warbot's leg and slapped the charge against the pilot's compartment. He triggered his hoplon shield and ducked down behind it.

Nothing happened.

He'd forgotten: *his shield was offline.*

A monstrous hand grabbed him around the waist and heaved him up into the air. A second hand *crushed* everything from his pelvis down, *broke* his legs off, and threw the shattered remnants away. Pain circuits cut in, and he screamed, firing his carbine at point blank range into the bot's chest, stitching it with little molten craters. His pain circuits maxed and cut out when they grew too intense. Critical warning symbols flooded his HUD.

Do or Die?

Embrace the power of 'and,' he thought, and triggered the shaped charge from a distance of ninety centimeters.

* * *

Epilogue

*D*ear Mr. and Mrs. Jakobou,
It is my sincere regret to advise you that your son Karlos was killed in action on May 23rd, 2634, standard calendar. I served with him in the Hellenic Augmented & Robotic Defense Corps and he left service a few years after I did. He went by the callsign "Kratos," was a fine soldier, and an essential part of my team.

Karlos didn't speak about his family often, but I know he was grateful for the time the Lakonia Project bought him among these stars that we call home.

We recently undertook a contract to rescue and extract a number of VIPs from Montoya Three. You may be familiar with the chaos and anarchy that has consumed the planet there and have probably heard some terrible stories accusing me and my team of horrible things. Please rest assured we are innocent of what we are accused of—our mission was, in part, to save the lives of two dozen innocents trapped on the planet's surface as their planet tore itself apart around them. We arrived on planet and witnessed The Urbicide, but we had nothing to do with it. We are being blamed for it regardless.

Our lander had already extracted the civilians, but there were so many we couldn't all fit in one lift. As we waited for our own extraction, we came under attack by an enemy mecha and some supporting forces. Several of us were damaged in the fighting, as the mecha out-massed us ten to one. Kratos was damaged, disabled the mecha's legs with demolition charges, and then damaged again. Our weapons were too light to destroy the mecha, and, heedless of the danger, your son charged the warbot. Karlos was a highly trained sapper and used his last demolition block to stop the threat. He couldn't escape the danger radius of the explosive and died in the blast.

Karlos was my friend, and, despite his synthetic exterior, he remained very human inside. By my count, his skills, knowledge, and expertise helped Myrmidons Inc. save more than three hundred fifty innocent civilians from violence, capture, slavery, or worse. It was never about the money for him—whatever he earned, he reinvested right back into the company.

Enclosed are his personal effects. He has personally been cited by three heads of state and five ambassadors, and he has received civilian honors in four systems. I am enclosing the medals, ribbons, plaques, and real pulp-paper accolades he received over the years. The last one, the Windsor Meritorious Service Cross, is new, and is the second highest award Rideau issues. You will note that it is in the shape of a Greek cross—I believe this is deliberate—and is one of the first instances where an allied military medal was issued to someone who is technically a civilian.

I understand they will be interring his remains at the Leonidas Cemetery on Attika, at a date and time to be determined when you may attend. Duke North, Governor General Listowel, and Ambassador Mylette plan to attend and honor your son's sacrifice. I wish we could meet, but allegations by the Escobaran government mean bounty hunters are searching for us, and our presence would put everyone at risk.

Per his Will, I am further enclosing a draft for fifty percent of the value of his shares of Myrmidons Inc. The remaining ¥6,556,762 is being donated to the Children's Hospital, Cybernetics Division on Sparta Four. He said you'd understand.

My deepest condolences,
Damien Xanthopolous, C/S Bellerophon
CEO, Myrmidons Incorporated

* * * * *

Jamie Ibson Bio

Jamie Ibson is a new writer from the frozen wastelands of Canuckistan, where moose, bears, and geese battle for domination among the hockey rinks, igloos, and Tim Hortons. After joining the Canadian army reserves in high school, he spent half of 2001 in Bosnia as a peacekeeper and came home shortly after 9/11 with a deep sense of foreboding. After graduating college, he landed a job in law enforcement and has been posted to the left coast since 2007. He published his first short stories in 2018 and more are slated for 2019. He's pretty much been making it up as he goes along, although he has numerous writer friends who serve as excellent role-models, mentors, and occasionally, cautionary tales. His website can be found at ibsonwrites.ca. He is married to the lovely Michelle, and they have cats.

# # # # #

Yellow in the Night
by Philip Wohlrab

Now

Undisclosed Military Installation

*O*h *boy, were we in trouble.*

I knew the moment we hit the target, and it wasn't what we thought it was. When the Undersecretary for Civilian Security, Democracy, and Human Rights walked into the small conference room? I knew we were fucked.

"Major Holt, do you know what you have done?"

"Shot a bunch a bad dudes in the face, oh, and your boss," I replied.

"Yes, the President wasn't too pleased to find out her Secretary of State was shot by the U.S. Army," he stated in a cold voice.

"Well sir, she shouldn't have been vivisecting a young girl," I said, my voice dry as the Sahara, "and Mr. Wallen, you should know that my 'plants allow me to see you behind that smoked mirror. You might as well join us."

I could hear, and sense, Wallen's shock. He wasn't used to working with Phoenix Team and had only a limited understanding of our capabilities. The under-secretary harrumphed at that, but I couldn't care less what he thought. I was tired, dirty, and desperately wanted a drink—oh, and to unsee everything I had just witnessed over the last forty-eight hours, so fuck him.

* * *

48 Hours Ago
Undisclosed Military Installation

"Come in ladies and gentlemen; we have information on a target of opportunity, and we don't have a lot of time to plan this, so shut up and sit down." The voice was gruff, coming from Colonel Vandermeer, a short, solid, woman. "This is Mr. Wallen. He is going to be the liaison from the State Department on this case. Mr. Wallen, if you would be so kind?"

Wallen stepped forward, a short guy, greying at the temples, and a tad heavyset. The first thing I noticed about the guy was his furtiveness.

"Uhh, so thank you Colonel. Umm, troops, I am Mr. Wallen, and as the Colonel said, I am your liaison on this mission. The information for it came through sources connected to the Bureau of Intelligence and Research." I scratched my head at that one, I knew they existed, but our ops were usually generated by other alphabet soup agencies, not State Department. "We have intelligence that a Red Banner team is holing up in a villa outside Punta Prima on the island of Menorca; what it is doing there, we aren't sure, but it may be related to last month's attack on Toulouse. Red Banner forces have been known to operate from the Balearic Isles before, but usually only as a transfer point, given how little of the area is actually patrolled by Spanish or French authorities."

"Excuse me sir, but how do you know these guys are Red Banner or connected to Toulouse?" Sergeant First Class Ben Tooley asked.

Mr. Wallen appeared annoyed to be asked that question, and it clearly showed. He said with a sneer, "Uhh, we have our own means of developing sources, and I would rather not go into that, uhh," he glanced at Tooley's collar tabs, "Sergeant."

"Be that as it may Mr. Wallen, Sergeant First Class Tooley raises an excellent question," I said. "Look sir, we are the very best at what the Army has to offer in terms of Special Forces; this mission profile as presented so far is a job for local forces. Red Banner isn't known to have any synths or 'plants. Why do you need us? This sounds an awful lot like overkill to me."

Mr. Wallen still had the annoyed look on his face, but he went on, "Well, Major, we suspect that there are others mixed in with this Red Banner force. We suspect operatives of the Chinese People's Liberation Army's Siberian Tiger Forces are with them."

There was a collective deep inhalation of breath from my group. The Siberian Tigers were one of the many PLA Special Forces units. They were good, and just as implanted as we were, with combat enhancements.

"Have you been able to confirm this?"

"We think so. Our operative on the island reports that there are Chinese nationals in Punta Prima."

"Is this the guy running your source?"

"No, he is independent of the source; that came in via other means."

"What other means?" asked SFC Tooley.

"I am not at liberty to discuss those."

There was a grumble at that from my troops; I was annoyed too, but we needed more information to plan so I moved the conversation along.

"What information do you have on the villa, its local environs, how big it is, any security systems or drones?"

"I have prepared a packet on what we know of the villa; it will be forwarded to your 'plants once it has been scrubbed by your security screen."

Wallen was referencing getting information through our firewalls. The dangers of cyber warfare were understood as far back as the early 21st century, but cyber warfare had advanced enough that a skilled hacker could take over bioplants. Because of those dangers, our 'plants were configured in such a way so as to not take incoming transmissions without being first scrubbed through our security pads. After a few minutes of interfacing and scrubbing the downloads, the information was directly transmitted into my brain, as well as those of my team. As I scanned through the information, I wasn't impressed.

"Mr. Wallen, there are hardly any details on the villa here. Nothing about personnel, other than perhaps five to six guards. Hell, there is nothing on whether they have drones or jaguars. The last thing I want to do is hit this place and find 150 pounds of combat-enhanced angry kitten trying to eat my face," I said.

"Uhh, you guys are a Phoenix Team; don't you have things that can counteract?"

I pinched the bridge of my nose for a moment before answering, "Mr. Wallen, have you ever been on an op before? Do you know what you are asking?"

"What? An operation? Don't be ridiculous; that would be dangerous. That is what *you* guys are for."

I glanced around the briefing room and motioned to where two of our cats lay snoozing on their perches. For their part, the two cats looked content and sleepy.

"Mr. Wallen, those are Pixie and Babou. Notice anything about them?"

"They're your combat cats, but I fail to see where you are going with this—"

"Right. They are our scouts, and they are better than drones; they have senses that electronics can't duplicate. They communicate with Sergeants Muhler and Jenkins there, who are our cat specialists. The problem is that if the Red Banner guys have Jaguars, or—the gods forbid—the PLA Siberian Tigers have one of their Great Cats, they are both orders of magnitude bigger than even Brutus over there." I motioned to the Combat Cougar lazing on his bed. "What kind of car do you drive Mr. Wallen?"

Wallen was startled by the question but answered anyways, "A Honda Civic, why?"

"Well Mr. Wallen, a Chinese Great Cat is as long as your Civic, and masses almost the same." I was exaggerating, but not by much. He visibly gulped while I went on, "So again, Mr. Wallen, have you told me everything there is, or are you holding stuff back?"

"Look, Major, I have given you all the information I know." Here Wallen glanced down at his feet, and I knew he wasn't being honest. "All I can say is that it's a Red Banner team mixed in possibly with some Siberian Tiger Forces guys. We need you guys to fix this before we have another incident like Toulouse."

"Alright, what makes you think these are the guys that blew up the Airbus production facility?"

"Well Major, we have imagery of what appears to be Red Banner guys exfiltrating the area. CCTV caught their getaway vehicles going down the A61 to the A9, and eventually escaping to sea via the port at Valras-Plage. Overhead imagery shows boat traffic that appears to be heading for Menorca."

"What is your reliability on this?"

"Seventy-five percent."

I gave Mr. Wallen a sharp look at that. I don't mind kicking doors and shooting bad guys in the face, but let's face it, the US taxpayer has spent on average about 25 million bucks on each of us. I couldn't believe the DoD was going along on this, based on this level of intelligence. I couldn't believe that Colonel Vandermeer was sitting there not interjecting either. My team was sub-communicating their disbelief on our private channel amongst themselves. I had to tell them to can it, so I could think.

"Alright Mr. Wallen, we will take it from here. If you have any further intelligence that you can pass along, or that comes up, send it our way. In the meantime, we have a mission to plan. If we need something more from you, we will call."

I motioned for him to leave the briefing room, but he didn't look pleased with being dismissed. He was some kind of "big cheese" at State; but here, he was nothing more than a source. He gathered his few things and stalked out of the room. The team gathered around the holo-table so we could pull up the satellite data for Menorca. I touched a few controls and dropped the magnification down onto the town of Punta Prima. It was located on the southeast corner of the island, a small resort community for the rich and powerful. It didn't always used to be that, but with the changing world economy, only the rich and powerful could afford the island anymore.

"Seems a strange place for a bunch of terrorists to hole up," remarked Staff Sergeant Lauren Jenkins. "Why go to a place that is the playground of the rich?"

"Well, given the amount of recruiting that Red Banner does among the children of the wealthy, I can see it," remarked Tooley.

"I never got that, why would you seek to overthrow the very system that provides your wealth?" asked Staff Sergeant Hailey Muhler.

"For some, it is pure adventurism, a way to get a new high." I scaled the overhead imagery in to a zoom level we could use. "For others, they feel guilty about their wealth and seek to find some kind of meaning in their lives. It isn't a new phenomenon, and most of their parents see it as a way to keep the children distracted. It isn't like Red Banner has ever managed to be successful, nor do they cause much damage, which is why I have to wonder why we are being included in this at all. This is like dropping a sledgehammer on a gnat. The only thing I can think of is that the Siberian Tigers really are there, but that's an odd play for them. China owns most of Airbus now, why would they blow up one of their own major production facilities?"

Tooley said aloud what we were all thinking. "Boss, this one stinks. I don't know what State is up to, but I have a feeling we are getting into something that isn't what's being advertised."

"Agree, so what that means, Team, is we need to be on our toes. Fortunately we have the cats to help out, but we need to be prepared, too…"

* * *

36 Hours Ago

Outside Punta Prima, Menorca

One of the nice things about Menorca was that most of the island had gone back to nature. As the world economy collapsed in the 2050s and the population died off, there were fewer and fewer people to populate Menorca, and it gradually turned into the playground for wealthy European or North African elite. Operationally, this was a two-edged sword for us. Sure, there were fewer people to hide from, but that also meant there were far fewer vehicles moving around on the island. This meant we would be walking, but first we had to get on the island.

The blast of cold air hit me, though my body barely registered it due to the combat suit I was in. The suit acted to enhance my already otherwise enhanced body. As the ramp on the MC-214 hit its stops, we shuffled forward and leaped off into the darkness. It was a bloody long way to fall before popping my chute, but this way we stayed under any possible surveillance systems...or so we hoped.

The team deployed from the aircraft in a fan, with the cat handlers at the rear and the trigger pullers at the front. Babou and Pixie were joined to Muhler and Jenkins via a specialised harness that kept the two Ocelots from moving around or snapping at their handlers. Brutus was too big for this arrangement, so the Cougar had been trained to make jumps tethered to his handler, SFC Anthony. The big cat was splayed out like the rest of us, with his own small chute designed to drop him at the same rate as his handler.

I could see the LZ through my enhanced night vision, which resolved the world into shades of blue and white, making everything stand out in sharp detail. It gave me a god's eye view of the island from the height we jumped at, and I took the opportunity to look over the target site as well. For some reason, though, the area wouldn't resolve into the sharp detail of the rest of the area, and I began to get a headache.

"Can anyone get a good look at the target?" I asked over the sub-vocal net. Normally, I wouldn't have risked even the microburst transmission, but this mission was seriously spooking me.

A chorus of replies in the negative came back, and SFC Tooley said something about it making him vaguely nauseous. I filed that away; perhaps the Chinese were fielding some new anti-surveillance tech that interfered with 'plants, but something was definitely messing with the team's enhancements. I stopped thinking about that as the LZ rushed up toward us.

I bent my knees to absorb the shock of landing. Our chutes were designed with our enhancements in mind, so we fell at a much faster rate than an unenhanced human could tolerate. The carbon and graphene fibers that were bundled into our muscles, and the strands fused to our bones, greatly enhanced both the strength and flexibility of our bodies, meaning we could run faster, jump further, and generally take hits far better than unenhanced humans. That didn't mean it still didn't hurt like a son of a bitch when I hit the ground at forty-five miles an hour.

"I have to find a better line of work," mumbled someone over the team net. It sounded like Muhler; she was rated 'expert' in dark humour.

I let it slide, because while technically a violation of comm discipline, it did much to diffuse the tension that had built up from our experience on the drop in. We collected our chutes while the cat handlers freed their charges of their jump harnesses. For their part, the three cats began to aggressively clean themselves for a few minutes while we prepared our gear. Once everyone was ready, we moved out; we had five klicks to cover to the target site.

The cat handlers released Pixie and Babou to range ahead of us. Every sensation, sight, or smell the cats experienced was transmitted via a bio-feedback loop to their handlers, making them the perfect semi-autonomous drones. The handlers, for their part, could direct their cats where they wanted them to go, or what they wanted them to investigate further. The cats were just as enhanced as the humans, being stronger, faster, and more capable than their natural counterparts. Brutus for his part was kept close to our team, where he could augment our combat power. The decision to use cougars and ocelots was partly because they were native to North America and therefore easier to acquire a sustainable population from wild specimens, and partly to preserve both species from extinction. Thousands of the great cats had been raised in vast wild preserves, while only a few hundred were utilized in the program for combat cats. Nature, for her part, was also helping the situation as humanity's population decreased exponentially.

"Sir, the cats are acting funny," reported Sergeant Muhler in a worried tone.

"Funny how, Sergeant?"

"Sir, there is noise in the bio-feedback, like a buzzing. I thought it was just me, but Jenkins and Anthony report it as well. The cats are all acting spooked as well. Babou is only out about half his normal distance from me, and is hesitant to get any farther away."

"Pixie isn't even that far out," SSG Jenkins added. "She stopped about half the distance away from Babou and won't go any farther, other than in his direction. She wants to stick close to us, or to him, and is refusing to investigate anything I tell her to."

"What about Brutus?" I asked.

SFC Anthony, a tall, powerfully built man, even for a Phoenix-enhanced human, had a funny look on his face. He gestured at the cougar, which was slinking along just ahead of our team. "That cat has faced jaguars, combat drones, and everything in between. He has never been freaky about any of that, but he isn't himself either. He's edgy like I have never seen him before."

"Could there be a great cat spooking them?" I asked.

"Boss, I don't think so, I…well the cats have all seen other combat enhanced animals before, and we train them for that. No, I think it's something else," replied Sgt Muhler, her tone even more subdued than normal.

"Alright, well, we still have a target to hit. You all will just have to do the best you can with the cats. Sergeant Tooley, let's get on with this."

"Yes sir."

* * *

28 Hours Ago
Punta Prima, Menorca

We had made good time covering the distance from our landing zone to the perimeter of the villa, and by good time, I mean it was miserable. As Menorca had been systematically depopulated by the elites of the European Union, the local populace had been displaced, and the island had largely gone back to nature at first.

But then the resort developers had moved in, and they had created an artificial environment of what they thought Menorca *should* be. That meant vineyards and orchards were spread out everywhere along our potential routes in. While in theory that meant concealment, there were all kinds of automated drones running around maintaining and monitoring them. The automation was to cut down on the number of necessary humans involved, which reduced the chances of the rich coming into contact with anyone who wasn't a servant of theirs.

For every meter we went forward, we would have to detour three meters in another direction to avoid one of the automated little devices. I wasn't too worried about the terrorists having hacks in on the devices. Red Banner was rarely if ever that sophisticated, but with the Chinese potentially involved, *everything* was suspect. They were masters of electronic and cyber warfare. Worse than the drones though, was the terrain. Mostly open, with neat orderly rows of trees or vines laid out, we actually had little cover or concealment along our route march. The orchards weren't awful, as we could flow through the trees, but the vineyards were more of a problem, as we had to crawl down the rows of vines, staying low and out of sight. We would have tried going around, but unfortunately those were large open areas, and no amount of adaptive camo makes you completely invisible on all the spectrums.

Our cautious approach seemed to work, because the team had finally went to ground on a slight rise overlooking a villa that was backed by one of the orchards.

"Sir, I make out eight individuals—so far—around the villa's exterior wall. They all appear to be locals; I don't make out anyone that is enhanced. Jesus, is the Kalashnikov ever going to go out of style with revolutionaries?"

I chuckled at that and responded, "Probably not, Corporal Ferrer." I was still concerned that neither Pixie nor Babou were doing their usual scouting, but the closer we got to the villa, the more reluctant they were to range out at all, and now both cats were perched by their handlers, tails swishing in agitation.

"Okay team, we are going to hold up here, I want everyone on a 50/50 rest cycle while we observe the villa. Keep an eye out for the Chinese, but if we don't see any during the day, we may risk sending in a few drones of our own to scout the place further. For now, even numbers sleep, odd numbers on watch. We will trade off in four hours."

There were murmurs of assent from my team of fourteen troops.

"Even numbers, sleep now." With my command, each member of the team assigned an even number fell asleep in mere seconds. This particular enhancement allowed us to be well rested, putting us to sleep on command, and we could wake up on command without the groggy effects normally associated with waking up. The command triggered our combat drug implant to dump a sleep or wake up chemical into our system. There was a penalty for screwing with the body that way though, and when we would return from mission we would all need to sleep for a 36-hour period while the body healed itself from the effects of the combat drugs.

"Odd numbers, energize now." This command dropped an awareness stimulant into our systems that was developed by the Rip-It Energy company. I personally didn't like the stim, but I knew it was vital after having been up for the last thirty-six hours. We then settled down to watch the villa.

* * *

25 Hours Ago

Punta Prima, Menorca

"Sir, movement on the road up to the villa."

"Roger, Corporal, I see it. Looks like three 15-Pac vans."

Moving sedately up the road were three black Mercedes vans, their windows tinted so as to mask the contents of the vehicles. Against normal eyesight, and even most sensors, that would have been an adequate mask, but Phoenix doesn't use just any sensors. The first two vans were packed full of people—mostly *young* people. Something else though, was in the third vehicle, something that was interfering with even my 'plants.

"Sir, what is this? These aren't terrorists." Sergeant Jones, a shooter on the odd team said.

"I don't know," I replied hesitantly. "This mission stinks."

"What do we do, sir?"

"We continue to observe. We will still hit the place tonight, but I am going to want answers when we get back. State hasn't been truthful with us."

"Why, sir? I mean, why hit it if the mission isn't what they told us it was going to be?" asked Sergeant Cochran. She was a long-service member of my team, and I knew *she* already knew the answer, but Ferrer and Arazi were new and too junior to ask. The gods bless intelligent juniors; by asking the question that the new troops couldn't, she was allowing me to explain my rationale to them.

"Well Sergeant, *whatever* is going on down there, those people are clearly in the wrong, and while this might not be the terrorist group we think it is, I am concerned about the number of unaccompanied children that were in those vans. What are they doing here? What is their purpose, and why are a bunch of heavily armed mooks bussing them around?"

"Right sir, so this has potentially turned into a rescue mission?" asked Cochran.

"Yeah, we are going to have to be careful going in there."

"Roger sir."

From the villa we could hear sounds of yelling and kids crying. One wail was particularly piercing. Our augmented hearing couldn't pick out what was being said, but we could hear that there was a lot of commotion and a lot more adults than we could see were down there. The third van backed up to a garage, obscuring whatever was in it as it was offloaded. As the van doors opened on this third vehicle, I was looking directly at it, and I felt as if someone had shoved white hot needles behind my eyes. I grunted in anguish, and I wasn't the only one.

"What the *hell* was that?" asked Cochran sharply.

"I...I don't know," I replied. It hadn't just affected us either. The kids down at the villa collectively let out an agonized wail. Worse, the sleeping members of my team and the three cats all stirred as well. Fortunately for us, the guards around the villa couldn't hear us on the ridge, not with the terrified screams coming from the villa's courtyard.

"Fuck it, I am calling this in. *Even team, wake,*" with my command the members of even team woke up instantly, though they all looked disturbed, as if their sleep hadn't been restful like it should have been.

"Sir, what's happening?" asked SFC Tooley.

"The mission parameters are blown, and I am going to risk calling it in. Sergeant Cochran, get me a link to higher headquarters."

Sergeant Cochran reached over to fiddle with her PRC-3TB radio before saying, "You're up on the net sir."

"Whiskey Base, this is Phoenix Actual, I need to talk to Storm Actual," I mic'd.

A few anxious minutes went by before I got a reply. I knew I was breaking protocol, and running a risk of detection by not just potential adversaries, but also allies that were unaware we were operating in their yard.

"Phoenix Actual, this is Storm Actual, you had better have a damn good reason for contacting me."

Despite her gruff voice, I could hear the worry in Colonel Vandermeer's voice.

"Storm Actual, I think we have been sold a false bill of goods. We haven't observed any terrorist cell, nor any Chinese special forces types. What we have seen so far is a very large human trafficking operation, involving approximately thirty or more kids. But there is something else, something is playing merry hell with our sensors and implants."

"Are you one hundred percent sure there are no Chinese special forces present?"

I sighed, and then keyed my mic, "I cannot say that ma'am."

"Understood, orders from State are to proceed with the mission."

I sighed again. "Ma'am, in light of the changes I am requesting on-call air support. Also, let the Navy know we are gonna need more extract if I am bringing a bunch of kids out."

"That's a negative on air support, Phoenix. Per higher, that would up the mission profile too much. We will let the Navy know to expect more for extract. Continue the mission."

"Roger, ma'am," I reluctantly answered.

The rest of my team looked at me. Even the *cats* looked at me. They could see I was not happy, but because of the screens, they hadn't heard my conversation with higher.

"What is it sir?" asked Tooley.

"We are still a go, and no air support. We are going to have to do this the hard way."

"Roger sir, perhaps you and odd team should get some rest, we can take over watch. I assume you still want to wait for darkness, correct?"

"Yeah, but I am moving the timetable up. We will hit them just after midnight, rather than waiting for 0400. We kill the...terrorists, or whoever they are, and secure the villa until the Navy arrives for extract. I don't want to risk them having the kids any longer than necessary. Who knows what is really going on in there?"

"Roger sir, continue rotating watch shifts every four hours?"

"No, switch it to every three hours, and make sure your team gets some food in them."

* * *

16 Hours Ago
Punta Prima, Menorca

Despite getting a broken six hours of deep sleep, I wasn't feeling rested, and I could tell the rest of the team was just as edgy. When I had been asleep, I had terrible dreams of things slithering in the night. Shapeless, formless horrors grasping for me and my team. But now, thankfully, I was awake, and the Rip-Its did their job of chasing away the fuzziness. I was hitting them hard on this op, and I knew I was going to pay a terrible price for that, but I needed something to chase away the shapeless things.

"Boss?" Sergeant Cochran looked disturbed. "I got a bad feeling about this."

That phrase had meaning behind it. Sergeant Cochran had been on my teams for a long time. She was an excellent trigger puller and had a keen sense of when things were about to go sideways. More than once that feeling had made us approach a problem a different way, and we had survived because of it.

"Right, well, we still have a mission to accomplish, so let's get this thing done. Sergeant Tooley, any changes down there?"

"A handful of cars came to the place and dropped one or two occupants. None of them appeared armed, and if I had to guess, I would say they were big players or some other high value target. Boss, these guys aren't Red Banner."

"What makes you say that?" I asked, not because I doubted SFC Tooley, but I wanted to hear what his reasoning was.

"Red Banner are typically college-age individuals with revolutionary ideals. Sure, they are content to blow up the occasional police station—or military post—but I have never heard of them dealing with kids in any way. They largely avoid hitting civilians, unless they are somehow connected to the establishment in some meaningful way. Yes, they're wielding Kalashnikovs, a revolutionary favorite, but other groups use them as well. Most of the people we have observed down there haven't been college aged, but older. None of them have the right look. If I had to guess, they are private security of some type mixed in with traffickers."

"Did you see any high-tech stuff while I was out?"

"None sir. These guys are pretty low-tech, most look like thugs."

"Okay, that settles that it. Arazi I want you to deploy your drones. Muhler, Jenkins, are the cats still acting funny?"

"Babou won't leave my side at all," replied Sergeant Muhler.

I looked over at the two ocelots, and sure enough, both were crouched beside their handlers. They leaned up against them and were the most agitated I had ever seen them before. So was Brutus, and this still spooked me.

Why were the cats acting funny?

"Sir, drone one is up," reported Corporal Arazi.

A flat black disc, two inches thick, and five inches long, hovered above the corporal before moving out toward the villa. The small drone was followed a moment later by an identical device. Corporal Arazi was bent over a small pad and was using it to direct the drones to different areas of the villa. One of the features built into our helmets allowed us to grab a friendly drone feed and direct it to our heads-up device. Sharp HD video filled one portion of my helmet display as drone one moved closer to the garage the van had backed up to several hours earlier. It was dark now, just after local midnight, and the villa, surprisingly, wasn't lit up. The guards moved around, but it was only a small force of them, and they appeared to be using old fashioned night optics attached to Kevlar helmets. They didn't look like much with their old-fashioned body armor and their even older rifles. The drone's audio sensors clearly picked up a conversation between what looked like the guard unit commander and one of his lieutenants.

"Yes, the ceremony has begun. The Master will be pleased," rasped the commander in an accent I couldn't place.

"The time is right for the King's return," said the lieutenant.

What were these guys talking about? The only king these days is the one in England, and I doubt he is here. The two men continued to talk, but the drone kept moving toward the garage. And then it died.

"Arazi, what happened?" I asked.

"I don't know sir, there was no warnings coming from the drone, it just dropped."

"Okay, what about drone two?"

"It is still up, I am trying to get a look through one of the windows on the upper floor, the one with the yellow glow coming from it."

"Roger, I am having trouble linking it to my HUD, can anyone else bring it up?"

There was a round of negatives, and Arazi wasn't sure what the problem was. He began to fixedly stare at his pad, and from where I was positioned, all I could see was that the screen had turned yellow, but I couldn't make out anything on it.

"Arazi, what do you see? Arazi! Arazi! Arazi?"

I tried to get his attention, but he just clutched the glowing pad, bringing it closer to his face.

"Carcosa," he breathed out in a whisper.

"What?" asked SFC Tooley. "Arazi what did you say?"

To my horror, I watched as tears began to roll down Corporal Arazi's face, which took on a terrified aspect. As he began to scream, Tooley, who was closest, reached over and grabbed the corporal. Tooley was able to get his hand over Arazi's mouth, but I could see the commotion had garnered the attention of at least two of the guards down in front of the villa.

"Take them," I commanded.

Two muffled shots later, and both of the gate guards were down. Tooley and Ferrer managed to hold down Arazi, as the team medic, Sergeant Clifford, slapped a syringe into Arazi, and the corporal went limp. In the commotion, the pad that displayed the drone feed had been broken.

"What they hell happened to him, sir?" asked Clifford.

"I don't know; he was looking at the pad when he freaked. I can't explain it. But we don't have time to figure that out. Sergeant Jones, stay with Arazi and establish the extraction point. The rest of us, strike plan delta, go! Go! GO!"

My team flowed down the ridgeline, all except Jones and the incapacitated Arazi. With surprise mostly blown, we only had speed and violence of action to push us through this. My lead shooters, Ferrer and Massa, took down the guards that had come around the corner of the villa's outer wall in response to the gate guards going off the air. Neither of the guards knew what hit them. I was surprised they hadn't turned on the flood-lights; surely the guards were fully alerted to our presence.

We made it to the wall and stacked to either side of the gate, making sure not to hug the wall too closely. Even team had point, and on the command of the team leader, SFC Tooley, the point man went through the gate, followed closely by four other team members. The two even team cat specialists, SSG Jenkins and SFC Anthony, held back with SGT Muhler from my team joining them. I wanted the cat specialists concentrated for the moment since the cats weren't acting right. My odd team followed the even team through the gate with the cat specialists bringing up the rear.

There had only been two other guards in the courtyard when even team came through the gate, and both were down. Pools of blood expanded from where they had fallen.

"Tooley, head toward the left side entrance, I am going to take my team through the garage."

"Roger boss."

Before either of us could execute, Brutus let out a challenging scream, joined by Pixie and then Babou. It startled all of us into a momentary pause, and the garage doors exploded outward in a hail of splinters. The courtyard was perhaps a hundred feet from the gate to the house, and three hundred feet wide. The garage was attached to the right side of the house, connected to the gate by a well-paved driveway. We went to ground as three...*things* raced out of the garage.

I could only form an impression of gnashing teeth, flashing antlers, and legs that didn't move right. A heavy musk smell preceded them, and it was overwhelming.

I—and everyone else—opened fire on the creatures. A mixture of rifle and machine gun fire washed across the charging things—to no discernible effect. No, scratch that, it made them *angrier*.

"*What the hell are those?*" someone screamed. One of the beasts reached Ferrer and lowered its huge head, driving its pointed antlers into Ferrer's chest and heaving him off the ground. Ferrer shrieked in terror and agony while the beast bellowed at us in challenge. Ferrer desperately tried to pull himself off the antlers until the beast shook its head, tossing him ten yards or more. Sergeant Clifford stopped shooting and raced over to his limp body. The other two nightmares flanked the first, each adding their own dissonant howl, and the right one charged Cochran. She emptied her magazine into the creature's face—to no effect—and it slapped her aside, tossing her 10 feet to the left. The creature continued its charge until it reached down and grabbed SSgt Massa. Massa wasn't a small guy, standing at over six feet tall, a broad-chested bodybuilder type, but the creature handled him like he was a rag doll. It ripped Massa's right arm off at the shoulder joint, which should have been impossible given the carbon and graphene enhancements. Massa shrieked in agony until the creature sank its maw into Massa's neck and bit his head clean off.

"Oh my God, what *are* those things?" Jenkins screamed.

Her scream caught the attention of one of the beasts; it lined up on her and charged. To her credit she didn't freeze, but instead leaped out of the creature's way and back 12 feet. Pixie had followed her, and the cat yowled a war cry of her own as the beast reoriented on SSG Jenkins' new position. As it continued the charge, a low sleek shape took the creature in the side, knocking it to the ground. Brutus let out a howl of triumph as he sank his fangs into the right haunch of the beast. SFC Anthony moved up, firing as he came with his 6.5mm rifle. The creature tried to rise up, but Brutus tore a great big chunk out of its right leg, severing muscles and tendons. The creature screamed in agony for a change, and Pixie attacked. The two cats slashed and bit at the thing as both Anthony and Jenkins unloaded their magazines—once again—into its tough hide.

"Why won't you *die?*" Anthony screamed as he kicked it viciously in the spine. Something popped *loudly*, and the lower half of the monster went limp.

246 | IBSON & KENNEDY

"Why don't bullets hurt it, but physical attacks do?" cried Jenkins.

No one had time to answer her, as we had the other two to deal with. Seeing my rifle was useless, I pulled out my knife. This was no tactical folder, but instead a fixed blade that doubled as a short machete. I had never really used it as a weapon until now. The beast was distracted, having forced Sergeant Cochran to the ground. It didn't seem to be trying to eat her, but...*something else*. I didn't really want to think about the implications of what I was seeing. Instead, I leapt forward and plunged my blade into the base of its skull. It sank into the creature's flesh and I could feel it scrape across bone. The beast let loose a furious bellow and backhanded me with its antlers as it turned. I sailed through the air, landing like a sack of potatoes. I didn't see it, but my distraction gave Cochran enough time to roll out from under the creature as it reared back. She saw where my knife was stuck in the creature and she jumped at it, putting all of her considerable strength behind the blade. It must have found the sweet spot, for the creature's breath exploded out of it, and it collapsed, lifeless.

I rose up in time to see the three cats acting in concert take down the third beast, and then my troops fell upon it, blades flashed, and it too died. I felt my chest around the area that the beast had hit me, and I could see where it had cracked my combat suit. I could also feel a grinding pain in my ribs and knew something wasn't right there. My body would heal them at a much faster pace than a normal person would, but broken ribs still suck. I fiddled with my medical panel for a minute and relief washed over me as a pain reliever was dumped into my system.

"Teams, report," I commanded. I put a boot on the back of the dead thing's shoulder blades, took my machete in one hand, and the antlers in the other. By forcing the antlers up and away, I was able to rip my blade free from the base of its skull.

"Even team, Ferrer is in bad shape, multiple chest punctures, and at least one collapsed lung. He has lost a lot of blood as well, but Sergeant Clifford has stabilized him for now," reported SFC Tooley.

"Staff Sergeant Massa is dead, and I am covered in monster slime," said Cochran in a shaky voice. "Everyone else is good."

"Roger, Clifford and Romero, get Ferrer back to Jones, then double time back here. I have no idea what those things are, but there are a bunch of kids here, and I am not going to leave them in the clutches of a group that keeps things like that around."

The teams looked spooked, but they all nodded, and the cats at least looked a little more at ease.

"So...what now, sir?" asked Tooley.

"We aren't splitting up; we go in together through that front door. If it presents as any kind of threat, we kill it. Cochran can you raise higher and see if we can appraise them of the situation?"

"Sorry sir, but all my outside comms are down. All I get is static. Been like that since the moment Arazi went nuts."

"Riiiight," I drawled out.

The air, which had seemed so charged with electricity while we fought the beasts, became suddenly still. The whole team picked up on it, and from back at the collection point we could hear Arazi begin to rave again. That shouldn't have been possible with the drugs Clifford had given him.

"Fuck this," I said in a heated tone, "let's get this done and get the fuck out of here. Romero, take point on that door; the rest go in with the cats once again bringing up the rear."

I took my place in the center of the stack as we breached the front door. Upon entering the large front hall, I could see that the interior was decorated in a romanticized Victorian fashion, which is to say, it was cluttered with faux-old *stuff*. The front hall had four rooms adjoining it and a grand staircase ascending to the second floor. It appeared to run the full length from front to back of the house. There was no movement in the hall, nor any real noises other than us. Troops broke off to cover the four open doors, while others covered the staircase and upper landing from the ground floor. Pixie and Babou, at the direction of their handlers, split off and went into the two front rooms, while Brutus stood in the center of the hallway with his handler, ready to go in any direction. We quickly cleared the ground floor and discovered a second stairwell leading down into a basement.

"Which way boss, up or down?" asked Tooley.

"We go up, all the noise is coming from up there. Once we clear the second floor we can come back down and clear the basement."

"Roger that, alright boys and girls, you heard the man. Stack on the stairwell."

We didn't bother with stealth at this point, everyone had to know we were here. I was growing more agitated at the *lack* of response from the occupants, and I didn't want to give them any more time for whatever it was that was more important than responding to a commando raid. We moved up the stairs at a fast pace and spread out upon topping the landing. Again, there were four doors, two per side, with a door at the back of the upper hall that appeared to lead to the third wing of the house. Noises that sounded a lot like chanting and screaming were coming from the doors on the right side of the hall. I didn't bother with the left side, but instead we went through the front right door.

"Holy shit," I breathed out, having stopped dead in my tracks. My team had gone through the door, but something was affecting our judgement, and rather than going through our well-oiled entry drills, we piled through the doorway in a mob. I tripped over Romero when he drew up short, not letting us through, and then I froze too.

Spread out before us was a group of perhaps twenty people. All of them were clad in yellow robes, and they faced an...*altar* at the front of the room. A young girl, naked, was held down by two big men flanking the altar, while an older woman carved intricate patterns into the girl's chest with a vicious dagger the length of my forearm. The girl was screaming in both agony and terror. The room was lit up in this sickly yellow light, which made me nauseous just to stand in. But it was what was *behind* the altar that stopped us in our tracks. A grotesque figure in yellow, that even now I can't describe, but perched upon his head was a nightmarish crown.

"*Too much, it's too much!*" shrieked out Corporal Romero. The trooper toppled to the floor, vomiting, twitching as though in a seizure. The...thing at the back was aware of us now, and it had locked eyes on my downed soldier.

It was Brutus who broke the spell. The cougar leaped at the nearest cultists, yowling his battle cry. He dragged down the first shrieking cultist. Brutus tore her apart before the other cultists started to react. All of them lifted daggers, identical to the one that the "priestess" was using at the altar. As if with one will, they attacked en masse in a deathly silence that was only punctuated by the chanting of the priestess and shrieks of the girl.

I opened fire at the cultist nearest to me, and just like outside, my rounds had no effect. The others in the team discovered that their guns were equally useless. But they had been forewarned by the fight with the beasts outside, and my men and women pulled their blades—fighting knives and tomahawks—and went to work. The fight was vicious, and I watched as three cultists dragged down Alexander with supernatural strength. It should have been impossible; there was no way they should have been able to force him down, but they did. The knives rose and fell, each time more stained with gore, but there was nothing I could do for him as I had to deal with the cultists attacking me. Gripping my rifle in one hand, I leveraged it against my single-point sling so as to wield it like a club. This allowed me to block the first cultist with my rifle while I snapped my machete free of its scabbard and stabbed the second cultist through the eye. The man cackled madly even as the blade drove home, until I could feel it hit the back of the man's skull and punch out the back. I jerked the blade free, and the cultist dropped as if he were a puppet whose strings had been cut. With him out of the way, the other two cultists attacked simultaneously, and I had to back up and away from them, while using my rifle and knife to parry the swings of their daggers. SFC Anthony stepped in behind them and swung a deadly looking tomahawk into the back of the neck of the woman on the left, taking her head clean off. That gave me a chance to hack down the last cultist.

The cats weren't idle either. An ocelot normally wouldn't be able to take down an adult human, but there wasn't anything normal about Pixie or Babou. Both of them turned into whirling dervishes, slashing vulnerable tendons and hamstrings, while Brutus grabbed a cultist and mauled the bastard. We were all bleeding from one wound or another by the time the last of the yellow-clad madmen dropped. With each death, the hideous King appeared to wane a little bit, until he was nothing more than a shadow behind the altar. The priestess had stopped carving her malefic sigils on the girl's flesh and seemed to be pleading with the Shadow King, while her two assistants moved toward us with murderous purpose.

I was tired and had been stabbed and beaten; I had no desire to fight these two as well. I pulled my sidearm, a 10mm pistol, and shot the first man. The other assistant stopped in his tracks and looked at his dead companion, and then back at me. I shot him as well, but this time three inches below his belly button. It occurred to me that not two minutes ago, our bullets were having no effect. This change of events was as much a surprise to him as me—apparently—because the man folded up and hit the floor sobbing in agony. There was mocking, cruel, laughter from the shadowed Yellow King, and the priestess turned back toward us.

"My Lord, why do you abandon us?" she cried out plaintively.

"*I do not...reward...failure!*" it hissed back at her.

I walked up to the altar and looked down at the ruin of a child lying on it. The girl was mewling in agony, and had lost a lot of blood. Before I could say anything, Sgt Clifford was at my side, his aid bag already open. Seeing that the girl was in good hands, I looked back at the diminished priestess, whom I belatedly realized I recognized.

"Madame Secretary," I snarled.

She looked up at me, tears running down her face.

"You're...American military?"

"Yes," I stated simply.

"I command you to stand down. Do you know who I am, who I am connected too?"

"Yes, ma'am I do."

I shot her through the face.

* * *

Now

Undisclosed Military Installation

"You might as well join us." Wallen, the weasely little shit, stalked into the small conference room. The smell of fear poured off both of these two, and it was beginning to give me a headache.

"Major, you decided to be judge, jury, and executioner, and in the process killed the highest-ranking cabinet level secretary in the country. Care to explain yourself?" asked the under-secretary.

"As I said, sir, your boss shouldn't have been carving up a girl in offering to whatever the hell that was."

"We think it was an Old One," Wallen said, in all seriousness.

Both the under-secretary and I turned to stare at him.

"A…what?" exclaimed the under-secretary.

"An Old One. Your boss was dealing in some really arcane shit, man, and it cost her life."

"Man? Have you lost your damn mind? One, don't call me "man," I am the under-secretary, and two, you cannot tell me you believe this nonsense about magical beasts and some kind of cult, can you?" asked the under-secretary, though his tone ran from angry to more plaintive, as if he was coming to the realization that something truly horrific had occurred.

"Believe it? Hell this is my *job*. Look you two. My agency, for all intents and purposes, doesn't exist on any flow chart in the government. We clean up messes that other people make, messes that go beyond the veil of normality. We were tracking that Secretary Axton was dealing with things she shouldn't have been. But what my agency lacks are the internal resources necessary to handle messes of this magnitude. Usually some pathetic dude in his basement finds some arcane text on the internet, and tries it out. We kill them, unless the ritual goes awry and they kill themselves first, usually in really horrific ways. But when the powerful get their hands on this stuff, and they have the resources to really do it right? I'm sorry I had to lie to you Major, and to your team, but we had to clear this nest out before it could unleash truly evil things."

I gave Wallen a cold hard stare and didn't speak for several moments. Then clearing my throat, I spoke up. "Mr. Wallen, you sent my team in with no warning of what it would encounter. In the process I have three dead, one who has gone insane, and a third who is going to be in counseling for a long time due to being sexually assaulted by that creature. Give me a good reason why I shouldn't tear your head off right now!"

My voice rose in anger as I addressed Wallen, and I stood up, hurling the chair away. Wallen flinched back from me, and began to stammer something, but it was Colonel Vandermeer that brought me back to my senses.

"*That will be enough, Major!*"

"Yes, ma'am," I said. I dropped into the position of parade rest, though I did have the small satisfaction of smelling the scent of urine coming from Mr. Wallen.

"Again, I am sorry, Major, but there was no way we could have warned you about what your team was really getting into. Pretend, for a moment, that I *had* told you. Would you have believed me?"

I will give Wallen a small amount of credit, he hadn't emptied his entire bladder.

"So, what do we do now?" the under-secretary asked.

"My advice? Reveal the Secretary for the scum she was," I said.

"Absolutely *not!*" the under-secretary shouted. "No way in *hell* are we saying anything of the sort. For one, no one would believe us. For another, that would just tell every wannabe demon cultist that it *works.*"

"The Secretary had a skydiving accident while visiting the Punta Prima resort on Menorca. Due to the gruesome nature of the accident, there will be a closed casket funeral," suggested Wallen.

I was disgusted by it all. I popped out of parade rest and begin to leave the office in search of a stiff drink.

"You weren't dismissed, Major," the under-secretary said coldly.

I wheeled back to him. "Sir, *with all due respect*, you don't need me anymore. My team does. We are going to go get *very* drunk, and try like hell to forget this whole affair."

"Make sure you do, Major," Wallen tried for subtle menace, but it fell flat.

I wasn't so subtle.

"Mr. Wallen don't let our paths cross again. *Ever.*"

With that, I left to find that drink, bury my dead, and take care of my living.

* * * * *

Philip Wohlrab Bio

Philip "Doc" Wohlrab has spent time in the US Coast Guard and is a medic in the Virginia Army National Guard. He earned the title "Doc" the hard way in Iraq in 2010. After two tours to the Sandbox he returned stateside to take an instructor assignment with the Guard, where he continued to train the next generation of medics. He earned a Master of Public Health in 2016. He has since left full-time service and currently works in the Department of Defense as an Adaptive Wargaming Analyst.

# # # # #

The Chaos of Well-Seeming Forms
by Rob Howell

I opened the pressure door to the New Pittsburgh West-Alpha-12 communal dome and an embrace that would have broken most people's bones slammed into me.

But I was not most people.

Nor was Eric Allardeck, the man who had swept me up. It was a good thing, since I massed well over two hundred kilos.

"Where you been, you lazy hussy!" He laughed. "I mean, Staff Sergeant Fielding."

"Command, Sergeant Allardeck." I shrugged. "You know how it is, even with the truce and our passes."

"Yeah."

"Now put me down, you oaf."

Once on my feet, I looked past him to see people filling the area, generally organized into two groups. The first group, my family, the Fieldings, glared at Eric and I from the left side of the room, faces filled with thunderous rage. The Allardecks matched them on the right.

The only face not filled with rage was my Aunt Beatrice's, but then, she had always been an odd one.

The Fieldings and Allardecks had been feuding since first landing. One cubic meter was all it had taken to make our great-grandfathers mortal enemies, but Mars has its own sense of whimsy. When the Federated States consolidated New Pittsburgh, its governor saw no reason to make two sets of domes with separate water and air to go to this section of the city just because our families hated each other. In the decades since they arrived, neither family conceded their original steading nor moved.

And so, the families walked in groups to the other areas of New Pittsburgh. They also made sure there was no evidence for anything resembling assault, nor as had happened, the occasional murder.

The only others in the dome that morning worked the various kiosks that served the communal area with espressos, smoothies, and soy pastries. Those people huddled nervously instead of offering their wares, watching with wide eyes because this morning we had asked both families to come out at the same time.

We turned to the families and our Internal Dynamics Mk. V-M2 hands (right for me, left for him) clasped together, almost of their own volition. Oddly, they had been our first touch, other than thumps on the training mat, so they seemed more loving to us than our real hands. We stood close to each other, wearing joyful smiles.

The families started to rumble. Our enhanced hearing could easily pick up "Damn Allardecks" and "Fucking Fieldings" from various relations.

"Shall we?" he whispered.

"Absolutely." I glanced up. My father was spitting fury. I winked at him. "Who goes first?"

"You're prettier."

I laughed and turned to the onlookers. "We're so glad you could be here. Eric and I have asked you all here because—" I hesitated, then glanced up with my real eye at Eric.

He smirked. "Tonya and I have asked you all here to witness our wedding."

The screams of outrage forced us to dampen our hearing.

Aunt Beatrice, of course, chuckled. I focused my vision to read her lips, which clearly said, "Romeo and Juliet."

Eric gauged the Allardeck reaction. "How long should we let this go on?"

"As long as they need, though we might want to stand in the middle. We don't want them to actually fight."

"Leave that until the wedding reception." Eric laughed again.

I loved that laugh, though it had seemed arrogant and mocking the first time I had heard it.

But Martian Defense Force basic training had a way of cutting through things, especially since cadre had taken great glee in matching us together. They knew, of course. Everyone who had walked Oppy's Trail was aware of our feud.

We stepped forward, letting our hands separate.

My father stomped up to me. My improvements had not changed my height much, so he still towered over me. On the other hand, his finger jabbing into my breastplate surely hurt him more than it did me. I simply ignored what he said.

Mom, as always, used crueler weapons. "Tonya, dear. Surely you don't want to disappoint your father like this. Didn't we raise you well? Don't you know we tried?"

"Yes, Mom, I do."

"Then surely you see that this is just a mistake, one that's easily fixed, you know?"

She was from a completely different family halfway across Mars, but she had taken to the feud easily. I never knew why.

"It's not a mistake, Mom."

"But, he's…an Allardeck. You're so much better than that."

The uncles on both sides had already started making threats, and a fight would happen soon. Fortunately, Eric and I were the only ones in the families who had served in the MDF during wartime, so no one else was enhanced. We could, and did, move to separate our clans faster than anyone else. Two hundred kilos had its uses after all, even in the light gravity of Mars.

I looked over at Nick Allardeck. "I know you'll never like it, but Eric and I will be married."

"I'll not allow it."

"You have no choice."

He glared at us with narrowed eyes. "I'll not allow it," he hissed again.

Eric said essentially the same thing to my dad. Dad's reaction was much the same as Nick's.

I glanced up at Eric. We had expected it, so we had planned for it.

He grinned. "You do it. It'll be more fun that way."

I turned to all in the dome and cut through the snarling. "Your choices are as follows. One, come to the wedding and witness our joy. You may not like it, but we'll have a feast to remember since we're eligible for the Enhanced Couple Marriage Bonus. Or two, you can choose not to come. However, I, for one, will expect all Fieldings to give us our traditional wedding O-credit, whether you come or not."

"And I expect it of the Allardecks," Eric said with a snarl.

"So, come eat an actual cake, or give us your oxygen for nothing. Your choice. The wedding is tomorrow."

"Ridiculous!" snapped Beatrice.

"That's your choice, Aunt!"

"Not that, you idiot. *I'll* be there in my best. But you've given me hardly any time to get *you* ready."

"I'll just wear my uniform."

"Ridiculous!" she snapped again. "No niece of mine will get wed in anything but the gown I wore when my Fred made me an honest woman." She chuckled with a sly smirk. "Well, mostly honest."

Eric laughed. "You better do as she says, love. I'm sure as hell not brave enough to argue with that one."

I laughed, though I saw the comment had made Nick almost snarl.

Eric saw the look too. "Do you have something to say, Dad?"

"None that a fool like you will listen to."

Eric moved to him and they walked to the side. Nick spoke decisively, his fist repeatedly smacking his palm.

Beatrice took me by the shoulder. "Don't worry, lass. That one's stronger than his father. Besides, we've barely got time to fit you."

She looked over the rest of the family. "Now get to work, you all. We've a Fielding to wed, and we're damn sure going to look good doing it."

Behind me, I was startled to hear Nick suddenly say essentially the same thing. I glanced back. His face was still red with anger, and his eyes burned into mine, but he clearly was not going to let the Fieldings show up the Allardecks.

Beatrice herded us back into our warrens with the ease of long practice. We went back to her section of the warren. She claimed a much larger area than most, but she was also our clothing mistress. The rooms she ruled included a large area with several good sewing machines and immense storage for supplies. Her piles of fabric included some she had bought—at ruinous shipping costs—from Earth, including silk, cotton, and linen in weaves more advanced than Martian fabric printers could produce.

"Stand here," she commanded. She looked at the various young nieces and cousins who had followed her. She pointed at four of them. "You will stay here. The rest of you, go assist…*elsewhere*."

The others scurried away, happy to be released from Beatrice's critical eye.

My aunt now marched to her low-pressure chamber, a small area kept at Martian atmosphere and filtered completely clean of particulates. Nearly every warren across Mars had several because they so good for long-term storage. She pressed on its control pad, and after a moment, it sent out a zipped bag. Reverently, she took the bag and laid it on her primary work table.

Inside was a gloriously white wedding dress.

She whispered with that sly smirk to me, "I do so hope you're not a virgin, but let's have you wearing white anyway, shall we?"

I blushed. "As you wish, Aunt."

"Yes." She smiled and held the dress up to me. Then she looked at me expectantly. "Well?"

"Well what?"

"I can't fit it to you while you're wearing that uniform, though you always have looked dashing in it."

I chuckled and stripped to my skivvies.

"That's better." She held the dress up to me again. "Hmmm. I think we need to take the bosom in a bit."

I glanced at her chest quickly.

She chuckled. "Well, let's just say my Fred had few complaints on that topic. Of course, I was not so firm in other areas. I'll have to take in the hips as well. You're five centimeters taller than me, too, so I'll need to let out the bottom hem."

She turned to the cousins. "You! Measure her arm length."

One of the girls complied. "Sixty-four centimeters, Aunt Beatrice."

"Not surprising. Your arms are longer than mine. That'll be a bit trickier, but we'll make do."

The rest of the afternoon and evening consisted of me standing around while Beatrice, and eventually, my parents, told me what to do while they made preparations.

* * *

A nd such preparations!

The West-Alpha event hall looked incredible, as I suspected between our two families the hall boasted every flower available in all of New Pittsburgh. Even in wartime, there was room in the hydroponic areas for some flowering plants, and they filled the hall with their aroma.

Each had brought out their ceremonial china, too, much to the relief of the caterers. No one had anticipated a fancy wedding, and the caterers had brought utilitarian, fully-recyclable table settings that were far too prosaic for the splendor in the hall.

Everyone who entered took a moment to appreciate the hall, inhaling with wide, gleaming eyes.

The primary question buzzing throughout the day had been who would officiate our wedding. Fieldings asserted it would be Neo-Catholic. *Had to be*, of course. *Pshaw*, or some curses to that effect, answered the Allardecks. The groom was a Calvinduist, and that settled that.

That had been the first question we had answered after Eric had proposed to me. I treasured the memory.

"Ah. Ummm," he dithered. It had been a rare moment of uncertainty for him. His proposal, moments before, had been...spirited. As had been my response.

"Spit it out, Sergeant!"

He grinned. "I thought you preferred the other option."

"Gonna be a short engagement, you keep that up, boy."

He had laughed. "The officiant?"

"Ah. Well, that's easy enough."

"Oh?"

"We just let the MDF assign us a duty chaplain."

"Perfect. That's settled." He had smiled that bad boy grin of his. "Shall we continue to discuss that other option?"

I had laughed and proceeded to show him which I preferred.

When we found out the officiant assigned to us was an actual Orthodox Jewish rabbi, we insisted he perform the ceremony in Hebrew, not English. Our implants translated Hebrew easily enough, so like always, we understood each other and what was going on. But our families would never understand why we were getting married, so they might as well not understand the ceremony.

Fortunately, both of us wanted a short ceremony with a big reception, so little time for everyone to get bored.

Scrounging was Eric's speciality—had been so before his first enhancement—and he had helped the caterers provide a spread worthy of the Fielding-Allardeck feud. Actual salmon, canned to be sure, but something that had swam in an Earth ocean. The best created beef, both steaks and hamburgers. Of course, we had tomatoes, since they had taken so well to Martian hydroponics, but we also had grilled asparagus, which had not. Scrambled eggs from real chickens. So much more.

And the cake. A cake! Big enough to feed both families. Made of actual flour and chocolate and sugar and eggs and milk. Hideously expensive. Might have cost more than a year's salary for some of my relatives.

So worth it.

We put the buffet table down the middle, accessible from both sides.

We also set up a bar between the two groups. We did not splurge as much here, though there was Terran wine. Martian liquor was what most drank anyway.

And we stood in the gap between our parents and families.

I could not believe how I looked when I tried on the dress for the first time. I would never be beautiful, especially since the piece of shrapnel had sliced up through my cheek and eye.

But I was resplendent in that dress.

Eric's eyes widened when he saw me, and his were not the only ones. Beatrice stood with a smug look. The MDF rabbi grinned quickly, then resumed his professional face and began the ceremony.

Just in case, both Eric and I set our weapon scanners to warn if anyone pulled a weapon, but the promise of cake seemed to make even this feud pause for a bit.

The only tense moment came when the two of us stamped on glasses after the Seven Blessings. The crunch startled various relatives on both sides out of their inattention, though the sight of the rabbi instructing his young assistant to sweep up the glass calmed everything down.

For several hours, our families reveled, separated only by increasingly depleted chafing dishes. Then, when the two of us were ready, we had the rabbi flip a coin to see which family would leave first. Dad called heads, it fluttered down to tails, and the Allardecks left first. The MDF rabbi decided to walk with them to West-Alpha-12 just make sure no one set a trap.

It had happened before, after all.

Once the rabbi sent a message it was clear, my family returned to their warrens.

The hall was a mess, but the caterers had already started to clean up. We did not wait to watch them split the leftovers into two equal portions, one to each family. No, we had pressing business elsewhere.

The best hotel on Mars offered rooms to couples getting married. It knew they would get a bunch of O-credits as wedding gifts and it gave a slight discount if you paid in oxygen. A good deal for all, since their O-bill had to be incredible.

The honeymoon suite was all we could have hoped for. Our own private room. Not a bundling closet, our usual location for previous opportunities, but a *real* room with a *real* bed. And a bathroom with unlimited hot water.

We sat on the bed. Despite our enhancements, we were both exhausted. They had not yet invented an implant to deal with emotional fatigue.

"Well, no one got killed." Eric smiled.

"And only one injury, which frankly was my uncle's own fault. Noob mistake in Martian gravity. Forgot he wasn't on Earth."

"Will his knee heal?"

"I didn't check, but mom didn't seem worried."

"Good, no one really should get an implant if they don't have to."

I smiled wryly. "Anyone break your record yet?"

"Not yet. I've still got more enhancements than anyone else."

"Thought so. My first rule in this marriage is that you're not allowed to get shot anymore."

"Anything you say, my love." He laughed at me. "And not for nothing, you got more enhancements than most. You don't get to get shot either."

We shrugged with rueful smiles. Getting shot was our job, after all. Once a soldier received his first enhancement, which automatically included an implant to properly run it, he was statistically much more likely to survive combat. So, command gave us more training, called us Special Forces, and kept sending us out. We kept getting wounded, which meant more enhancements. With each new add-on, our odds to survive any single engagement kept getting better.

But they sent us to every battle. Sooner or later even the best odds run out.

Our titanium hands touched as we remembered absent companions.

Eventually, I smiled slightly. "Oh, I suppose I'll agree to that. It does seem fair, after all."

Eric kissed my cheek with a tenderness no one in the MDF suspected he had. Then I kissed him with no tenderness at all.

I leaned back with a broad grin on my face. "You remember, though, that not every part we got is fake, right?" I spread my legs. "In fact, I seem to recall you have something that's quite sufficient in its natural state." I checked my implant. "We've got 27 hours, 17 minutes, and 43 seconds until we have to report back. I suggest we use our original parts for every single second we can."

Eric's laughter was as mocking as I could ever remember, but this time, he mocked the world.

We made full use of the private room, which had cost quite a bit of our O-credits. But what else were we going to spend it on? By this point, we barely breathed oxygen at all, anyway.

* * *

I woke up.

Something was wrong.

My implant radar showed no major troop movement, so the Chinese were not attacking by land. I accessed the Command feed. The position of Federated States and Chinese warships above Mars had not changed. I saw life signs in various places, mostly sleeping cubicles at this time of night, though the hotel bar was full.

Thank goodness, the truce wasn't broken.

However, Eric stood looking through the window at the Meridiani Planum.

"What's wrong?"

He did not move.

"Honey, what's wrong?" I got up out of bed and went to him.

He shook, like he was having a seizure. I reached out to him in terror.

Slowly, in sharp jerks, his head swiveled to face me. Tears streamed from his original eye.

"What is it?!" I tried to handshake implants, but he would not let me in. He shrugged my hand off his shoulder.

"Eric, talk to me."

"I...My father—" He blinked his good eye and suddenly talked as if to someone else. "I can't. I can't do this."

"What?" I grabbed his arm and twisted his two hundred and fifty kilos around. "What can't you do?!"

He put a hand on my cheek. "My implant OS. He got the MDF codes." He paused, then said through clenched teeth. "And when we got ready this morning, my nephew…" He yelled to the ceiling. "No!" He shook his head. "I won't do it." Then he yanked his human arm down to hold his artificial hand. He turned away, staggering toward the door.

Could Nick have done that? I shook my head. Didn't matter, someone had done something.

I threw on my MDF uniform and went after him. He appeared clearly on my radar, though he could have blocked me with his EW suite if he had chosen.

He ran on a direct line to the West-Alpha-12 communal dome. There, in the center one had to choose. Fielding or Allardeck.

His icon stopped. I raced to catch up.

His icon took a step toward the Allardeck pressure door. I breathed a sigh of relief. But then it halted again.

I burst into the dome. "Eric!"

He glanced back, a sick look on his face, and tottered toward the Fielding entrance as if dragged toward it. Then his implants and muscles started working together and he straightened up.

He yanked open our door before I could get to him. He closed it after him.

I chased straight through, and he was waiting for me. The punch from his titanium hand sent me rebounding off the door. The door crumpled slightly under the impact.

Fortunately, he struck me in my breastplate, and he retained enough control to avoid putting all of his strength into the punch.

I bounced back, scything my leg at his ankles. He jumped over the move, lashing back with a side kick. I slid the kick past me with my enhanced arm, and then punched just above the back of his knee, where the implant connected to what remained of his right thigh.

Even with my human hand, only strengthened with calcium supplements, he felt the blow, as that had always been a tender spot.

We reset and circled each other.

His human eye stared in horror. His enhanced eye merely gauged my next move.

He shuffled forward, holding his bruised leg back. Then he snap-kicked at me, which I knew he would follow with a sweeping leg kick and a series of punches. It was a combination that had won him many a bout on the training salle, and he had used it at least once in combat that I had seen.

Fortunately, though, I had seen it enough to know just what to do. I feinted to my right and jumped to my left, pushing the sweeping kick past me. Then I hammered into his back plate three times with my titanium hand, bouncing him off a plastic interior wall.

Other than cracking the plastic, the blows did not do much, of course. I was trying not to hurt him, but sometimes heavy impacts forced our implants to react. I hoped that might give him time to regain control, but even if that was possible, those blows were not sufficient.

My father and three uncles came to the door leading farther into the warren. They were all armed, but their hand weapons probably wouldn't bother Eric in the slightest.

Eric started toward them, but I tackled him, yelling, "Get the fuck outta here!"

Eric kicked me loose from his leg, but in the time it took to do that, my relatives stepped back, closing the door.

Thank goodness.

We rose and circled again. He tried another move I had seen before. The results were similar to the first combination.

He tried again.

I realized his implant was fighting with ingrained moves. What little control he retained meant his implant could only use maneuvers Eric had practiced with or which came with our basic martial arts uploads.

I had to fight out of the norm.

Our training emphasized aggressive fighting. Usually, we were faster and stronger than our opponents, and we ruthlessly took advantage of it in battles.

But not now.

I backed off and circled around. I hesitated and feinted. I zigged, when our training told me to zag. I struck not when it seemed right, but when it seemed wrong. It slowed me down, but also confused his implant.

I hammered a side kick into his ribs when he overextended, then got a hold of his arm and flipped him onto the ground.

He eluded the elbow smash, rolling out and around to crack the back of my enhanced leg.

Enhanced or not, it hurt, and I backed off to give my implant time to deal with it.

Then he charged at me. The charge was as reckless as I could have hoped. I feinted the wrong way according to our training, then took his two hundred and fifty kilos and flung them against a wall as hard as I could.

I picked the wall carefully. It was not one to the outside, where it was -66C today in the Martian atmosphere, now up to almost five hundredths of an atmo after thirty years of Federated States' terraforming. No, it was the heavy wall that separated us from the Allardeck warren.

Over the years, both sides had drilled many a hole to slide through a microcam. But those were small and subtle. The hole he created when I slammed him into the wall was not.

He folded the heavy sheet plastic back into an Allardeck storeroom, making a gap over a meter square. There had been a shelving unit against that wall. It slammed into another and all of their contents crashed to the ground. The crash sent vibrations bouncing throughout both warrens.

My enhanced hearing dampened the crash, but immediately returned to full sensitivity. I heard shouts of alarm from both warrens. I routed an emergency message to all the Fieldings to stay where they were, which I should have done much earlier anyway.

Eric shook his head. I stepped back.

Please, let that have worked.

His human eye cleared for a second. He started to relax, and I stepped toward him. But then the enhanced eye focused on me again.

I had given up my advantage, and he took the chance. His kick knocked me against an exterior wall. I felt it crack, ever so little, but enough that the air in the compartment started trickling toward it.

My enhanced hearing heard the fans in the environmental controls kick in to adjust. Microcracks were a common problem in New Pittsburgh and easily fixed. Accidents happen, after all.

But his follow-up punch was no accident. I managed to push it past my head and his titanium fist drove through the exterior wall. The trickle increased to a steady stream. Not enough to completely depressurize everything, but clearly as much as the environmental system could handle.

Alarms appeared on my implant. Not that I had time to pay attention to them.

I eluded his next attack, rolled away, and got free. I resumed my earlier tactics. He pounced again, but again I moved away. And again, but this time he lunged a little too far forward. I started to take advantage of his lack of balance, but he was too quick, so I stepped back out of range once more.

Suddenly, something yanked me back. I broke the grip of a hand reaching from the gap in the Allardeck wall, but not before Eric jump-kicked at my head. I got my shoulder up, barely, but his kick hammered it. My collar bone and shoulder socket had been enhanced years ago after a shell fragment went through them, but my humerus was still human.

And now it was broken, making my arm useless.

My implant automatically eliminated the pain signals and sent healing nanos to the location, but they would need days to do anything. Like as not, they would simply replace the humerus after all of this.

If I had an after.

I circled away from the wall, now clearly seeing Nick Allardeck leaning through the hole with a nasty, triumphant snarl.

"Kill her, Eric. Kill her now! Then all the Fieldings!" he shouted.

The shout stopped Eric. He turned, slowly, fighting every centimeter, toward his father. He tried to move that way, but his body, his enhanced body, betrayed him.

He turned back to me and suddenly, as if the effort to get to his father had drained all of his will, came at me again. His titanium hand shot toward my temple. I moved to block it, but it had been a feint, and his kick hammered into my already broken arm.

My implant was unable to completely block the pain, and I gasped. His eye cleared momentarily when he heard me gasp, and his next strike came in slow enough I could lurch away.

"Now, Eric, finish her off!"

I realized Nick had a pad in his hand. Between yelling at Eric, he kept jabbing at it.

His control over Eric?

I shifted to my left, then my right to avoid Eric's strike. I did not try to attack, merely to elude.

It was not the way of the MDF Special Forces to elude for long, and his implant kept anticipating a strike.

And strike I did, but not at Eric. Instead I rolled out of an attack—right over the broken arm—relying on the implant to dampen the pain and sprang at Nick. His reflexes were only human.

276 | IBSON & KENNEDY

I grabbed the pad out of his hand and slammed it to the ground, shattering it in a startling burst of plastic and components.

Bouncing back into my stance, I looked at Eric with hope. He was shaking his head. His eyes narrowed again, though, and he launched another attack.

This time, I responded as the MDF had trained us. I led with a kick at his knee. The kick pushed the titanium joint back with a crunch. Then I slammed my titanium arm into the side of his head.

The control on his implant broke for just a second. But only for a second, and he flipped me sprawling in front of the crack in the wall. His father reached down. I batted his hand out of the way as I continued to roll into another stance.

But my broken arm slowed me. Eric was right there to hammer a series of punches at my breastplate. They would have killed a normal human, but fortunately my armor did not—quite—break.

My implant noted: *Breastplate Integrity Compromised.*

No shit.

I had no time for a fancy move, so I just punched with a short jab to his nose.

It knocked his head back and I had time to get back to my feet. I turned my right side toward him, shielding the wounded shoulder and putting my enhanced arm forward.

He jumped at me, this time with an odd hesitation.

The jab might have done something.

I caught his leg and slammed him to the ground. He bounced, twisted out of it, and came down with a hard thrust at my left shoulder.

I pivoted, pulling him along his line of attack, and then pirouet-ted around him to reset.

His eyes were clear, but the implant still controlled his muscles.

"Kill me," he hissed.

"What?"

"You'll have to kill me."

He kicked out. I blocked it.

"I can't..." He shook his head. "Too much—Too many im-plants."

He kicked again, this time crunching into my titanium-enhanced thigh. My implant redirected that pain as well, but I staggered back, trying to regain my balance.

Eric did not take advantage of the opportunity, though. Instead, he swung at his father. Nick ducked and the wall took part of the punch, but I heard him cry out.

Still alive. Too bad.

My lover turned back to me; his eyes flickering in and out of con-trol. He bounced into a combo; one I had never seen him use before. It startled me.

His kick struck my titanium leg, sending more warnings into my implant. The next punch added more warnings.

But I was able to block the follow-up attack, making him slightly off balance. I stomped on his ankle, bending it out of shape. No doubt, his implant sent him a series of warnings too, but unfortu-nately bent titanium joints could still be used, even if awkwardly.

Still, it staggered him.

He glanced at me. Then at his father, who had pulled himself back up, blood streaming down his face.

"Do it, Eric. Finish her off. Finish all the Fieldings off."

He stared at his father with loathing, but he still could not gain control. He hesitated.

"Do it!"

He twisted back into a stance, and then glanced around as if shaking his head to clear it.

"Eric!" both his father and I yelled.

Quicker than I could have imagined, he struck.

But not at me.

He rushed Nick and ripped open the wall between the two families. Essentially, the two rooms were now one.

Startled, his father staggered back onto a pile of debris. Eric ignored him and jumped back toward me. In my stance, I stepped back to avoid Eric's next assault.

However, he turned to the hole his fist had made in the exterior and yanked it, turning the small hole into a huge opening to the outside. One well beyond what the environmental system could control. One well beyond any normal patching could fix in the time we had.

"No!" I yelled into the wind, but he was not done.

He jumped straight up to a hatch in the dropped ceiling. There he hung for a moment with a sick look in his eyes.

I realized what he intended. "Eric, you'll kill us all!"

He glanced down at me. A teardrop fell, seeming to levitate as it accelerated at only 3.7 meters per second squared in the meager Martian gravity.

We stared at it until it splashed onto the ground.

I looked back up at my husband.

"I can't stop. I must kill all the Fieldings. I just can't stop," he whispered. "But I can also kill the Allardecks. My family doesn't deserve to live."

"No!"

"Forgive me, love." He pulled himself into the crawlspace.

I jumped up to chase. He was ahead of me by several meters. I crawled after him as fast as I could, which was difficult with a broken arm. He reached the joint air system.

I rushed at him. No finesse in this charge, just everything I could do to stop him from breaking the environment system that was the only hope of both the Fielding and Allardeck families.

He watched for half a second, and his ambivalence almost allowed me to reach him.

But right before I got to him, he wrenched the pipe apart. I slammed into him, driving him down through another access panel. We fell through the ceiling onto the floor of the communal dome.

I landed on top of him, my good arm pushing at his head and my titanium knee on his breastplate. Even in the light Martian gravity, the impact sent alarms all through my implants. The alarms on his implant must have been worse, because his head and neck curved at an odd angle.

"Kill me, my love," he whispered. "Kill me, then save them all."

"I can't."

"Please. I must die."

"No." I shook my head.

"Please. I beg you. You're the only one who can save me."

His enhanced arm reached at my throat.

"You see? Even now I seek to kill you. Don't let—" His eyes burned with terror and love. "Please."

I rose. Cries of panic came from behind me as the families realized the warrens were decompressing.

"Save them, my love." His hand groped after me. "Kill me so you can."

I stamped once, twice, thrice at the base of his skull with my enhanced leg.

The first did little. The second filled his eyes with love. The third crunched through his skull. His love ebbed until his eyes stared at me with nothing behind them.

No time to grieve.

* * *

I wrenched open the door into the Fielding warren. It was hard to pull with only one arm and the loss of pressure on the other side. I ran toward the room where Eric and I had fought.

My uncle ran past, pushing along cousins.

"Dad!"

"He's back there organizing," snarled the uncle.

"Good."

Idiot! Speaking of organization. I have a comm implant for a reason.

"Sergeant Fielding to all emergency services. We have an emergency decompression in West-Alpha-12."

"We see it. Don't you Fieldings know how to use the foam canisters? You know, the blue and yellow cans in every exterior room?"

"We had other things on our mind," I snarled.

"Fine, we'll send the patch team since you can't be bothered."

"Listen to me, asshole. The breach is too damn large. It can't be patched in time. If you don't send medtechs and low-O assistance in the next two seconds, I'll make sure that every bone in your body has to be enhanced. Got it?"

"What—"

"Send help right fucking now, Mars damn you!"

And to hell with radio protocol.

I left him to it and ran back in. I got two kids under my healthy arm and brought them to safety.

I did it again.

And again.

But the air pressure was essentially gone. My implants' O2 sensor flashed at me. I had reserves and hyper-efficient lungs, but this was more than even that could handle.

Don't think about what it will do to unenhanced humans. Just go help.

I found dad. He had made it most of the way back but had tried to flee carrying mom. I picked them both up and ran out with them.

By this point, most of my family was out, coughing and wheezing. I saw most of our kids. A few Allardecks had made it out by this point as well, but hardly any children.

I hesitated for a half-second, but there was no choice. I ran into the Allardeck warrens.

I did not have to worry about arguing with them, as I would have normally. The Allardecks had more things to worry about than a

Fielding. I grabbed every kid I could find. I basically threw them out into the communal area and went back.

I had been given over a dozen enhancements over the years. I was, in many ways, superhuman. But even so, my body could only be pushed so far.

My oxygen reserves fell to critical levels. The human parts ached, but the internal painkillers helped with that. Then they fell to critical levels too.

Warning after warning showed up on my implant. I ignored them.

I saw Nick Allardeck. To his credit, he was trying to help two of their children flee. However, he staggered to the ground, dropping them. I grabbed the two kids and left him there.

Fucking Allardeck.

I pushed through the Allardeck pressure door. In the communal area, O2 was plentiful. I staggered back to my feet, taking stock and breathing deep.

So few.

I did not see Beatrice.

Without thinking, I pushed the pain and fatigue away and dove back into the Fielding warren. She was not in her area.

My wedding dress was, though, hanging in front of a window overlooking the Endeavor crater. It flapped in the wind. The red Martian light from the window colored it an ethereal crimson.

No time to grieve, dammit!

I finally found her on the floor in our home school, which happened to be on the far end of our warrens. In her arms, she cradled the girl who had measured me a lifetime ago.

So blue.

I grabbed them anyway and staggered down the hall.

Then my oxygen reserves gave out.

I tried to breath in the remaining atmosphere.

Not worth the trouble.

I ran onward, holding my breath. The door was only thirty meters away. Twenty. Ten.

But the door was shut and would not open.

I set them down and pushed.

I got it open a crack, but it slammed back.

No time for this.

One last try. I pushed with all I had. It opened a little, and then enough for me to get some oxygen. But the crack was only about ten centimeters wide, and the oxygen was not enough. I could feel the door slipping. In desperation I pushed again, and got it back to about ten centimeters, but no more.

I put my back to the door and pushed with both legs, and I could feel it move out again.

Yes!

Then my real leg shattered under the force, and I fell down, the door pushing me back into the warren.

I reached out with my right arm to catch the join. But the air pressure kept pushing the door. In agony, I realized the door was bending the titanium.

In front of me, neither my aunt nor the girl had moved.

Still, so blue.

I remembered Eric's tears and waited for it to end.

The world started getting darker.

Then the rescue teams arrived. Their hydraulic opener succeeded where I had failed. They wrenched the door open, and my arm was free, though curved and wrong-looking.

I tried to rise but could only get to my knees.

The first person in a pressure suit tried to pull me, but I waved him off and pointed behind me. He nodded and picked up the girl. Another handed me an oxygen mask. Then he picked up Beatrice.

I sucked in all the O2 I could. With some oxygen, I was now able to rise and hop out of the warren.

People filled the communal area. Many were lying on the ground or against the wall. Medtechs moved hastily around, looking grim.

I finally made it to my parents. I collapsed to a knee next to my mom. Dad was also there, holding her hand and crying.

"What happened?" he asked.

"I think Allardeck tried to get Eric to kill me by hacking his implant. In the end, Eric caused the decompression."

"What!"

I nodded. "Eric fought it. I'd be dead if he hadn't. He gave me a chance."

"I'll kill him."

"Eric's dead." I pointed across the room, then covered my face. "I killed him."

"Not him, his father."

"He's probably dead. I don't know for sure, but he's still in there."

"Allardecks!"

"Leave it be, Dad. We can hate each other tomorrow."

"How many did you save?"

"People? Or Allardecks?" I snarled.

He grimaced. "People, I guess. I don't want to kill most of the Allardecks." He spat. "Nick, though."

"I don't know. Dozens, I guess. I could replay the recording on my implant, but not now. Please, by Mars, not now."

He put his hand on my shoulder, his face troubled. "We'll have to see it someday."

"I'll just download it. I don't think I ever want to see it." I looked over at my aunt. A medtech was covering her with a blanket. "So much I don't need to see ever again."

He looked at my shattered leg and crushed, curving arm. "You could hardly have done more."

"I guess."

"I don't see how you survived at all."

"I'm part of the Martian Special Forces, now," I spat out. "We don't *get* to die. They'll just give me the new model arm and replace the leg. Everything'll get fixed right up, and I'll be back to going wherever they need someone to be shot."

My mom coughed, and we both turned to her. She lifted her hand to touch my face.

"Saw…saw you."

"Stay quiet, mom. You'll be fine. Just rest."

"Love you." Her arm fell back to her chest. Fortunately, I could see she was breathing.

My dad stroked my hair, just as he had done when I was a kid. Just another completely human Martian kid.

I held mom's hand.

"I have to go. Stay here," he said.

I nodded.

I shut out all the noise and just stayed there.

Then, finally, hospital gurneys arrived in sufficient numbers. They lifted mom up on a gurney and I rose, standing again on one leg.

They saw my leg for the first time, and with horrified noises rushed to get another gurney for me.

I waved them off and hopped over to Eric. I curled up next to him, holding my dearest love.

Medtechs came up to me.

"Sergeant, you're hurt. We have a gurney, and we need to get you looked at."

"I'll be fine."

"Yeah, probably so, given the readouts your implant is feeding us, but you've got to come with us." He glanced at Eric with sad eyes. "We'll take care of him."

"I love him."

"We know." He reached out a hand, braced to help up someone with my mass.

I kissed Eric on the cheek and let them help me sit on a gurney.

And it was such a relief. My adrenalin subsided, and all I could do was cry in long, loud sobs.

"Tonya?" My father had returned, escorted by my uncles. They had troubled looks on their faces. "Tell me again what happened."

"Someone, I think Nick Allardeck, hacked into Eric's implant and forced him to attack me." My eyes turned cold. "Couldn't have me for a daughter-in-law, I guess."

"I sort of understand that. I didn't want Eric as a son-in-law."
My dad's face turned grim as he looked around the dome. "But I
don't understand doing what he did. How'd he do it?"

"I don't know exactly. The truth is each enhancement is just one
more component of us. Just like any other computer part. They're
wired into the implant that's connected to our brain."

They glanced at each other.

"That's what we thought," he said. He looked around. "You
saved so many people here. And you've done us proud in the MDF.
All those awards."

"Yeah. Useless pieces of paper and ribbon."

"I guess." He fidgeted.

"What is it, Dad?"

"Honey. I love you."

The uncles nodded. One said, "We love you."

"What, then?"

Dad's lips twisted. "We love you, but..." He gestured to the
dome. "What Eric did here was evil."

"Mars damn you! No one would be alive now if Eric hadn't
fought the implant to give us a chance! Don't you get it?" I started
up off the gurney. "He's a fucking hero!"

Dad shook his head. "None of us, Fielding or Allardeck, would
be dead now if it weren't for him. At least, what he was at the end."

"What do you mean?"

"Tonya, we're scared of you."

"You're scared of me? But—"

"Not just you. It's Eric and the others like you." He glanced
around at the rescue efforts. "Honey, you're not my little girl any-

more." He pointed at my broken leg. "You'll be even less her when they fix that."

"But, I'm still me!"

"Maybe." He bent his head for a moment. "But we don't know that. You knew Eric, but these aren't the deeds of the man you knew. They're of someone else, and we don't know if you'll ever be someone else. Someone who could do... *this*."

He glanced at my uncles. They nodded. "We love you. But you're no longer welcome in our warren. We just—" Tears came down his cheeks.

My implant flashed a new alarm: Analgesic Supply Exhaustion Imminent.

"We just can't," he continued.

I stared at my dad, my soul falling to pieces around me.

Then, thankfully, the analgesics failed. A shattered leg and crushed arm drove away the anguish of my well-seeming form.

* * * * *

Rob Howell Bio

Rob Howell is the creator of the Shijuren fantasy setting (www.shijuren.org) and an author in the Four Horsemen Universe (www.mercenaryguild.org). He writes primarily medieval fantasy, space opera, military science fiction, and alternate history.

He is a reformed medieval academic, a former IT professional, and a retired soda jerk.

His parents discovered quickly books were the only way to keep Rob quiet. He latched onto the Hardy Boys series first and then anything he could reach. Without books, it's unlikely all three would have survived.

His latest release in Shijuren is *Where Now the Rider*, the third in the Edward series of swords and sorcery mysteries. The next release in that world is *None Call Me Mother*, the conclusion to the epic fantasy trilogy *The Kreisens*.

You can find him online at: www.robhowell.org, on Amazon at https://www.amazon.com/-/e/B00X95LBB0, and his blog at www.robhowell.org/blog.

# # # # #

Forty Acres and a Mule
by Luke R. J. Maynard

The gunship touched town at Miyagino just after midnight in a gravel parking lot barely big enough for a dozen cars. The base commander had been kind enough to clear the lot, but not to such a distance that the whine of the engines didn't set off a couple of car alarms coming down. Valentine had slept most of the way in, but the chorus of sirens and chirps was enough to break the monotony of the jet engines and pull him back from his dream. He straightened up in the chair and shook the cobwebs from his head as his neural systems came back online.

"What the hell is that?" he muttered. The gray-haired, heavyset pilot shrugged with his eyebrows, since his shoulders were hard at work holding things absolutely still.

"Touchdown momentarily, agent," said the pilot.

"D'you set us down in the middle of a goddamn toy store?"

"Sorry about that, Chief. Bit of a tight squeeze." The pilot grimaced as he brushed the antenna of a satcar with one of the stabilizers.

Valentine peered out the window. "It is at that. *That's* all you've got in Sendai? My second wife had a shoe closet that big."

"That's all we've got," said the pilot. "The Japanese don't take too kindly to our presence after the Kuril Wars. After that gong show on Broutona, we're lucky they let us keep a P.O. Box for fan mail."

"You get fan mail?"

The pilot laughed so hard the wheels bounced as they hit.

"No," he said.

"Don't worry about it," said Valentine. "I'm not looking to build a summer home here. We'll be in and out before they know we were here." He clapped the pilot on the shoulder. "Thanks for bringing me all the way out here, Major."

"No one else I trusted to fly under the grid," said the pilot. "You want something done right…"

"You going to check in with the folks on duty?"

"I'll see to it, Mr. Valentine."

"Good man." Valentine palmed his pistol, fingered the sensor until it came online, and holstered the live weapon as he reached for his briefcase.

"You expecting trouble, Chief?"

Valentine slid open the door. "It's only trouble if you don't expect it. Give my best to base command."

"You're just going to walk off down the street?" asked the major incredulously. But before he could get it out, Jimmy Valentine had done just that.

* * *

The beer here came in half-liters, in cases of 20, which made the math easy. Terry Cullen had always been good at math. Six cases by four, stacked six high to a flat:

fourteen hundred and forty kilos per lift. Terry's skeleton was sustained-carry rated to sixteen, which should have been a fine buffer. Only he figured that some pencil-necked bean counter in Logistics had failed to account for the weight of glass, and the weight of three thousand bottle caps—and that was why Terry crunched painkillers like candy and had a wicked buzzing in his legs when he bent at the neck now. It's why his maintenance bills, physio, chiro, nano, had all spiked in the last year.

Then again, it was why cybernetically altered super soldiers earned two thousand yen an hour to the regular stock boys' nineteen hundred.

A cut above, my ass.

As a high-end Class 4 Mule, at least, Terry had been fitted for stealth as well as carry strength. The other Mules on the assembly line whined at the joints as they loaded truck after truck. Terry felt the uncomfortable heat and buzz in his joints, but the whole system was quiet enough that he could hear the metal fire door unlatch even over the hum of the conveyor belts.

With a sigh he set down a ton and a half of booze and hit the red stop button on his conveyor belt.

"I don't say nothin' till I see a badge," he began—but stopped when he caught sight of Jimmy Valentine's shadow. He stepped back, and his hand went instinctively to his hip.

"What the hell are you doing here?" he snapped.

Valentine raised his eyebrows. "Wow," he said, nodding to Terry's weapon. "A pricing gun? You going to kill me with *that?*"

Terry laughed in spite of himself, but felt the little machine in his hand, weighing it. It definitely had some metal in it. He put it back in the apron's holster, beside the pocket for sale stickers.

"I've killed tougher men with less," he said.

Valentine looked absently around the warehouse. "I gotta say, this is not the end of the wholesale beer industry I thought I'd find you on. I figured 'consumer' was probably your end."

Terry smiled. "You can waste all the time you want on the ground here," he said. "Make all the jokes you want. If my people see me talking to you, Mister Tanaka will cuss me out, maybe put me on bathrooms for yapping on the job. Your people see you talking to *me*..." he let the threat hang in the air. He was just about to restart the conveyor when Valentine slapped a honey- brown envelope down on top of his next flat.

"What's that?" he asked.

"What do you think it is?"

"Not enough money," said Terry, and brushed it off the top of the flat. Valentine caught it, opened it.

"You think I'd bother printing a cheque?" he asked. He stuffed the paper into Terry's hand. Servos thrummed away silently as Terry tore it open.

"Office of the Judge Advocate General...A pardon? Is this real?"

"Not yet, it's not," said Valentine. "Needs a signature and a seal. But I can get them."

Terry's heart dropped in his chest, and his mouth went dry. "I'm not eligible."

"Times have changed," said Valentine. "Or they're about to."

"I don't like where this is going," said Terry.

"You won't like where you're going, either."

Terry read the letter in disbelief. "You sound mighty confident," he growled.

Valentine folded his arms. "And when am I this confident? When are the only times?"

Terry sulked like a kid made to apologize. "Sure things and chicken wings," he spat out, under duress.

"Now, do you s'pose I came halfway around the world, to a blackout zone, for cheap wing night?"

"No, sir."

"You s'pose I came for a sure thing?"

Terry gritted his teeth. "Maybe I'm not that easy to read anymore. Maybe I'm not a sucker anymore, either."

"There's worse things to be than a sucker," said Valentine. "Kid, you've always liked to make me sweat. If that's what you want, we can stand here twenty minutes, trade some witty repartee, and you can come 'round once I started talking about Samarkand."

Terry froze.

"Or," Valentine went on, "you can take it for granted that I wouldn't be so supremely confident your answer was 'yes' unless it was. You can give your notice right now, or not, and follow me back to the gunship I got parked at Miyagino with the meter running, and we can pull chocks by the time you've heard enough to agree with me. What's it gonna be?"

"Give me the elevator pitch," said Terry.

"I'll give you the fast rope pitch," said Valentine. "We found Crate 14. It's in Uzbekistan. I'm putting together a cr—"

He was interrupted by the hiss of Velcro torn open as Terry pulled his apron off.

"Tell me on the way," he said.

"I told you," said Valentine. "I *told* you, Terry."

"Shut up and take me there."

* * *

T hey were already hustling like hell when the alert went off. It was silent to the casual pedestrians, who took note of the hulking *gaijin* but didn't seem to care over-much as he shuffled past them in his massive, steel-plated Mule exo-skeleton. But Valentine's neural network was still linked to the Security Council's blackout frequencies, and though he couldn't understand the words so well anymore, there was no question they'd been found.

"We've got to move," said Valentine, and he took off. Terry engaged and braced himself for a tremendous leap. The whole apparatus threw itself forward, then again, and he bounded ahead of his companion on the straight road.

"Don't wait for me," said Valentine. "Response time is seven minutes. We're cutting it tight."

The gunship was rumbling away, ready to lift, when Terry bounded into sight of it. A half-dozen bodies—local MPs, probably—littered the gravel parking lot where it idled. An angular, severe-faced woman in iridescent dragonskin sat dangling her legs off the side of the gunship. She looked up as he raced in; her sidearm made a graceful circle on her hip as she spotted him, drew it, recognized him, and holstered it in a single smooth motion.

"Izzat you, Disco?" he asked. She half-smiled.

"D'you bring me a beer?" she responded.

"I'm going to get a lot of shit for that, aren't I?"

"As long as it keeps being funny."

"Look, it was a job. Not much work for Mules after the Service. A guy's gotta eat. I was out of this game. So were you, if I recall."

She shrugged. "Sometimes getting out's the best way to survive still being in. What'd you do, leave the old man behind?"

"He's right behind me," said Terry. As he reached the helicopter, he looked down at the bodies. "I don't suppose you ever considered nonlethal countermeasures?"

"Gosh," she said innocently. "I just knocked 'em all out with pepper spray, is all."

Terry narrowed his eyes. "Uh-huh." He looked down. The one at his feet was face-down, but an exit wound like a grisly rose blossomed out the back of his head.

"The really strong stuff," she said.

"Uh-huh."

"You know…for bears."

They sat in silence for a moment. In the cockpit, the major was barking commands into a transmitter and was two switches away from being airborne. Valentine was quick on his feet, and his internal organs were top-of-the-line. He wasn't even winded when he rounded a corner and came into sight.

"Dammit, Disco," he spat. "I told you not to come out of cloak."

"You needed an exit," she said.

Valentine looked at he bodies. "An exit," he muttered, breathing hard. "Exit. Like a door or a window. Not a goddamn ten-foot hole in the side of the house."

"Is this everybody?" The major asked, calling back to them.

"We're on," said Valentine. "Go!"

The ship was up in ten seconds and hit its ceiling beneath the grid in twelve. The major threw the jets to horizontal so abruptly that it dropped two dozen feet as it took off. By the time Valentine caught his breath, they were halfway across Sendai Bay.

Terry was eager to talk. He jerked his head toward the pilot. "Is he all right?"

Valentine looked up to the pilot. "Hey, you got some heavy metal you can stream through that headset of yours?"

The major nodded. "Just give me a tap if you need anything. We'll be back on the carrier in about seven, eight minutes." The galloping drumbeat of something loud and crunchy crackled into his headset, almost loud enough for Valentine to make out the tune.

"We're good," said Valentine.

"So you wanna tell me where we're going?" Terry asked. "You wanna tell me why I just left Japan with you on ten minutes' notice? I could've used an hour to grab some underwear and a toothbrush, at least—say goodbye to some friends, maybe."

Valentine raised an eyebrow. "You made friends?"

"It's a figure of speech," said Terry. "Out with it. Somehow after we botched a once-in-a-lifetime raid, you got us a second shot. I wanna know how."

"Zee knew what he was doing," said Valentine. "That's how."

Terry rolled his eyes. "I should have known. Knew what he was doing, right. That's why half of Uzbekistan is radioactive now."

"Hear him out," urged Disco.

"Far as we knew," said Valentine, "Zee nuked the whole valley. We couldn't contend with the artillery and couldn't get to the target, so he wiped the valley, everything died, and the drones made it out with the cargo."

"That's the long and the short of it," said Terry.

"That's the short of it," Valentine corrected. "The long of it is that he left us a failsafe. Sniping into an explosion, he called it. Two payloads, the first so big that nobody saw the second go in. Long story short, those mountains have been baking in their own gamma rays for years—and it's only ten years on that his trick paid off.

We've always known what he used—at least, we thought we did. Karpov and the Atomic Energy Commission knew exactly what the half-life at ground zero was going to be. All he had to do was stash the cargo somewhere, wait a decade for things to cool off, and go back in and get it. Only, there was a second payload, a targeted payload with a different half-life. Something stupid like sixteen thousand years."

Terry frowned. "You know, five years on a team with nuke assist, I should have learned a little more about the science."

"Think of it this way," said Valentine. "You're getting a homing signal from a transmitter. You know where it is and how to get it. But everything in the whole city puts out the same signal. Every cat and dog, every fire hydrant. Every candy bar wrapper, every cigarette butt. Everything within fifty miles is a clone of your homing device. But they're putting out a signal from shitty dollar-store batteries. Underneath it all you've got one transmitter powered by name brand. All we had to do was wait until the radioactive static decayed—until the fallout from Zee's nuke crapped out."

Terry nodded. "That's brilliant. So we've got a pinpoint."

"Affirmative."

"We're going for it?"

"Affirmative."

Terry grinned. "Fucking legend. Waleed al-Zee. He's the smartest nuclear cook the Service ever had, you know that? He's never going to live this down."

A shadow passed over Valentine's face. "No…he won't. He died eighteen months ago."

"No."

"Cancer. About four kinds of it."

Terry nodded, half-numb. "All magic comes at a price."

"I don't need to tell you we're pulling this one for him."

"No," said Terry. "Not for Zee. Only for me. I imagine Disco's the same. I imagine all seven of us are."

Disco nodded solemnly. "All four."

"What?"

"You, me, Valentine. Turner's waiting for us in Uzbekistan. That's it. Cameron went Fed. Binnie was retired by a land mine in Siberia."

"What about Ghost?"

Her mouth drew tight. "Ghost settled down."

"Bull shit." He enunciated both words for emphasis.

"My hand of God. Got married, bought a house in Vermont. Two point four kids, the whole deal. And then committed suicide in the back yard."

Terry bit his lip. That one stung.

"Well," he said sadly. "That…seems fair. Couldn't have been any other way. The only person who ever could have snuck up on Ghost…was goddamn Ghost."

Disco chuckled, but not happily. "Goddamn Ghost," she agreed.

"I guess there's no getting the band back together," he quipped.

"This ain't a high school reunion," Valentine reminded him. "It ain't an Auggie nostalgia tour. It's the last stage of a very long mission—a mission that I remind you is still active, however long you've been slingin' beer. What it means on the world stage, I don't much care. What the Chinese or the Europe A.I. Trust or the Pentagon think doesn't mean a damn thing—except insofar as I have not yet found my way to a beach chair in Hawai'i, and one day I might like to. All we have in front of us is a simple drop mission and the chance to make right on a promise to ourselves, for Zee, or for Ghost, or for the peace of mind of your immortal soul. Whatever you got in the tank to get this job done, you get it done. So long as they do not stand between me a sunset in Waikiki, your reasons are not important to me."

"Fine," said Terry. "What's the op?"

"The crate's in a collapsed cave in the center of the Boysuntov, in a network of military excavations the Americans call the Anthill. We need you to do what a Mule's always done. We need heavy kit, and we can't trust a bot or an ATV to go where we need to go. We need to be in and out on a tight clock: if we wait for safe levels of radiation, Karpov sends in his people and audits the cargo, maybe moves it again. He can't go for it while it's still kinda-sorta lethal, so we're going to dose up with anti-rads and make a couple days of it, no more. When we get to the excavation site, we need you to bust us in. It's not glamorous, but it's a vital ops role."

"Opposition?"

"Automated only, light to moderate," said Valentine. "The Anthills are a deadlands, but they're patrolled by drone. The tech on those bad boys has gone up a ways since the twenties. I'd prefer no contact—but we're not exactly sending you in with a pricing gun."

"Funny," Terry grimaced. "Who's bankrolling?"

"Does it matter?"

Terry thought about it. "I like to know who I'm running for."

"New Persia, mostly," said Valentine. "Probably CIA. They have an interest if you go far enough up the chain. There must be somebody stateside, otherwise they wouldn't have the INS to get you that pardon. But don't worry—we're strictly outsourced."

"Yeah, 'cause that's what I'm worried about," Disco chimed in. Valentine smiled at her.

"It's the tax evasion that'll get you," he said. "CIA, NSA, MI-6, ISIL…only initials I was ever truly afraid of are the IRS."

Terry shrugged his massive bionic arms. "I was just kidnapped," he said. "Shanghaied. I was not under the impression that I was getting paid."

"If I recall correctly," said Valentine, "there was supposed to be some gold in Crate 14 too."

Disco smiled. "You think it's like to make us rich?"

"Maybe," said Valentine. "Maybe. But hopefully not so rich as to be somebody's problem."

* * *

Turner was waiting in Tashkent with the gear, as they planned. Most of the fighting was south, around Samarkand, and they had plans to skirt the worst of it and head straight up into the mountains. He'd quartermastered for the Service long enough that he knew what to get them, and the proximity of an active war zone without too much UN oversight made the Fergana Valley a veritable candy shop for a man of Turner's refined taste in tools of destruction. Dog-tired from the trip in, they crashed on arrival and woke up to an array of dust-covered flight cases like a live-fire Christmas morning as Turner hauled them out of the closet

"Blackout M4 for the lady," he said, opening the first of the cases. "Right lovely for an infiltrator. Light, easy carry. Nice fellow at the swap threw in a suppressor, because a lady never tells."

Disco turned up a corner of her mouth. "Won't do much good without—"

Turner lifted the first layer of packing foam; the mags were underneath. "Subsonic blackout rounds on the left, the finest in leisurely flight and gentle arrival. Obnoxious armor piercing on the right, if you fancy giving something a little more than a love tap."

She smiled. "You do plan ahead."

Turner looked to Terry. "Now you, since Valentine had to be a spoil-sport and open his presents early…" he lifted a case onto the table. "For a sidearm…how's the standard Desert Eagle suit you?"

"Just fine," said Terry. "For my purse, maybe. In case my ankle gun jams and I gotta use something small."

Turner went back to the closet. "You're a hard man to satisfy," he said.

"Come on, man. You know what kinda shit they were making ten years ago. You know what kind of firepower you can plug into a Mule Rig."

"Oh, they certainly did play around," said Turner. "See which kind of walking tank could strap on the biggest, noisiest piece. Seemed like a bit of a pissing contest to me."

"Only contest I was ever good at," said Terry.

"They did try and make you walking dump trucks a shorty carbine for Vulcan rounds, didn't they?"

"They didn't try," said Terry. "They *did* it. Those things were great."

Turner went back to the closet. "I hear they never got past the prototype stage."

"Pyrith Arms folded in the early thirties," he said. "But I hear a couple got out into the wild."

304 | IBSON & KENNEDY

Turner grinned like a very satisfied snake as he hoisted a heavy case off the closet floor. "I hear some idjit just bought up the last one," he said.

Terry opened the case, beaming. The gun was a low, squat, massively fat-barreled thing, fitted with a forearm brace and collapsible stock that would interface with the plates of his rig and feed the recoil straight into his frame. He cracked open a magazine thick as a family Bible and looked at the rounds with alarm.

"That'll do," he said.

Valentine came out the bathroom, already dressed and half-kitted, brushing his teeth. He almost choked and had to spit in the kitchen sink.

"Jesus Christ, Neville, don't encourage him."

Turner shrugged. "I knew what he'd want."

"I'm heavy infantry," Terry said. "I need the heavy gear."

"You're heavy infantry," Valentine grumbled. "Not air support. That shit belongs on a fighter jet."

Terry shouldered the gun proudly. He probably wouldn't have been able to one-hand it at all without the rig. "You might be glad for it if things go south," he said. "Biggest thing he could find me."

"If you need something bigger," said Valentine, "try learning to aim better."

"I trust you gentlemen are satisfied?"

Valentine nodded and checked his own hardware. "I knew we brought you along for something." It was the logistics, he knew, that could make or break a mission.

"I'm none too happy with the underwear situation," said Terry. "I'm a boxers kinda guy at home."

Grunting from the strain, Turner hauled a little diesel generator out of the closet as well. "Don't push it," he said. "Just put down your new toys and load up the bloody vans."

* * *

The plan was to drop in from above, swift and stealthy, like in the movies—only it was an empty desert and cloudless skies, the drones could see by night, and there was nothing stealthy about any of it. For the price of one airlift from the PMCs who still funnelled ammo, socks, and expired MREs into the hills around Samarkand, Valentine found them three desert-battered Volkswagen camper vans, stained with just enough of the local flavor to make the trip in *real* stealth. They'd been at it too long now to suffer any amateurish pretense to coolness in the face of practical objectives. A little before dawn on the first day, they were off the main roads and into the desert, and Terry blasted Wagner's *Ride of the Valkyries* from his smartphone for irony's sake as they rolled downrange at twenty-five miles an hour.

Turner had found them maps, and geosyncs, and the usual boy-scout toys, and even though they stayed mostly in sight of each other over the next four days, they had picked out a rendezvous in the foothills to gear up, down their anti-rads, spend the night throwing up, and head up into the Anthill at dawn. Disco had a heavy foot and the van with the best suspension, and she was the first to arrive. Having brought most of the support gear, she had the tent up and the three-tower Geiger imager going by the time the others arrived. She'd brought her civvies and luggage for a quick departure—nobody expected to stick around for a drink when it was done—and they found her hunched over the Geiger's central display, drenched

306 | IBSON & KENNEDY

in sweat with a lavender floral print shirt draped over her head to keep the sun off.

"How are we doing?" asked Valentine.

"Not too shabby," she said, tweaking the dials. "It's too windy to get a sharp image right off the bat, but we should have more detail over the next couple of hours." She pointed up into the mountains to the southeast. "Our big gamma bloom is that way. More or less, give or take a mile or two, everything's exactly where it's supposed to be."

"Is that pink?" Terry asked, grinning.

Disco didn't look up from her dials. "Fuck you, it's purple," she snapped.

"Are those little flowers?"

"Oleanders," she said. "They're poisonous." She pulled the shirt off her head, wiped down her neck, and threw it back into her van. "What's for dinner?"

Turner slammed the squeaking door of his own van and tossed her an orange bottle of pills. "For dessert, Love," he said, "the finest in gourmet nanotherapeutic anti-rads."

"Tasty," she said.

He set down his duffle bag, rummaged through it, pulled out a few glossy brown packages and started handing them out.

"And for your main course dining pleasure," he said, "you blokes are treated to—looks like Number Four. Cheese and Vegetable Omelet."

Disco cracked up. Terry shot him a look that could peel the paint off a tank.

"Seriously?" he said. "Ten years out, I come back to a Vomelet?"

"Mister Valentine's getting on in years," said Turner. "Thought he might appreciate a little bit of the old country."

Valentine shook his head with masochistic fondness. "They haven't made these in twenty-five years. I didn't know they started making 'em again."

"Oh, they haven't," said Turner. "You can't reboot a classic."

Valentine opened his package, revelling grimly in the stink of it. "Where did you even find these?"

Turner smiled. "Let us just say that I know a guy, who knows a guy, who knows another guy, who knows someone who hates you and wants you to suffer."

Disco leaned against the bumper of her van and downed her anti-rads as she tore open her dinner. Terry sat down beside her.

"You're a braver man than I, Lady," he said.

She shrugged. "It's all gonna be in the dirt in a couple hours anyway. Better not to waste the pizza."

Terry nodded. "I do like the pizza."

She cracked her water bottle and leaned in, lowering her voice. "We stayed with Turner for a week while Valentine tracked you down. This stuff is all he ever eats."

"You're kidding."

"Whole cupboards full of the stuff. No wonder he's so lean."

"Well, we've all gotta do something to keep in shape, once we hit his age."

Disco looked at him. "You're his age," she said.

Terry shrugged. "Yeah, but carrying weight's what I do. You're wired as infiltrators. Targeting systems, collapsible joints, modular weapons. All that James Bond shit. I've got one job—hauling freight at speed. I've put on twenty-five pounds easy since the last time we did this. Doesn't matter. My fat ass is rated to sixteen hundred kilos sustained carry. Three thousands of burst weight. I'm basically a superhero."

Disco shook her ration bag in earnest. "You will be," she said, "after this much gamma radiation. You want my apple butter?"

He took it, obligingly, though nothing in the whole bag tasted good. He didn't care who ate it; neither did she. That wasn't the point.

"Six years I worked in that factory," he said. "Did you get to see it?"

"I stayed with the ship," she replied.

"I never know where you are. Six years I worked in there. Fifty weeks a year. Thirty-five hours a week. Two hundred flats an hour. D'you know how much beer I shovelled?"

"I'm not the one with the calculator in my head," she said. "Ask Valentine."

"Don't have to," said Terry. "I did it once. Six billion, forty-eight million, give or take. The greatest advancement of my age, the greatest military cybernetic field unit ever engineered, dedicated to the most sensitive and important operations ever conducted on foreign soil. And where did I end up? Where did all this tech end up? In a warehouse. Moving six billion bottles of cheap Japanese lager."

Her armor shimmered as she shrugged. "That's a lot of beer," she said.

He nodded absently.

"I don't know what it takes a civilian to get their drink on," she said. "Three beers, maybe four. But six years of that—I imagine you made a lot of people very happy."

Terry almost smiled. But she opened her ration pouch and there was nowhere in that whole hellish desert to hide from the stink.

"I imagine so," he said as he downed his pills.

* * *

They camped early, soon as their stomachs had settled, and started upward at three in the morning to make the most of the chill. You had to go up before you could go down, but up was nothing. Up was child's play. Terry's incredible atomic exoskeleton did most of the heavy lifting—literally, as they'd emptied all three vans onto him before making the climb. Living at sea level for so long, he found himself breathless and gasping in the thin air as he went, even with his augments doing the hardest of the work. Disco and Turner were both supremely conditioned and made their way in silence and easy grace. Valentine, owing to the sophisticated powers of his Class 6 internals, led the way without so much as breaking a sweat.

Terry thought back to his days before the augments, to the rock climbing at Devil's Lake, a lifetime ago. He recalled the burning thrill of hauling himself up with his own natural strength, the effort with which he scaled a mere four hundred metres above sea level. He would fly up those rocks today—Mules were built to take any terrain under any weight. He would do it effortlessly, like Superman beneath a hot yellow sun. Even now, as he swooped back down to sort out Disco's climbing harness, the heroic trumpets rang in the back of his mind. But his muscles really never ached with delicious strain anymore, and he did not feel heroic.

Having summited the outer wall of the mountains, they came down into the Byzantine trenches of the Anthill, and the moving parts of Terry's arms and shoulders slotted themselves tightly against his bioflesh as he squeezed through passages barely wide enough for an ordinary man. He moved as fast as the others—even faster, maybe—with only seven or eight hundred pounds of kit to slow him down. But no matter how strong they made him, there was only so much he could do against the tight fit of the rocky channels. His pack towered over his head and came down to his calves; it was twice as wide as his shoulders, and when he reached the top he had a set of ski poles to walk with—not because the weight was too much, but because it was harder than it sounded to balance with a pair of Harley road bikes strapped to your exoframe.

Before they'd gone a mile in, Terry could see the problem. The Anthill was littered with what must have been mercenary encampments at one time. Stray barricades, shelters, utility stations, and bits of gear littered the trenches wherever they had fallen. Whole walls had collapsed; the place had been blown to hell. Someone had been through for things of value, at some point—either Karpov's mercs, in the early days, or intrepid villagers who'd cut their lives short in the deadly hills for a chance at a heavy Russian gun. They understood, well enough, that the hills made you sick—but a life cut short by ten years was a fair trade for a Russian cannon that would bring you fifteen years' pay on the black market, if you were poor enough and desperate enough. More than once, he passed the skeletons of those who hadn't made it home.

The damage got more extensive the farther in they climbed. If there had been open caves, they were so much rubble now, and that's why they needed him. In a different world, the Anthill was a living maze, stationed throughout with mercenaries and fanatics, cult soldiers to Karpov's mad sectarian ambitions. Ghost and Valentine would have come alone, done this whole thing their way, gotten in and out without a shot fired. But it wasn't their world anymore: it was a dead land, a land of emptiness and broken promises, and those were Terry's specialty.

They caught sight of the first drone six miles in, a shimmering black and silver bug fluttering its rotary wings against the light of a rapidly approaching dawn. Valentine pressed his back against the rock wall and motioned Turner to point, signalling the takedown.

"About a hundred and ten yards," he said. "Have you got something in a nine iron?"

Terry set down one of his packs and hauled out the scrambler. "Make it count," he said.

Turner shouldered the scrambler and made some final adjustments. Disco engaged her cloak as she moved up: for a moment, Terry's eyes were the closest and she seemed to disappear entirely. Then, as she dialled in the drone as her main threat, her primary cloaking sensors targeted the drone alone, and a few buggy traces of her body and poorly reflected rock came and went as her less exact secondary systems took over for all other onlookers.

"One shot," whispered Turner. "Do it right."

He shouldered the scrambler, locked on and hit the drone with a burst of interference that took out its comms. The weapon was silent, seemed to do almost nothing, and the drone's antennae twitched as it searched for a satellite connection, darting upward and turning sideways as if to reach for a signal.

"Hit it," whispered Valentine.

The deep, muffled *pop* of Disco's rifle went off as she hit the drone. The thing sparked brightly in the light of dawn, but did not fall. It came about. She fired again, twice more.

"Cover!" shouted Valentine.

Terry's rig wasn't suited to heroic dives, but the trench walls were deep and the drone was at a tough angle. It didn't seem to have tagged Disco; it went straight for the largest moving object and spat out a grenade. The blast echoed in the trenches and reverberated throughout the mountains. Its flight pattern shifted, rising fast as it came toward them.

"Heavy fire!" called Valentine. "Give me heavy!"

Terry was out of practice and slow to disentangle from the rubble. A couple hundred pounds of rock had come down on top of him and he had to jerk one arm free while he covered his vulnerable head with the other. Disco shouted something at him, but his ears were ringing and he was in no mood to give them time to clear.

The Baby Vulcan prototype looked absurd in his hand as he drew it off his rig and locked it into his shoulder. It felt more like a grenade launcher than a carbine, and beneath the Mule Rig and the heavy cargo on his back, Terry felt like one of those absurd, stylized space soldiers with a tiny head and enormous, clumsy hands as he engaged the forearm support. But the assist engaged as the gun came to life, and it read him as he raised it, and it wasn't bad for kick as he pumped an anti-material round square through the drone's armored fuselage, tearing a chunk off it and spinning it almost out of the air.

"There's your hole!" he shouted, half-deaf from his own cannon. He didn't know if she heard.

Beneath the freakish underwater ringing of his ears, he could make out the little pops as her next couple of shots went off. Even his hand cannon didn't down it, but its innards were more sensitive than the thick plating that covered them, and by the time she'd put four more rounds into it, the blades had stalled, and the thing was in free fall.

Turner winced and touched his ear. "There goes the bloody element of surprise."

Valentine watched it fall as his eyes relayed calculations to his neural systems. "Terry, go get me that. The rest of us need to not be here. Now."

Disco checked her watch; she had it synced to the imager rig at camp. "Fourteen hundred meters to the dig site," she said. "Can we make that?"

"Piece of cake," said Valentine. Turner hauled out the St. Christopher medal around his neck and kissed it for luck as he engaged cloak and took off.

"Catch up, Terry," he said and took off running.

The drone had fallen about a hundred yards away, though it hadn't tumbled neatly into the trenches. Terry had to leap up and out of the trenches to find it on the mountain's original skin. The armor was thick—so thick that it had kept the innards together in the fall, and only the rotors were damaged. The grenade launcher had broken in the fall, and the 40mm shells had scattered across the rock like a half-dozen deadly eggs. These he scooped into one of the bags before he seized the drone and headed back toward the others, bounding across the tops of the rock. This far out, it wouldn't have been easy to pick them out in the trenches below, especially moving in stealth. Even Valentine had a way of slipping through unseen, though he wasn't specced as an Infiltrator like the others. But he knew more or less where they were headed and promised himself he'd set up comms as soon as they were inside.

From the top of his leaping arc, he could make them out against the sunrise. The shimmering silver would've looked nice at market, but out here in the field it was tactical stupidity. Then again, as he counted the drones closing in—ten, fifteen—he wondered about the value of stealth, and how much it weighed against the value of rank terror.

"Simple drop, he says," Terry grunted as he dropped back down into the trenches. "Stupid easy, he says."

In the trenches, Turner and Disco weaved in and out of each other's steps with such slick precision that even Valentine had lost track of which shimmering figure was which. It was like a shell game with invisible shells.

"Where are we at?" he breathed.

"Three hundred metres to the dig site," said one of the shimmering spectres with Disco's voice.

"Friendly behind you," Terry called out before darting into view. When his blood was up, he could run in the rig better than he thought.

"You got it?" Valentine asked. Terry nodded and held it up.

"There's about twenty of those things headed this way," he said. "Probably more I can't see."

"We didn't have much choice," said Valentine. "I wanted this to be quiet, but jeez, look at this plating. It's next-level. They didn't have drones like these ten years ago."

"Later," urged Terry. "We have to move."

While they paused to catch their breath, Turner had unpacked a drone of his own. It looked laughable next to the military bots—a little plastic number with a cheap webcam mounted on the front—but he'd clearly done some aftermarket work on it.

"What's that?"

"Mouse on a stick," said Turner. "Buy us a little time, maybe." He set the drone in his hand, accessed a little app on his phone, and frowned. "No signal," he said. "It's like some proper idjit just fired a scrambler, innit?"

"Come on, Turner," Valentine ordered.

Turner kissed the drone, set it to random flight, and turned it loose before tearing off after the others. "Go with God, little man," he said to it as it whirred away into the sky.

Disco had hit the dig site and was changing out her magazines when the others caught up to her.

"Going heavy?" Terry asked her. She tossed him her suppressor; it was still uncomfortably hot.

"Stow that," she said. "Stow these, too. These lady farts aren't going to put a dent in one of these things. She threw her subsonic magazines to him, one at a time. He swung down his rig and found a place for them.

"What, you picked now to reorganize?" said Valentine, taking down his own rifle. "This is your moment, kid. Punch us a door right—"

He stopped. He got down on one knee.

"Jimmy?"

"Have a look at this," said Valentine. "Who d'you suppose put a hole there?"

It wasn't much of a hole, but it was enough. The mountain wall showed signs of erosion and water damage here; there was a cave mouth, or at least there had been at one time. The whole mountainside had been covered by a collapse, sometime after the trenches, but sometime before a thin layer of desert moss had started to come back to the soil. It was clear enough where Terry needed to carve them a path, but just below the cave-in, to the side of the main rock-slide, an opening had been carved out in the lighter debris, barely wide enough for a man's shoulders.

Terry squinted in the dim light. "What is that, it's been braced?"

"Carbon fiber," said Valentine. "Looks like a backpack frame."

"Can you get in?"

The air was split by the sound of twenty sirens, howling in perfect dissonance, as the drones closed in. If there were any within a half-mile that hadn't registered the gunshot, they were on their way now.

"I can. You can't."

"Get in there," barked Terry. "I'll think of something."

"The hell with that," said Valentine, shouldering his assault rifle. "Get some of those rocks down here, make me a barricade."

Terry complied instantly, with the instincts of a soldier. He was on his second stone by the time the stupidity of it all set in.

"They've all got forties on board," he offered.

"And what have we got, pricing guns?"

Terry cursed under his breath, but tore into the boulders, hauling them into place. At the outer opening of the cave mouth, Turner had taken down his face mask, hauled in a deep breath, and exhaled a cloud of wide-spectrum smoke that filled the alcove. Some sly English witticism sparkled in his eye, but the last time he tried to speak while dropping the smokescreen, he'd nearly choked to death.

"Contact!" shouted Disco, and the fight was on.

Terry wondered as he shouldered the Baby Vulcan, just where Disco went for her quiet when the fighting began. Everybody he'd ever run with had a Quiet Place, when they'd fought enough. He was surprised to find that now his wasn't his breathing, and it wasn't the way he centered himself by pushing his tongue to the roof of his mouth. It was the conveyor belt, the monotonous twisting and turning platform where he'd worked for the last six years, the simplicity of motion and the meditative trance of engaging and disengaging, flexing and relaxing, as the enhanced biomechanical supports that woke him in the night aching and reeking of metal carried him through day after day. It was a trance unto itself, a ballet of monotony, and as the drones came in, he put a quarter-pound bullet in one, then the next, with the methodical regularity of a factory worker lifting crates. Squeeze, center, place. Squeeze as he lifted the flat. Center, as he moved it to the conveyor. Place, as he released.

Place, as he redirected to the next drone. Center, as he locked it in his sights. Squeeze, as he put it down. He'd feel the kick of the Vulcan that night, if he lived to nightfall. It thumped hard against his skin when it bucked, and the exhaust seared his face and fingers. There was no mechanical skeleton, no hydraulic assist to get around that. It wouldn't be terrific. But then a shell burst too close to him, rocking his ears and slicing his cheek with a spray of limestone, and there was no time to think about the future. Just place, center, squeeze.

Rocked by only the occasional grenade, they spent the next few minutes pinned by a hail of bullets, firing back when they could. With armor-piercing rounds and no less precision, Disco brought down her fair share, now that stealth was no longer an option. Every grenade that landed kicked more debris into the air; every whizzing bullet curled Turner's smokescreen in interesting ways—and the drones seemed to be programmed for solitary recon and defense work, not for squadron combat. Twenty grenades at once, in a coordinated pattern, might have buried them and ended their expedition right there. But with only six grenades on board, the drones didn't launch unless they locked—and the more of the mountain they kicked up, the harder it was for them to get a solid lock. Bullets, though, they sprayed with abandon, and everybody took a few center-mass before it was over. A few of the scales from Disco's dragonskin had burst, showering her chest and her arms with the iridescent ceramic gel that filled the little cells. Terry's shoulders were dented and his massive arms deeply scratched where he'd taken shower after shower of rock and shrapnel. He wondered if Valentine still had a maintenance guy. His thoughts drifted back to that pardon, ominously waved—and, he hoped, not left behind in the factory. If he could get back Stateside, maybe he could have a maintenance guy too.

Disco knew what they'd brought for ammo—it was, as she'd said, a thousand-bullet situation, and she kept firing in short bursts with precise abandon until it was clear nothing was shooting back. She signalled the all clear and Valentine responded in kind. Turner grinned out of the side of his mouth, and said something witty, though Terry's ears were still ringing hard, and he didn't catch it.

Valentine moved them close enough that he could shout to them. "That ain't a half of what they got in the air," he said. "There's plenty more to come if we don't get this thing and get out of here. I think we're hot from here until I tell you otherwise. Might as well use the power tools, now."

The pack broke down quickly, and Terry remembered just how much he had hauled up with him. Jackhammers for the little people, a compressor to power them, and a generator to power the compressor, and diesel to power the generator. Again it was the logistics of the feat that separated the pros from the amateurs: twenty minutes of setup could've been the end of them.

He remembered to set up his comms with them, but it was a moot point once they started jackhammering. Between them it was a five or ten-minute job, and even Valentine had to admit the hiding place was a good one. The mountain range was lethally radioactive, patrolled by heavy drones, and had probably been bombed by Karpov's private jets just to seal in the goods. This was no place for grave-robbers, no team that could have moved the requisite equipment to such an impossible location the old-fashioned way. And yet someone had cut into this cave already. Muscles and servos surging, Terry rolled down the boulders for them. He grabbed and tossed the rocks as the team broke them up. And all the while, he nursed the feeling in the pit of his stomach that someone had already come—that the whole trip would be for nothing.

"Does it bother you," he asked the others as they shut down the hammers, "that somebody might've beat us to the punch?"

"Course it does," said Valentine. "But not as much as you'd think. Karpov stopped being a warlord years ago. He's an emperor, now. He wants a shadow empire across Central Asia, and every year he's closer to having one. Ten years ago, he thought whatever he buried up here was the way to get it."

"Well, genocide seems to have served him in a pinch," Turner observed.

"Even so," said Valentine, "he's a big fan of whatever he's hid down this particular hole. Do I want it? Sure I do. I might have a buyer. I know for sure you do, Neville. Do I want to retire on a beach in Waikiki? Sure I do. But do I want it more than Karpov does? Maybe not, because I'm not insane. I do know I want him *not* to have it. So if some local outfit has come in here and low-tech'd it out of here—if a couple of grave robbers and Sherpas somehow came up here and disappeared it all—I can live with that."

"I want my pardon," said Terry. "Even if there's nothing at all down this hole." Turner put a comforting hand on Terry's enormous shoulder. It was cold and clammy, but Terry couldn't feel it.

"We'll get it done," he said. "I have contacts, too, who appreciate that the Service is still sending us, where and when they can. We are respectable gentlemen, now."

Disco spat into the dirt. "Keep digging."

The monotonous clack and crunch of the rocks began to echo hollowly. Beyond the wall of rock, dusty rays of light began to stream onto the smooth cavern floor. With a few heavy lifts, Terry opened the hole wide enough to squeeze his shoulders through. Without the generator, without the heaviest parts of the excavation kit, he could move a lot more freely. Against Valentine's protests and Turner's calls for stealth, he was the first one in.

"About time," he muttered. The rocks around the cave mouth crunched and crumbled as the others made their way in. As if shaken, as if roused from slumber by their harsh entry, the whole mountain groaned and trembled beneath them like an ancient man settling into an ancient throne.

"What the hell was that?" Disco asked. Valentine was silent, his sensors working overtime. "We've got company," he said, and then the flash-bang went off.

* * *

For the first time since his surgery, Terry couldn't move his arms. He woke up in a panic, his heart racing, drenched in sweat. It was dark beyond dark down here, a dark so thick you could taste it. He was strung up strappado-style, with his massive arms wrenched behind him, and only the massive steel plate across his shoulders kept both them and his ribs from tearing to the point of torture. It was ingenious. The bionics didn't seem to be responding. He might try to pull free on his own, to twist the plastic straps or jerk his way free under his own strength. But he was balanced precariously with fifty pounds of steel and carbon already fused to his frame, tapped directly into his spine. One wrong move, one botched attempt to pull free, and the delicate balance might slip. The extra weight of his hulking metal body would tear him apart.

A burning light struck his face as a figure walked through the dusty cave. Her figure was a woman's figure, small and fit; but her face was hidden by a gas mask, and by the glare from her miner's headlamp.

She studied his face, he thought—then turned to Valentine, who was tied and gagged—more than gagged—on the floor of the cavern. He had a gas mask, too; but Terry saw from the way it fogged that it was blocked for air. His internals were working full-time just to keep him alive. A man with basic innards would have suffocated by now. He couldn't remember what happened to those like Valentine, and that troubled him immensely.

The light multiplied as others came into the deep cave. Six, seven men, all wearing the same headlamps. All of them armed, all of them heavies. He tried to place the company, but he was too long out of the game, and too rattled by what had happened. The little woman looked so out of place among them—unless—

"Terry Cullen," she said. "As I live and breathe." She killed her headlamp and doffed her gas mask. Lit only by the lights of her men, she smiled in the darkness as the reflected constellation of a half-dozen xenon lamps glittered in her almond eyes.

"Hello, Ghost," he said.

At the sound of her name, Jimmy Valentine looked up from his place on the cavern floor with nothing but betrayal and heartbreak in his eyes. He was still putting it all together in his mind, but he didn't need to. He'd been in the business long enough to know how these confusions resolved.

"You boys have a lot of nerve coming back to Samarkand," she said. "I thought you'd retired."

"Heard you'd retired," Terry shot back. "Permanently."

Ghost shrugged. "A condition of my new employment."

"You're here for Crate 14?"

"The other condition of my employment," she said, smiling.

Terry cast his eyes around the room as best he could. "Who are these guys?" he asked. "You find yourself a new team?"

Her laugh was still musical. "I've been spoiled for good teams," she said. "No. They're Chinese nationals. They work cheap and don't ask questions. They speak a lot of Mandarin, and no Arabic."

"Didn't think it was your way to trust mercs outside the Service," said Terry.

Ghost weighed the observation with a lackadaisical half-smile. "I suppose if I'd trusted them," she said, "I would've told them about the radiation."

Something about her coldness frightened him. It made no sense. He'd seen Disco put down a half-dozen men less than a week ago. He was fine with it. But there was always something off about Ghost. Terry took a deep breath, centered himself, and pushed his tongue against the roof of his mouth. He jerked his head toward Valentine.

"How come he's gagged, and I ain't?"

"Because there's nothing you can say to me that I'm afraid of."

"Go to hell," he said, and she smiled.

"Case in point."

As the men milled about, coming and going from the deep cavern, one of their headlamps flashed across an old wooden crate. Terry tried not to look, but he'd always been a terrible liar.

"You want to see it?" Ghost asked him. "It's smaller than we thought. All that fuss over such a little box." She flicked her headlamp on in her hands, shone it over like a flashlight. Crate 14 was about a foot in every direction, small enough that Terry could have shouldered it in high school, before his surgery, even before he bulked up for the Reserves.

"There ain't no gold in that box," he said, despondent.

Ghost raised her eyebrows. "Is that what he told you?" she asked. "Jimmy, did you tell poor Terry this was all for a little box of gold?"

Valentine's eyes were black pits of anger.

Ghost walked over to Terry, ran her hand over his head, and stroked his little dark curls affectionately.

"You see?" she said. "This is why he's gagged and you're not."

Terry spit in her face. "Don't do me no favors," he sneered, with as much venom as he could muster. She backed away, genuinely surprised, and wiped her face with the sleeve of her fatigues.

"Ew," she said. "Uncalled for."

"What's uncalled for," he said, "is you rolling on us for Iskander Karpov."

Her smile faded. "I don't work for Karpov," she said.

A mask of confusion passed over Terry's face. "Then how come I'm strung up like a fish?"

One of the soldiers came in, whispered something to her in Chinese. She nodded and motioned for the others to come in.

"You're here for the things my new employers want very badly. There's other interested parties."

"Look, Valentine doesn't even care," said Terry. "He just wants to get it away from Karpov, whatever it is. You want it? Take it. You work for somebody else, just take your prize and go. But leave us out of it."

She scoffed. "You think that's how this ends? You think I can just let the three of you walk out of here?"

Terry smiled at that, transparently pleased. Ghost's eyes widened and she motioned to one of her mercenaries, who called for the others. They came in, hauling Turner with them, and threw him onto the dusty earth. She gave them an order and made the hand motion for a perimeter search.

"Something up?" Terry asked.

"You didn't come alone," said Ghost. "You've got somebody on the outside to give you an hour and see if you don't come out. Well, we're leaving. Now."

"I'll pack my things," said Terry.

"You think you're coming with us?"

Terry shifted uncomfortably in his hogtied position, trying to ease the pressure on his joints.

"I ain't that lucky," said Terry. "I think you're going to take off with that crate as quickly as you can. You're going to get the hell out with most of your crew, and you're going to leave us behind. Maybe you'll leave behind a couple of the guys you like the least, with orders to dispose of us as soon as you're somewhere safe."

She smiled at him, cocked her head as if she were considering it.

"You're not that lucky either," she said. In a smooth motion, she pulled her pistol and popped two rounds into Turner's head.

There was no question of saving him—no question of anything. She was close enough for a contact shot, but wise enough not to give him the opportunity to slip it. The people they'd run with over the years—especially Terry and the other Mules—had had such a pissing contest when it came to large-caliber weapons that her little 9mm didn't seem like much. But Terry'd been hit by a 9mm before, more than once. You only called it "small caliber," Turner had told him once, until you took one. What was left of Turner went down in an instant, showering Valentine's horrified face with blood. Ghost pivoted and let the little gun's recoil guide it up toward Terry's face, and Terry's shout of alarm came from a place he didn't know and meant something he couldn't really understand.

Ghost's team were cheap hires, and they didn't really know her. Maybe they expected her to leave them unattended, to delegate their execution to some bargain-basement soldier-of-fortune and be on her way. Maybe they took her for a little woman with a firm strategic will but weak stomach. Or maybe they were just asleep at the post— but they never saw the execution coming either; they flinched and recoiled as the shots rang out, then relaxed as they began to make sense of the situation. That was the moment she turned to put a bullet in Terry's head—the only moment Disco could have chosen to do her thing.

The roof of the cave was uneven, thick with stalactites, mottled with thick shadows and no shortage of anchor points. As she came down, Terry had the unpleasant experience of staring straight down the barrel of Ghost's gun as the muzzle flashed. But Disco came down already spinning, and the cloak had trouble with spinning; it never really gave the perfect illusion of invisibility, just a queer shimmering mass of light as the muzzle flash lit up a hundred flashes of her dragonskin at once. She was already spinning when the hollow point tagged her in the shoulder, exploding in a shower of multicolored light, and the force of it kicked her around the cable even faster, accelerating her rotation as her onboard targeting locked, locked, locked.

Resisting the urge to move as Disco wiped the room was the hardest part. Every nerve in Terry's body was screaming to hit the deck, but with the weight of his exoskeleton precariously balanced, it would have been a fatal mistake. He closed his eyes, imagined himself loading flats of beer, and trusted in his team.

A few of them got shots off in the darkness, but they didn't do too much good. The flash of gunfire and sparking ricochets was enough to return fire by, and Disco emptied her magazines into the room. The mountain shook and echoed ferociously with the sound of gunfire, and the overpowering stink of powder and death filled the cavern. When they were out, Disco's guns seemed to appear in mid-air as she let them fall and kicked back up the rope in a shimmering flash of nothingness and disappeared.

Valentine had been waiting for his moment too. He had a dozen onboard ways, of course, of slipping out of his restraints—just none that were stealthy enough to deploy while he was being watched without risking everything. His wrists were bleeding a sticky concoction of blood and nanofluid where the blades had come through, but he wasted no time in yanking a rifle from one of the mercs and kicking Ghost's pistol away into the shadows. Like every other hostile, she'd taken two to the chest, but Disco's armor piercing rounds had only gone clean through the vests of the others. She was gasping for breath, probably nursing a busted rib, when Valentine put his boot on her wrist and the muzzle of his new gun against her throat. With his free hand, he reached up to tear the gag off. His hand came away bloody—worse than bloody. With disgust, he threw the tangle of nerves and bloody wires to the ground.

"Fuckin' turncoat," he hissed. "I thought you were dead."

"Well played, Jimmy," she gasped. With the room neutralized, Disco slid down her drop rope and began gently cutting Terry free from his precarious position. She took her time, sawed meticulously with her knife. If he fell, she didn't have the strength to catch him.

"There was no play," Valentine said. "You dumb traitor, there was no play. Just the job. We came for the crate. We came to set things right. That's all."

She wasn't lying, as it turned out: she didn't work for Karpov. Valentine didn't need enhanced hearing to pick up the distant rumble of Karpov's drones tearing apart the men she'd sent on a perimeter check.

"You killed one of your own," he spat, jaw clenched furiously tight. "Not just an Auggie. One of your own brothers." He twisted her head, hard, with the end of the gun toward where Turner's body lay. A profound sadness crossed her eyes—but not nearly enough of it for Valentine's liking.

"This is so much bigger than the Service," she tried to explain. But Valentine would have none of it.

"I should leave you to rot in one of these caves," he said. "I should drop you to the bottom of the Dark Star and phone it in to Karpov. See if his men get to you before something else in this god-forsaken pit gets its claws in."

Her eyes were defiant. "Don't you want to know who I work for?" she asked him.

He took a sidelong look at Turner's mangled face, the lifeless body, the blood-spattered St. Christopher medallion, and ended her the same way without a drop of remorse.

"Not especially," he said.

Terry's external mechanisms had been scrambled, and he hauled himself over only with immense difficulty. It was like moving with suitcases strapped to his arms on a fused spine. Disco tinkered with his rig as he walked, hoping to get his systems back online from whatever Ghost had done to him.

"You all right?" Terry asked.

"I'm not," said Valentine. He lifted his hand from the back of his neck and Terry grimaced.

"What the hell happened?"

"Ricochet off the rock, I think," he said. His eye twitched.

"Valentine, it's bad. Real bad. How are you alive?"

"I'm not," said Valentine, though the words chilled him to the bone. "I've just got a hell of a last-stand switch. Redundant cognitive systems, the works. I think I just lost half my brainstem. But vitals will hold out as long as the chipset has a little juice in it. I'm not an Infiltrator, Terry; I'm a Class 6. A fat lot of good it did me, in the end."

Terry nodded, a little horrified. Outside, another grenade came down on the retreating mercenaries.

"You never did tell me what they made you for."

"That story's not likely to get told," said Valentine. "This is not—how things were meant to do."

They looked down at Ghost's body, at Turner's.

"You find out what she was doing here?"

Valentine tried to shake his head, but the mounting was too flimsy now. "No," he said instead, holding it on. "It's not going to target to me."

Terry looked at him, confused. "What?"

Valentine rolled his eyes. "Secondary aphasia," he said. "It's a memory defect, an artifact of the damage. My brainstem's shot, my chips are puppies. A lot of wrong words while the neural cistern shuts down. I haven't got long. Vital systems burn out last. Language is one of the first to drop as I go dark. But don't respect me to burn you a watercolor painting, either."

"We'll get you out of here," Disco urged him. "Turner knew people in Tashkent, in Samarkand. We'll find you somebody."

"I doubt you could find a vacuum cleaner repairman out here," said Valentine. "Much less a doctor for what I've got. Anyway, no. I didn't shake who she works for. Don't worry. If it's big enough, they'll find you now that she's dead. But they won't find me."

"Come on," said Terry as his exo finally came back online. "I can carry you. We can all get out of here."

"Not so fast, hotshot," said Valentine. "We've got a box to move."

"No need to move it," Disco replied. "I can rig it to blow, either now or when Karpov opens it. We don't need to sell it; we don't need it on the black market at all. Just take it away from him. Just give him that final kiss-off."

"Let's do it," said Valentine. "Prep the charges. But just once...let me see it. Let me open it 'round, and see how much our lives were work."

Terry lifted him gently, like a massively strong toddler cradling a paper doll, and carried him to Crate 14. As Disco prepped an entry charge and retrieved the diesel fuel confiscated from Terry's massive supply unit, Terry wedged the tips of his fingers against the top of the crate and pulled. He didn't have to lift hard—Ghost or someone on her team had already been into it.

"What have we got," asked Valentine. "Christmas ornaments?" He laughed in spite of himself, until he coughed up a handful of blood and had to stop.

"I don't think so, boss," said Terry.

There in the box, nested in a bed of straw and Styrofoam, were a few dozen pieces of broken stone and clay, catalogued by yellowed paper slips with Arabic writing.

"What have we got here?" Terry asked. "A box of rocks?"

"Antiquities," Disco corrected him. Outside, the firing had stopped. She motioned to the front cavern, and Valentine blinked his eyes.

"Go careful," he said. He reached out to handle one of the artifacts, then looked as his blood-drenched hands and thought better of it. He smiled weakly.

"I know where these came from," said Terry. "They've been missing a long time."

"Karpov's wanted a claim to the region for years," said Valentine. "He may just have one here. There's something—look at how many! Something to give him...legitimacy with the tribes."

"Or something to bankroll his move from warlord to emperor," breathed Terry.

"Maybe it's magic," grinned Valentine. "A magic idol down there somewhere. Some kind of Indiana Jones doohickey. A magic lamp with a genie in it."

Terry shook his head. "Now I know you got your brain blown out," he said. "But it might just be worth more than gold, after all."

Valentine coughed. "It sure might be."

Terry looked at the charges Disco had left for him. "We can't blow this junk up. We just can't."

Valentine smiled sadly. "No, we can't. You've got to carry it out. This is more important than anything I could've imagined."

"Soon as Disco gives us the all clear, we're gone, man."

"All clear," she called in answer, her augmented hearing picking him up in the eerie silence of the cave that had been alive with gunfire only minutes before.

"That's it?" Terry asked. "No hostiles?"

Disco was breathing hard when she came back. "Nothing a little pepper spray couldn't fix. Pack up, get him up, and we'll get going. Those drones are headed back to duty stations. If we move quickly, we should be able to get out nice and quiet."

"Oh, quiet," said Valentine. "That's been cooking for us real well, so far."

Terry sealed the crate, dumped the generator and jackhammers, made room for it in the massive Mule Rig, and strapped himself in.

"I hope you remember where we parked," he said.

* * *

The way down was harder than the way up, especially with Valentine as delicate as he was. They bandaged his neck and splinted his head on, and marvelled at the intricacy of the internal systems that had been exposed. Whatever he'd been built for before joining the Service, it wasn't proper military combat. Whatever he could do, it made him a deadly soldier and a natural team leader. But that wasn't his primary function, the way that Disco was an Infiltrator and Terry a Mule. Whatever he was, his story was lost to them now. A few hours into the climb, the light had faded from his eyes, his famously sharp sight and hearing were gone, and his speech was so garbled by a stuttering, nonsensical aphasia that they could barely make anything out.

Across the foothills, down miles of forsaken, radioactive trails, Terry carried his load with a grim sadness. He knew how it would end. He knew there was nothing to be done. But there was no talk of leaving him, not while he was anything even half-alive. The Service didn't work that way.

They took most of the guns, just to keep Karpov's mercenaries from scavenging them when they finally sent in an inspection team to see what kind of expedition the drones had put a stop to. They took the water, and they took their civilian go-bags. They left the compressor and all the hardware they might have had cause to use, but didn't. They took the diesel fuel, and Terry made ready to burn Valentine's go-bag unopened. That was the way of it. He wouldn't need it where he was going now—and it was never their place to know who he was, or who he'd wanted to be when all this was over.

They laid Valentine down in the shadow of the Mule Rig and gave him some water, and debated with silent eyes whether it was time to let him go. Disco must have come up from espionage; her eyes said yes. But Terry was a military man, and his said no.

The day's desert heat had beaten down for hours on the unprotected vans. Terry sat in the shade with Valentine while Disco made the rounds of the three vans to see which one she could get started. As one of the dusty starters whined away, Valentine gripped Terry's arms with a sudden urgency and hauled him down to eye level, fixing him with frightening intensity.

"Tell me my night," he begged, reaching a splayed hand toward his go bag. "Tell me, quickly."

With his face tight, Terry brought the bag over. Valentine tore it open, rummaged through things that Terry would never have imagined him owning: cufflinks. A tie embroidered with tiny cats. A palm-print bathing suit. Fruit-flavored gum...the kind the kids chew.

A honey-brown envelope.

"Tap him," Valentine urged weakly, handing over the envelope. "Tap him, Cullen."

Terry thumbed open the envelope. It was an American pardon, signed and sealed, with his name on it.

"This ain't real," he said, shaking his head. "No way you had this the whole damn time."

Valentine closed his bloody hands around Terry's tightly as a van engine coughed and rumbled to life. "Didn't I say you." He grinned. "Chicken wings."

"Chicken wings," said Terry. He clutched Valentine's hands as long as Valentine held them back. He held them until he realized they'd locked on his like that, clenched shut like the legs of an insect in a hot window. He smoothed out Valentine's gnarled fingers. Folded his hands onto his chest. Closed his eyes.

The van engine revved, smoothing out.

"Come on!" Disco called. "Terry, we've got to go! We can bring him."

Terry pocketed his pardon, doused Valentine's go-bag in diesel fuel, flicked his Zippo and tossed it in. The diesel wouldn't ignite easily—not till the fire hit the primers or the stack of identity papers really got going. But it was a hot day, and the air was still. It would all go up eventually, with or without the diesel. None of it lasted forever.

The passenger door was so sticky that Terry had to activate his bionic assist just to screech it open. He wedged his metal shoulders tightly into place, slamming the door shut behind him. He studied, intently, how the hell he was going to make the seatbelt work around his massive frame. Anything he could to avoid eye contact.

"Terry," Disco said, not dispassionately. "I said we can bring him."

"No," said Terry. "We can't."

Disco wrenched the transmission into first and kicked the ungainly little bus down the trail toward the main road. Grief and anger set her jaw tight and stung her eyes as sharp and sure as desert sweat. What was there, after this? What was there, but dust and road and the red rage of the lowering sun?

Crate 14 rumbled in the back seat, buried ignobly under a folded tent and a case of MREs. The treasures of a vanished empire rattled within. But if Disco knew what it all meant, she didn't let on.

* * *

There was still sand in the assist mechanisms, grinding in the joints. No matter how many times he cleaned it out, a grain remained behind. He moved a little slower, now. His shoulders and back ached a little more. But that was why they paid the cybernetically altered super soldiers twenty bucks an hour to the regular stock boys' seventeen.

The way of life was different here. Nine to five meant nine to five, and if you were on the lot a minute past, you were 'ama'ama. A sucker. A gullible fish. But there were worse things to be than a sucker.

Big Noah had been coming to get him earlier and earlier. "Pau Hana, my friend," he called. "Time to punch out."

"It's ten to five," he said. "I've got ninety more flats to hit quota."

"Quotas are for sissies." Noah laughed with a fat grin. "Come on, Terry. It's New Year's Eve. You don't got a party to get to?" He held his smile until Terry reluctantly returned it.

"A little party."

"Well get going!" said Noah. Terry loaded one more flat on the conveyor belt, just to make the point that he didn't take orders anymore. As he was clocking out, Noah handed him one of the little souvenir boxes from the cargo he'd been sorting. Inside was a cheap plastic hula girl.

"For your dashboard," he said. "So you don't look so gosh-darn grim all the time."

Terry left the lot a proper sucker at three minutes after five and headed downtown. The old highway was six lanes wide and skinned the coastline all the way in. Behind a row of low houses, he caught glimpses of the sea—brown and silty out to about fifty feet, then glittering sapphire blue for a thousand miles beyond.

It took him a long time to find parking, and for a minute, he thought somebody had beaten him to their picnic table. Then she turned to him, and the sun sparkled off the iridescent dragonskin beneath her little dress, and her smile lit him up like a pinball machine.

"Hey," he said. "I barely recognized you."

"Hey, you," she said, and kissed him. "How was work?"

"Work was work," he said. "You know. Forty acres and a mule."

She grinned at him sarcastically. "Are you the mule?"

He smiled. "Figure of speech," he said. "I guess you wouldn't know. Forty acres and a mule—that's what they promised the slaves, when Lincoln freed them. For all their years of slavery. Forty acres and a mule, that's all."

"And did they get it?" she asked.

He raised his eyebrows thoughtfully. "Oh, sure, some of 'em did. Those who were farmers, they did okay. Those who had other jobs—house slaves, rail workers, furnace men—they didn't have much use for a mule, couldn't much take to a trade they didn't know. But plenty were farmers already. Some stayed and worked the land they had worked their whole lives. But they did it for themselves, now. Not for anyone but their own selves."

"And that's how work was today?"

"That's how work was," he said. "Same as ever, only…better, somehow." He ruffled her short hair with his hand, cast his eyes down her body. Those parts of her armor that came off were off. Those parts that didn't were a part of her. Odd as they looked in a little sundress, he wouldn't have them any other way.

"Hey, is that lavender?" he asked. She slapped his hand off the strap.

"Shut up, Terry," she snapped.

"Miss Kadie, is that a sleeveless sundress?"

"You know goddamn well what it is. And it's Disco, if you keep on like that."

"Okay, okay," he said, retreating. "How was *your* day?"

"Baby steps," she said. "I found an archaeologist at the Sorbonne, who can maybe do something with the broken tablet. Tell us what it is, what it says. And I've got a buyer lined up for that fertility goddess I've been keeping in the bathroom."

"About time," said Terry.

"I liked her," she replied wistfully. "But I guess it's time for her to move on to someone new, now."

She smiled slyly at him, but he wasn't looking. He fussed in his pocket for something.

"Terry, what?"

"I got you something." He pushed the little hula girl into her hand, flicked its ass, watched it bobble.

"Oh, hell no," she said. "Not in my house."

"What? It's a good luck charm."

"I've had plenty of luck," she said. "Best not to push it."

Even in the dead of winter they had a lot of daylight left. They swapped the last of their war stories, and by the time it was dark they had moved on to sports, to the news, to the newsletters in cybernetics. There was talk of government grants for people who wanted to risk bionic reversal therapy. But they'd had some fatalities, and a few of the clinical trials had come down with Gibson's disease, and there were no easy answers, yet.

"Maybe not in our lifetime," Terry admitted.

Kadie smiled warmly. "But maybe in someone's."

"Would you do it again?" he asked. "After all the places we've been—if you had it to do over, would you get Augged all over again?"

She thought about it. "The unstoppable soldier of the future?" she said. "I think so. When you get right down to it...I don't know how to do anything else. How to *be* anything else."

He put a massive arm around her, and she squeezed it affectionately. He'd never felt particularly handsome, but did like his arms. They'd carried a platoon's worth of artillery, once. They'd torn the doors off Humvees, punched through concrete walls in Beirut. They'd cleared out mountain tunnels, carried wounded friends, and cracked skulls. They'd torn down the steel flagpoles and bronze statues of wicked men. They'd changed the world, as much as a part of him could change anything. He hoped it was for the better.

"I don't know, either," he said. "But we're learning. Always learning."

"We'll get there," she said as the sun slipped away. The sky hummed in eerie harmonies as a hundred firework drones shot up from the boats. With a thunderous roar and a blazing red fiery burst, the festivities began.

"Soldiers of the future," he agreed.

She smiled up at him wistfully. At last, in the coruscant glow of a blazing sky, he caught the spirited gleam in her eye.

"I suppose that can mean a lot of things," she said. "The future."

* * * * *

Luke R. J. Maynard Bio

Luke R. J. Maynard is a writer, poet, scholar, lapsed medievalist, musician, and wearer of sundry other hats in the arts & letters. Born in London, Ontario, Canada, he received his PhD in English Literature from the University of Victoria in 2013, and his Juris Doctor at the University of Toronto's Faculty of Law in 2019.

Luke's first CD, *Desolation Sound*, was released in June of 2018. His first novel, *The Season of the Plough*, will be released by Cynehelm Press in July 2019. Luke currently lives in Toronto.

# # # # #

Imperfect Mind
by Jason Cordova

A Kin Wars Universe Short Story

I did not cry when the men wearing dark suits took me from the Holding Home in the dead of night. Tears had stopped being a thing years ago, after my parents had deposited me on the steps of the rundown building the day after my third birthday. Faint memories of their angry faces haunt me on occasion still, but the sadness was long gone. Which was a good thing. Showing weakness in that building meant you became prey to the older, bigger kids.

Since I was technically an adult when the Praetorians arrived, I had been expecting it. I did not fight or resist. That would have been a futile gesture. I merely lowered my head and acknowledged that I was no long the responsibility of Sister Verona or the others who took care of the Imperfect children. There were no belongings for me to gather except for an old, ratty sweater I had received the previous Restoration Day. Sister Verona was not a cruel woman, though. She made certain that I could keep the clothes on my back, much to the annoyance of the Praetorians who were there to remove me from the premises.

341

Instead of moving me to another city, as I had expected, they took me to a military base on the outskirts of town. From there I was thrown into a shower, which terrified me initially because it was a waste of water. I also burned myself, since I'd never experienced hot water before except for cooking. The Praetorians didn't seem to care, though, and had me scrub every inch of my body with a strange lotion, including my head. That was far worse than the hot water, but eventually every single hair on my body fell off. My armpits and between my legs were bare skin for the first time since I had started maturing at ten. Since I typically wore my hair on my head short anyway, it didn't bother me that much. Losing my hair between my legs bothered me greatly, though. The more I looked like a boy, the safer I'd be.

Unfortunately, standing naked in the middle of a room of Praetorians, it was hard to hide that I was not a boy, especially with everything bared. They didn't stare and gawk, like most of the older kids did when they found out I was a girl. The two men simply continued to go about their business, making certain I was clean and hairless. It was terrifying and painful, yet not nearly as bad as I had been expecting it to be.

We whispered in the dark about what happened to kids like us, the genetically imperfect, after they were removed from a Holding Home. The stories about being sold into slavery for rich men and women to be used as play toys haunted our dreams. Even the sisters who watched over us didn't help, reminding us to be careful when we walked out their doors because bad people wanted to harm us. We didn't understand. We couldn't, not really. We were kids, innocents. The warnings did nothing but infect our dreams, temper our hopes, and lead us to the realization that we were a subclass of human, not even worthy of being treated as equals. Over the years we accepted this, understood our role in the great society that was the Dominion of Man.

After the showers, I was led into a room where a bunch of men and women wearing long white coats waited. They looked me over and inspected me, making sure that my imperfections were not clearly physical. They weren't. I was born with Duane Syndrome, which affected my eyes. The men and women didn't seem concerned by this, though, which was odd. I knew my eyes were different. Always have. It affected the way I saw things at times.

"She's a good candidate," one of the gathered people declared. A woman, and from what I could tell, she seemed to be in charge of the group. Everyone else nodded in agreement and seemed pleased with her decision. I didn't know what I was a good candidate for, only that it was better than being sold into a gangster's brothel. Still, standing there in the middle of a group of strangers with nothing on made me a little nervous. She must have seen this and clucked her tongue. "Get her into a medical sheet. We'll begin the implant procedure immediately."

"Implant procedure?" I asked, becoming warier by the second. She tried to smile at me in a comforting manner but obviously wasn't used to dealing with people because it more resembled a grimace than anything else.

"Yes," the woman replied. "I am Doctor Pulvere. This is a test facility for a new combat weapon, and we were looking for volunteers. The Praetorians tasked with watching your Holding Home mentioned that you were available, healthy, and expressed an interest in helping, so here we are."

"Oh," was all I could think of to say. It wasn't like I really had much to offer anyway. I was an Imperfect, a genetically inferior human being. My life was worth less than everyone else's, so why not offer to help? I'd always been like that as a child, eager to help others with the chores. It kept the beatings from the bigger kids to a minimum. "Okay."

"Excellent!" she clapped her hands excitedly. "Doctors Hiram and Keebler will prep you in the next room." She turned and looked at the Praetorians still on either side of me. "Your services are no longer required. Thank you."

The Praetorians left and two men, the doctors I assumed she had been talking about, led me into a smaller room off to the side. There was a sheet which I could put on to cover my nakedness. I quickly donned it and sat down on a cold metal stool as the two doctors moved behind me and began to inspect the back of my head. They argued quietly for a few moments before one of them held the top of my head still with one hand. With the other he drew a small circle and then added something to the inside of it.

They rubbed their fingertips over my smooth scalp for a moment before murmuring something. I couldn't understand them; their accents were thick and heavy. I knew that some accents in the Dominion were strong on worlds within the Core, but I'd never actually heard any of them before. On Solomon, everyone sounded about the same. Wanting to ask but not knowing how, I simply remained mute as they finished their brief examination. Standing me back up, I was returned to the large room. Instead of a large group of people waiting for me, there was a small bed on wheels and a lot of lights. Tools were gathered on a small tray next to it, and Doctor Pulvere stood waiting. She wore a strange mask and gloves and was now covered with a sheet very much like the one I wore. The doctor motioned for me to lay down on the small bed. I began to, but she instructed me to flip over onto my belly instead of lying on my back.

The pain I experienced over the next two hours was something that I could never properly describe. The best I could manage was that it felt as though electric wires were being dragged across my brain inside my skull. It was excruciating, and despite the shots they gave me, I felt everything. I was crying but unable to move because of an injection they gave me in my spine before the surgery began.

They cut open my head in the back where the doctors had drawn earlier and put something inside me. There was a lot of pressure behind my eyes for some reason, and I could hear the doctors talking about something, but the words made no sense to me. I tried to tell them that the pain was too much, but nothing came out but tears. They poured out of my eyes and dripped down my nose, falling to the tiled floor where they pooled over time.

After what felt like an entire lifetime, they were finished. Intellectually I knew that only two hours had passed, because the doctor's words became understandable again once the pressure behind my eyes went away.

"No time to waste," Doctor Pulvere told the gathered group as they wheeled my bed out of the large room and down a long corridor. I was slowly beginning to get the feeling back in my hands and feet as we arrived in a very dark room. Lights came on, and I tried to wince but couldn't. My face hadn't recovered yet from the injection and was frozen still. "Here we are. Let's get her into the mask and don't forget the goggles this time! The way the last test subject's eyes melted almost made me lose my lunch."

Unceremoniously they hoisted me off the bed. I almost threw up, but since I really didn't have control of my body just yet, I merely felt sick. My heels dragged along the rough surface of the floor, and I could almost feel the skin cracking from the friction. If it kept up for much longer I knew that there would be two trails of blood from my heels opening up soon. Fortunately, they reached their destination before that point and stopped dragging me.

An oxygen mask was put on my face and secured, then a pair of goggles went over my eyes. The air which poured into the mask and filled my lungs was richer than anything I'd ever breathed before, and the feeling in my legs and arms came back. I could see decently well through the goggles. Uncertain what was planned next, I allowed the two men carrying me to lift me off the ground completely.

They removed the thin material covering me, and I was naked once more. The two men didn't seem to notice or care as they focused on their task. I was then placed into a large device that seemed too big for my tiny body. It quickly dawned on me that it was human shaped, but much larger than the average human body. I could feel the tubing from the oxygen mask on my shoulder. I wanted to squirm, but the device I was in seemed to be more restrictive than I thought it would be.

Suddenly, I felt something warm and slimy at my feet. I struggled as the sensations made their way up my legs, passing my kneecaps. I began to panic, but then I heard Doctor Pulvere's voice in my head.

"Relax," the woman whispered. I suddenly realized that her voice wasn't in my head, but next to it. A helmet of some sort lowered down over the top of me, and I was sealed inside. The goop continued to crawl up my legs and touched my thighs. I squirmed uncomfortably. "This is a gel designed to protect you once you're inside the mechanized infantry suit. In a moment you will feel a slight pinch in the back of your head, and then you will see everything that the Mark One sees."

Mark One? I had no idea what that was, but I fought the urge to panic as the gel substance reached my stomach. The only blessing of the strange sensation as it crept up my body was the warmth. That was actually nice, though a part of me began to wonder just how far the gel stuff was going to go. A minute later I found out just how high it would go.

Completely submerged, the panic returned. However, before I could focus on the fact that I was probably going to drown in a moment, a horrible pinching sensation made me scream. It was loud and echoed throughout the warehouse. Light assaulted my senses, and my skin felt cold and clammy. Bulky and heavy, I was no longer a tiny and underfed young woman. I was something far bigger, monstrous. Unable to hold back my emotions any longer, I began to bawl my eyes out.

"Shh, it's okay," Doctor Pulvere tried to calm me down as my cries seemed to echo throughout the cavernous room. "You're suffering from temporary sensory overload. Let me dial back the receptors, then you can adjust to the new sensations."

The room suddenly wasn't too bright, and my skin didn't feel as heavy or strange. I was normal, but not. I looked around and found that while I was unable to move my head, I could still see all around me. The warehouse seemed small compared to what it had felt like a moment before. Even Doctor Pulvere, as tall as she'd been when I'd first been led into the operating room, was tiny as she stood behind a metal desk. There was a long fabric-encased line which extended from the back of the desk to somewhere behind me.

"What happened?" I asked between sobs. Doctor Pulvere winced and pressed something I couldn't see at her desk. I tried to soften my voice and regain control of my emotions. "Doctor?"

"Much better." She nodded, ignoring my question for the moment. "Now try to lift your right arm."

Carefully, I lifted my right arm in front of my face and gasped as I saw that instead of my normal dark brown arm, a giant robotic one was before me. Instead of panicking like I had before, I instead focused on my breathing as I inspected the arm.

It was a flat, dull gray color with large plates of what I figured was armor stacked on top of one another. Bulkier than what I thought robotic arms should look like, it took me a few moments to realize that I was looking at armor covering my body. I was seeing with the robot's head somehow, though I was at a loss to explain it.

"How am I seeing this?" I asked Doctor Pulvere.

"The implant nodule in your head is called a cortex implant," she explained. "It allows you to interact with the Mark One suit as a second skin instead of actually wearing it. It should feel more natural than standard combat armor. It's our prototype mechanized infantry suit."

"Okay," I muttered and lowered my right arm. I did my left next, and then we worked on walking. It quickly became apparent that I was overcompensating, to which the doctor simply told me to walk normally.

"Don't make exaggerated movements," she told me again and again as I struggled through the movement tests. Eventually, after much trial and error, we figured it out, and I was moving around the warehouse as only a five-meter-tall mechanized infantry trooper could.

WE DARE | 349

"I like this," I admitted after I trotted a few steps, quickly pirouetted, then landed on my right foot while kicking out with the left. It was a move I'd perfected while in the Holding Home to protect myself if a boy refused to accept "no" for an answer while delivering the maximum damage to his male bits. After the time I made Jarl vomit and pee blood for two weeks, the other boys at the Home stopped harassing me for good.

"You are naturally graceful," Doctor Pulvere told me. I could feel my face heating up in embarrassment inside the suit and was glad that I had both the breathing mask and helmet on to hide in. She continued on, unaware I was blushing. "If you had been Perfect, you probably could have trained to be a dancer."

"But I'm not," I said as I stood upright. The suit definitely felt more natural to me now than before, and it mimicked my movements perfectly. I didn't even have to think about it anymore, I simply *did*, and it followed suit, mimicking my motions at the same time I performed them. The doctor had been right; it did feel like a second skin.

"No, you're not," she agreed with my previous statement. I wasn't mad about it. It was simply a fact of life.

"What else can this do?" I asked, curious now as I strode over to where Doctor Pulvere was at her computer.

"The suit can handle weapons as well, such as heavy machineguns and even recoilless anti-tank rifles," she replied. I nodded, pretending to know what she was talking about. I had no idea what a recoilless anti-tank rifle even was, though I was a little familiar with the term "machinegun." I'd seen a vid once where the hero had one and had fought the evil villains, agents of the Caliphate. Very noble death at the end for the hero, and the love interest moved home to care for their beautiful Perfect child. Doctor Pulvere continued, seemingly unaware of my ignorance. "We are designing a rotating cannon for the arms but we're still working on the physics of that, plus identifying the attachment points and where to place spare ammunition. We might make the arms bulkier and simply allow it to be stored there. We're working on that."

I still had no idea what she was talking about, but it sounded like she did, so I changed the subject. "This should have blades on the arms or something, for stabbing faces. What about knives sticking out when I make a fist?"

"I like the way you think." The doctor grinned. She typed in something on her computer and looked back up at the suit. "Definitely something to keep in mind for future upgrades to the suit. How do you feel about a field test?"

"A what?" I asked as I felt a certain giddiness envelope my senses. I'd experienced something like this before, when one of the boys had smuggled in some Blizz and we had sat in the cellar later that night, tasting the stuff. It made my brain tingle with pleasure, and I'd done some stupid stuff afterwards with the older boys. I didn't have that desire now, thankfully, but it still made me feel really good.

"Go out into the field and test this," she asked again as she continued to type on her keyboard. Oddly enough, I felt the need to do this. The tingling sensation disappeared and was replaced by a desire to serve. I couldn't explain it, but the desire to go out and fight was appealing. I was nodding inside the suit before she had even finished asking the question.

"Yeah, we can go and break bad people," I suggested in a cheerful voice. Doctor Pulvere looked up at me for a moment before slyly smiling. Making her happy made *me* happy for some reason, so I was really beginning to understand her. I pressed on. "Maybe we can go kill some pirates or something?"

"Kill?" She asked, obviously amused. "Pirates? There are no pirates on Solomon."

"I..." here I paused, uncertain. I almost seemed to *know* that pirates were, indeed, on Solomon. Somehow, with no rhyme or reasons, I could even pinpoint where they were on a map. It was scary, but I decided to speak up anyway. "No, they're here, on the planet's surface. I can show you on a map."

"That's okay, I believe you," Doctor Pulvere said and smiled. She took her hands away from the keyboard and stretched her back. "While we were talking, I found a pirate's base that is reputed to be on this world. It has been hitting colonist's resupply vessels regularly and they have what seems to be a den near here. The marines are too busy to do anything, and the Navy can't drop kinetics onto their base without disrupting the atmosphere. This seems to me the ideal situation for the new mechanized infantry. How about it? Do you want to try it out?"

I was nervous, but ready. "Yes. Only one problem, though."

"What's that?"

"I don't know how to use a gun," I admitted. She smiled again, and I immediately felt more confident about my abilities. I don't know what it was about this woman, but she could motivate me to be greater.

"I think you know more than you realize," she commented as she turned back to her computer for a moment. Satisfied with whatever she had typed in, the doctor began to walk toward a set of wide double doors at the other end of the warehouse. Noticing that I wasn't with her, she stopped and glared at me. My heart dropped as I saw the disappointment in her eyes. I couldn't let her down. I followed loyally behind. I would take down the pirates and protect the Dominion. It was expected of me.

"Where are we going?" I asked the doctor.

"To get you a weapon, then send you in to kill some pirates."

My heart leapt into my throat. It was something I'd always wanted to do, and now I was getting the chance to do it. The strangest thing about it all, though, was that I knew deep down that this was wrong, that I'd never even given any thought to fighting pirates before. Now, though, it didn't matter. Killing pirates was my only mission in life. I would kill all the pirates or die trying.

Doctor Pulvere led me to a smaller room where four rather nervous looking men wearing identical uniforms were waiting. I had seen something like what they had on in a vid once and immediately recognized them as marines. I had to duck to get through the doorway even though it was almost seven meters high. There was more than enough room for me to stand upright to my full height once inside. This, of course, made the men back up warily. Either they had never seen someone as large as I was, or my suit scared them. Either way, it pleased me to see other Imperfects like these marines respect me. Being reminded that I was the ultimate authority on behalf of the doctor made me feel amazing, powerful. I smirked inside my suit. *Those pirates don't stand a chance*, I thought as Doctor Pulvere began to explain to the marines precisely what I needed.

I had no idea what a Ma Deuce was, but when the marines began to bolt a massive gun on my left arm, I couldn't help but feel a little giddy. It made that arm a little heavier than before, but I managed. The marines then attached two large circular drums beneath it and began to feed the belt with all the ammunition on it into the machinegun. The drums each weighed over two hundred pounds. To compensate for the added weight I leaned more to my right. It was awkward but I managed.

"Yes, that'll do nicely," Doctor Pulvere stated as she inspected me with a critical eye. She appeared to be pleased, which made me all tingly once more. My brain was on fire with the amount of pleasure I was receiving at her apparent satisfaction. I was more than ready to go and kill every pirate in the universe, and anyone else that the good doctor needed dead. She smiled and I about died of orgasmic bliss. "You ready to go, young lady?"

"Yes!" I nearly screamed. The sensations were too much. I needed to kill, needed to rip the heads off of every single enemy of the doctor.

"If you think about a map, one will appear in your vision," she told me. I tried to think of a map and, just as the doctor said it would, one appeared. It showed a blue glowing dot in the middle with a red X to the left of center. It actually wasn't too far away, from what I could tell. "That red X might appear to be close, but it's actually ten kilometers away. Your suit has more than enough fuel to make it there, destroy the pirate den, and return. If you pivot left and right you'll see the position of the X will change."

I did so and, sure enough, the X moved. However, so did the marines who had helped attached the Ma Deuce to my left arm as the barrel swept across their heads. They yelled and managed to avoid being brained by the long barrel of the machinegun.

"Sorry!" I apologized and pointed the barrel upward. Suddenly it dawned on me that I didn't know how to fire the blasted thing. I looked over at the doctor, ashamed. "Doctor, I'm…I'm sorry, but I don't know how to shoot this machinegun. I've failed you."

"It's okay, child," she whispered and gently reached over and patted my hip. "Don't do it now, but when you're ready to fire simply clench your left hand and hold it shut. The machinegun will fire until you unclench. Just be careful. You only have twelve hundred rounds of ammunition before you're empty. Try not to blast through that in one go, okay?"

"Yes ma'am," I said in a respectful voice, recalling what Sister Verona had told me about politeness when dealing with Perfects. I loved the doctor, of course, but extra politeness never hurt. "Do I just go to the X spot and kill everyone in the pirate's den?"

"Yes dear, that's precisely what you need to do," she said and smiled. Oh, it was glorious! I would die for that smile. "Don't fail me."

"Never!" I gasped as stronger emotions raced through me. I lumbered awkwardly out the door and back into the training warehouse. The map on my screen showed me that another route out of the building would get me there faster, and I would fit through it. Plus, it would keep me away from the administration points, which filled me with a strange sense of dread.

I moved away from the military base and deep into the wilderness around the city. I'd grown up in the city but had never stepped foot outside the city limits. I didn't know of any other Holding Home kids who had snuck out of the city and ever come back. We could only guess as to their fates. Dead? Maimed? Eaten by wild animals and then worn as skins? All of us kids had no idea.

Now, out on my own and within the Mark One suit, I knew that I was the top predator around. There was nothing that could actually hurt me in the wilds. The pirates might have machineguns that could do something, but I had absolute and perfect faith in Doctor Pulvere and her suit. She wouldn't fail me, not in any way, shape, or form. This suit of hers was perfection.

As I raced along, the former euphoric sensations I felt faded, and soon I began to crave some sort of communication with the doctor. Strange as it was, it paled in comparison to the anger which was beginning to build. Every second away from the doctor caused my rage to build. I vowed then and there to kill every single pirate I found. They were the reason I could not stay in the presence of the doctor and bask in her brilliance.

As my hatred fueled me, I realized I was rapidly closing in on the position marked on the map. The suit helpfully zoomed in, and I could see the pirate's den from over a kilometer away. It was what I had expected it to look like, with a wide-open field for pirate ships to land on and lots of defense towers. I figured that if I could see them, they should see me soon enough. I needed to correct this.

Not knowing how far the rounds in the Ma Deuce could shoot, I decided to creep in a little closer. Unfortunately, I knocked down a small spruce tree and startled a herd of deer which had been bedding down for the day where I was walking. They were on their feet and bounding off toward the pirate den in a flash, which caused the guards atop the towers to glance in my direction. I was close enough now to see the absolute shock and surprise on their faces.

"I guess that's close enough for the Ma Deuce," I murmured as I aimed the machinegun up toward the closest tower. A small reticle appeared on my screen, showing me where I was pointing the barrel of the gun. I realized that if I fired now, the only thing I would hit would be the concrete support structure and not the men ten meters higher. I adjusted and clenched my fist.

What came forth from the barrel of the Ma Deuce was unlike anything I had experienced in my life. The muzzle flashed brightly as I poured forth hate from the barrel and into the bodies of my unwitting targets. The two pirates in the tower seemingly came apart at the seams as the rounds tore through them. Bright red blood splashed radiantly into the clear blue sky, and I could see entrails and gore dripping down the side of the tower, a beautiful yet macabre painting of death and carnage.

"Oh…wow," I whispered and relaxed my firing hand. The Ma Deuce stopped spitting out rounds immediately. A small screen appeared in the corner with what appeared to be a bullet in it. I quickly figured out that this was how much ammo I had left in the drums of the Ma Deuce. I blinked in surprise as I realized I'd fired over fifty rounds at the tower. If there were hundreds of pirates in the den, I'd run out of ammunition long before I got to kill all the pirates. I'd need to be more careful in the future.

Ahead I could see smaller figures on the ground scrambling as the alarm sounded. Since they were obviously aware of my presence I decided to run to the den. If I could get there quick enough, then I could potentially stop them from getting better prepared. It was a trick I learned at the Holding Home. If there's no other option available, attack.

The first thing I discovered was that the Mark One suit was *fast*. I had been quick before, since it had allowed me to roam the streets of New Haven without being molested by creepy strangers. The ability to outrun even the gangers had come in handy on numerous occasions. Now, though, I seemed to fly across the open ground, my heavy steps leaving large footprints deep in the soft dirt behind me.

A group of pirates appeared in front of me, seemingly out of nowhere. The suit's reticle appeared in my eyes and the Ma Deuce came up almost of its own accord. I squeezed off a few shots and watched in satisfaction as two of the pirate's heads exploded into a fine red mist. The others started shooting back, and the Mark One's armor was tested at long last.

Unsurprisingly, the suit held up under the barrage of gunfire. My senses tingled as it dawned on me that Doctor Pulvere's design was working perfectly to keep me alive. I had promised her that I would kill each and every pirate I found, and it was a promise I intended to keep. I stopped running, leveled the Ma Deuce, and let it rip.

The results were predictable. Eight dead pirates, one living Imperfect encased in a massive armored suit of death. There was nothing that could harm me.

I jerked violently as something exploded against my right shoulder. The suit warned me that I had been hit with a grenade, fired from a distance great enough to prevent it from identifying the source. Remaining still meant becoming dead, so I started sprinting at an oblique angle toward the den. Two more explosions blew up a small cloud of shrapnel and dirt before me. Near misses, but they enabled the suit to locate the shooter at last. It was a young woman, no older than I was, firing from a concrete bunker about forty meters ahead. I sighted her head, aimed carefully, and squeezed off a single round. The shot removed her head from the body's shoulders. I looked around and moved in further.

A warning light told me that the suit had suffered some external damage on the right side from the grenade. I couldn't fix it, but since it didn't seem to be affecting my shooting or movement, I ignored it for the time being. I figured that once I was back with Doctor Pulvere she could fix it. I hoped that she would accept my apology and not be too disappointed in my damaging her suit.

As I got closer to the pirate den I realized there were a lot of concrete bunkers which were close enough together to make me very suspicious. Figuring that the majority of the den was underground somewhere, and that I needed to find an entrance, I began to search for a building which looked like it would lead underground. Here my history as an Imperfect child left to their own devices on the streets of New Haven paid off.

Past experience told me that every ganger who roamed the bad parts of New Haven needed somewhere to operate out of. One of the things that kids in Holding Homes always knew was how to spot them. It would be someplace that would look plain and boring, not the slum housing falling to the ground or ritzy high-rise towering into the sky. Nothing to draw attention to it, either good or bad. These buildings, usually squat and almost always ugly, were where ganger bosses like to store their goods, be it drugs, stolen property, or anything else that caught their eye.

The best bet for most of us kids was to avoid them. Gangers seemed to take perverse pleasure in tormenting young Imperfect kids, even going so far as to kill them for sport. There used to be a gang a few years back that ran underground fights between young kids. They would give them long knives and tell them to kill each other, or they would be killed instead. These fights were always to the death, and lots of gambling went down during these events. Fortunately, the Praetorians eventually stepped in and stopped them before I was old enough to get caught up in the fights. Still, I knew of many Imperfect men and women with long, ugly scars running up and down their arms from these underground battles.

I looked around and quickly spotted the most likely building. Unlike some of the others that appeared to be rundown and abandoned, this one had a few boarded-up windows but otherwise was in decent shape. What convinced me, though, was the men who kept coming out of the building in spite of its relatively small size. Either they were packed in there tightly or there was another entrance I couldn't see.

As the pirates came out of the building like ants out of a kicked anthill, I realized I was missing an opportunity and started firing. Large holes appeared in the wall of the building as some of the rounds from the Ma Deuce punched through the person I was shooting and impacted the wall. I painted the formerly white stucco walls red with the blood of the pirates.

They started falling back inside in search of protection, so I continued to walk my stream of gunfire into the doorway. There the bodies began to pile up as they struggled to run and escape to the safety of the building. The pirates were struggling to climb over their dead and wounded in an attempt to flee. I removed that hope with more well-placed shots and continued to fire until there were none left moving.

I glanced at the counter and saw that I had fired over one thousand rounds already. Dismayed, I vowed to be more discriminatory when it came to shooting in the future. With less than two hundred remaining and an unknown number of bad guys still to be found, I would have to make every shot count from here on out.

I continued to approach the building but couldn't hear anything on the inside. Visually sweeping the bodies in from of the door, it became apparent that a lot of them weren't dead but merely wounded. Knowing that the doctor would be displeased with my efforts if I left anyone alive, but at the same time realizing I needed to conserve ammunition, I simply began to step on the heads of the wounded.

It was over in a brutally short amount of time.

I ducked into the building and looked around. I could see a small trapdoor in the floor in the corner of the large open room, which was exactly what I expected. However, it quickly became apparent to me that I had no way of getting down there easily. Carefully maneuvering myself inside the building, I stayed crouched low enough to not destroy the roof. It wasn't painful since the suit was doing all the work, but it still felt awkward with the Ma Deuce and the nearly-empty ammo drums on the left throwing off my balance. Still, I managed, and finally ended up standing over the trapdoor looking down into a dark tunnel.

After a few seconds of inspection, I determined that I probably couldn't fit down into the hole. Still, I needed to clear the underground tunnel for any more pirates. I looked around the room for something that would give me an idea. As I stared at the stucco walls it dawned on me that while I might not necessarily be able to drag anyone out, I could definitely bury them within. The walls looked more than heavy enough, and I knew that they were pretty solid.

It didn't take me more than ten minutes to tear down the house on top of the trap door after I closed it, ensuring that any pirates trapped in the tunnel were stuck. For good measure I piled the bodies of dead pirates on top of the house, as a message to any who might come after to help them. It was a long process, not because of the weight of the bodies, but because I wanted to ensure I got as many dismembered parts together as I could beforehand.

Doing this continued to give me unimaginable pleasure and more than once I had to stop and breathe as the shaking became too much. There was just something so exciting and marvelous about pleasing the doctor by killing pirates. Nothing I had ever experienced in my life could top the sensations that coursed through me at that moment.

A noise from my left drew my attention. It was another pirate, though this one was encased in some sort of heavy lift device. I'd seen them before during construction projects in New Haven. Twin lifts extended from each arm and enhanced the wearer's strength tenfold, and the support legs could help move tons of equipment fast inside of an enclosed area. This one appeared to be modified slightly, with thicker arms and a protected driver's area.

I brought my Ma Deuce up and targeted the driver's compartment. Clenching my first, I unleashed hell onto the last remaining pirate that I could see. The large rounds from the Ma Deuce bounced harmlessly off of the lifter's arm. The person driving that thing must have figured I would try something like this and had been prepared. I left the gunfire taper off as I began to trot toward it. I was down to six rounds now, which was silly. I'd wasted a stupid amount of what little ammunition I had left trying to shoot a walking tank like me.

Not like me though. The lifter was slower, and while I knew it was probably twice as powerful, I could maneuver. It would be a nasty fight if I got in too close and let the lifter grab me with one of those arm lifts. I remembered what the doctor had told me earlier about being graceful and put that to use.

I bounded into the air and lashed out with one of my armored legs. The extended reach of the Mark One allowed me to stay just out of range of the lifter. The pirate inside apparently couldn't compensate for the extra movement and staggered to the right as my suit's foot connected solidly on his left shoulder. It spun but I was already moving quickly behind the lifter, bringing the Ma Deuce up to fire. I only had six shots left and needed to make each one count. I started shooting into the back of the driver's carriage, trying to keep each shot at the same point of impact to weaken the armor.

Unfortunately, none of my final shots penetrated the lifter. One, however, did ricochet back and impacted the helmet of the Mark One. I felt the impact above my head and winced, glad that I was shorter than normal. My ears were ringing from the bullet bouncing off my suit as dizziness threatened to overwhelm me, and I struggled to stay upright.

The lifter must have sense my moment of weakness because the pilot managed to grab me with the lifts and the two prongs which stuck out of each arm locked into place. One had managed to grab my left arm, pinning it down to the side and rendering it useless while the other had encircled my waist. I struggled to escape but the power behind the lifter was too much. The prongs began to close shut, and the Mark One suit started to creak and groan in protest as the lifter applied more pressure.

It was becoming difficult to breathe the more the lifter squeezed. I was enraged because if I didn't kill the driver of the lifter, I would have failed the doctor. Her disproval would kill me more painfully than anything the stupid pirate could manage. I was running out of options, though. I was stuck, and with only one arm free there was almost no way for me to gain leverage.

For a moment I wished I could see inside the protective case of the lifter, so I could look into the eyes of the person who was about to kill me. It was denial on my part. I couldn't believe that I was going to die and fail Doctor Pulvere like this. Anger, confusion, and fear flooded my mind. There had to be some way I could at least take the person inside with me.

As my fury grew, I realized that there was a raised edge on the side of the protective driver's cover. The clamps around my waist grew tighter still, and the suit began to malfunction. I was in near agony as the forks slowly pressed in on my pelvic bone from either side. The pressure grew greater as the suit's protection started to fail. There wasn't much time. I had to kill him, and now.

With the last of my strength, I managed to dig the suit's fingertips beneath the lipped edge. I yanked it once, twice, but nothing. Howling with pain and anger, I tried one final time. It crumpled and the armored cover was torn asunder, revealing a very confused and alarmed man on the inside.

At that same moment I suddenly felt cold all over my body. Numbness hit my entire lower half as I felt *something*. I couldn't see anything below a certain point but the suit helpfully informed me that everything beneath my pelvic region had been removed and the cortex was administering neural blocks to prevent me from feeling any pain. It also told me that I was bleeding to death and had but a few minutes at most before I died. More than likely I would be dead in seconds.

"That sucks," I whispered as blackness began to fill the edges of my vision. I was ashamed. I would fail Doctor Pulvere. *No you won't!* something inside my mind screamed. *You have one chance. Use it!*

I eventually succumbed to the pain, but not before I used the last of my strength to reach out and crush the skull of the last pirate with my hand.

* * *

"I read your report, doctor. Very impressive. Well done that your little Imperfect eliminated that troublesome nest of political undesirables. Tell me, how did the suit perform, in your opinion?" Emperor Solomon Lukas II asked impatiently as Doctor Lucinda Pulvere finished analyzing the data on her screen. The ruler of the Dominion had only just seized the Blood Throne three years before, and with the fourth anniversary the following month, the paranoid ruler wanted something to show Parliament that it was *he* who controlled the empire. The mechanized infantry suits were supposed to solidify his hold on the Blood Throne and drive away any pesky contenders and claimants, most especially his older sister, Sarah.

"The suit works just fine, Your Majesty," Doctor Pulvere told him as she looked around the room. The emperor had insisted on absolute privacy for this meeting, yet the man who had orchestrated his grab for the throne, Lord Matthias Samuels, sat off to the side. Emperor Solomon either did not care about Lord Samuels' presence or, more than likely, wanted him there. Doctor Pulvere had no idea why, though. "More armor might be handy, or I'd recommend that they do not engage in close quarters combat in the future. The primary weapons system operated ideally and flawlessly. The implant nodule worked well after some time of disorientation for the subject, and the cortex worked perfectly in conjunction with the suit, as expected. The patient was susceptible to all programming changes and was eager to please the more input she received. However, blind obedience might not always be the best. Perhaps just reinforcing positive behavior toward an ideology? I don't know yet; we'll need more tests to determine that. There might also be some flaws when the later generations and upgrades are introduced. I believe we should install some sort of loyalty subconscious programming to prevent acts of violence against the royal family. This way nobody can usurp control of them. The amount of rage the subject showed during the last few minutes of fighting allowed us to measure some very interesting patterns in her brainwave activity, sire."

"Such as?"

"The angrier she became, the more effective the cortex and suit worked, Your Majesty," Doctor Pulvere explained as she pulled up the data and transferred it to the emperor's computer. He glanced at it in a cursory fashion, making it abundantly clear to the doctor that he did not understand what he was looking at and was waiting for her to explain. After a pause, she continued. "The brain transferred the data far faster as she fought her way into the rebel's base. I would recommend in the future we come up with a way to test brain wave patterns to find the right fit with our Imperfects. Of course, we'll have to figure out if these mechanized infantry suits are going to be marines or fall under Navy jurisdiction…"

"Neither," the emperor stated as he glanced over at the nominally quiet Lord Samuels. The Justice nodded in agreement. "We're working an amendment into the Constitution to have them fall under direct command of the sitting ruler only. Call them a royal guard or something. Limit their numbers, but only I can command them, or someone at my behest, like a general or something."

"Commandant." Lord Samuels spoke for the first time, his eyes glinting as he turned to look at the doctor. She felt insignificant under that reptilian gaze. "It has a better ring to it. Instills both confidence *and* fear, a wise combination in these trying days."

"Fine, sure, whatever." The emperor waved him off. "Tell me, doctor…how many more of these suits can we produce?"

"A lot, Your Majesty," she readily admitted. "Now that the last of the cortex issues have been worked out, we simply need the go-ahead to find a contractor to build them."

"Excellent," the emperor nodded and stood. Doctor Pulvere, not anticipating the move, stumbled to her feet, grabbing her carrying case and nearly dropping her computer as well along the way. She tucked it inside and secured the case. Lord Samuels was already up, which infuriated the doctor. The old lord from Corus was a slimy individual. "You're dismissed, Doctor."

"Thank you, Your Majesty," Doctor Pulvere bowed deeply at the waist and backed away. As she passed the required ten-meter mark, she turned and began to walk out. As she reached the door, however, the emperor's voice stopped her short.

"By the way…whatever happened to your Mark I prototype suit that the girl was wearing?"

"Recovered, Your Majesty," Doctor Pulvere stated. "It didn't give up the ghost. One of the doctors on my team suggested calling it a Ghost suit, but I disagreed and thought that it was inappropriate to name it at this time. The girl inside, though, didn't survive."

"Ah…so your secondary project failed?"

"Not quite, Your Majesty," Doctor Pulvere corrected mildly, choosing her next few words with utmost caution. "Her brainwave patterns were remarkably clear, and what we dug out of the cortex is almost a completely fresh mind. We have our best scientists working on the artificial intelligence program now, using her as a template. Fifteen, twenty years and we'll be able to create a fully functional AI. We've already established a lab on the world where we did the field test, Your Majesty."

"Very good," the emperor nodded. He glanced at Lod Samuels before continuing. "Oh, what are you calling it? The AI program, I mean?"

"We were thinking of naming it after the girl whose brainwaves we're using, Your Majesty," Doctor Pulvere answered. "Almost like a backhanded compliment, even though she *was* just an Imperfect."

"Color me curious. What was her name?"

"Sfyri."

* * * * *

Jason Cordova Bio

A 2015 John W. Campbell Award finalist, Jason Cordova has traveled extensively throughout the U.S. and the world. He has multiple novels and short stories currently in print. He also coaches high school varsity basketball and loves the outdoors.

He currently resides in Virginia.

Catch up with Jason at https://jasoncordova.com/.

# # # # #

Bag Man

by Jack Clemons

The gentle vibrations sounded like the rattle of an insect's wings. They pulled at me across the gulf of soft sleep, the constant buzz of plastic on the varnished wood of the bedside table. My eyes opened reluctantly as if fighting the reality of the vibrations. Reaching out by memory without opening my eyes, I grasped the thin plastic of the phone.

I forced one eye open to view the dimly lit screen. I didn't recognize the number, but that wasn't uncommon for me. My thumb hovered over the screen briefly as I mentally composed myself to take the call. I rolled over onto my back among the cool tangle of sheets and blankets that made up my solo sleeping arrangement. Not that I minded sleeping alone. It was one of those things I had learned about myself in the wreckage of two divorces in 5 years. Sleeping alone is a luxury few truly appreciate.

As I sat up in the bed, I swiped the screen to answer the call.

"Hello," I said, keeping my voice as neutral as possible

"Yes, am I speaking with Mr. Drake?" the controlled female voice on the other end of the line asked.

It was a work call, but that wasn't surprising. The reason this phone sat next to my bed was so that I could be on call. I checked the time. Barely ten pm. I hadn't been asleep for an hour. I briefly considered raising my fee.

"You are. How may I help you?"

"I was given your number by a friend at UB&W. They recommended you as a specialist in adjudication."

I reached over and palmed a control switch on the bedside table, bringing the lights up in the room slowly to not be too jarring. Upham, Burke, and Waingro wasn't the name of a mid-sized law firm but it was designed to sound like one. It was a single office in the bad part of town with a secretary and a sole proprietor.

William "BillyBoy" Goldstein was a disgraced and disbarred former corp lawyer who had been drummed out of his profession for what he called, "Getting caught doing what everyone else was better at hiding." I had never asked him for the details, and he never felt like giving more than that. That being said, he was a man who lived enough in both worlds that he had seen the need for a niche role in helping facilitate the corporations when it came to legalities even they weren't willing to break. To that end, he maintained a stable of various specialists. He farmed our skillset out to the highest bidder and took both a healthy finder's fee and a flat 10% of our net profits.

So, for "Miss Cool and Collected" to be name dropping "BillyBoy," she was confirming her need for discretion and violence. Her timing of the call meant this was a matter of some urgency. I processed this as I rubbed my face in a movement that stretched back to the cavemen. Touching skin to try and trigger some deeper core in myself.

"Ahh, yes. Is there a timeframe for your matter?" I asked, swinging my legs free and onto the floor.

"I am afraid the matter is quite urgent. Are you available for a face-to-face meeting?" Her voice never wavered, strong and precise. She likely wasn't the one with the issue, I guessed. Some corporate trouble-shooter who had probably been asleep an hour ago herself, before a more frantic call had reached her.

"I am, where at?" I walked toward the closet, my feet moving silently through the plush carpet. "And, of course, there is the matter of my fee for such urgent meetings."

"I will send you an address. As to the fee, we were informed as such. Ten thousand credits have been deposited into the indicated account. We do ask that you arrive quickly, as the matter is quite timely."

"Of course." That was a hefty amount. About my maximum consulting level fee, not that I thought that was where it would end. All for me to wake up and go see someone. I had done a lot worse for a lot less. "I will be on my way shortly."

"Excellent." The call ended abruptly.

I tossed the phone back onto the bed as I opened the memory plastic door of the closet. Dilating at the touch of my finger, the coded door revealed my wardrobe. I glanced at the suits briefly. Each one a bespoke masterpiece that cost more than I used to make in a month slinging cheap bootleg TriDees and Narco injectors. If this meeting had been scheduled during business hours, these suits would have allowed me to drift among the sea of corporate drones without a second glance. But, to me, these were merely a camouflage of a different sort. One of the first lessons I had ever been taught on my rise from Street Sicario to my current lofty position of Corporate Bagman.

372 | IBSON & KENNEDY

"You have to be able to move in both worlds, and their world won't come naturally. So pretend, disguise, and lie. Do it until it becomes second nature. The easier it is for them to forget what you are, the better you are at your job. Just never forget yourself."

Instead, I dressed in a loose casual manner that would see me well in almost any environment. Dark jeans, a grey mag-sealed double breasted shirt with a mandarin collar, black running shoes that pulsed a dull red on the sole with each step, and a tan all-weather jacket. Reaching down, I pulled free one of the dark green hard plastic military cases that rested in the closet. I rarely kept all of my working supplies here, but I kept enough hardware on hand for personal use.

I selected a thin Smith and Wesson semi-auto with a concealment holster and slipped it inside the waistband of my jeans at the one o'clock position, attaching it to my belt. A spare magazine and auto-knife went into my left-hand front pocket. While it was unlikely this meeting was an ambush, you didn't make it in this line of work without a layer of paranoia helping you get dressed.

I gave myself the once-over in the mirror. No matter what I did, I would never get rid of the look of being "The Heavy." Tall and muscled but not comically so. I was glad for the long sleeves and high collar to cover the gang tattoos of a previous life and the cybernetic enhancements of this one. My dark black hair was cut in a severe near-military fade, my beard trimmed and squared off. The edging of gray was showing more and more. For some, it was a matter of self-consciousness; personally, I took pride in it. Neither my father nor grandfather had lived to see gray hair.

I walked out of the spartan guest room I slept in and was assaulted by my curator's garish, trending TriDee motifs. I didn't mind the art; I just didn't feel the need to stare at it every night before drifting off to sleep. The decorator's name was Sarah, and we had met eight months ago at a party thrown by a friend of a friend. I had seen her across the room and immediately been infatuated. She was tall and pale, her red hair cut into a side shave to show off the intricate Celtic knotwork tattoo that writhed and moved with the beat of the music. I can still remember her sheer red dress that left just enough to the imagination.

That night, we fucked. Afterward, her hands traced the scar tissue and black carbon fiber of my cybernetics. She told me she could work when and where she wanted, or not, but whatever she did had to be "spiritually fulfilling." She asked me what I did for a living, and in a haze of drugs, booze and post-coital endorphins, I told her.

There were many names for my profession, but they all boiled down to the same thing. In earlier times, I would have been called a sellsword, ronin, soldier of fortune, or mercenary. Now the masters who hired my services preferred to dress it up in a different way: Security Executive, Conflict Adjudicator, or Contractor. The street called us Kordats, Freehires, and of course Bagmen. But it all meant the same: people of resolve for hire to the highest bidder.

Rather than making her run off, she found it fascinating. She told me later it was our auras, something about her being wind and me being fire. I didn't really understand it then, and I still don't now. But the balance was there, and for now she was in my life, and we enjoyed each other. I know she'll grow bored someday and be gone...and I would be left with an apartment full of art and a head full of memories.

She was stretched out on the floor, nude, wearing a full body sensory harness and laying on a RealDee response blanket. Judging by the sounds she was experiencing some sort of sonic trance sequence that she had informed me was all the rage currently. I had tried it. Honestly, it had felt like dancing with a Muay Thai fighter for forty minutes while the music buzzed in my ear. It was the latest thing for the Neo-Druids in their Club/Temples, but really not my bag.

Her lithe body twisted and turned in a way that was both erotic and religious, worshipping some goddess of fertility in a mix of synth wave and bass-boosted music. The Atlanta skyline outlined her through my floor-to-ceiling windows from thirty-seven stories up. Buckhead's neon and LED lights mixed with what stars were powerful enough to beat the city haze.

I didn't interrupt her; we didn't have a "goodbyes" type of relationship. She likely wouldn't notice me being gone 'til tomorrow at some point, and I needed to be in work mode, not thinking about what we last said to each other. That had happened with Wife Number Two. Thinking about an argument had led to a lot of time in the surgery stack. Lesson learned: keep your personal life locked away. It can and will get you killed.

So I walked out of my apartment.

The armored glass elevator plunged down, allowing the city's lights to play over me. The night had just begun in earnest, changing the city from the corporate jewel of the south into the party tourist location that had made it famous. Taverns, bars and pubs, clubs and lounges, parks, restaurants, street meat vendors, diners, and dives all roused from their dormant states. Likewise, partiers, punks, tourists, thrill-seekers, and mischief-makers took over Late Night Atlanta. Like the first hit off an opium pipe, the city breathed in vice and exhaled experience. It was in these streets I had grown up, where I had killed my first man, and where I had evolved into what I am now. Descending from my apartment to the streets below felt like falling from heaven.

The soft ding of the elevator pulled me away from the now-subterranean view. I was still somewhat groggy. As I turned and stepped into the garage, I saw my BMW sedan sitting and waiting. The elevator had informed the E-Chauffeur in my car I was coming down, causing the vehicle to activate its electric motor and drive to the elevator. The sleek black and red paint showed off German engineering for the modern enthusiast who could afford it. I slid into the driver seat. The door sealed behind me, and I looked into the phone for the first time since the call had ended. The address was north of the city in Kennesaw. Not overly surprising, and at this time of night I could be there in 45 minutes.

"Liz," I said as I slid the phone into its cradle.

"Yes?" The voice was sultry and sinful. Not a factory option; I'd had the default personality removed and a hacked variant placed in its vacancy. Not only was it far more secure, it matched the car better.

"Get us on 75 northbound and get Ivan on the phone. Call until he answers."

The Beemer's electric motor hummed as the autodrive engaged. The streets were wet from a late December rain, creating reflective surfaces in every puddle. The E-Chauffeur matched its speed with those posted, leaving me to brood as I listened to the muted rings through the car's speakers. I had known Ivan for three years and employed him for two. He wasn't Russian, but the influx of refugees from the Sino Conflict meant that the streets were learning all sorts of new slang. He was younger than me, and when I first met him, he barely had any cybertech. So I paid him half in cash and half in "chair-time" at my preferred mechanic.

Now, he was running so many mods he barely qualified as human. Cybernetic addiction was another thing you had to balance in this life. You could run internal comms, sensors, weapon enhancements, subcutaneous body armor, organic weapon mounts, and limb replacement. A common mistake—that much tech meant you were going to flash every sensor in a three-block radius. And any decent CeeCee will fry your shit, turning off vulnerable systems one by one. Keeping your anti-intrusion software up to date could be as pricey as turning your body into a living weapon.

Personally, I preferred a more subdued approach. My hardware was all non-network reflex, strength, endurance boosters, and a few other "dumb" systems that allowed me to be protected from intrusion and offer minimal footprint to sensor sweeps. Of course, there were the replacement body parts; those had been necessary as the years of damage took their toll. And that didn't even account for all the possible chemical cocktails. Living at the bleeding edge was expensive, but that's why I charged the prices I did.

The speakers pinged, drawing me out of my thoughts.

"Yooooo!" Ivan's voice was cheerful, and the sound of thunderous music could be heard even through his voice filter. "You out tonight? I am at Typhoon!"

"We have work. You sober?" I asked as the car took another corner smoothly. A group of young ladies were walking down the street, flesh, holograms, and minimal clothing drawing my eye. One turned and blew the car an exaggerated kiss.

"Shit man, yeah mostly. I can drop a hypo but that will mess with my reflexes."

"I am headed to meet the client, call Zipline. Go get a work van. And some tool boxes. Meet me at Landmark. Sober up there."

"Da, what's the gig?"

"No clue. Pack for a little bit of everything. There seems to be a timing issue, so I don't want to go back to the lockers if we can help it."

"Seems nexus. You want back up for the meet?"

"No, they seem relaxed enough. Besides, the down payment is already in the bank."

"Skuller, see you at Landmark."

He hung up, and my BMW slid onto I75 north. The 16-lane freeway cut through the entire state, offering those so inclined easy surface travel to Tennessee or Florida. It had also made Georgia a smuggling hub for over a century. Drugs, people, guns, and all manner of illicit goods made their way through the country on I75. Atlanta didn't mind as long as the right palms were greased and enough busts were made to show the housewives who gave a fuck that the Dot-Gov types were "doing something."

My first jobs, once I had been inducted into the Cartel, had been driving loads of "product" from Jacksonville to Lexington. I knew this interstate like I knew my own hand. I could still remember my hands on the wheel, tweaking on meth, listening to older Sicarios in the passenger seat tell me the ways of the world, as salsa-pop pumped out of the speakers. My vision blurred to the tune of the beat. It hadn't seemed like a bad way to spend one's teenage years, and that's why the Cartel recruits from high schools. By 18, I had killed men for less money than I now spent on a haircut and massage. When you grow up with nothing, you really don't have much to lose.

"Manual drive. Release governor. Sport mode active." I watched the steering wheel extend from the dash as I touched the accelerator, and I felt the gasoline engine kick on. The twin turbo V6 growled as I began pushing into the light traffic, watching the speedometer climb to 140KPH.

"Anything else Papi?" The voice sent a light shiver down my spine. You could practically feel the virtual teeth biting on your earlobe.

"Yes, Playlist 4. And back it off about twenty percent there Liz."

"You're no fun." The car pouted as it dutifully activated the playlist.

I dodged around a slow-moving cargo hauler and pressed harder on the accelerator.

* * *

The drive back from Kennesaw was faster than the one there. The meeting had gone predictably; now all that was left was to convince my crew. The Landmark Diner was one of those long-standing Atlanta traditions that seemed almost ageless. A large-scale diner planted in Buckhead that, during the day, catered to upscale families and corporate workers looking for a meal with a wide variety of menu options. But, much like the rest of the city, as the sun set, it took on a new tone.

The front of the restaurant remained brightly lit, attracting partiers heading out for the night, and, later, partiers recovering afterwards. But in the back...we who plied our trade in violence and vice could enjoy a more private and secure environment.

I breezed past the receptionist, who was lost in the holo drama before her. I walked through the mostly empty dining room and stepped through an unmarked door near the bathrooms that most people would assume was storage. It was not, and the sonic wash of the noise dampener came over me like a baptism of hidden vice. The backroom had been a well-known comedy club, but the years marched on, and as the need for private dining had increased, the establishment had responded. Now the darkened room was lit by contrasting blues and reds making facial recognition software iffy at best. Sonic dampeners kept conversations localized to their tables, and patrons desiring maximum anonymity could rent booths with force shields.

I glanced around those in the open and saw a number of familiar faces. Herold "Limerick" Jones was at one table, surrounded by a host of hangers-on. He was a local WaveRapper who fancied himself a player in the underworld. Our dealings had all been public and polite. Our mutual acquaintances had informed me that his lyrics weren't just for show, and he was more than happy to get his hands dirty. Neither I, nor my clients, had any desire to hear of *my* work on a chart-topping hit.

Four armored police officers sat at another table. Their gear marked them as elite APEX rapid response and crime suppression specialists. When plans went sideways, and you didn't have an exit strategy, they happened...a normal patrol officer wasn't a threat to a man like me, but these cops rode Mil-spec VTOLs, and ran as much cyberware as any Street Soldat I cared to think of. I looked over their faces, since their armored helms hung from the back of their chairs like mirrors. I recognized two and could tell they recognized me. We had a checkered history, as men who had seen each other through their holographic gunsights tended to have. But all of us viewed it as happenstance of the profession, and this place was as sacred as any church or temple. Out on the streets, they would crucify me if they could, but a good meal is hard to come by late at night and no professional rivalry was worth endangering that.

Last, I spotted my party. Posted in the corner booth, Ivan was stretched out with half a plate of wings, and a growing pile of bones next to it. I calculated the amount of time he had been here, based on the speed at which I knew he ate and how many wings remained. Close to forty minutes.

Ivan had been tall and lanky at 6'8" and 200 lbs. Then he'd added half again his natural body weight in augments and cyberware. Those hadn't bulked him up, so his long spindly limbs had earned him the street name of "Scarecrow." He didn't care for the nickname; his ego demanded he be Ivan the Great. But even that wasn't good enough. He was "Ivan the Greatest of All Time, Goddammit," which, of course was shortened to Ivan the Goat behind his back.

He was wearing typical Soldat combat clothing, a clashing mix of Sino aesthetic and "Formal Slavic Business Wear." His Kamayhara combat gi was an eye-catching blue and had been covered by cyberware sponsor patches. His tight, slash-resistant pants, black, were by Adidas. Multiple refugee cultures had collided with unrestrained American capitalism and resulted in some very strange fashion trends.

Ivan looked up at me with a broad grin on his face. His companion turned to see me with an expression more sly and reserved. Zipline was a Circuit Cowboy I had used for few jobs. His specialty was Direct Action Network Manipulation and Intrusion. His skills would have landed him a comfortably extravagant lifestyle in any corporation, however that would have required a shift in lifestyle that Zipline clearly wasn't embracing. His skinny, scar-covered body spoke of a life of alternating chemical and technological addiction. His clothes were tattered cargo shorts and a denim vest bearing currently-trending Trailer Park SlamRock patches. His hair had been replaced with the interwoven tech-dreads of processors and spare RAM, giving him onboard computing power to rival most 20th century supercomputers.

Of course, keeping that kind of tech safe in the trailer parks full of factory burnouts and junkies wasn't easy or cheap. I had seen Zipline's personal cluster of trailers before. Layered active and passive defenses ranging from less-than-lethal minefields to auto-turret controlled shotguns loaded with monofilament razor shells. I had been curious about why he still lived there. His freelancing clearly provided more than enough for him to move to a safer environment, but he had merely shrugged and said he didn't want to be removed from the real.

Sliding into the booth, I reached over and palmed the privacy screen, causing an opaque white field to block out the rest of the room. I glanced at their faces, hungry and almost feral. My jobs never paid small, and these boys knew that came with risks. But on the ragged edges of society, you rarely get opportunities to break out of your station in life. These two men knew that to do so meant the application of violence and acceptance of risk.

"What's the *rabo*?" Ivan asked, pushing aside the pile of dead avian remains in front of him.

"Recovery of an asset," I said evenly, pulling out a disposable tablet, "and retribution on those that took it."

I quickly entered an eight-digit code, opening the tablet. Ivan picked it up and began flipping through the pages of the brief. Zipline had likely already hacked the pad; he was just polite enough not to talk about what he found. He compulsively hacked every device he laid his eyes on, so I didn't bring my personal phone out when he was around.

"So break it down, Hoss," Zipline said in his overly exaggerated southern drawl.

I cleared my throat and took a second to run over the details as they had been fed to me. The scene hadn't been an entirely unfamiliar one. A stoic patriarch, the weeping matriarch, and their cluster of supporters; the story was only new in the minutia.

"Sometime around noon today, a Bankhead drug den was robbed. They did the typical sweep job looking for drugs and cash. When they didn't find enough, they started taking people."

At that moment I selected a file and pressed play. Shaky tri-dee clawed to life as a desperate cameraman caught precious frames of a masked man shoving a young girl who had been gagged and bound into a cargo van. I froze it on the best frame of the girl's face.

"Video was taken by the asset's boyfriend."

"Excuse me," Zipline said stubbing out his Pall Mall. "What does some drugged out slag have to warrant our kind of response?"

"The asset is the daughter of a very prominent figure in local politics. If he involves police in this matter it gets discovered his daughter is a burned out junkie who performs in online porn shows."

Perking up at that information, both leaned in. Scandal and corruption meant even healthier paydays. Plus, who didn't like hearing about the woes of their social betters?

"Who is he?" Ivan asked.

"No one you voted for," I countered.

"You know I can't vote." He pouted. Ivan had caught a charge early on, and it was a sore spot. For a known killer, having a felony record for attempting—and failing—to break into an AutoBurger kiosk during a three-day drunken binge? *Less than intimidating.*

"Anyway," I said, slightly annoyed at the deviation; they knew I wouldn't discuss client details if it could be helped, "we have been charged with getting her out of the current predicament and returning her to her family."

"So, who took her? And why?" Ivan asked, taking a pull off a bottle. "Also, where is she?"

"Learn to read faster," Zipline quipped. "Boss, this ain't gonna be that easy. The Towers are no fucking joke."

"Fuck man, The Towers?" Ivan moaned.

"Yes," I said icily. "The Towers. Get over it. It's why you get paid the big bucks. The good news is the hard work is done for us. The family tagged the girl with a tracker on her last trip to rehab and had the family investigator track her once the boyfriend informed them of what occurred. He traced her to the tower and has sat on her this whole time. They move her, and he will inform us."

"So who has her? Why did they take her, anyway?" Ivan asked. He pointedly was not reading the brief as a rebuke to Zipline's jab.

"Tower gang called 47 Ronin. And, as far as we can tell, they grabbed her and three other females, likely in hopes of selling them."

"Yeah, I know those guys," Zipline said. "They're a burned-out shitty MC. Made up primarily of Russian refugee kids who have a hard-on for Jap samurai culture shit. They used to be an up and comer, 'til a few months back. Half their number either got cut down or got hard time."

That part hadn't been on the brief, but I wasn't surprised Zip had that kind of intel. Guys like him had a vast array of informants and intel sources. He was as much an information broker as he was a combat hacker.

"Shit was gnarly," he continued. "Deal gone south with some crew of dudes I had never heard of before, turned to gun play, and it just so happened that an APEX VTOL was nearby. Gunfight became a massacre, and ever since, the forty-seven Ronin are more like nine. Hearing that they are robbing Trap houses and dabbling in human trafficking doesn't surprise me one bit. These dudes are speed freaks with some bare bones milsurp augments."

"Know any of them personally?" I asked.

"Yeah," he answered, lighting another Pall with a propane torch.

"That going to be an issue?" I kept my voice flat and didn't move. This world was made of questions like this, determining if someone was mercenary enough to take on someone they knew personally. I could feel muscles tensing and aching for the comfort of the grip of a handgun, but I forced myself to remain calm.

"Nah," Zipline said, expelling smoke across the table. "I *know* him. I don't *like* him."

"Good. Got us an in on these guys?" I asked as my muscles relaxed slightly. There was still all the chance in the world that Zipline was setting me up to stab me in the back. But, like I had told him, the risk is why they pay me.

"Yeah, like I said. Speed freaks. I can drop a Wave asking for a load of trentameth for pick up. These guys are likely mid-meth-ride and will be up for another two days."

"Do it. There is a bonus if we get her back before anyone finds out she is gone."

"Yo," Ivan interjected. "So we go in and get the girl, what do we do about the Ronin?"

"We kill 'em all. Contract is pretty clear about that. Client wants this washed away like a bad dream." I pointed at Ivan. "Me and you go in, handle them, grab her, and walk out. It's The Towers. No one is going to give a shit. Zipline runs intrusion and overwatch."

"Nexus," Ivan said, "What is the payout?"

"30k each for y'all. Expenses out of my end."

"I don't think y'all get it," Zipline interjected. "Y'all got the easy slice of pie. The Towers are a jumbled mess of private networks, honey pots, bear traps, black ice, and server bombs. Place isn't secure; it's just fucking dangerous. I could end up a Toaster Strudel if one of those ICE counters slips me up."

"Oh, like, our fucking end of this is easy?" Ivan growled. "Remember the meth'd Russians?"

"Zero out. Both of you," I said calmly. "The money is good. If shit gets *oblicuo* I might consider a combat bonus. But let's not pretend that risk is a new concept."

They both looked at me, Ivan's augmented eyes a stark contrast in matte black and metallic gold. Zipline's were still his original organic, murky green ringed with bloodshot white. The Tri-Dees would have you believe violent men would follow their leader because there was some deep spiritual connection that made them want to follow them into hell. The reality is we all did it for our own reasons, and my leadership was more a trait of tactical ability than any thrilling heroics.

"Alright, I am in. But if I fry processors I expect coverage," Zipline stated sourly.

"That's covered in expenses," I said hitting the tab out button. A weak Tri-dee sprang to life showing the itemized list and total. I waved a preloaded card and added a 20% tip.

"Now let's get going. I'd like to be home at some reasonable time tomorrow."

The security field wavered and disappeared. I stood and started walking to the door, noting that the table of armored officers were gone, their unpaid tab lazily dancing in the air over a table covered in dirty dishes. I heard Ivan and Zipline slide out of the booth and follow me, Zipline tossing a wave to Limerick and his entourage.

Outside, I saw the cluster of cops standing near an empty clearing of the parking lot, smoking and obviously waiting on their ride. The path to our van took us past them. I silently whispered prayers to a god who, if He were real, would want nothing to do with me, and that my compatriots would act like the professionals they were paid to be.

As we passed, I felt one set of eyes track on me and follow. I ran my memory trying to think where I had last seen the somewhat-familiar face. As the memory came to me I heard the voice. He had all the measured authority a badge and gun gave you. Trained in the academy to command respect and obedience from the frightened and weak willed.

"Well, well, well. Mr. Drake. What brings you out and about tonight?"

"Officer Anderson," I said, turning, flicking my eyes to my two compatriots, hoping they got the message to stay calm. "Just another late dinner with friends."

"Uh-huh," he vocalized condescendingly. "Where you working tonight?"

Our last encounter had not been an overly kind one, and in the end, he had been forced to concede the point that police authority only extended so far. So, his needling right now was less a threat and more a statement that he knew what I was and didn't care for it.

Of course, I didn't much care for him either.

"Oh," I said opening the sliding door of the van and stepping in. "No place with a high enough income bracket for you to care about."

I closed the door before he could reply and turned to Zipline.

"Get us rolling."

He didn't say anything; he just shifted us into gear and slowly rolled the work van out into the night.

* * *

The back of the van was a strange mix of rituals. Ivan sat with his back against the wall of the van, his feet bouncing in rhythm with whatever SlamSalsaPop song filled his ear buds. Long ago, he had confessed to me that the moments before a hit were the hardest for him, so he pretended like it wasn't happening. Zoned out with his thoughts on how he would be spending his share, it was an almost sexual look for him.

I looked decidedly less serene. Stripped to the waist, my body was racked with micro tremors and was drenched in sweat. I watched as the auto injector fell from my hand soundlessly—over the pounding of the blood in my ears, I couldn't hear *anything*. The cocktail wasn't one of my making. I had learned it years ago from Sicarios trained by the Mexican government, back when they gave a shit about fighting the century old drug war. A combination of chemicals and nanos would let me operate at peak combat efficiency. I would move faster, feel less pain, react quicker, and process the world around me better. But like everything in the world there was a tax to be paid. And that meant not only a hard shock to the system as it was carried through my veins and distributed throughout my body, but also a wicked hangover in the next three days...which was about the same amount of time before I would be able to go to sleep.

I breathed deeply in and out. Pushing air from my body and feeling the tremors slow and finally subside. I reached under the bench I sat on and pulled out a black duffle bag. I had packed and repacked it over the years. My quick and dirty work bag. If the job wasn't a specialty gig, this bag would likely get me through it. As I unzipped it, I saw Ivan staring at me.

"What?" I asked, overly hostile. It wasn't that I particularly gave a shit if he looked at me or not, but the drugs left me aggressive and snappy.

"*Nichego* man, that shit never looks fun," he said coolly, "or healthy."

"Berserk really isn't something done for pleasure," I said, trying my best for a flat response, not that I pulled it off.

"Yeah, I get that. But typically you dose up two or three hours before we smash someone. You about to walk in there looking like a fucking *Ángel muerte* junkie."

He dug into his jacket and pulled out a green-tipped vaporizer. Pressing it out to me as an offering he continued. "So chill, man. We are going to have to be glass smooth before this thing turns to *kinzhal.*"

My initial reaction was to smash it down and inform him he could get fucked—which told me he was likely correct—so I took it and drew deeply off it, letting the THC concentrate flood my lungs in a cloud of water vapor.

"Thank you," I coughed out.

"*Nyet*," he said, leaning back.

I returned myself to the task at hand, hoping the THC could stabilize me for now. I considered the hardware and tools in the bag. Hard and soft goods massed in an organized jumble. The mixed smells of sweat, lubricant, gun powder, and pine freshness (from the tree shaped car fresheners I had thrown in the bag) assaulted my nostrils in a familiar wave.

I glanced up and consulted Ivan's hardware and considered how to best compliment it. His Remington 230 short barrel auto-shotgun sat across his lap, a compact and brutal weapon that made up for its lower capacity with the sheer brutality of its 10-gauge buckshot shells. The short shotgun was a popular home defense weapon for those worried about the threat of cybernetically augmented foes. Ivan had a fondness for the gun, despite its punishing recoil. He'd also taken a pair of compact Glock handguns from the office, one tucked into his pants by his belt buckle with a cheap holster, the other stuffed into the pocket of his bomber jacket. Ivan's theory revolved around disposable firearms and gear, cyberware over hardware.

Once, we had been deep into our cups after a successful hit. Sitting on a boat in the middle of Lake Lanier, our blood-soaked clothes and hardware sinking quickly into the murky waters in our wake, he got philosophical. "*It's America, man; guns are the one thing we aren't running out of anytime soon. Whole country who made with the things.* This here is Cordite Country."

I disregarded the compact Beretta SMG—Ivan had indiscriminate mayhem covered. What I needed was accuracy and utility. I opened a side panel and removed a padded case. Inside rested a Sig 430, customized by the company's elite Grey Division. They'd taken a basic service handgun and made it a tack-driving weapon worthy of any high-end special-ops types.

The gun featured a low-profile, frame-mounted, red dot sight, ported and compensated barrel, flared mag well, retextured grip, and reworked trigger. All these features gave a well-trained, discerning shooter a super-compact and accurate weapon in an easily concealable package. Its 11mm cartridge allowed for a number of different load options for the various threats in the world. I selected four extended 20-round magazines. Two were filled with flesh and augment-shredding micro-explosive hollow points, the other two with armor-piercing rounds.

I fitted myself with a gun belt and filled the pouches with ammunition, knives, emergency medical gear, and a breaching charge before sliding a magazine into the Sig and racking the slide. I slid it into a PHLstar holster I had mounted to the right of my belt buckle, the aggressive rearward cant of the holster allowed for a faster draw, even if it was slightly harder to conceal.

Next, I pulled on a thick black shirt. The 3mm thick shirt felt much like a 20th century wetsuit and was nearly skin tight, but its honeycombed features would act as reactive armor. It should stop most frag, spall, and lower velocity ammunition. In addition, I slid in two titanium plates, one front and back.

My light-up sneakers were stylish, but also a poor decision tactically, so I replaced them with a set of black Altama combat moccasins. Finally, I pulled on a loose-fitting hoodie emblazoned with the logo for a local chain of restaurants. It may have seemed like an odd thing, but it was comfortable, hid most of the hardware, and they really *did* make a tasty burger.

"Towers are coming up," Zipline said from the driver's seat. The front passenger seat was filled with his intrusion rig. "Once I drop y'all off, I'll find a parking spot. They are in Tower 3, Nineteenth Floor, Suite Twenty-Nine. Don't take any fucking risks with these guys."

I looked up from my preparations and caught Zipline's eyes in the rear-view mirror.

"Cornered dogs fight harder," he stated, meeting my eyes.

He was right. This gang had once been a powerhouse, content and rich off multiple schemes. Now, they couldn't even pull off a simple heist. They were like a rabid dog riding a meth high, and if they felt pressured or threatened, they would go to guns.

"They're expecting a purchase. Once they pop the door, I am hitting it with a sonic charge and following a 12-Bang in. We burn them down, grab the girl, and dip. This all goes according to plan, it should be a milk run."

And with that, we were there.

* * *

With the influx of refugees from both sides of the Sino conflict, Atlanta had few options for placement. It had finally been decided they would take the former Six Flags Over Georgia theme park and convert the 300 acres into a "Rehoming Solution." They'd redesigned it to transplant the refugees into a place they could make a new home, with low-income housing and open-air markets that would foster new businesses and create a thriving community.

The concept was presented as, "A bold new direction in housing for the less privileged." Politicians and corporate types were on all

392 | IBSON & KENNEDY

the right talk shows saying all the right lines. The public bought it hook, line, and sinker. Those of us who are considered undesirable laughed at the whole show. We knew what was going to happen.

The first tower had a full ribbon-cutting ceremony with Vladimir Ivanovic, a 16-year-old Russian refugee, holding the scissors. Smiles all around. The kid's story was a touching one—his mother and father killed in the fighting, making his way to America with his sister and grandmother, his English was just broken enough to be endearing. He was on all the morning talk shows and became a three-minute celebrity.

The third tower wasn't even open yet before Vladimir was found dead.

The story was different every time I heard it, but a dozen bullets found their way into the kid in the middle of an apartment-turned-drug-den. The news didn't cover it, because his three minutes were up. It was better if The Towers project completed without scandal, and the news knew who paid their bills.

A total of twenty towers were planned. Eight were completed, but the ninth sat half-finished in a skeletal husk. By that time, all the towers had become such horror shows not even the corporations could keep the stories under wraps. Much of the money intended for the refugees had found its way into bonus checks for corporate types and campaign funds for politicians, a few paltry arrests were made, all approved by the lords on high, and the damage was done. More importantly, the grant money was all gone, so The Towers were left to their own devices and became what they were destined to become all along.

Now multiple factions lived, worked, and fought over them in a tale as old as time. Gangs, prostitution, drugs, weapons, and anything else you could desire could all be found there. Police rarely went into them, and the corporate owners could barely be bothered to maintain them, let alone pay for privatized security firms. So, instead, the police watched the exits, the message clear: "Stay where you belong."

As we walked down trash-strewn walkways, we were greeted by the few dwellers of The Towers still up at this hour. Junkies, drug dealers, and hookers looked us over and, in most cases, immediately directed their eyes elsewhere. While we were obviously outsiders, our cyber augments and clear gun bulges also clearly marked us as apex predators. We were allowed to pass without challenge.

Once inside Tower 3, we looked around the deserted area that was once supposed to house a bustling marketspace full of restaurants, theaters, stores, and other shops a self-contained society might need. Now, all that was left was a gun shop sitting behind armored glass and a bar where even the heaviest sound proofing couldn't contain the pulsing, hard bass.

We made our way toward the elevator bank. Designed to raise and lower dozens of citizens at a time, they had once been glass and glow bulb lit. Now years of abuse and neglect left it with chain link and armored neon bulbs. No one joined us as we slowly rose into the air.

"Place is more and more depressing every time I come here," Ivan said looking out of the elevator across the open air chasm at the other side of the tower.

"Out of one warzone into another," I replied blandly. The plight of refugees was occasionally a drum beat by the wealthy elite who liked to pretend they gave a shit, but the reality is they wanted someone else to do the hard humanitarian work. They never beat the drum long, just enough to get the social currency they needed from it.

A noise buzzed in my ear. A micro bead bio-communicator was slowly dissolving there.

"It's Zipline. I'm in."

"How do we look?" I asked, adjusting my gun belt.

"Good. Tower is quiet tonight. Not too many active users. The floor above the target is pure black ice. I think someone is running an offsite server farm there."

"Weird" Ivan said, as he checked the load in his shotgun.

"None of our business," I stated as the doors opened. "Zip, we clear?"

"All cameras down, and I will start suppressing all phone service when you hit the door."

"Golden."

We made our way down an off-shoot hallway. Barely lit, graffiti-stained walls, and the smells of food and humanity beat down on me, tearing at my brain, but I focused myself toward the target door. A nights' work was finally coming to fruition. Soon everything would come down to my team's skills vs. the other side. My muscles trembled as adrenaline mixed with the drugs already there. My gut tingled like a virgin on prom night.

The door to Suite 29 was a hardened security door with a cheap video intercom drilled into the wall. The door itself was covered in painted Kanji and Cyrillic. I reached into my pockets and pulled out a sonic breaching charge. Pulling off a protective cover, I adhered it to the door and placed the detonator in my left hand.

"Ready?" I softly whispered.

"Ready," Ivan breathed, palming a 12-bang and hiding it behind his leg.

"*Ready,*" Zipline stated calmly.

"I have control." I nodded at Ivan, who reached out and hit the buzzer.

Crackling with cheap audio feedback, a voice on the other end said, "*Who the fuck are you and the fuck you want* Gaijin?"

"Zipline sent us," Ivan said calmly. "Said y'all had grade alpha crystal."

"*Yeah we do. Y'all got cash?*" the voice asked.

"Duh." Ivan looked disinterested. Of course when most of your face was mostly cybernetic, that was fairly easy. He lifted a wad of cash in the hand not busy holding a flashbang.

"*Hold on a fucking tick,*" the box.

"Stand by," I whispered.

Ivan tensed, getting ready to hurl the device into the room. I waited, trying not to look overly threatening in case they were still watching the camera. The sound of grinding metal told us the door was being unlocked, and I felt the tension escape. Now was my time, the time I was made for. Gone was all doubt, all fear; now there was only the fight.

"*Execute. Execute. Execute!*" I said and detonated the charge.

* * *

Door breaching was as ancient as warfare and engineering. Defenders always want to keep attackers out, and so as long as men had invented doors, other men had found solutions to getting *through* them. Battering rams, hammers, picks, crowbars, and bombs. Bombs were *great* for removing doors, but they were also the most dangerous to the attacker.

The sonic breacher eliminated the issues of over pressure, fragmentation, and flame that traditional 20th century door charges had. Instead, they sent a rapid series of ultra-high frequency pulses through the door that shook the surface so hard it practically disintegrated.

Of course it would be beyond unpleasant if you happened to be touching that surface that was being attacked in such a fashion. The Ronin gang member who had been unlocking the door screeched as his hand was vibrated to the point that his bones and muscle up to his shoulder were liquefied in a flash.

I kicked the remains of both the door and Ronin out of the way and stepped back so Ivan could do his part.

"YEET!" Ivan screamed as he hurled the 12-bang into the room.

The hallway shook and flashed as if in the middle of a rave thrown by a Norse god, each flash bright enough to be seen through closed eyes and each bang left one feeling as if they had been slapped across their entire body. Even I, someone who had trained with them extensively, had to hold onto my focus with everything I had. I was only in the *hallway*, anyone in the room would be on the ragged edge of sanity.

As the tidal wave of sound and light ended, I drew my Sig and went through the door. Behind me, I heard the boom of Ivan's riot gun as he finished the doorman. The suite had a large common room, a hallway, and smaller rooms branching off. Opposite to me, across the common room was a glass sliding door leading to a balcony. Behind the glass two men clawed at the air, disoriented by the flashbang.

I shot them through the glass.

The first, I centered my red dot sight on his chest and stroked the trigger, fast. The first micro-explosive hollow-point impacted the plate glass door and exploded. The resulting pop of the embedded charge shattered the glass, allowing the following rounds to pass nearly un-molested. As each round found their mark, they penetrated several inches and then detonated, opening up massive wound channels and driving tiny slivers of shrapnel throughout the body. The target jerked and folded to the ground, an oozing wreck of a body.

My eyes tracked to the next, who was starting to claw for some sort of chest mounted holster. I rotated my body like a turret, finding him through the optic. I settled the red dot on his head and stroked the flat trigger once. A spray of red and pink filled the air. Watching a human being having their strings cut was always unsettling. All functions stopped, and the body went from being alive to simply another bag of meat. Gravity took full effect, and the body dropped out of my sight picture.

Taking the briefest of seconds, I looked at the first man on the balcony I had shot. He was still moving slightly, and I shot him in the head. While likely overkill, I'd rather kill a man twice over, than get shot in the ass by one who was only partly on his way out.

Ivan had been right behind me after dispatching the wounded door man, and I was damn happy for that. He had covered my blind side as I had engaged the men on the balcony, and he'd caught one coming out of the kitchen with some sort of long gun. Ivan's shotgun had splashed the man's innards and third rate cyberware across the wall.

My instincts screamed for me to move, and I dove behind a couch as a stream of full-auto fire tore through the space I had inhabited. The deafening roar of the weapon filled the room. Tufts of couch stuffing and faux-leather filled the air as my concealment-not-cover was clawed at by the fusillade of rifle rounds. I crawled forward, desperately trying to not be where the gunman had last seen me. Getting the end of the couch, I could see the fire was coming from one of the bedrooms. I yanked my pistol out and emptied it into the doorway, causing the shooter to retreat deeper into the room.

"You with me?" I heard Ivan roar.

I rolled over so I could access my magazine pouch and quickly reloaded my pistol. Worried we might be dealing with a barricaded enemy, I selected a magazine of armor piercing.

"Yeah, I am here," I stated calmly.

"Good. Let's get this fucker. *Shchit* up!" Ivan said.

I turned to look at him. The burst of fire had clearly hit him, his coat was in tatters and his shotgun was on the ground. He shook out his left arm, causing it at first to twist and bulge as the synthetic skin on it distorted, stretched, and finally ripped. From within, a thin ballistic shield sprang into life. Covering his vulnerable torso and head, it wouldn't be able to take many rounds, but would be more than enough to cover him pushing the door. His right hand drew his first Glock from his waistline.

"Moving!" he spat furiously. Ivan hated getting shot.

"Move!" I stated, coming to my knees and firing at the problematic doorway.

Ivan moved forward behind his shield. As he got closer to the door I stopped firing, stood, and followed him, slipping behind his armored bulk. I was protected but blind. Ivan stopped before crossing the threshold. I reached up and squeezed his shoulder hard with my left hand. With that, he exploded into the room taking a hard left. I went forward to cover my sector. I heard a burst of gunfire followed by several muted pops.

I stayed focused on my sector. This had once been the master bedroom, but it was clearly now more of a work room. Cheap memory plastic tables and chairs held weapons, clothes, and...projects. In my sector I had no one living, but I could see movement under the crack of a door in the corner.

I risked a glance over my shoulder to check on Ivan. The gang member who had opened fire on him was slumped into the corner, half a dozen ragged holes in his chest and a smoking Kalashnikov in his lap. Ivan stomped his head in with a cybernetically enhanced kick. As the body began to spastically twitch and gurgle, Ivan turned to me and flatly stated, "Clear."

I spoke, pointing my weapon at the door. "Movement. Door."

He nodded, dropping his half-empty Glock to the floor. He reached over and disconnected the spent shield, leaving it on the floor, exposing a skeletal arm of carbon fiber bone and steel cable muscle. He drew his second Glock awkwardly from his jacket pocket. I positioned myself to the side of the door.

"Kick," I ordered tersely.

Ivan obliged me with his gore-covered foot, leaving an unpleasant-to-see-and-smell, dark red smear across the already stained door. As the door flew off its hinges, I glanced in. It was an adjoining bedroom. There were surplus bunk beds and a Ronin gang member stood in the far corner. He was using a frightened girl as a body shield. I looked at him through the optic of my pistol as I used the wall as cover. He had driven his machine pistol into her head and had his finger on the trigger.

"Fuck you, cocksucker! Y'all come any closer, and I will blow her head off!"

His voice was panicked. His face flush with fear. Our eyes locked as the situation played. As keyed up as he was, if I took the shot, there was a very real likelihood he might squeeze the trigger and kill the girl. It was a desperate plan on his part and ultimately...a flawed one.

"Yeah…. But she isn't the one I am here for," I said and pressed the trigger.

* * * * *

Come Up Screaming
by Kevin Ikenberry

A Runs In The Family Short Story

2265

Rally Point Broadspur

Radin

"Guidons, guidons, this is Saber Six. Short count follows. Break." Captain Mairin Shields released the transmit button on her helmet for two seconds. The Greys possessed particle beam weapons and ships that were faster-than-light. They could undoubtedly find and direct weapons onto human radio transmissions, and old habits died hard. The procedure wasn't taught in any of the modern Terran Defense Force schoolhouses. It came from a memory imprint grafted to Mairin from a long dead ancestor. He'd been a tanker and cavalryman, too. Mairin volunteered for the experimental procedure more for the benefits of perfecting her myopia and eliminating her crippling allergies than the three-hundred-year-old memories. She hadn't wanted a soldier's life. Combat taught her the TDF was grossly outmatched. After the victory at Wolc, due in no small part to her newfound abilities and memories, she'd realized at the very least that she could make a difference for the soldiers under her command. Losses were to be expected, but as a commander, the ability to protect and lead her troopers in spite of the chaos and bureaucracy around them was enough to keep her in uniform. She depressed the transmit switch again. "Three, two, one, engine start."

Mairin felt the thrum of the Slammer magtank's turbine engines come to life from the hull. Around her, the seven other tanks in her makeshift troop started simultaneously in an attempt to mask the number of vehicles under her command. Her unit was the Division Cavalry Troop for the 56th Armored Division, Terran Defense Forces, and her mission was simple: screen the main effort's route of march and provide forward reconnaissance. The Fighting 56th marched toward Springfield, a human colony that had reported an overwhelming Grey attack six days before and had been radio silent ever since. Had the planet been scorched to embers, the outcome of the colony would have been known. The Greys seldom left a planet unscathed, and yet Radin's lush grasslands and rolling hills appeared none the worse for wear as they surrounded the wrecked, smoldering colony.

Orbital intelligence couldn't confirm the presence of a Grey "jack," the tetrahedral shaped carrier used to drop armored forces, but there were more than five hundred vehicles in defensive positions on the ground above Springfield. From her location screening the western flank of the attack, Mairin lowered her binoculars and frowned. Visual confirmation of anything other than the Grey division encircling the compromised township had proved fruitless. Her cavalry protected the main effort's advance and provided what reconnaissance they could, but without seeing anything in the gentle, wooded hills above Springfield, there was nothing she could do to calm the gnawing, twisting feeling in her stomach.

The sensation was familiar enough. Ever since her imprint procedure, the prospect of combat operations triggered a fierce reaction—a combination of feeling hyper-alert and focused, while physically charged enough to sprint up Mount Everest. Adrenaline prolonged the effect and amplified her ability to think and react faster. For the last four months, she'd experienced the familiar nervousness and exhilaration in advance of combat. The unfamiliar rumbling in her stomach wasn't hunger, nor sickness, which bothered her.

What are you trying to tell me, Grandpa?

Technically, the memory imprint came from her maternal great-great-grandfather, but she shortened the moniker to keep it simple. Of course, the imprint never really spoke in a voice she could audibly hear, but it manifested in her mind. Most of her direct interactions with it were unconscious triggers of soothing memories, experiences, or strange sensations focused on adjusting her instincts. Her stomach soured more while she watched the division massing to attack.

"All Renegade elements, this is Durango Six Actual, your orders are to attack the Greys and drive them out of Springfield. Retake the town, search for survivors and all items of interest. Report all intelligence requirements. Good hunting."

Mairin felt her gut twist again. Durango Six was an odd callsign for a German Brigadier General. As much as it reminded her of General Talvio, her regular commander and his penchant for cowboy-isms and 19th century American frontier demeanor, Mairin knew that her presence on General Steinhauer's flank was partly her own damned fault. Since dropping her cavalry on the hair-brained orders of her battalion commander at Wolc, her forces had gained both notoriety and success. When Steinhauer decided to liberate Springfield, he called Talvio and asked for the cavalry to guard his flank. Talvio had been happy to assist. Mairin wondered if the two men were friends and decided against it. General officers, from what she'd seen, only seemed to look out for themselves. The reality was more that Talvio realized that her immediate commander, Lieutenant Colonel Bob Coffey, was an idiot who couldn't find his ass with both hands and a map. If he didn't give Mairin a break from her commander, they'd end up in a mess the TDF would solve by relieving the entire chain of command, Talvio included. Her vacation from Coffey appeared to be an even bigger shit storm of a combat operation.

"Durango Six, this is Gaucho Six, crossing phase line Lincoln, time now." Mairin glanced at the pilot's kneeboard she'd strapped to her right thigh. Gaucho Six was the lead battalion in the coordinated attack. Mairin stood up on her seat and climbed to the top of the track for a look around.

Mairin raised binoculars to her eyes and swept the hills above Springfield one more time. Seeing nothing, she lowered herself through the hatch and into the tank. Her feet found the seat below and she dropped neatly into a sitting position, cueing her intercom as she did.

"Crew report."

"Gunner ready," Lee replied from his position immediately in front of her knees.

"Comms ready," Conner replied from across the wide breech of the auto-loading electromagnetic rail gun that dominated the inside of the turret.

"Driver ready," Booker replied from his position in the hull.

Satisfied her crew was ready, Mairin touched the intercom button again. "Gunner, index sabot and arm all weapons."

"Sabot indexed, sabot loaded," Lee replied. "Master Arm is armed."

Like clockwork.

She pushed the transmit button in the opposite direction. "Saber elements, this is Six. Main effort is hitting the objective in about two minutes. Get ready to advance the screen at my command."

The company of eight tanks chimed in one by one as Mairin powered up her command and control console and saw the icons of the main effort now forward of the small creek they'd named Lincoln and racing toward the Greys' defensive perimeter. Through the deep thrumming of the tank's repulsors and engine, Mairin felt concussive waves from artillery shells falling on the Greys' position. With a glance, she confirmed that Gaucho Six, Lieutenant Colonel Maurice Davis of the 2nd Tank Battalion, was in contact with the Greys, and massed friendly artillery fire slashed through the defensive lines.

"Driver, move out. Steering cues are active."

"Yes, ma'am. I've got good steering," Booker replied. "Gear three selected."

Mairin tapped her console and sent the move out command silently to her vehicles. All eight icons representing her troop turned green on her tiny screen and moved south, paralleling the attack. Eyes on the battle to her right, Mairin couldn't help but look into the hills over and over again, each time her stomach twisting on itself.

They have the high ground, I get that. What are you trying to tell me?

Mairin connected her helmet's communications platform to the operations network and heard the command to lift and shift artillery fire from the massed point. Immediately after that call, she heard the 2nd Battalion commander's deep drawl again.

"Durango Six, this is Gaucho Six. Avalanche. I say again, avalanche."

Mairin gasped. The attack had breached the Grey perimeter, and the little bastards were in full-fledged retreat. Her stomach folded itself in two and then two again. She reached up to close her hatch and paused. Without thinking, Mairin stood again on her seat and stared into the hills. The three closest hilltops to Springfield held her gaze for twenty seconds.

What are you doing, Mairin? There's nothing—

A bright flash at the top of the central hilltop stopped the thought cold. The intense purplish burst was a Grey particle cannon. Mairin stabbed the transmit button.

"Durango Six, this is Saber Six, Papa Kilo on the high ground!"

No sooner had the words came from her mouth, than the entire central hilltop and downslope facing Springfield erupted in a hail of inbound laser and direct munitions fire. The TDF attack stalled in a matter of seconds under the fusillade of enemy fire. The Grey vehicles in retreat stopped and fired into the forward battalion, scattering the tanks into the tight corridors and thoroughfares of Springfield.

The concealed Grey strongpoint had been there all along, waiting for the attack. Once again, intelligence failed them. *How many times is it going to be this way?* Mairin dropped into the tank and zoomed her display in on Gaucho Six and engaged a direct laser link.

"Gaucho Six, Saber Six. Shift artillery to cover your move. I'm on my way." She disengaged the laser and found the operations network again, but she hesitated. There were only two options. The main effort would counterattack through the strongpoint, or they would retreat. In either case, Mairin knew she had to move the screen forward and maybe even draw fire from the strongpoint to protect Gaucho Six and allow them to move.

"Saber Six, Gaucho Six. Comms lost to Durango Six. CAS is negative on this position. We're cut off—"

Mairin popped up through the hatch one more time and realized the main effort had not only stopped but pulled back beyond Phase Line Lincoln, leaving Davis and his battalion cut off inside what had been Springfield and under slowing, but intense fire. As she watched, particle cannons fired down from the adjacent hilltops. Springfield lay surrounded on three sides, and the forward tank battalion was pinned down and unable to move without risking severe casualties. The operations network was eerily silent, and the main effort sat motionless outside the maximum effective range of the Grey weapons. Stymied.

Worthless.

Afraid.

The trap perfectly executed; the Greys could hold off the main effort at will. They knew human weaknesses to the letter. The enemy had all that they needed to take the field—all it took was time. The TDF wouldn't attack and risk further casualties. They would retreat from an unwinnable situation. Her stomach settled and an intense calm washed over her as the word floated from her ancestor's imprinted memories and into her mind.

A honeypot.

Sonuvabitch.

* * *

The silence broke, and Mairin heard Lieutenant Alex Ulson's voice in her ears. "Six, this is Red One. We have good terrain to the southwest. Should get us closer to Springfield without exposing us. Permission to recon forward a bit?"

Mairin nodded. "Granted, Alex. Stay in visual range of Red Two and stay ready to backtrack as fast as you can. Stay behind the high ground to our three o'clock."

"Copy all, Six. Permission to dismount and get closer?"

Mairin shook her head. "No, Alex. Stay on your track."

I'm not risking you out there, she finished silently.

Ulson didn't immediately reply. Mairin knew what he was thinking, and she really couldn't blame him. Scouts pushed forward in search of information to detail an enemy's position and strength. As the supporting cavalry to the main effort, reconnaissance was a part of their job, but not within Steinhauer's construct. Mairin's orders were simply to protect the western flank and ensure that more Grey forces didn't surprise them.

Nobody's coming.

Mairin blinked and shook off the thought. Leaning forward, she pressed her eyes to the extension of the gunner's sight and saw what Lee saw as he connected the main gun's sighting system to one of the Condor autonomous vehicles overhead. Mairin saw her position clearly, but there was good enough terrain to hide her cavalry until the time came to move. She watched Ulson's tank creeping forward. His tank's gun tube pointed off to the southeast, down a likely enemy avenue of approach through a quiet, wide valley. The idyllic scene, complete with a meandering stream widening in the distance, seemed out of place with the carnage in Springfield. In every operation she'd seen with the Terran Defense Forces, the shadowy enemy used lower terrain for either an attack corridor or a way to retreat off the battlefield. They protected such avenues vigorously and never dug into defensive positions along the high ground. Their very threat was predicated on rapid shifting, unified movement in the attack. Defensive positions were only for what the intel pukes called tactical pauses.

They aren't moving, and they're not going to.

Mairin snorted. *There's only one way to find out, Grandpa.*

"Red One, this is Six. Stay where you are. Let us catch up to you. Break," Mairin released the transmit switch and pressed it again a moment later. "Guidons, this is Six. Move out, staggered line formation. We're pushing the screen farther forward."

No sooner had her tank lurched forward than Mairin heard Steinhauer's voice in her ears. A glance at the commander's information console told her it was a private laser connection. At least she hadn't pissed him off enough to make an example of her on the wider network.

"Captain Shields? What are your intentions?"

Mairin crouched on her seat and poked her head above the ring of her independently rotatable turret. She swung her machine gun to a firing position that guarded the extreme eastern flank as the column pushed forward. "Sir, I'm moving the screen line forward. The immediate valley to my left is not what the Greys are interested in holding."

There was a span of three seconds before the general replied. "I'm trusting you, Shields."

His tone was obvious. He didn't trust her and the cavalry at all, and here she was moving her combat forces closer to the enemy position while they surrounded the stranded forward element. "We're not poking the nest with a stick, sir."

Steinhauer actually chuckled. "Point taken. What are you looking for?"

"The point where they engage us or if we can see how they got there in the first place. Nothing seems out of place up here, sir. The Greys either came into those positions from the rear and did a spectacular job of camouflaging their infiltration or—"

"Or they've been there all along. Days. Maybe months." Steinhauer sighed, and Mairin could almost hear the thoughts circling through his mind. "Springfield is the largest human colony on this planet. What would they want in sequestering it like this?"

Mairin shook her head and didn't answer. There was nothing more dangerous than a second lieutenant with a map or a general officer asking a rhetorical question. Intelligence officers loved answering that type of questions—combat leaders knew better. As the silence dragged on, Mairin considered pushing the transmit button. The terrain around Ulson and the other lead tank erupted in a flurry of small bomblet detonations.

"Shellrep, sir. Enemy bomblets. They're ineffective." Mairin watched the vehicle condition indicators for her tanks stay green even as they reported multiple impacts. She dropped fully into the tank and slammed the hatch closed above her as the mortar shells continued falling. In a heartbeat, the sporadic firing grew in intensity until it sounded like someone throwing shovel after shovel of gravel at a tin roof. Still, the vehicle indicators remained green.

They're harassing you. Seeing if they can make you stop.

Conner piped up. "Ma'am? Laser comms are down. We're UHF only."

"Copy."

"Line of sight is obscured," her gunner said. "Driver, back off the gas."

"Roger," Booker replied, and the tank slowed more than half its original speed. "I have radar visual on all our tanks."

Mairin glanced at the display. The long curve of the hill to their west slowly dropped toward the valley floor. Their cover would be gone in a matter of moments. When it was gone, the Greys would stop lobbing bomblets and engage with direct fire. "Red One, this is Six. Stop before you get into the open. We can take up defensive positions once they turn on us and bring the attack down the—"

Bright flashes from the distant hilltops flashed again. "Six, Red One, papa kilo fire on the objective. They're hammering the forward battalion."

Jaw clenched in sudden anger, Mairin fought the urge to punch the turret wall. *They've got the advantage in the defense. If we had coordinated artillery and air support...*

She let the thought trail off as a memory floated up quickly. A classroom. A man in the dark green camouflage of the Army of the 1980s stood at a lectern. On the wall was a screen and a crude graphic of an attack.

"This is what the Russians would face if they came through the Fulda Gap, people. A steadfast defensive position, though, isn't enough. If they can't gain superiority in the artillery fight or the airspace, they'll stall, and we'll pick them off one unit at a time."

Good God.

Mairin stabbed the transmit button. "Guidons, full stop. Back up one hundred meters and coil. Move!"

Her tank slammed to a stop, and Mairin almost bounced off the commander's display. As her vehicle shot backward, she watched Conner snap to his rear-facing vision block to guide the driver. In less than thirty seconds, the eight tanks sat in a loose circle with their gun tubes pointing outward for full security. The bomblet rounds stopped immediately.

You realize your bomblets aren't effective, but we've stopped. You want to see what we do next.

Noted.

Mairin frowned and shook her head. The Greys had the advantage of the high ground and excellent fields of fire. They could harass anything in the valley. That meant two options. Artillery and aviation. Steinhauer was a proponent of mechanized forces in the attack and a staunch opponent of Fleet aviation. He had twisted the words of the politicians to describe it as a combat disabler on more than one occasion. His relationship with artillery was warmer by comparison, but he believed that artillery was only as good as the maneuver forces that employed it.

That's my in.

With three quick taps on the command screen, she saw the main effort reconstituting for a counterattack. There were two options for her forces after the broken screen. The Greys knew she was there, and they harassed her enough to believe that her rearward movement was indicative of a full retreat. They were wrong, and she could either sit and support the main effort or she could press forward and attack. Either way, she could leverage the regimental artillery by acting as a forward support observer team in name only. The cannon-cockers knew where the enemy was and what to fire on them. All

Mairin had to do was give Steinhauer an excuse to let them loose, but under her control.

"Laser is up."

"Get me Durango Six Actual."

"Button two UHF. He's calling you." Conner smiled. Over the crew intercom, she could hear her entire crew trying not to laugh.

"These things always go well, huh?" She laughed. "Just don't record this one, Conner. Got it?"

"It's SOP not to, ma'am. You tend to be more colorful when you know the CRD is off."

The crew recording device was a combat record for the vehicle that was supposedly incapable of being disabled. Conner had done it within minutes of their drop on Wolc a month before. A quick "hippocket" class with the rest of the unit had fixed all five vehicles.

Mairin winked at the young communications specialist. As she touched the transmit button, her smiled faded, and the cold, calculating part of her mind took over.

"Sir, request permission to act as a fire support team," Mairin said. "I think I've got a way to skin this cat."

Steinhauer's response was immediate. In the background, she heard a cacophony of shouted commands and intense fire. "We're withdrawing by fire, Shields. Prepare to displace and return to Assembly Area Baltimore."

What? You're not massing to attack?

Instead, Mairin asked "Sir, say again? We're retreating?"

"We are withdrawing by fire, Shields."

"There's no difference between them, sir. All you're doing is lobbing a few rounds over your rear decks to make it look like you're firing." Mairin seethed and instead of listening to that quiet part of

414 | IBSON & KENNEDY

her brain that told her to follow orders and do what she was told, she cut loose. "There's a forward battalion cut off up there and who knows how many civilians! Now stop the retreat, give me command of the artillery, and get your forces into the fight!"

"One more word, and I'll relieve you, Shields! How dare you accuse me of—"

The connection dissolved in a burst of static, and Mairin snapped her eyes to Conner. "Get him back."

"I can't. Termination at the receiving end. No connection."

Mairin looked back at the commander's display. In the center of the main effort's formation, exactly where the command group should have been, were a half dozen flashing black icons. The operations network was a frantic mess of reports of particle cannon fire at a much farther range than ever observed before. A central cannon picked off targets seemingly at will. The remainder of the regiment was in full, unorganized retreat.

"All Durango elements, this is Sierra Five. Apocalypse. I say again. Apocalypse. I have assumed command of the field. Pull back to Baltimore and reconstitute. I say again—"

Apocalypse? The whole goddamned mission failed?

Again, the connection terminated in a burst of static. Mairin looked at Conner. "They're targeting UHF! Emergency laser traffic—flash it at every unit you can and order them to relay it, Conner. Do it."

"That means that—"

"Yes!" Mairin yelled. "It means we'll be radio silent. If we don't, the Greys are going to kill off every goddamned vehicle that tries to take command of the situation. That includes us!"

WE DARE | 415

"Roger, emergency laser engaged." Conner said. "Radio silence, all units. Greys targeting UHF. Relay to all by type. Reconstitute at Baltimore. I'm repeating it."

Mairin listened to the operations network grow silent. In a matter of thirty seconds, there wasn't a human voice on the frequency.

That's one problem solved.

Mairin pushed her laser connection to Ulson. "Alex?"

"What the hell, ma'am? They've figured out UHF comms?"

Mairin nodded to herself. "Direction finding of radio transmissions isn't that hard to do, Alex. We've done it on the battlefield for a few hundred years, but not quite as effectively as the Greys just did. They've simply never targeted it before."

"No kidding." Ulson replied. "What do you want to do?"

"We've got the main effort in retreat to Baltimore. That leaves us and the trapped battalion in Springfield." Mairin replied. "We don't know what's still there and without UHF the likelihood of getting a laser fix on Gaucho Six from this position is somewhere between slim and none."

"Which brings me back to my question, ma'am."

"Two options." She forced herself to take a deep breath. "Retreat and cut the main losses or find a way to get our people out of Springfield."

"I'm for Option B," Ulson said. "But we can't do it by ourselves."

"You're thinking what I'm thinking then," Mairin said. Looking at their position, the idea came about quickly. "Okay, here's what we're going to do. Move your tank out of this position and back to the north about two hundred meters. You should be able to get a direct laser on the artillery battalion on the north side of Lincoln."

"Roger. I see what you're suggesting. What do I tell them?"

"Give them a fire for effect order on the central gun."

"How will they know how to hit it?" Ulson paused. "They'll need targetable coord...oh."

"Yeah, I'm going forward to target it, but you're going to have to broadcast UHF, Alex. That way I can track it and they can kill it. If you broadcast as you move this direction, maybe just before you reach the high ground, they might not be able to target you."

There wasn't a response for a minute. "What's our other option, ma'am?"

"Air support, but that means UHF, too."

Or does it?

"Standby, ma'am." Ulson dropped off the frequency for fifteen seconds. "Ma'am? I've got a drop ship twenty kilometers to the north. I can have them broadcast on UHF. They've got a much better chance to get to cover, and we can bring in the artillery on the particle cannon."

Mairin nodded, impressed. "That's the second problem covered. But we're going to have to have more than artillery to make this work. We're going to need close air support. We're going to have to get the exospheric pilots down here to do some business."

"They won't like that, ma'am." Ulson sighed. "I wish the Lancers were here."

"That makes two of us, Alex." Mairin replied. "Switching to Ka band. You have command until I talk the Fleet out of staying in orbit again."

"Good luck with that, ma'am." Ulson clicked off, and the laser connection terminated.

"Ka is up, ma'am. I have the *Sapporo* overhead. The window is six minutes and thirty seconds."

Mairin tapped her screen and found the callsign list. The *Fleet Battle Platform Sapporo's* flag officer was a rarity among the Fleet—a pilot who actually flew more missions inside atmosphere than out during his flying days. If there was a single ray of hope for Gaucho Six and the civilians trapped in Springfield, he was it.

Mairin scrolled through the callsign list with her finger and found it easily. "Katana Six Actual, this is Saber Six in command of cavalry forces on the surface and declaring an emergency. I say again, Katana Six Actual, this is Saber Six in command of forces on the surface and declaring an emergency. I need close air support vectored on my position. Acknowledge. Over."

"Saber Six, this is Tanto Six, all communications for this vessel and its occupants are handled through the command bridge, and you are in violation of—"

The connection terminated in a heartbeat leaving dead, silent air on the transmission. "Saber Six, this is Katana Six Actual. What do you need? Over."

Admiral Kamagawa's voice was quiet and measured. She'd never spoken to him or any other fleet officers of significant rank, and for a split second, her stomach rolled inward on itself and a fleeting, terrifying thought crossed her mind that she'd really screwed up in calling him before she recognized that she was talking.

"Katana Six, this is Captain Mairin Shields in command of TDF cavalry forces to the southeast of the area of operations. The main attack has stalled, and the TDF is in retreat. There is a battalion-sized element of armor trapped in Springfield. The Greys have set up a honeypot complete with multiple particle cannons on the high ground. I can't determine how many there are in the higher terrain, and I can't get in and get that battalion out without air support." She took a breath. "Sooner is better than later. I think we can break them, over."

"You think you can rescue the battalion and defeat an enemy dug in on the high ground with superior weapons?"

The question was a quiet challenge. Mairin stabbed the transmit button. "Affirmative, Katana Six, but only with coordinated air and artillery strikes in support of the main effort."

"You have command of the artillery forces on the ground?"

Mairin bit her lip and trusted Alex to do what she'd asked. "Affirmative, sir. They're preparing to emplace the guns now. Though some orbital artillery wouldn't hurt in this situation."

"You are danger close for nuclear strike, Captain Shields, and the civilians trapped in Springfield would suffer needlessly. I will not have that."

There was something in the man's voice, something she knew was not a familiarity with the subject but a pained recognition of what she was asking. She took a breath. "I'm not asking for a nuke, sir. I'm asking for non-nuclear munitions. I know the *Sapporo* and the other platforms have the capability. If you have them, I'd really like them employed on the Grey positions."

"The concussive forces are potentially too dangerous for unprotected civilians," the admiral replied but she could hear doubt in his voice. Mitigating risk was the hardest part of a commander's work, and it never ended.

"Sir, the Greys have laid siege to Springfield. If we want anyone alive there, TDF forces or not, we have to act now. We'll do what we can to alert Springfield."

Kamagawa replied but Mairin wasn't listening. On her display, the enemy situation updated, and a slew of red triangular icons descended from the western defensive position and into Springfield itself.

"Katana Six, the Greys are counterattacking Springfield. If you can support us, please send it now. Saber Six, out."

No sooner had the connection ended than Alex Ulson's voice was in her ears. "Ma'am? I talked to the artillery commander."

"What did he have to say?"

"There's good news and bad news, just like always."

Mairin smirked. "How bad is the bad?"

"You're not going to like this at all." Ulson paused for a moment. "Relaying graphics to you now."

Mairin shook her head and realized that Conner stared at her, his mouth agape. "What is it, Conner?"

"You just 'out-ed' an admiral, ma'am."

"So?" Mairin smiled. "Sometimes a breach of radio procedure is enough to get the point across, Conner."

God, please let me be right about this.

* * *

Mairin studied the display for half a minute following Ulson's report. The artillery managed to find a covered position where the particle cannons wouldn't be able to immediately target them. That was the good news. The bad news was that only one battery had more than fifty percent of their remaining rounds to fire. Collectively, they were at thirty-one percent combat effectiveness and while they hustled to redistribute rounds and fuses, they wouldn't be able to keep up any type of suppressing fires for very long.

There had been no additional communications from Kamigawa, either. As much as Mairin wanted to believe the quiet admiral with a reputed spine of steel would help them, the most precious resource on Mairin's side, time, passed quickly.

"Ma'am?" Conner blurted. "I've got Ka coming in calling for you."

Mairin made a "give it" gesture with her left hand. A deep male voice with a very African accent called, "Saber Six, this is Storm Eye One, over."

"Storm Eye One, Saber Six. What's your traffic?"

The voice came back a moment later. "Storm Eye One has two sections of three Vindicators loaded for close air support operations moving your direction. We are fifty thousand meters above you, bearing of zero niner zero from your position and descending to a low-level initial point. We're coming in nap of the earth and as fast as we can. Primary target is Grey forces in Springfield."

"What about the particle cannons?" Mairin blurted without touching the transmit button. *Don't they get it?*

"Saber Six, this is Katana Six Actual. Relay special instructions to Gaucho Six elements in Springfield any way you can. Hammers deployed. I say again, hammers have been deployed. Three shots. One for each hilltop. ETA is two hundred seconds. Once they've hit, you have command of the mission. Secure Springfield, Captain Shields."

"Yes, sir," Mairin said. "Breaking for Storm Eye One."

Holy fuck! He did it!

"We are with you, Saber. ETA is four minutes." The man's voice was as quiet and confident as Kamigawa's, but vastly different. "Relaying expected attack plans to you now."

Mairin tried not to grin. "How many passes do I have you for, Storm Eye?"

"One, Saber. We have instructions to hit the targets and resume an intercept mission in the event a Jack appears."

One pass; haul ass. Got it.

Mairin nodded to herself. Fair enough. "Copy, Storm Eye One, welcome to the party."

"It's only a party with proper fireworks, Saber Six. Approaching initial point, going UHF silent. ETA is three minutes forty-two seconds. Mark. Storm Eye One, out."

Mairin checked the updated commander's display. "Interface, update the mission timers."

<<Acknowledged. Timers are active. Red One has a laser lock on Gaucho Six.>>

"Get me the attack profiles from those Vindicators as soon as they're close enough."

<<Acknowledged. Estimate data receipt at the ten nautical mile initial point.>>

"Just get it when you can," Mairin replied. Smart systems never seemed to be all that smart when built by the lowest bidder.

Mairin swiped the icon for Ulson's tank and opened a type window. With his laser engaged on Gaucho Six, he wouldn't be able to hear her. Instead, she typed.

Alex. Tell them Hammers are deployed. Less than three minutes. Once they hit, we're on the attack.

A moment later the window blinked. *Roger, Gaucho Six wants to know what's a hammer?*

* * *

"Say again, Saber One?" Lieutenant Colonel Maurice Davis shook his head as he hit the send button. *The* Sapporo *dropped a non-nuclear, kinetic weapon on the Grey cannons? I didn't even know we had those things.*

The reply appeared on his screen. "Roger, sir. Three projectiles are inbound from orbit. Arrival in two minutes, fifty-five seconds. Once they hit, and you ride out the shockwave, be ready to move. There are two companies of Grey tanks about four hundred meters from your position on the attack. They're coming up a creek bed."

Davis looked at his flickering command display. The enemy icons weren't there, nor were any of the data for his vehicles and crews trapped in Springfield, but he could see the terrain well enough via the topographical map display. The Greys wanted to use the lower ground for ease of movement. They wanted to move fast, but they could easily be stopped. All he had to do was figure out how many vehicles were left, if they could fight, and how much ammunition they had.

Piece of cake.

"Okay, Saber One. Copy all. Our heads are down. When the shockwaves pass, we'll come up screaming. Gaucho Six, out."

"Saber One, laser disengaged."

Davis disengaged the transmission and spoke aloud in the turret. "Interface? Status update?"

<<Negative communications in all bands. Laser comms with Gaucho Seven have not been restored.>>

I knew I shouldn't have let him get out on foot.

Command Sergeant Major Benan Mashali was one of the best non-commissioned officers Davis had ever known. Tough in a fight and a class act in garrison, Mashali took an old soldier's creed to heart. He wanted to ensure that his troops were informed and ready. He also wanted to make sure they followed their commander's orders. With that in mind, the young Turkish sergeant major had dismounted his magtank and crept through the shattered avenues of Springfield looking for survivors. Alone.

"Find him. Anything but UHF. Relay that across the battalion." Davis glanced across the turret at Sergeant Stratmann. The young kid held his broken right arm across his chest. Blood trickled down the right side of the communications specialist's face. He'd been unable to fire the auxiliary deck gun from his hatch, and operating the comm panels took him far longer than normal. He'd been right-handed, to boot.

<<I have located Gaucho Seven. He is currently with White Three. Bearing three zero one at one hundred and eighty meters.>>

"Laser lock on White Three."

<<Unable. Debris.>>

"Then how in the hell can you tell he's at White Three?" Davis shook his head, exasperated. The Interface was a great improvement for command and control systems, even if most of it was PFM. Pure Fucking Magic.

<<White Three is in communication with Green Two.>>

And we have line of sight to Green 2.

"Can we talk real time or just via transfer?"

<<Transfer only. That is not a recommended course of action.>>

Tell me something I don't know.

Davis sat forward. "Emergency text to Green Two. Have Gaucho Seven move to Green Two and connect via external comms. I need to talk to him ASAP."

<<Standby. Message sent.>> The Interface went silent and returned five seconds later. <<Message received. Gaucho Seven en route to Green Two. ETA is one minute forty seconds.>>

Davis glanced at his malfunctioning display and frowned. Even the clocks were damaged beyond repair. There was no way he'd know when Mashali would get there and—

"Gaucho Six, this is Seven."

"I need you back on your track. Fleet has dropped kinetic weapons from orbit. ETA is any second now."

There wasn't an immediate response.

"Benan?"

"I'm here, sir. I can't make my track in that time."

Davis felt his heart jump. "Then climb aboard Green Two. Ride this thing out from there and—"

"No time, sir." Mashali snorted. "Been an honor."

"What are you doing, Sergeant Major?"

"How close is the air support? Fleet wouldn't have tasked a kinetic drop without some kind of air support even for a BDA. That's your best chance to get the battalion out of here." Battle damage assessment, a frivolous measurement of combat efficiency reserved for staff pukes and rear echelon motherfuckers, was about the only reason the Fleet would support the Terran Defense Forces in combat operations anymore. The days of combined arms warfare had lost out to the concept of finite control—when a general had a specific set of playing pieces and didn't want or ask for help from anyone else lest it show weakness. The whole bureaucratic bullshit made Davis, and thousands of other commanders, want to vomit.

"My clocks are all FUBAR, Benan." Davis replied, his voice thick with emotion. "I can't tell how much time you have."

"Doesn't matter, sir. Was a pleasure serving with you." There was a high-pitched whistle in the transmission that sounded almost like feedback, but Davis knew it wasn't. He didn't need a clock, or a microphone to know what was coming.

"Alpha Mike Foxtrot, Benan." Davis said and terminated the connection. He looked at Stratmann and pushed the intercom switch. "Crew, brace for impact!"

Davis reached for the hand hold mounted along the turret wall with his right hand. His hand never made it before the ground lurched in six directions at once. His helmet bounced off his sight extension hard enough that he saw stars as the shockwave roared over them like a tsunami.

* * *

Mairin tried to see the tungsten rods fall through the sky, but there wasn't anything to see. One moment, the three Grey particle cannons were firing at targets within Springfield, their purple particle beams vibrant and clear against the dark green vegetation. In the blink of an eye, the three hilltops erupted in simultaneous geysers of earth and foliage. Shockwaves raced down the hills and tore through the town. High ground between her position and the impacts took some of the brunt away, but the shockwave was enough to buffet her Slammer so much that repulsor overheat warnings rang out like the tolling of funeral bells.

The tank slid backward and listed hard to the left as the blast wind rushed over them.

No more than five seconds after the impacts, the shockwave barreled through her tanks and shot down the valley behind them. Mairin tapped the intercom switch on her helmet. "Crew report and vehicle status."

"Gunner, all systems nominal."

"Comms, working on available channels. Laser is down."

"Driver, repulsors heating, but shutters are closed."

Unlike the dust that choked her ancestor's tank filters in the deserts of southwest Asia, the Slammer came equipped with shutters that covered and protected the facings of the filters themselves. They'd be okay if the Slammer could move forward and get increased air into the repulsor systems. The longer they stayed immobile, the greater the threat.

Mairin looked at the wide-eyed face of Specialist Conners. "Give me everything, Conner. UHF, VHF, whatever we have."

"Yes, ma'am."

Outside, the massive cloud of debris, rock, and dust blotted out Radin's sun and wispy high clouds. There was nothing to see in any direction more than a hundred meters or so away. She used the independent camera view to swing around. Her tanks were all there, but two of them listed badly on their repulsors and threatened to ground themselves.

Dammit.

"You're up, ma'am."

We'll see if we can talk, I guess.

And then fight.

Yeah, Grandpa. We'll fight. First things first.

"Guidons, this is Six. Vehicle status?"

Ulson answered immediately. The connection was strong, despite the exceptionally polluted air. "Ma'am, Red 3 and White 2 are down. Everyone else is okay, repulsors are running hot, but we're ready to fight. Over."

"Copy, Red One. Move out. I say again, move out. Line abreast once we clear the end of the valley. Red 3 and White 2, ground your tanks back to back and maintain security and comms." Mairin glanced at her combat display. The Grey armored column continued to march toward Springfield. "The Greys are still coming, folks. Red One, take us out. Weapons free and good hunting."

The Slammer moved forward effortlessly. Booker adjusted the repulsors, and the tank glided more than a meter above the terrain at fifteen kilometers per hour. Mairin tapped her display and keyed a relay of the driver's radar display system to her console. Everything appeared to be working as advertised. Booker once told her that the system was good enough that he could see everything inside of a black hole. It appeared the young man was right.

The valley opening yawned ahead. She saw Red One take up the left edge of the line abreast. Red Two and Red Four joined him. Booker took her tank into the center of the formation and the White elements formed on her right side. Mairin tapped the display and found a private UHF channel for White 4, First Sergeant Livingston.

"Top, your kids doing okay?"

"Affirm, ma'am. They're too new to really mess up. I've got them and will provide overwatch. Give you and Lieutenant Ulson freedom to maneuver." Livingston's lilting Jamaican accent belied any nervousness he felt. Mairin knew from experience the man was even better than his word.

"Roger, Top. Stay ready to fight."

"Always, ma'am," Livingston said. "Are we doing the right thing?"

The question surprised her, both in its timing and in the hesitation she heard in Livingston's voice. He'd been rock solid on Wolc and in every single interaction they'd had.

"What do you mean, Top?"

"Going after that stranded battalion without the main effort?" Livingston asked. "We don't owe them anything, and finite control says we handle our mission and let the higher commander—"

"No," Mairin interrupted. Livingston fell silent. "I don't give a damn about finite control, Top. What matters is that our friends are trapped inside Springfield. They matter. The higher ups use finite control as a way to accept defeat. We don't. We're not going to quit on this mission, and we're damned sure not going to let any more of our brothers and sisters die in there for no reason. We take it to the Greys, and if we die trying to get them out, so be it. I would want someone to be willing to risk their ass for me like I'm willing to do for them. No one else is going to."

There was silence for a moment, and then Livingston responded. "Then we sound the charge, ma'am."

Damned right we do.

Mairin watched the display—Red One appeared to fade in and out with the wafts of thicker debris. "Red One, watch your—"

"Contact, front left!" Ulson reported on the troop main frequency. In cue with his report, Mairin saw Red One's main gun chuff out a round. The vehicle suddenly swung hard left. The radar confirmed a large rock formation Mairin recognized from the drone reconnaissance feed. They were on the outskirts of Springfield and really deep in the shit.

Cover. We need cover.

Mairin stabbed the troop frequency. "Guidons, break left behind those rocks. Red One, push all the way to the end of the formation and secure that side of the objective. White elements follow me and prepare to hold this side of the formation. Move!"

Ulson's section raced into the clouds and disappeared. Booker steered her tank into the area behind cover and drove forward enough that the White section could enter and get cover before slowing. Mairin was already on the button. "Top, pivot your section and prepare to support by fire."

"Copy."

There was a harsh burst of static in her helmet, and Mairin flinched. She looked at the commander's display and saw all of her vehicles were still online. Whoever was trying to transmit was on the division frequency. There was something there, but she couldn't hear it or make sense of it.

"Clean that up!" Mairin stared at Conner who almost leapt back to his communications controls. Five seconds later, Mairin could make out the voice and it brought a smile to her face.

"Saber Six, this is Redleg Six. I have radar feed from the Condor and am targeting the Grey armored column. More than ninety targets moving your direction. Permission to fire? Over."

"Redleg Six, Saber Six. Fire for effect. Give me everything you've got."

Here we go, you little bastards. See how you like being fish in a barrel.

Mairin glanced at the tactical display. There was one more ace up her sleeve, and it was time to play it.

"Storm Eye One, Saber Six. Have a ball on the tee and ready for a game. You in?"

"I never liked golf, Saber Six. But for you, we'll be on station in one hundred twenty seconds."

"I have artillery inbound, Storm Eye One."

"Good thing we can fly around it, Saber Six. Standby for danger close support."

"Copy," Mairin said, suddenly nauseous. Eyes mashed closed and fingers tight on the stabilizing handles of her seat, she grunted. "Copy, danger close."

* * *

T he memory was clear, but fast. Familiar, unrelenting heat pressed in on her from all directions as she walked. A platoon of Marine infantry marched ahead of the armored column, and she'd dismounted to talk to their commander face-to-face. Someone screamed, and weapons roared to life. The whoosh of a rocket-propelled grenade split the air above her head. She dove for the sand.

Ambush.

She saw cover, a waist-high concrete wall, ten meters away. Instead of high crawling, Mairin shot to her feet, took three quick steps and flung herself behind the wall next to a young Marine screaming into a radio.

"Whiskey Two One, clear danger close. I say again, clear danger close."

Overhead, a Marine Cobra gunship appeared low and fast over the squat Afghan houses. The folding fin rocket pods came to life, and the entire street erupted.

* * *

"M a'am?"

Mairin blinked. "Yeah?"

"Redleg Six called his shot."

Mairin stabbed the division frequency transmit button. "Shot, out."

"Splash in five seconds, Saber Six. Second battery firing now. Shifting for CAS. Over."

In the swirling debris, fresh explosions tore into the armored force that Mairin could not see with her eyes or the Slammer's thermal targeting system. There was too much interference with the sensors.

You need to see them to hit them, girl.

The second round of artillery slammed into the Grey advance as Mairin tried to see what the Condor could relay. There wasn't much.

"Saber Six, Storm Eye One on station and descending. Keep your heads down. The Greys are still marching."

"Copy," Mairin replied. "Can you relay targeting data, Storm Eye One?"

"Unknown, Saber Six. Once I roll out, I'll see what I can do. Thirty seconds."

But he can at least see the enemy. That's a point in our favor.

"Six, Red One. Some clearing down here. The wind has picked up from the east. I can see almost to Gaucho Six's position."

Mairin startled. *I'd forgotten about them.*

432 | IBSON & KENNEDY

"Comms?"

"Working, ma'am," Conner replied. "Red One has a laser lock on him. They're up and moving."

A millisecond later, her command display updated with information. She could see the charging Grey column clearly, more than fifty vehicles still moving fast toward them. Gaucho Six was there with three tanks.

Charging into the Grey's flank.

Sonuvabitch!

"Six, Red One. On the attack. Covering fire!"

No, no no!

"Red One, hold off. CAS inbound!"

There wasn't a response. On the display, she saw the six Vindicators take up their attack patterns in two three-aircraft formations. Her eyes flitted to the icons for Gaucho Six and Red One. The two formations charged at the Greys from the northern flank and the forward echelon head-on, respectively. If the Greys saw it and stopped, they'd be sitting ducks for the Vindicators.

<<Storm Eye One has reached their initial point. Six nautical miles from target. Mission data link integrated.>>

Mairin reached for the transmit button and hovered her fingers over the radio controls. Where her stomach had twisted and turned on itself was an ethereal calm.

Wait.

Just wait.

Mairin sucked in a breath and held it as Storm Eye One rolled in on the Greys, and the two armored columns pressed forward. The Greys stopped and attempted to engage both forces at once.

Her mind calm, a voice not her own sifted up as if she was dreaming. *The window is open, Storm Eye. Punch those fuckers in the throat.*

* * *

Mairin watched the first group of three Vindicators roll in via the commander's display and the mission data link. Two of the aircraft flew line abreast at an altitude so low the system couldn't indicate it with precision, leaving a NULL reading. The third lagged behind the leaders by a couple of kilometers at a slightly higher altitude. Mairin guessed it was for mission analysis or suppression of enemy air defenses, but it ultimately wouldn't matter. If the first two couldn't get in and hit their targets, none of the others would. At the six-nautical mile mark, the two aircraft executed quick banks. Storm Eye One rolled twenty degrees to the left while his wingman rolled thirty degrees to the right, giving them dispersion. Each of the aircraft climbed and immediately, the Greys turned their weapons toward them, but to no immediate effect, as the two aircraft paralleled each other toward the Grey position.

"Interface, how fast are the Vindicators going?"

<<Five hundred knots. They are set up for a long-range toss profile.>>

Mairin watched their distance and time to target populate on the display. Three miles from the target, they rolled over and pulled down toward the target. Storm Eye One's path was straight into the Grey column while his wingman banked hard left to put his nose onto the same column.

<<Hack. Storm Eye One has dropped munitions.>> A second later, the Interface chimed again. <<Hack. Storm Eye Two has dropped munitions.>>

Breath held in her chest, Mairin watched the indicators for weapons track flick on immediately. Both Vindicators executed hard-right turns at full power and raced low over Springfield to the north.

"Saber Six, Storm Eye One is clear."

<<Weapon time of flight is ten seconds.>>

"Saber Six, Gaucho Six. Attack stalled. Need assistance and covering fire."

Hang on, sir. It's almost there.

Mairin studied the attack profiles of the incoming Vindicators and realized that Storm Eye One had given her a wide berth for artillery. The aircraft accelerated low and fast away from the stalled main effort. "Redleg Six, fire mission, same coordinates and effects. Multiple batteries. Over."

"Saber Six, we were hoping you'd say that. Shot, over."

Mairin grinned. "Shot, out."

"Splash in fifteen seconds. Good luck."

We're gonna need it. Mairin watched the Greys' line erupt with multiple explosions as the Vindicator's bombs fell on them. The explosions resounded through the valley, and there were several secondary explosions as well.

"Splash in fifteen. Cleared and switching." Mairin stabbed the comms button. "Red One, charge. Everything you've got. White elements roll out and sweep in from the north. Artillery incoming for cover in ten seconds. Move out!"

"Red One, on the move!" Ulson yelped on the frequency. As one, her tanks charged into the dusty, cloudy terrain with their cannons blazing.

"Saber Six, Storm Eye One. I have targeting data. Can your interface connect?"

Mairin didn't even have to ask. <<Confirmed. Data downloading. Enemy positions updating now.>>

The Grey armored column's positioning data came in in droves. The sixty Grey vehicles remaining were clearly identified. Better yet, Mairin knew that the Interface would feed the positioning information to the gunner and nearly automate the fight. With targets designated, Lee could laze and blaze, as the saying went.

That means your head is in the outside fight, instead of your turret. Mairin blinked. The information came so fast that she barely felt there was time to breathe and yet, her mind was clear and focused.

Get on it, girl.

Mairin nodded to herself. "Driver, move out."

"On it!" Booker replied.

<<Red One has pierced the enemy forward line.>>

"Get me there, Booker. Gear five. Fast as you can make this beast go."

The Slammer shot forward as Mairin stabbed her private channel. "Alex, SITREP."

"Red One, we're charging through Six. Greys are slagging right and left." Ulson replied with a whoop. "Gaucho Six and his tanks are back in the attack now. We've got them!"

<<Next Vindicator section is thirty seconds out and targeting the rear of the Grey formation.>>

Mairin tapped the all frequencies button. "Red One, Gaucho Six, this is Saber Six. Vindicators inbound now. When they engage, tear the Greys a new asshole. Saber Six swinging to Gaucho Six's right flank. Let's sweep the field. Out."

No sooner had she cleared the transmission when the division frequency crackled to life. "Saber Six, Gaucho Six. Thanks for the assist."

"Gaucho Six, we're not out of the woods yet, but I hope you'll do the same for me or someone like me one day." Mairin opened the upper hatch and stood in her seat. Hands on the venerable XM2 machine gun's firing handles, she swung the gun over the front slope of the tank and grasped the handles tightly. The damned thing bucked like a mule and she wanted to make every round count to the extent that she could.

"That's what it's all about, Saber Six." Davis replied. There was a quiet satisfaction in his voice. "That's what we do."

A glint in the swirling clouds above caught her eye and Mairin watched the second section of Vindicators roll in. Lee and the Interface found a new target, slewed the main gun and fired. Ulson and Davis coordinated their attacks and the pilots perfectly executed their mission and raced up into their patrol routes. Mairin heard the Division network come to life and saw a slew of friendly blue icons flicker to life on her display and move toward Springfield. The sudden cacophony of command blanketed her, but she was calm and content both in mind and body. Actions were natural. Decisions were easy. Even with the memories of a man she never knew racing through her mind and the challenge of leading troops when their leaders didn't want to win failed to matter to the joy in her heart. The Greys might have the advantage, but they couldn't dominate the human spirit. Especially hers. Her ancestor knew what it took to win the field, and she knew he was right about the war and her place in it.

Truth be told, there was no place else Mairin Shields wanted to be.

* * * * *

Kevin Ikenberry Bio

Kevin Ikenberry is a life-long space geck and retired Army officer. A former manager of the world-renowned U.S. Space Camp program and a space operations office by, Kevin has a broad background in space and space science education and continues to work with space every day. He is the author of the Peacemaker novels in the bestselling Four Horsemen Universe (*Peacemaker, Honor The Threat, Stand or Fall,* and *Deathangel*) as well as the award-nominated Protocol War series (*Sleeper Protocol* and *Vendetta Protocol.* Kevin's other works include *Runs In The Family, Super-Sync,* and *Chasing Red.* Kevin is an active member of SFWA and International Thriller Writers and lives is Colorado with his family.

* * *

Author Note:

This story takes place in a six-month interlude that appears in the novel Runs In The Family and features that protagonist, Captain Mairin Shields, as we learn how she learns to listen and ultimately trust the memory imprint of her great-great grandfather and the advantages it provides on the far future battlefield.

# # # # #

Angel

by Robert E. Hampson

A shadow moved across the bedroom window, a deeper shade of darkness against the overcast, moonless night outside. It moved to the dresser, resolving into a figure searching for something in the dark—picking and replacing several items before finding the object of the search. Next, it moved to the nightstand, pocketing an object that emitted a single red light—the sole light source in the room other than the pale clock numerals and the faintest of light from the window. It was that nebulous period of time often called "oh-dark-thirty," and the figure seemed to be taking pains to avoid awakening the only other occupant of the room. The shadow stopped at the side of the bed, looking down where a sleeping figure stirred and made a faint sound.

Martin kissed his wife gently on the cheek. Claire brushed a hand in the general direction of her face and pulled the covers nearly over her head with a muffled "mmmpf." He smiled to himself, and having long familiarity with the bedroom, stepped out into the dark hallway, closing the door behind him. With the same silent tread, he slipped into his daughter's bedroom and knelt next to the child's bed. Carefully moving a favorite stuffed rabbit, he kissed Sally on the cheek as well, this time eliciting a sleepy "Daddy." He leaned over and hugged her, then placed Bun-Bun back into her reaching hands. She hugged the toy, turned over, and was back to sleep immediately.

Martin left the room and moved through the house to the garage, all without turning on a light. The duffel was exactly where he had left it the night before, right next to the door into the garage. The garage door was well maintained and opened with little more sound than Martin had made inside. His dark-adapted eyes found the dashboard lights of the car almost too bright; fortunately, he had disabled the interior lights, or he would have to adapt all over again. It was a long drive into San Antonio, and he needed to be there by dawn.

It was a warm night, and he kept the air conditioning off, preferring instead to be able to smell the salt air giving way to the earthy aroma of South Texas ranches. The call-up notice in his pocket indicated that he could expect to be away from home and family for at least six months. There were times he regretted the fact that Claire's job had taken them to Corpus Christie while he still had to report to Joint Base San Antonio for drill and guard weekends. On the other hand, it was Claire's job that paid for the nice house on the inlet, and there was interstate highway the whole way to S.A. The only real problem with the long drive was that it made him introspective, and that was a good way to have an accident.

The taillights ahead had been far in the distance but were getting closer. Was that one set of red lights? Or two? They were getting a *lot* closer, and might be stopped in the middle of the road. Martin slowed down and moved further to the right to pass the vehicle stopped practically in the middle of the left-hand lane. He caught a brief glimpse of two vehicles, an animal carcass in the road, and someone shining a bright flashlight on the mangled front end of one of the cars. It was dangerous to stop in the middle of the road like that. They needed to put out flares, reflectors, or something. Flashing lights ahead signaled the arrival of the highway patrol. The car passed traveling in the opposite direction, and Martin could see it in the rearview mirror as it crossed the median and approached the accident. He looked back ahead just in time to see an animal dart in front of him. Dog? Wolf? Coyote? It didn't matter as his car swerved off the highway at too great a speed.

* * *

"Buddy, are you okay?"

Martin awoke hanging upside down. A bright light was shining in the window. He reached down—no, *up!*—to release his seat belt.

"Hold on, you're gonna fall!" the voice said. The door was pulled open with obvious effort, and a hand reached in to provide support.

"Ugh." Was about all that Martin could manage as he half fell, half crawled out of his car. His head hurt. There was a stinging sensation on his forehead, and a feeling like getting kicked in the belly. He stood—carefully—and looked at the vehicle. It wasn't as bad of some of the shit he'd seen, but it was bad enough; he wouldn't be driving the rest of the way to San Antonio.

"Buddy, y'all might wanna siddown, yer kinda cut up an' bleedin.' Ah called th' nine-one-one, an' they're sendin' an ambulance." The man pronounced it 'amble-lance' marking him as one of the locals, probably a rancher. Now that Martin was out of the car, he could see the other person. Worn blue jeans, checked shirt, but heavy work boots instead of cowboy boots. He was just taking off the pair of heavy leather work gloves he'd used to handle the sharp metal edges of the door. More likely a drill-hand from Eagle Ford. That meant he was just another early morning commuter like himself.

Back down the highway, he could still see flashing lights at the *other* accident. It hadn't been that long, then. "How—wha?'" He tasted blood, and his tongue was swollen. He'd probably bitten it in the accident.

"Ah seen y'all swerve, then head off'n the side'a th' road. Ya rolled three-four times jist as Ah was comin' up. Y'all lucky—don' look as if th' air-bag popped. Coulda' kilt ya!" Martin looked, and sure enough, there was no popped-balloon appearance of airbags, no dust, and no ozone smell. "Look, y'all okay? Ah gotta git ta th' rig. Boss'll dock me if'n Ah'm late." The reflected blue and red light started to move, and there was the sound of a distant siren. "Looks like Trooper's headin' up, he'll take care' y'all."

The man gave a wave, headed back to his pickup truck, and took off before Martin could manage more than a muttered, "Thanks." The highway patrol car's arrival was followed soon after by the county's Rescue Squad, fire truck, and ambulance. Clearly they'd been prepared to have to extract him from the wreckage. It was almost anticlimactic, sitting in the back of the ambulance while the EMT put 'butterfly' wound closures on several cuts. "Sir, please hold still!" the EMT said as Martin kept trying to look past the tech at a Highway Patrol officer talking to the tow-truck driver.

"Don't 'Sir' me." Martin mumbled automatically.

"Sit at attention, Soldier," barked a voice behind him. Martin stiffened at the commanding voice and sat perfectly still, allowing the tech to finish the bandaging. Out of the corner of his eye, he could see the other patrolman. Tall, broad-shouldered, slight thickening at the waist, shaved head under the Smokey-the-Bear hat. He looked like every Drill Sergeant that Martin had ever known. As he walked around into Martin's line of sight, his expression softened a bit. "You're going to need some fresh ACU's before you report, Top."

Definitely a DS, Martin thought as he looked down at his scuffed and bloody uniform. "Yes, sir. Sergeant Major will chew me out, for certain." He would have to get his things from the car before they towed it away. It was why he was fidgeting for the tech to finish.

The officer turned to the tech, "That's a lot of blood, you're sure he doesn't need to go to the hospital?"

"There's no active bleeders," the EMT replied. "You'd think he'd have a concussion or something, but there's no sign of it. Not even a lot of bruising. We'd just send him to San Antonio anyway."

"Officer, I'm due in to Camp Bullis this morning. I'll report in and then head to Med Battalion. They will want to look me over anyway." He looked over at his car, being dragged onto the flat bed of the transport tow truck. "I might need a lift, though."

The officer noticed his glance and then grimaced. "True. Y'all better grab your gear. I'll run you up there, that way someone can keep an eye on you and make sure you report to the doc." He gave Martin that look that drill sergeants always gave when they didn't really believe a story.

* * *

Martin came to attention in front of the colonel's desk and saluted. "Sergeant First Class Martin reporting, sir!"

Colonel Wilkinson returned the salute and commanded: "At ease, Sergeant. Are you feeling okay? I have a report here from the

Highway Patrol. That was a nasty accident; you could have been killed, from the description of it."

"Ibuprofen and water, Sir. I also changed my socks."

Wilkinson laughed, then stepped around his desk. "I have a briefing to give, and I want you to listen in. We'll talk after." The two exited the office and went down the hall to a meeting room.

Martin was still in a bit of shock from the rapid-fire pace of events. It had gone pretty much the way Martin had promised the patrolman. Upon reporting in to the battalion at Camp Bullis, his First Sergeant had ordered him to report to the medical bay. He'd been poked, prodded, and x-rayed over the course of several hours, then sent back to finish in-processing. Back at the Battalion HQ, he received a message to report to the brigade offices at Fort Sam Houston, 15 miles away in the heart of the city. Being ordered see the colonel was a bit unusual, as was the 'invitation' to an urgent briefing, let alone the mysterious, "we'll talk later." He took a seat in a folding chair near the back of the room, along with several other senior noncoms. Most of them wore medic insignia, the same as Martin, so whatever was about to happen, it looked like it would involve combat-related injuries.

Once the room filled, the colonel stepped to the podium, the lights dimmed, and the 32nd Medical Brigade emblem projected onto a screen. There was a faint whisper of, "death by PowerPoint" that appeared to come from the middle of the room—Lieutenant Country, most likely. The senior noncoms shared glances, and a few rolled their eyes—*someone* would catch hell from command by the end of the day.

"No, this will not be a typical boring PowerPoint, Lieutenant!" Wilkinson fixed a glare on a young officer in the fourth row. "There has been an incident. It has not hit the news yet because officially, no one has come out of the affected area." He clicked the control, and the slide changed to the now famous Object that had appeared in the space above Earth several days prior. Successive images showed a shape detaching from the apparent interstellar craft. "We assume that this was a landing craft or shuttle of some sort. It landed in Western Virginia, near Roanoke, yesterday afternoon. Satellites picked up evidence of explosions, and high altitude surveillance shows some sort of machines moving around. However, we have had absolutely no contact with the area. Most of the communication circuits are operable, but no one is answering.

"An infantry company from a National Guard battalion— Stonewall Brigade, actually, doing Annual Training on Fort Pickett— was dispatched; they arrived in the area two hours ago. They reported encountering a large number of vehicular accidents and dead civilians—some of the accidents appear to have been caused by the rapid onset of whatever killed the people there. The company pushed into the city, and reported seeing small, floating machines that emitted a white beam that killed whomever it touched. They took over 90% casualties, with only one squad's worth of survivors. They were able to E-and-E back to the NG Armory in Lexington. One of the senior Guard medics from Pickett has family in the area; we called him in to check the survivors. He also had a chance to examine a couple of the dead as well—drivers and a truck captain that had been killed while still in the transport vehicles.

"We don't know how, yet, but we know that the machines killed those men with a white beam that took their life without doing any external damage. The victims bled out for no apparent reason. The one thing the survivors had in common was that they had sustained serious combat-related injuries in the past two years. Those injuries required surgery and hospitalization, right here in the hospital over at San Antonio Military Medical Center (SAMMC). However, while they were seen here at SAMMC, they were also first treated in the field by combat medics, which is why I asked for the senior Sixty-Eight Whiskies to be here. Gentlemen and Ladies, we are here to brainstorm what it is that may have allowed those troops to survive this encounter. National Command Authority has authorized a recall of all units on leave and the mobilization of the Guard." Wilkinson stopped as an aide entered the room and handed him a note. He read it briefly and continued, "And it is confirmed. The President has declared a State of War. We don't even know who the enemy is...yet; however, we do know at least one of his weapons, and that some combat vets can survive. We need to get a handle on this, and we need to do it now. You were each given a briefing packet with an assignment to a working group. Get started."

Wilkinson looked up, and it seemed as if he was looking directly at Martin. "Dismissed."

As the room emptied, Martin noted that the colonel spoke briefly to his aide, who then made his way toward him. "First Sergeant Martin?" the aide asked. "Follow me; the colonel wishes to speak with you." The aide took Martin directly to the brigade commander's office.

Once again Martin came to attention in front of the colonel's desk.

"Sit, Martin." Wilkinson indicated a chair in front of the desk. "I just wanted to ask you a few questions. The squad has been evac'ed here to San Antonio and admitted to Brooke Army Medical Center, so BAMC cross-referenced any data relevant to the survivors. They found an interesting connection: all six had previously been treated for combat-related injuries, including surgical procedures by Dr. Tobias Greene. Two were treated at the 41st Combat Support Hospital, twenty-one months ago." He looked up at Martin and pushed two pieces of paper across the desk. "Here are their files. I believe you were attached to the CASH at the time."

"Sir?" Martin wasn't certain how to respond. It was always best in that situation to just follow the officer's lead, so he looked at the files. "Yes, sir. I was attached to the Forty-First up until 18 months ago, but I do not remember these soldiers. It was an Active Zone, sir."

"Relax, son." Wilkinson told him curtly. "You aren't being grilled; I'm trying to check out a hunch. I believe you assisted Toby Greene, is that correct?"

Martin relaxed, but only slightly. "Yes sir. I had just been re-classed Sixty-Eight Charlie and was a surgical nurse for the CASH. We had four trauma surgeons. Dr. Greene got the hardest cases. I only worked with him for about four months, though; I rotated home soon after he rotated in."

"I see." Wilkinson went back to looking at the tablet. "And did you work with his surgical nanobots?"

"Not directly, sir; he did the actual programming for surgical procedures."

"But did he ever mention the Phase Two 'bots?"

"Yes, sir. He made it a point to talk with all of the line medics and nurses. He said he was working on a tool to put in the hands of the First Responders." Martin looked at the officer. "Sir, my understanding was that it was still in development."

"According to information here, they were developed, but not widespread." Wilkinson, put the tablet back on the desk. "Last question. Were you ever exposed to the nanobots yourself?"

* * *

"Martin! Marty!" The beeping sounds sped up. He was in a bed, and something was blocking his throat.

There was a figure bending over him, dressed in green scrubs, mask, and cap. "Relax a minute. Let me get this tube out." There was a gagging sensation, and the tube was removed from his throat. A squeeze bottle delivered a small amount of water to his mouth. The doctor flashed a light in his eyes, then pinched the skin between his thumb and forefinger. "Good. Sensory responses are normal. Marty, do you know where you are?"

Martin tried to respond, but could only get out a croak. A nurse came in with water and ice chips. While he rehydrated, the doctor explained recent events.

"You're telling me I died?"

"Technically? No, Sergeant, you were only 'mostly dead'..." Dr. Greene's face was almost unrecognizable behind the surgical cap and mask. His wireframe glasses with the attached surgical magnifiers were distinctive, though, even if Martin had not recognized the eyes. "...And as you know, 'mostly dead, is still partly alive!' Your heart stopped, not unusual with the electrical shock you sustained. Also, it's pretty easy to restart. I gave you something to fight the burns and fluid retention. You should be back on your feet in a couple of days."

"A Princess Bride reference, how thoughtful, Doc!" He remembered the vehicle bringing casualties into the CASH. The 41st Combat Support Hospital was a unit with a long and distinguished history. It had been deactivated for decades, and then reactivated when the smoldering war they were in heated back up to full-on combat. The troops had called it "Sand, gravel, and shit—just like a cat litter box." The derogatory label: the Litterbox stuck. Unfortunately for those same troops, it was worse when it rained. The vehicle hit a rock, bounced, slid on a patch of mud, and hit one of the poles supporting the overhead power lines. Martin was a medic and nurse precisely because he *was* one of those people that ran toward danger—rather than away from it. He'd gotten the casualties out of the back, and then tried to extract the driver. He had seen the electrical arc, but he had a soldier to save. "…And the 'something to fight the burns,' would that be some of your little buggers?"

"Actually, I'm not sure 'little buggers' is a term you should be using in front of an officer, Marty, but just perhaps...yes, it's possible that I injected some of my nanobots to scavenge the dead tissue and repair the leaky blood vessels that occur after a shock." Greene smiled; you could tell by the creases around his eyes. "There's a project in the works to get them into the hands of the line medics, just that little bit would go a long way toward stabilizing casualties. I'm not sure you should tell anyone that, though; we don't have approval for this, yet." He patted the bed. "As I said...a couple of days as a slacker in bed, and you'll be back to being annoyed at me in the OR."

* * *

"Y ou were saying, Sergeant?" Wilkinson's forehead was furrowed, and he was looking at Martin strangely.

"Yes, sir. I believe I was exposed, sir." Martin hesitated. "I believe that Dr. Greene may have used the nanobots on me."

"As I suspected. You were put in for a Purple Heart, but the attending physician tasked with your evaluation could find no evidence of injury, and ruled it an accident. Witnesses said you had no pulse and a flat line on the defibrillator when they pulled you out, but no-one saw Dr. Greene inject you."

"No, sir. He said not to mention it. I considered it an order from a superior officer." Martin had not told anyone. The medal wasn't important anyway; he was just doing his job. "Sir, may I ask a question?"

Wilkinson smiled. "Yes, Sergeant, you may. This is not a hearing, but the information has been valuable."

"Sir, is this a problem? The nanobots?"

"No, but it may be a solution." Wilkinson sighed and sat back in his chair. "First, I have a report that two soldiers survived something that killed over a hundred men. The only thing they have in common is having been treated by Greene. Then you show up—a medic who spent several *months* with Greene—having been in a wreck that a highway patrolman told your CO you *should* have been seriously injured in, but you walked away with only dry cuts and bruises that appeared to be days old.

"When I put all of this together with information one of my surgeons brought back from a recent conference, I started to see a pattern. You can relax, Sergeant, we just need to find Greene and get him to safety. His file says he lives somewhere up near Roanoke. On the other hand," he fixed Martin with a forceful look. "You may be uniquely equipped if I need to send medics downrange. Meanwhile, I'm going to have you attached to SAMMC, but sending you back to Bullis. The good news is that it's a promotion, so call your wife, tell her you're okay, and give her the good news. Then get those Sixty-Eight Whiskey's ready to deploy; we're expecting orders at any time."

* * *

"**D**ude! You were dead! "

"Shut up."

"But, I mean, you're just like Zombie Jesus or something!"

"Look Corporal, go run laps, or go get us some 'Rip-Its'! Yeah. Get the Rip-Its. I've got to go back on at midnight."

"Yes Docfather! Whatever you say Docfather! Er, I mean Sergeant!"

"And don't forget your reflective belt!"

The CASH was mostly inflatable buildings, but a few bunkers had been dug in, and the low roofs had the advantage of being out of the mud the recent rains had made of the Litterbox. It was dark, and the off-duty medics were up on the roof smoking cigars and wishing for beer. The junior medic was still a bit green—a 'baby' on his first tour. The old-timers had all earned the label 'Doc' from rendering medical care while under fire. The senior medic was responsible for training the juniors, hence 'father' to all of the baby docs. Martin had the honor of being Docfather on this tour, and he was certainly not going to get down off of a dry roof as long as he had a baby doc to run through the mud and fetch energy drinks for the rest.

"He's right, Marty. You shouldn't even be in the Army anymore, you died! Instant ETS!" Sergeant Polo was just starting his second tour and would be taking over for Martin when he returned stateside in six weeks.

"Can it, Marco. You know they'd just cite 'stop-loss' at me anyway." Martin knew he suffered from 'short-timer syndrome'—the fear that the smallest incident would delay or hinder his plans to return home to wife, two-year old daughter, and plans for nursing school. "Don't jinx it, man."

"I know, but you realize that Captain Sanford tried to screw you over, right?"

"I *don't* need any *damned* medals, Marco! I was just doing my *job*."

Marco held up his hands. "Buddy, I'm just saying, Cap will screw you over. A couple of us talked to the SMAJ and you're cool, but maybe you'd better stick close to Major Greene for a few weeks. I think Sanford's afraid of him." He was silent for a while. "Damn. Zombie Martin. Has a ring to it, don't you think?"

Martin made a snorting sound. "Asshole."

There was a gurgling sound from Polo. Martin turned to look at his fellow medic—but Marco wasn't there. Martin was standing on top of the bunker, cradling an M4, and there was a mob on the ground trying to climb up. Zombies! They were all zombies!

There was Polo, and the baby doc, whatsisname...Stephens? No, Patrick...E4 Stephen Patrick. They were hissing and moaning, trying to get on top of the bunker, and Martin was just standing there holding his M4. If they looked like they were going to get up here, he'd have to start shooting. Now they were joined by Captain Sanford and Major Little. There were nurses in scrubs and doctors in white coats mixed in with the crowd, great big sores and open wounds on them all.

"Zombies. Hmmm, I never thought of that!" The voice came from behind him. Martin whirled, brought the carbine up, but lowered it when he saw Dr. Greene, in uniform, with a general's rank insignia, which was strange since he was a civilian...

"Sir, we have to..." but Greene wasn't listening, he was looking down at the crowd below.

"Strange, but I don't remember treating them." He pointed to a woman and child.

Civilians. They didn't look sick, though. Claire? Sally!

The zombies were climbing now. Polo was in the front, about to get hold of the roof line and pull himself up.

"You know what you have to do, Marty. You know you need to do it!" Now Greene was a zombie, too. He moved to the edge of the roof and reached down a hand and started helping the crowd onto the roof.

Martin brought up his M4. Time to rock-and-roll, time to...

Greene reached down and pulled up Claire, holding Sally, just a baby...

* * *

"Aaaaugh!" Martin woke up with a start, drenched in sweat. *Where had* that *dream come from?*

It had been a month since his conversation with the colonel. Most of Martin's time had been busy with certifications for the new medics and refreshers for the experienced ones. Added to Martin's load were a promotion and quite a few afternoons down at SAMMC, where med techs poked and prodded him, took x-rays, scans, and blood. Man, did they ever take blood. He was beginning to feel like a pincushion. They told him that the reason for so many blood tests was because they didn't dare put him in the MRI.

The tests confirmed there were indeed nanobots in Martin's body. It was a small amount, much less than if he'd had one of the major procedures in which the surgical 'bots were used to track and repair damage to blood vessels and internal organs. Nevertheless, the tiny machines were present, and the medical staff was reluctant to find out if they'd respond adversely to the strong magnetic fields of the Magnetic Resonance Imaging scanner.

Four-thirty A.M. Since he was now awake, he might as well get ready for PT and start the day. There had been many more landings in the past weeks, and word had finally gotten out to the public. After the initial panic, things had settled down, but with each new landing, there were more refugees to be dealt with. Fortunately, most landings were not in the major urban areas, so people were flocking to the cities. The president and various state governors had made announcements, trying to stem the tide, but had finally acquiesced and passed several emergency measures to declare "fortress cities" and concentrate essential services in defensible locations.

Pre-dawn was the only time to run during a South Texas summer, and Martin wasn't the only SNCO or officer running along the track out to the old airstrip and back. During the run, Martin planned out his day. Claire was coming up to S.A. to interview for a clinic manager job at one of the hospitals in the sprawling South Texas Medical Center. This job might allow her and Sally to move closer and be within the defensive zone planned for the city. He was taking a leave day to watch Sally during the interview, after which they would look at apartments and try to find a place to live that didn't involve refugee housing.

* * *

The interview went well, but not the apartment hunting. There were no available rooms to rent...at least nowhere that they would trust for someone who was effectively a single mother. As a fallback, Claire and Sally could stay with Martin's sister in Johnson City. It would be a bit crowded, but it was with family. Unfortunately, it was also outside the defensive perimeter of S.A., and at an hour commute, he'd still need a pass to be able to visit them, the same as if they were still in Corpus Christie. At least it would be an hour, and not three.

With the onset of evening, the heat of the day had started to fade, so Martin took his wife and daughter down to the Riverwalk for dinner and a ride on one of the tourist boats. It was amazing that there were still tourists, but some people obviously felt that as long as they ignored a threat, it wouldn't hurt them. They continued to party, and the locals continued to find ways to profit from them.

It would be Sally's birthday in a few weeks, and the soon-to-be five-year-old girl was laughing and enjoying the colorful lights, wonderful smells, and the mariachi music. This would likely be as much of a party as she would get, so Martin was trying to make it special. Claire had been to S.A. many times and was leaning back against Martin with her eyes closed. He had a 48-hour pass and had managed to find a hotel room for a single night. Rooms on the Riverwalk were already expensive, doubly so with the influx of refugees. He would have a night together with his family, then run them up to his sister's place tomorrow.

He hated that Claire would have to drive back to Corpus by herself; some of the reports he was hearing mentioned an increase in strange activity between cities. The army was beginning to consider armed convoys, just like they had done in the Litterbox, and every war zone before that. At least Claire had a decent vehicle if she had to get off of the highway—the insurance payment on the sedan he'd rolled had gone toward a safer, sturdier SUV. He just hated the idea of not being there to protect her and Sally if there was an attack—human *or* alien.

* * *

"Master Sergeant Martin, reporting, sir!"

"Sit, Marty." Wilkinson gestured to one of the chairs in front of the desk as Martin entered the office. The colonel was a little grayer and a bit more worn. It had been a long six months. "I just got the transcript of your debrief but wanted to hear from you directly. But first, have you had a chance to see Claire and Sally? "

"Yes, sir, I have. I also need to thank you for your assistance. They're a lot safer than in Johnson City, and much more comfortable in my parents' old house than down in the Dome." San Antonio was one of the few cities to have expanded since the Aliens arrived. The existing and reactivated bases, plus Medical Command and local infrastructure, had transformed Joint Base San Antonio into Fort San Antonio, and it was the principal 'Fortress City' keeping South Texas under protection. Unfortunately, the refugee housing situation had gotten worse with locals coming in from towns just outside the 'umbrella' of protection provided by F.S.A.'s armaments. Martin's parents had passed away several years ago, and his sister had kept the house, never quite willing to sell it. It had been in danger of being confiscated for refugee housing when the Army had claimed it for housing the dependents of Medical Command personnel. It was crowded with three families, but certainly more comfortable than cots and chemical toilets in the sports arena.

"Good. Glad to help." Wilkinson picked up the tablet on his desk, tapped at the screen, then looked up at Martin. "So. You were support on the convoy to Tucson, encountered the aliens, and they took out your air cover."

"Yes, sir. We first saw the little floaters, they attacked the aircraft, and when the energy beams did not kill the pilots, the Pawns retreated."

"'Pawns?'" Wilkinson raised an eyebrow. "I thought they were called 'Grunts?'"

"Yes, sir, they are, but unofficially, the troops call the little round floaters 'pawns' because they are always the first in, limited in mobility and pretty easy to pick off if you aren't affected by the killing beams. They call those 'Checkmate' beams, by the way."

"Of course they do; command's been using some German word, but the troops will do it their way. You're telling me that the infantry plays chess? Never mind. Continue."

"Sir. Next came the 'Bishops'—those are the larger floaters, kind of boxy, with the cutting beams. The choppers drove those off, but there were Rooks waiting for us up ahead."

"'Rooks.' I assume those are the mobile ground units? With the particle beams?"

"They are, not as big as a truck, let alone a tank, but they seem to have equivalent firepower. Their surface-to-air attacks are bad news for choppers, but their weapons don't depress worth a damn. If you get close enough, you can take them out. Unfortunately, once the air cover was gone, the rooks started on the trucks, and the pawns came back in to support."

"So, that was when you took the hit?"

"No, sir. Captain called retreat, and we were headed back to 'Paso. They moved the heavy beam weapons down to White Sands, so there's pretty good force projection there. Problem is—we would never have made it." Martin realized he was gripping the arms of the chair. He tried to relax; it wouldn't do to damage the colonel's office furnishings. Only generals were allowed to do that.

"I see. The Intel report said something about the mountains?" If Wilkinson had noticed the sergeant's tenseness, he didn't react.

"You have the Intel report? It's all in there. Mountains where they shouldn't be." Martin paused. "Sir, how well do you know southern New Mexico?"

"Not very. I've been to White Sands, and I've been to Fortress Tucson."

"Sir, it's flat. West of Las Cruces, headed toward Tucson, hills and mountains are something you see on the horizon. Not near I-10. About 50 klicks west of Las Cruces, though, we saw mountains, about five—six thousand feet high. The pawns, bishops, and rooks were coming out of caves at the bottom. The captain dismounted a platoon and sent them up to check. The platoon Ell-Tee wanted to send a trainee medic along, but I convinced him to send me instead. It was an unstable situation, and they weren't trained for it."

"They all know the risks, Sergeant; why did you dispute the lieutenant? His report says you refused to let the junior medics accompany the platoon. 'Borderline disciplinary offense' were his exact words."

"Trauma'bots, sir. I've had 'em; the accident last June proved they were still active. None of the trainees have gotten them—there's still not enough to go around. Anyway, it was an ambush; they had the checkmate beams right at the entrance. Hit the whole platoon, turns out half the troops hadn't been inoculated, either. I had five injectors with me, and managed to get at least three troops stabilized. Of course, then I stood up at the wrong time."

* * *

*D*amn it, it hurt! Like his entire right side was on fire. He half-turned to the two privates behind him. They looked shocked but were still standing. That was a start. He tried to bend over to check the three troopers on the ground; he'd managed to drag them into the shadow of some rocks and get them injected. They were stirring now. He tried to tell the two standing—no, crouching—privates to drag their fellows to back to the road. They might be able to move on their own soon, but for now they needed to *move!* The only problem was when he tried to speak and couldn't open his jaw, couldn't grunt, couldn't hiss at them. He made a vague motion with his left hand. Either they understood his intent, or they figured it out on their own.

Someone tapped his shoulder, the signal to move out. He turned to see who was still here, and as he turned, he saw the private's eyes go wide. He turned back, but it wasn't something behind. The kid was looking at *him*. He felt something wet on his face, tried to brush it with his good hand, but it was sticky, red.

There was a sharp stinging sensation on his leg. He looked down and saw the kid holding a tube that looked like an epinephrine or atropine injector, similar to the kind used for someone severely allergic or as nerve gas antidote. Smart kid...They'd have to hurry, though; Martin's vision was going black...

Beep. Beep. Beeeeeeeeeeeep. Beep. Beep. Beeeeeeeeeeeeeep.

"His readings are all over the place—first his pressure's down, then up! He's bleeding out, then it stops! His heart stopped, then came back on his own. What *is* this? Howard! Get some more O-negative in him!"

"Frankly, Doctor Witcher, I'm surprised he's even alive; I heard he took a beam full on. I've never heard of anyone surviving that."

"Some do." Someone else had entered the already-crowded operating room; he wasn't scrubbed in, but was carrying a tray draped in sterile cloth. On the tray was the autoinjector that had been administered in the field. "They survive because of these. Use this, Doctor Witcher; we just got a delivery of Greene's Trauma'bots from North Carolina." He nodded toward the resident, who picked up the injector, careful not to touch the non-sterile areas near the newcomer's gloved hands. "Nice to finally get some of our own. Read me the serial and lot numbers. We need to match the programming codes."

"So how come he survived the hit *before* the 'bots were delivered?"

"Luck." Wilkinson replied. "Luck, and Greene disobeying protocols with his initial surgical 'bots. This guy was exposed to an early prototype, not enough to protect him, but maybe just enough for us to save him."

"Lucky kid."

"Lucky, foolish, charmed. Whatever. He shielded two other soldiers when the convoy got hit."

"Damn. Brave, too."

* * *

"Not exactly the way the platoon sergeant tells it, Marty. Something about shielding half the surviving squad and walking back through the beam to its source, then using an M-4 like a club. That's another Bronze Star, Marty, if not Silver." He paused and then continued, "By the way, your count was off. You had six injectors. One of your trainees used it on you."

"Oh. So that's where it came from." Martin shook his head. "Sir, I don't want medals. I was just doing my job."

"The report says that, too. The captain wants to be very mad at you, but admits that he can't. Last question..." Martin had been looking down through the last part of the exchange. It was against regs, but Wilkinson had made it clear this was informal by addressing him as 'Marty' and inviting him to sit. When the silence dragged on, Martin looked up to see the colonel staring intently at him. "In the cave, Marty. What did you *see?*"

* * *

As the survivors retreated, Martin turned back to look at the cave entrance. The grenades they'd tossed had had an effect, except it was after the checkmate had fired. Once again, he tried to get a good look, while staying behind the rock formation.

Rock formation. Something was wrong here; something his subconscious was trying to tell him. Rocks. The rocks shouldn't be here. The caves shouldn't be here. Hell, this *mountain* shouldn't be here.

* * *

"I collapsed, sir. I do not remember anything between seeing the private and...and waking up in SAMMC. I've tried long and hard to figure out what it was that bothered me so much at the time; what I saw. The only thing I vaguely remember thinking was that the rocks were moving."

"Moving?" The colonel had a skeptical look.

"Seems odd, but a buddy of mine helped me find old satellite photos that accompanied the maps of the region. There are *no* rocks in that area—not even the ones we sheltered behind."

"Moving rocks." Wilkinson stood up, and Martin popped to attention. "Very well, Sergeant. It's no wonder DiNote didn't include that part in the report. Moving rocks—well, I've learned not to doubt you on most things, but we may have to chalk that one up to getting half-poached by a beam! Dismissed. Get back to training; you're still on light duty, so no convoys for the near future. "

* * *

"So, like, you've died *twice*, now?"

"Shut *up*, Carl."

"Yes, sir." The medic trainee was in awe of the Master Sergeant. The rumors that he had actually *seen* the aliens was the talk of the barracks. "But...what was it *like*?"

Martin turned to the Specialist and leveled his best senior NCO glare. "It was a *god-damned nuisance* and a *pain in the ass* because of wet-behind-the-ears Sixty-eight Whiskey-oh-ohs who can't figure out that you *don't* call a Master Sergeant, *sir*! And don't know which end of the auto'jector goes on the *damned patient*!"

"I don't have any more time to spend with you so I will say this *once more*!" He held up the six-inch long, half-inch wide cylinder. "*This is your Mark Three Field Deployable Trauma'bot dispenser. It is an autoinjector! That means it will *automatically* inject whenever the red button is pushed. *Do not push the red button* until you are ready to inject a patient. Do *not* inject *yourself!* Do we know which end of the injector goes against the patient, Specialist Mitchell? The *red end*, Mitchell! *Red* end against the patient, then press the *green* button! Can you do that? Good! Let's see you do that with the practice injectors!"

* * *

"Y ou *shot* me, Private!"
"I was shooting at the shark, Top! I didn't mean to shoot you."
"You still *shot me!* Damn, right in the gluteus. It's not bad enough you shot me, but you *shot your first sergeant in the ass*, Roeder! You've probably wanted to do that for a long time. Corporal Levitt, get this grunt out of my sight."
"It's probably only a graze, Marty, don't be a wuss. It's already stopped bleeding."
"I'm never going to live this down, hand me that autoinjector."
"Sure he shot you—but you'll get better!"
"Shut up, Levitt."

* * *

"D id it hurt, Daddy?" Sally was sitting on the side of the bed, trying to be a Big Girl and restrain her natural impulse to bounce all over everything. It was hard for a six-year-old to sit still.

464 | IBSON & KENNEDY

"Yes, Babydoll, it hurt, but only for a little while." Contrary to Levitt's opinion, it had not been a graze, and Martin had needed surgery to get out all of the bullet fragments. The trauma'bots he'd administered immediately after the accident should have been sufficient to get him back to duty the next day; unfortunately, the location of the injury made it impossible to sit, and he was still just a bit too weak to stand for long periods. He'd been transferred back to SAMMC and would spend another day in the hospital laying on his side and stomach. Since he was back in town, and Claire had recently transferred over to the sprawling military medical complex, she and Sally had been invited to visit.

Claire mainly stood frowning, particularly as she saw the slight grimaces of pain on her husband's face as Sally's restraint wore down, and she started to bounce on the side of the bed. "Honey, don't do that; the doctor said you need to sit still."

"It's okay, Babydoll," Martin reassured them both, but then gave Sally the sternest look he could manage. "But don't let Dr. Hoyt catch you! 'Ogg' might toss you in the air again!"

Sally turned from bouncing to giggling "Doctor Ogg!" 'Cro-Magnon' was the phrase most often used to describe the Emergency Medicine (Pediatric) surgeon. He was heavily built, with an olive complexion, thick dark hair, heavy brows, and perpetual five-o'clock shadow. Despite the caveman appearance, he was friendly and well-liked, particularly by his pediatric patients and their families. He was an old acquaintance from the Litterbox who'd become a family friend as their paths (and eventually, his and Claire's) continually crossed at SAMMC. He'd picked Sally up when they arrived and swung her around a few times. Martin was a bit chagrinned that *he* was not able to do so, but the doc had winked at him as he sat her down and whispered to Claire that he hoped it would dissipate some of the child's natural energy.

Claire's expression was clearly signaling worry to Martin. They wouldn't talk about it in front of Sally, but she was clearly concerned about the dangers in his new job. Taking over a company as First Sergeant was a lateral transfer from Master Sergeant, but a massive increase in responsibility. It would mean more time deployed and less time under the relative safety of the F.S.A. defensive net. Unfortunately, as the most experienced medic in the use (on others and himself) of the field-deployable 'bots, he would go where the Army sent him.

After they left, he tried to roll onto his back, to get the kinks out. The pain in his ass was receding, but the painful memories remained. They'd lost good men—grunts and baby docs, both—at Las Cruces and on the flotilla evacuating Galveston. They were having to give up too much territory to the Rockers. He turned further and reached into the rucksack Claire had brought him. The small bottles were well-padded, and she'd had no way of knowing he'd put them in there last week. The booze was strictly against regs, particularly in the hospital, but it was late, the nurses were at their station, and he wanted an anesthetic that would treat the pain in body and mind, alike.

* * *

"Doctor, he's waking up!" The nurse grabbed for the tray of sterile surgical instruments before the patient's sudden movements could knock them to the ground. The beeping from the various machines monitoring the patient became louder, more incessant.

"Put him back to sleep! Dr. Charron, set a four hertz stim for 10 seconds on the TMS...yes, that's it, place it right there above his temple." The beeping slowed and the operating room quieted as the patient relaxed. The surgeon turned back to the table. "Ok, soldier, back to sleep."

* * *

"Sir, you really shouldn't..."

"'M not a 'Sir,' Bab-by Doc. 'M a sargn't. 'M your *Firs'* Sargn't!"

"Yes, First Sarn't, but you really shouldn't be in here. Major says the CASH is moving; it's not safe here. We're abandoning the bunkers in place, so no one's been looking in here, but Cap'n Hamm's been asking for you."

"An' you din' wan'im t' see m' drinking? Hell, Baby Doc, you should know by now that the damn 'bots don't let you stay drunk. We all got a fresh dose before heading to the Swamp. What does Captain Hamster want now?" Martin walked over to the ice box, grabbed two handfuls of ice, dumped them in the sink, filled it with cold water and then plunged his head into the bowl of ice water. He held it there for about 20 seconds and then straightened back up and reached for a towel. "So, if no one is looking in the bunkers, how did you find me?"

"Sarn't Gutierrez said to look for you here. 'Go find Top,' he said. 'Find him 'fore the Cap'n does; he's looking for the logs for the drug lockup.' Sarn't said he didn't like the numbers, and won't sign off on securing for shipment 'til he sees the logs."

"Crap. Sounds like Second Bravo's been running their racket again." The senior NCO reached for the combat uniform top that had been balled up and discarded under the folding table. He held it up, shook it out, and donned it. He then grabbed a bottle of deodorizing fabric spray and lightly misted himself.

The young medic was looking around nervously around the room. "Sir...Sarn't. The cap'n might have seen me come in here. I need to get back to loading. "

Martin finished straightening his ACUs and picked up the plastic cups and empty bottles. He put them in the trash, adding more litter to cover them. "Go, Baby Doc. I'll see if I can't mollify the Hamster." Finished with the cleanup, he turned back to the medic. "...And tell Gutierrez that Second Platoon and I are going to have a 'Come to Jesus' meeting after this evac!"

* * *

Martin stood at attention, waiting for the officer to wind down. He knew it was serious; the officer had not called him 'Top' a single time. All he could do now was wait it out. There would be no excuses or passing of the blame. His headache was receding as nanobots readjusted the fluid balance in his tissues and eliminated the last remnants of whiskey from his bloodstream. He no longer *looked* like he'd been drinking, which was part of the problem: he and the captain knew that it was *exactly* what he'd been doing. Martin wordlessly handed over the written pharmacy logs. Network connections were intermittent and unreliable this far forward, so they'd resorted to written logs. Unfortunately, they were easier to forge that way. If Second Platoon *had* been selling drugs and nanos on the black market, he would make sure that each and every one of them pulled convoy duty until the end of this war!

There was a strange prickling feeling on his skin, the hairs on arms were standing up and there was a smell of ozone. Targeting beam! "Captain! Incoming! Down!" The office exploded as the beam disrupted molecular bonds, releasing the energy bound in the materials of walls, ceiling, and furnishings throughout the structure. Explosive beams meant there were rooks in the area; rooks meant a heavy attack underway!

The captain was down and bleeding, but still had a pulse. Martin pulled an auto'jector out of the holder on his belt. No medic, doctor, or nurse was ever without one or more of the pen-sized 'bot injectors. With enough 'bots in the system, even death was only a 'temporary inconvenience.'

Martin stayed low—crawling to the remains of the door to look outside and check the conditions. He ignored the stinging sensation coming from his own wounds. The rooks would be targeting vehicles next. The troops loading trucks were in the open and would be unprotected, body armor either packed or left in the barracks until time to leave. He noted soldiers sheltering behind the trucks and wanted to yell at them to get clear, but wouldn't be heard over the electrical crackle of the beams and the chattering of counter-fire from the perimeter defense guns.

His attention was drawn to a vehicle looking like an armored motor home with too many wheels. The wide, bus-length vehicle was the Mobile Surgical Contingency Vehicle—the CASH operated around the clock, there would be procedures ongoing, despite the bug-out. The RV interior was isolated with a separate stabilization system to allow surgery to continue without interruption even on the move. They might not even know there was an attack in process.

Martin reached down and lifted the captain in a fireman's carry. Damn, he wasn't very big, but he was solid. Shouldering the weight, he quickly made his way to the MSCV. The keypad on the door was a problem, he had to release the captain, then manage to enter the code, pull the door open, then pick the burden back up, enter the van, and place him on the litter outside the panel isolating the OR from the entrance.

Looking through the heavy glass, he could see the OR was indeed occupied; it looked like two patients on the tables, plus a doc and two nurses. Martin punched the intercom attention button, and the nurses looked up. "We're under attack, we've gotta move!" He could see the surgeon speak to one of the nurses, never looking up from his patient; the nurse looked at him and made the thumbs' up gesture. Good. He checked the captain again—pupils okay, breathing shallow, not bleeding too much except for a gash in the scalp. Head injury, probable concussion, but he'd keep.

Martin stepped up, and into the driver compartment. Fortunately, the designers had decided that anyone making it *into* the mobile OR would have reason to be there; thus, there were no keys, just a red button to start the engine. The OR was *heavy*, it required a gas turbine engine similar to the one in modern tanks; it was right underneath the driver compartment. No amount of insulation could disguise that fact. The driver's seat was mounted forward and center, with a nearly 270-degree view. He could see bishops and rooks off to the left. They didn't seem to be advancing, but there looked to be rocks moving behind them. If a queen was moving up, this location was *blown*. Time to boogie.

Martin grabbed the controls and set the vehicle in motion, south for now. Since Roanoke, the Army had kept the Shenandoah and New River valleys pretty clean. I-81 corridor was safe enough for armored convoys, but it was 50 klicks west, with the Blue Ridge Mountains in the way. This raid was probably coming out of The Swamp, but if a queen moved in here, they'd lose everything east of the Blue Ridge—probably all the way down to North Carolina. He keyed the nav system display. Autodrive systems worked extremely well when ninety-nine percent of the vehicles were off of the roads. With a good nav signal, the mobile OR could drive itself back to Texas.

The signal was good, but limited coverage—he had a good enough lock to get the vehicle through the gap to the Valley, from there it could probably at least find Knoxville, providing the 'sats didn't get knocked out. Mojave kept launching navsats, and the Rockers kept hitting them with—well, rocks. Ever since the Roanoke landing, they'd launched kinetic weapons at anything that approached the orbital vessel presumed to hold their 'King.' No one had figured out whether the occasional rock dropped from orbit was targeting—or delivering more troops.

Martin set the navigation waypoint and looked around. Most of the permanent buildings were gone—that was a given, but the prefab treatment areas were still standing, and probably still occupied. No matter what the captain thought of him, he still understood his responsibility. He arose from the driver position and made his way back to the door. He got the captain secured and prepped for either the surgeon in the back, or the recovery team that would be attracted to the driverless vehicle.

Time to jump. The vehicle was picking up speed, it was now or never.

Oh, this was truly going to suck.

* * *

"**D**ammit, Vinnie, he's waking up again! Dr. Gautam, I don't care what you have to do, hit him on the head if you have to! Get him back to sleep!"

"Doctor, he has more nanobots in him than any patient we've ever seen; they are scavenging up the anesthetics, and resetting his EEG rhythms, even the delta-wave induction is not having much effect." The voice paused, then continued. "At this point, we may have to EMP the whole lot just to get them to stop."

"No, absolutely not. That would just wipe my 'bots, too. Given that they're scavenging shrapnel from around his heart, that's just not happening."

"Normally, I'd send a reset and reprogramming signal to the old 'bots, but the monitor is picking up at least six different generations—some of them don't even have address codes for reprogramming!"

"Six? That's odd...BAILEY, patient record...Nurse, patient ID?"

"MXM1066A1732. Martin X. Martin, Doctor."

"Martin X...who does that to a child? Never mind. BAILEY, patient record, MXM1066A1732..."

A synthetic voice said: "Martin X. Martin, First Sergeant, Two Hundred Sixty-Fourth Medical Battalion, attached to Charlie Company, Training, Thirty-Second Medical Brigade..."

The first doctor's voice interrupted: "BAILEY. Advance to surgical record, summarize, detail level one."

The synthetic voice resumed, "Patient Martin, electrical shock while at Forty-First Medical Battalion; received undocumented Greene Mark I nanobots, record manually corrected at a later date. Hit by Rocker 'totung' Beam on convoy duty west of Las Cruces, major tissue disruption, perforation, and inflammation; received Greene Mark II surgical nanobots. Gunshot wound while escorting the Galveston refugee flotilla; field administration of RKHMedical Mark II trauma'bots, surgical follow-up with RKHMedical Mark III surgical nanobots. Prophylactic treatment with Greene Mark III preventa'bots prior to Operation Reclamation. Shrapnel injury, skin abrasions, road rash, retreat phase of Operation Reclamation; perioperative treatment with SAMedical Mark IV surgical nanobots. Prophylactic treatment with Geisszler-Greene Mark IV trauma'bots prior to Operation Enduring Homeland. Traumatic amputation, Operation Alamo; administered SAMedical Mark VIII trauma'bots for stabilization and transport; surgical support includes..."

"BAILEY. Cancel. Well, there's your answer, Vinnie. He's got more 'bots than an internet porn site. You're right; we might have to EMP him, just to get some semblance of control."

"I'll have to put him on dialysis if we do. Inert 'bots are a pain to flush otherwise. I can't guarantee he'll make it if we slow them down, though."

"Slow them down...Yeah, that's it! Vinnie, put him on heart-lung bypass, volume expand with the fluoro solution and chill him to six-cee. That should slow them and him down enough..."

* * *

Martin came to attention as the officer entered the small room. "Sir." When he saw stars on the uniform, he started to salute, but caught himself—given his current circumstances, it would be inappropriate. Martin's own clothing was a dull gray jumpsuit.

"Master Sergeant Martin." They moved to the table, took the chair and sat. He did not release the NCO to 'at ease' nor invite him to sit, so Martin stayed at attention, looking straight ahead. "You have a problem, Martin. Captain Hamm wants you court-martialed for dereliction of duty, drunkenness, conduct unbecoming, disobeying orders, assaulting an officer, abandoning your post, desertion, theft of Army property, reckless endangerment, and improper operation of a motor vehicle. Major Jackson—the surgeon you saved? He put you in for a Distinguished Service Cross." The general stopped for a moment. "Well, we can't have it both ways. Award is downgraded to a Silver Star; charges are dropped except for improper operation of a motor vehicle. For that offense, you are relieved of the position of First Sergeant, Charlie Company, 264th Medical Battalion." He gave a snort, almost a laugh. "And you're 'busted' to Master Sergeant."

As if just noticing that Martin was still at attention, the general grunted. "Hmph. At ease, Sergeant. Sit." Once Martin was seated, the general looked him in the eyes. "Son, what the *hell* were you thinking? First you knock out your commander, dump him in the MSCV, and send it off to Knoxville, then abandon the vehicle once it left the CASH!" There was silence for a moment. "You may answer, soldier."

"No excuse, sir." Despite being seated, Martin was still basically sitting at attention. He kept his eyes focused at a point over the general's head.

"So, you do not deny striking Captain Hamm?"

"No sir, I do not dispute the record."

The general snorted. "That's interesting, Major Jackson certainly did! His report says that the captain suffered concussive blast trauma, and there is no evidence of being struck. One of the MSCV nurses found the captain, still unconscious, strapped to a litter, hooked to an IV and already treated with trauma'bots. The ident code on the 'bots track back to injectors issued to you—not the CASH, not the Company, but to you, personally. Level with me, Marty. Did you strike Hamm?"

"No sir, I did not knock him unconscious."

"You didn't say you didn't strike him."

"No sir, I cannot guarantee that he was not harmed on the way to the MSCV."

"Uh huh. You had to drop him at the vehicle door."

"Sir?"

"Then you tripped over him."

"Sir? How?"

"There's a camera, did you not know that? Inside and out. Microphones, too. You talked to Wohlrab the whole time, even though he couldn't hear you. Now you got the whole headquarters company calling him 'Captain Hamster!' It's fortunate he'll be on convalescent leave for a while. Not his fault; really, he remembers nothing except dressing you down, and then he wakes up in hospital, is told he'd suffered a concussion and was found unconscious in a driverless vehicle. You were right, what you mumbled on the MSCV—he's not a bad officer, he just drew the wrong conclusions. He's seen the recording, too. It's a good thing you treated him when you did, that was a bad concussion; he almost didn't make it. The vehicle was intercepted by airmobile out of Radford; the same team picked your sorry ass off the ground, too. You were right about the attack, too, by the way..."

Martin realized that his standard response was getting worn out. "In what way, sir?"

"You said it looked like a queen moving in. You were right. We lost the CASH, but were able to push back and stop the queen from settling in. That at least allowed us to get in and extract the survivors. Between that beacon you set off on the MCV, and the aid you rendered on the ground, you saved a lot of people, Marty. You *just* need to *stop* getting banged up! I don't know how many times we can piece you back together."

"Perhaps that would be for the best, sir."

"No, Marty, it wouldn't—and if you talk like that, I *will* relieve you! We need you, and men like you who run *toward* danger, and not away from it." The general stood up, and Martin popped back to attention. "Get out of the prison grays and get back into ACUs. The captain doesn't want you anywhere near Charlie Company or any forward CASH. Not that he's still mad at you; in fact, he's pretty worried about you. He thinks you need time to get your head straight. I agree. You're going back to Brigade—Headquarters Company, not Training. But not for six weeks. You are on convalescent leave and referred to mandatory counseling." The general handed him a card with the Chaplain Support number on it. "Go see your family and talk to the padre. It's more than most of these boys will get."

* * *

"Martin. How do you feel?" The chaplain had been a Pastoral Care minister working out of one of the civilian hospitals before the conflict. Before that he'd been a Methodist minister, and before that an enlisted grunt in conflicts remembered only by their nicknames: the Litterbox, the Sandbox, the Rockpile, the Jungle, the Mohingga!, Skeeter Farm, the Pits, and many other combinations of grunt humor and disgust. He was familiar with the blank stare and the unwillingness to open up to anyone.

The silence dragged on. For a first session, this was pretty normal, but that was okay.

He could wait.

* * *

Martin barely recognized his parents' house. The master bedroom had been subdivided into rooms not much wider than a single bed. The smaller bedrooms now held multiple bunks. The common living areas were now smaller, partly given over to cubicle desks to allow the children to do schoolwork, while the kitchen had been enlarged—pushed out into what had been a covered patio but was now an enclosed communal dining room. Claire led him out the back to what used to be a detached garage. "We were storing the old furniture in here and got the idea to turn it into a 'guest bedroom' so that we could get the occasional private night when the spouses are on leave." There were portions of four families here: three adults, seven children, and an eighth girl with both parents on active duty. A night alone—or with a much-absent spouse—would seem like a luxury despite the lack of central heating and cooling. "We can have this for the weekend, but then I have to give it back."

He'd been able to spend time with his wife and daughter most weekends, as long as he was stationed in San Antonio, but this would be his first night out of a barracks in over two years. Sally was already eight, growing fast. His biggest fear had been that he would miss watching her grow up. He missed weeks at a time, but he had been here enough that visits were both comfortable and special occasions. The 'guest room' had a sofa, chairs, a small table, TV, and a movie player to facilitate 'family time' in every sense (particularly considering the selection of movies from family cartoons to more adult selections).

Right now, Sally was cuddled in Martin's arms on the old sofa, while Claire leaned against him. They were watching a cartoon from a few years back. It had been new, and Sally's favorite, when he'd been called to San Antonio. Was it four years already? Now she was asleep and growing heavier by the minute. He'd take her back to her bedroom, except she'd wake up the moment he moved. On the other hand, there was a very small room, not much larger than a closet, with a cot and portable crib for couples with infants and toddlers. As long as Sally had Bun-Bun, she'd be okay.

Frankly, Martin didn't mind if they all fell asleep right here. He was overwhelmed by the warmth and scents of his wife and daughter. Sally was soap and lavender, probably something in the shampoo. Claire's scent was much richer, flowers and a hint of musk. The child was warm and soft, but his wife seemed burning hot where they touched skin to skin. Claire turned and gave him *that* look. He'd need to put Sally to bed soon, so that Claire could do the same for him. It had been far too long...

* * *

He was jolted awake by the ground vibrations. The alarm sounded over his and Claire's cell phones, the house phone, and the TV. He could also hear the message repeated over loudspeakers mounted outside so that everyone in the city would hear:

"Attention, Crystal Dome has been activated. Please stay indoors. All civilians should seek shelter immediately and avoid the outdoors. All military personnel, do not return to duty stations; shelter in place. Do not go outside, seek overhead cover, do not look at the sky! Attention, Crystal Dome has been activated..."

"Shit, crap, shit, f—"

"Marty, language." Claire was up and getting dressed; Sally walked in, sleepy-eyed. They needed to get back to the main house, but the instructions were clear, avoid open sky at all costs. It was only ten yards back to the house; they could cover it in a sprint in seconds.

Unfortunately, Crystal Dome meant that the city was under attack by orbital weaponry—usually rocks, but also the orbital killing beam, the Totung. The Fort San Antonio perimeter presented a layered defense consisting of explosive, kinetic, and energy weapons, combined with an atmospheric "cloud" of nanoparticles designed to diffuse the energy beams. It tended to make the sky somewhat 'energetic,' to that point that even a few seconds exposure could be hazardous, somewhat like a full-day sunburn in seconds. Fortunately, any type of covering provided protection—including tents—as long as you stayed away from the roof and walls. The way to do this would be to make a tent, and make sure that Claire and Sally remained completely under it.

"Claire, get the sheets and blanket off of the bed. I'm going to hold them up over us; you hold Sally and make sure you stay completely under them. "

"Oooooooo. I'm a *ghost!*"

"Yes, Sally, let's play ghost! One big ghost, just make sure no one can see that it's you under the blanket." They would have to move more slowly than a sprint, but it would be under cover.

Martin opened the door. The sky was as bright as day, with flashes of even greater brightness. He could feel a prickling sensation where his hands touched the fabric. He made sure to keep it off Claire and Sally. He'd have to check them later.

Ten steps. Fifteen. Twenty. Should be there, but they were small steps. He stumbled on the threshold. Claire had been the one looking down; his attention was on the covering. He stumbled forward, into the door. Claire fumbled the doorknob and got the door open. There was a yell from inside the kitchen. Martin felt himself falling and pushed the other two forward, along with the blanket. His legs were still outside and exposed, he could feel the burning sensation on the back of his legs.

He was dragged forward and the door closed, cutting off the bright sky. Sally was laughing as she crawled out from under the covers. Claire looked grim while looking down at his hands. They were red and blistered. Fortunately, on-leave didn't mean totally off-duty. His first responder kit was in...the guest room. He could probably wait until the alert was over; there had never been an attack more than an hour or two in duration. For now, he would treat it like sunburn. This was South Texas; there would be aloe somewhere in the house. He checked Claire and Sally—no sign of redness, so they probably weren't exposed. He'd give them both a shot of the field 'bots they use for minor injuries. Once he could get his kit. Sally's dose would be tricky, but it wasn't the first time he'd treated civilians caught out in the Zone.

* * *

"So, you waited out an attack with your family. Was that the first time?"

"Yes."

"Was anyone hurt?"

"No."

"I heard you had to go outside during the Crystal Dome alert. Wasn't that dangerous?"

"No."

"Huh. Spoken like a soldier. Tell me, though, how did it make you feel, having to take your family out under the 'Dome?"

"I'm fine, padre. It's what a man does. He protects his family. This is my job. I protect my family, I protect the civilians, and I fix the grunts."

"Ok, Marty. This is good. Well, it's better. How's the drinking?

"Good."

"That's not an answer, Marty."

"It's under control, sir. Medical hit me with the latest 'bot mix. I can *not* get drunk, so there's no point to booze."

"Hmmph. Well, I suppose that's one solution. Very well, we'll talk to you again on Thursday."

* * *

"Attention, Crystal Dome has been activated..."

"Crap. Shit. *Damn* it!" Martin had come to hate the alert sound coming over the phones. Last week he'd thrown his phone against the barracks wall when it went off in the middle of the night. Unfortunately, it was one of the rough-duty military models. It just bounced.

The attacks had gotten longer and more frequent. There was a greater probability of a leak when the rocks and beams came falling out of the sky. The HQ and Training battalions needed to keep working no matter what happened outside, so the buildings that weren't already connected by underground tunnels, such as the SAMMC hospital complex, were now connected by tubes constructed from tent canvas. Martin heard the rapid footsteps as someone entered the building and ran toward the NCO workroom. He saved the spreadsheet he'd been working on and closed the laptop. A young soldier came running into the office, stopped at the door and saluted.

Martin sighed, "You don't salute me, Private." The soldier, barely more than a boy, held the salute anyway until Martin sloppily returned it. "Okay, report."

"Sir! Brigade Commander! Wants you! In! His Office!" The words came out in bursts, punctuated by short gulps of breath. The kid was *young*, he probably had an abbreviated Basic training. Martin's own drill sergeants would have marched, run, and drilled that out of them.

"It's okay, Private. Take a minute and catch your breath." Martin stood, grabbed his cover and laptop. "Do you need to accompany me? Or are you supposed to go somewhere else?" The kid shook his head and bent over, trying to slow down his breathing. "Okay. Stay here. When you're ready, get on over to Clinic and tell the intake nurse that Master Sergeant Martin suggests Asthma A12'bots. Come now, you can sit here in the outer office while I go see the general."

* * *

T he job had been hard on Wilkinson. He'd finally been promoted, but was considering stepping down for health reasons. Ironic for the commander of a Medical Brigade, but the war was wearing everyone down. As Martin came to attention and saluted, he noted the presence of another general officer in the room.

"At ease, Marty. General Odle was informing me about the plans to pull back the Fortress perimeter." Wilkinson sat, but did not invite Martin to do so. "I will be brief. We need to evacuate Bullis. Training Company needs to get in under the umbrella as we pull it back. The Crystal Dome perimeter is being contracted to inside the Loop. Their first sergeant was injured in the last attack. You may be surprised to hear that Captain Wohlrab requested you as Top—strictly on a temporary basis. Get out to Bullis, get the company moved down here, then you'll be back to your regular duties."

"Yes, sir. Will do, sir." Martin paused a moment. "Sir, may I ask a question?"

"Go ahead, Marty."

"If we're contracting the perimeter, what about civilians outside the Loop?"

Wilkinson ignored the question and gave the other officer a meaningful look. Odle cleared his throat. Martin had the feeling he had met him before, perhaps as a more junior officer in the Litterbox. "We don't have enough coverage. Dependents are welcome in the refugee centers. Other civilians we will accommodate as space allows. We may be down to tents on the fairgrounds. The perimeter is not absolute, those close in will still be protected; we just can't guarantee 100% coverage."

"Understood, Sir."

"Marty, I know your family is outside the Loop, but they're so close, it should be okay. If it's any consolation, our families are there, too."

"Yes, sir, understood. Claire mentioned seeing Mrs. Wilkinson at the market."

"Good, then. Get out to Bullis and get our boys pulled in. Dismissed."

* * *

"Go, go. Go! In the trucks! Now!" The latest alert had sounded 40 minutes ago. Most attacks these days ran for hours, and the longer it went, the weaker the fringes of the 'Dome. There was no chance of avoiding open sky. There was already evidence of lightning-like strikes just to the north, well within the perimeter of the training encampment.

It was 25 miles back to the SAMMC by road. Only 15 miles by direct line, but it wouldn't be enough. Crystal Dome was being contracted back to a 10 mile radius from the center of town. It would cover the core of the city and the Joint Base, but portions of Randolph and Medina Air Force Bases were outside the perimeter, not to mention all of Camp Bullis. The latest word from brigade was that the defense system was being overtaxed to maintain the existing umbrella long enough to evacuate those areas.

An extremely bright flash of light overhead was followed by a seeming shadow. Martin was the only person in the open by that point, trusting on his nanobots to fix any flash damage he might sustain. It was reckless, but he was damned if he would don one of the hot, heavy radiation suits. He looked up. No shadow, just a lack of energy discharges overhead.

No discharges.

He scanned what he could see of the horizon. No bright shield, but plenty of bright beams of light.

That meant...

"*Trucks move out now*! If you're not in a truck, get back to the bunkers! *Now! Now! Now!* Crystal Dome is *down*, people!"

* * *

"This guy again! Vinnie, what does it take to keep him from running into trouble? Why is he back on my table?"

"Brigade says he saved a lot of guys."

"Harrumph. Damned cowboys. Full of shrapnel. Again, Vinnie."

"A *lot* of guys."

"Okay, opening up..."

* * *

"Talk to me, Marty."

"*Talk* to me! Marty! Snap out of it soldier!"

"They're...they're *gone*, Padre!" Martin was sobbing, covering his face with his right hand.

"Your family? We don't know that."

"It's a fucking *crater*! They're gone...my family, the Training Company, half of the brigade. All the trainees are gone."

"You saved a lot of people, Marty!"

"Not enough. *I failed them, Padre! I failed* my family and all of the troops under my care. I'm still here. Why am I still here, Padre?"

"You *died*, Marty. You saved the captain. *Again*, I might add, and he knows it! You saved the five truckloads of trainees that were loaded before the 'Dome went down. You *walked* back to the perimeter with a soldier over your shoulder. Your *one good* shoulder, I might add."

"Fuck that. I've died *seven fucking times*! They brought me back every fucking time. 'You were only *mostly* dead, Marty!' 'We can rebuild you, Marty!' 'You're lucky, Marty!' Heart stopped? Electric shock will restart it. Bleeding out? We've got volume expanders, quick-clot, and nanobots. Lost an arm? No problem, we've been doing limb transplants for years!"

"You do realize I know about that last one, right?" The chaplain held up his right hand. The fingers were stiff, and the skin color changed abruptly below the wrist. "Works okay, I guess, but the fingertips are still numb. And by the way, it's *six* times, Marty."

"Seven, Padre. Everyone forgets the first time, in the fucking 'Stans. The 'Litterbox.' Hell yeah—applies to everywhere, now. Rocks, gravel, sand, litter, buried shit, and stinks all to hell." Marty gulped, rubbed his face again, and peered, red-eyed, at the chaplain. "*Seven times*, Padre. Once more and I'm an honorary *cat*! Fucking nine lives. What the hell do I care if my fingertips are numb? God knows I'm *all numb*, Padre!"

"Yes, my son. God knows. God knows you are hurting. God also knows about all of the lives you've saved. Perhaps you need to think about them, too. Remember the good times, and hold on to them. Honor their sacrifices by doing the best you can. You've shown so much courage. Be courageous, Marty."

"I've just been doing my job, Padre. It's the only thing I have left. The only thing I know how to do."

"I know, Marty. Pray with me."

* * *

The beeping slowed down. The instruments settled back to a normal rhythm. "And...*done!* Close him up, Anthony. How are his vitals, Vinnie?"

"BP is rising, heart rate slow, but steady. Respiration's still low, but Oh-two sats are good."

"That last spike had me worried, Vinnie."

"He was in pretty active REM sleep at the time. The chill slowed everything else down, but didn't seem to keep him from dreaming."

"I hope they were pleasant dreams, Vinnie. Good work, Anthony, keep those stitches tight. Number eight, huh? How does this guy do it?"

"You didn't see the Medal?"

"Medal? What do you mean?"

"The Medal, Mark. Some general came in and pinned it to the pillow when he was being prepped. Told us to keep it with him at all times."

"So that explains why the field generator was glitching. I'm surprised you allowed metal into the sterile field, Vinnie!"

"It's...the Medal, Mark. This guy's a real bonafide hero."

"Hah! Heroes are only Regular Joes in the wrong place at the wrong time, and no way out of the fire but straight up the middle."

"This guy died eight times and was brought back each time. I think that qualifies, Mark. That Medal shows that he ran toward the fire...and he brought a lot of other Regular Joes out with him."

"Understood, but I'm not sure that makes him brave or a fool rushing in where angels fear to tread."

* * * * *

Robert E. Hampson Bio

Dr. Robert E. Hampson wants your brain! Don't worry, he's not a zombie. He's a neuroscientist who is working on the first "neural prosthetic" to restore human memory using the brain's own neural codes. As a nonfiction writer and consultant, he uses his PhD to blog about brain science and to advise over a dozen science fiction writers. As an SF writer himself, he puts the science in hard-science & military SF, and looks for the SF influences in science. While not a zombie, he does know a few things about them, and will keep them away from your brain...at least until he can use it for his own nefarious purposes! He is a popular convention panelist who makes science—and science fiction—interesting and accessible to the public. Find out more at his website: http://REHampson.com.

Author Note:

A substantially shorter version of this story appeared in U.S. Army Small Wars Journal as "Where Angels Fear," a finalist in the U.S. Army Training and Doctrine Command Mad Scientist Initiative 2017.

# # # # #

To Dust
by Marisa Wolf

Part 1

The largest explosion she had ever caused ripped through the outpost with a voracity normally reserved for half-starved predators.

She didn't know how many she'd just taken out between the primary blast and the meticulously staggered secondaries. She'd stopped counting kills some half-dozen bombings ago.

Not counting didn't help any more than counting had, but it was always nice to make a choice.

Eight Months Ago

Devra pressed each finger to its respective thumb by turn, the deliberate pressure of the repetitive gestures managing to partially block out Shike getting to know the newbie. The fifth time through her cycle, her left hand knocked the biofeedback out of balance, and half the nerves in that arm sent up a fiery protest.

"What's your damage?" Shike asked casually—and too close to kindness—for her to want to hear.

Devra knew it wasn't the newbie's fault, being dropped off when she should have been picked up, tromping in from Command with his fresh orders and confused eyes. By the time he'd been down and processed, she could do nothing but imagine the arc of the drop-ship's departure, curving around this shithole of a planet to meet its jumpship, which in turn would slingshot its way out of this ass-end of a system off to some other hotspot.

She should have been well out of the system by now, deep into the wormhole express, safe to sleep until home. Instead, she had to lie on her too-thin bunk in the too-empty barracks she'd lived in for *far* too long and listen to yet another fresh recruit stumble his way through his mods.

"My damage? Oh, I got, uh, eyes." The slang threw him; must be the recruits called mods some other dismissive term now. Or he was just easily thrown, finding himself on the ground of storied Huvo with a handful of soldiers scattered around him.

Devra squeezed three fingers on her right hand against their thumb, a failed attempt to block out the sound of his uncontrolled blinking.

"We all got eyes, Junior." Shike laughed amiably, letting the new-bie laugh with him.

"To see above our spectrum. You know, uh, infrared. A little ul-traviolet."

"Be better if you got ears. We could use a little more radar. Ours is buggy." Gibbon pitched in from the other side of the barracks, trying to lure Devra into the conversation.

"Ours is supposed to be halfway to the gas giant by now, G. A little respect." Shike took his reputation as the peacekeeper of their team seriously, but Devra still could have kicked him with real joy in her heart. "That it, Rook? Dialed up your eyes, and they dropped you off into the longest-slog colonial shit storm we got?"

"My bones are—"

"All our bones are reinforced, Newbie. They don't make a solider soldier than a Huvo soldier." Turk this time, chiming in from the farthest end of the barracks, where he filled the doorway with his near-infinite sets of pull-ups.

"Oh." The kid stopped blinking to swallow a few dozen times. Devra seriously considered burning the barracks down to get some quiet, but it wasn't to be. The dry clay of this corner of Huvo wouldn't burn anyhow. "They made me a runner."

"Told you we were getting more twos." Shike leaned over to slap the newbie on the shoulder. "Nice, Junior. You get speed, distance, jumps, what?"

"Speed and jumps. I'm not all distance, but enough." For the first time, a hint of pride edged through the kid's nervousness.

"A little bunker-buster we got this time, folks. Get up and in and clear the path for Dev to blow us an exit, yeah?" Gibbon laughed, and Devra stretched out her hands, releasing the building white noise of her biofeedback loop.

"I clear out the bombs, Gibb, I don't set them." She'd said it a thousand times, but there was comfort in the old lie. If she couldn't go home, she at least had these idiots in her corner.

"Don't listen to her, Rook. She's a three and crazy as a four. Eyes, fingers, ears. Best bomb squad you could ask for, but she'll blow you up if you piss her off."

"Can never give a man fingers," Turk said, mournful.

"Don't ask why," Gibbon interjected, exactly too late as the newbie opened his mouth.

"Why?"

"We'd never stop pulling our own cords, y'know whatta mean?" As always, Turk cracked himself up, chortling even as he let go of the pull-up bar with one hand to make an age-old gesture.

Even Devra smiled, despite her best efforts.

"Or noses, ya smelly git," Gibbon added, flinging a fieldbook in his direction. "Don't know why they'd give any of us noses, but the sciencey types gotta keep showing off."

"Are you—"

"It's rude to ask a lady, newbie." Gibbon glared at him until he wilted, then laughed. "I got eyes, but not like yours. Distance instead of spec-range. No noses in our unit, thank all the little angels. Hear they're hell on cleaning duty."

"Gibb's the best sniper you'll see this side of anywhere," Shike said, hopping back onto his bunk and kicking one of the loose chairs they'd scavenged over the years toward the kid. "You want to sit for introductions? We got nothing but time, 'til the next orders come down."

Their new recruit was jumpy and all exposed nerves, but his hand snapped out and steadied the chair even as he blinked down at it. The sciencey types didn't mess around—his reflexes had to be good to be a runner, and they rarely sent half-adjusted mods out into the field.

Though they'd never missed a pick-up either, and here she was, done with the countdown of her tour and counting back up to some other mystery number. Devra tried not to fixate on it, but her hearing kept slipping into different channels, trying to spot the directive coming out of Command. No one had answered her yet, and if they were sending anything out to anyone, it was encrypted below her range.

Making a low noise in her throat, she sat up, shoving out the useless thoughts and dropping her ears back into vocal. Her idiots were showing off; both to welcome the newbie and to try and distract her, the least she could do was be a part. Devra swung her feet off the bed, plopping her elbows on her knees and giving Shike her best listening face.

"Should we start with the newbie, Shike? Not all of us met him at Command."

"Some of us were blocking the rest of us out with fingerbangs," Turk muttered, dropping from his bar and grinning at the rude gesture she flipped him in response.

"I'm, uh, I'm Dixon Gunner, specia—"

"Ok, no, shut up. Your name is absolutely not Dix Guns, you twat-faced child. Show your tag." Gibbon sat up nearly as quickly as Devra had, grabbing a boot and lifting it in mock threat.

"It's—no, no, it's Dixon –"

"It is," Shike interrupted, clearly as delighted as the newbie was embarrassed. "Somebody's parents wanted him to go world-hopping. Got him all colonial-forces-ready from day one."

"Gunner is the town." Dix stared at the floor, but his voice had steadied. "They give you the town name when you're abandoned and no one knows where you come from. The group home names the kids alphabetically. I came in right after new year, so I was fourth; had to start with a D. No one else was named Dixon."

"Are you shitting us with this, D-Guns?" Turk asked, wiping non-existent sweat from his face in an excuse to either hide his expression or show off the flexing of his abdominal muscles. Or, knowing Turk, both.

"Shit's bad everywhere, not just the out-planets." Dix shrugged, still looking down, and Devra made an effort to stop blaming him for Command's fuckups.

"Look, it got you the best name in the barracks. Too bad you didn't get fingers, Dix Guns. Coulda been worlds-class in porn." Shike's voice, almost too-kind again, didn't grate as much on Devra's nerves this time.

Dix lifted his head, a confused smile trying to tug free on his face, and Shike grinned, then clapped his hands.

"Right. Dix Guns, the crew. Crew, Dix Guns." They all chorused a hello, waiting in an expectant silence until Dix turned back to Shike, trying to figure out if they were all fucking with him. Which, of course, they were. After the joke landed, Shike pointed at himself. "Me, you know. Carl Shike, putting you all back together every time you split yourselves open. Eyes modified for zooming in on your little bits, hands for dexterity, but none of that finger sensitivity." He made an elaborately disgusted face. "Bad enough I get closeups of your assholes, you assholes; I don't need to feel 'em real good too."

Dix's smile got a little more comfortable, and Devra lifted her chin toward Gibb, giving him a little more time to settle. Much as her unit liked to joke, there weren't enough people running around with three modifications stacked through their systems for newbies to always be entirely at ease with her. Any one mod changed you a little, and things got exponential with each addition.

"Gibbon Merk, and no, I don't know why my parents named me after some extinct ape-monkey. They blew up on a shitty mining shift when I was schooling, so it's not some orphan tragedy like yours, but sad enough, all right?" Gibb winked at him, the tiny muscles around her eyes tensing as she shifted her pupils and tightened her gaze. "Eyes got done up for sniping, can see the stray eyebrows on your forehead."

Dix lifted a hand halfway to his face before he caught himself, and she winked again.

"Turk. They ramped up all my glands and some shit so I'm endurance and pretty much peak human." He gestured at the length of his body dramatically, pausing to pose and flex.

"He's the muscle, and the one I get to see inside of most often," Shike added, waving off the kiss-face Turk gave him in response.

Dix glanced at Devra and back to Shike, swallowing. She waited until he looked at her again, smiling her slowest, creepiest smile. As soon as his eyes widened she dropped the expression for something more natural, and was rewarded by both Gibb's snort and Dix's sudden realization that she was absolutely fucking with him.

"Devra Hegel. I've been on this planet since halfway through the fight. Eyes, ears, fingers. Biofeedback loop from my built-out fingertips to get in the guts of something and differentiate its workings even if I can't see it, frequency hopping to find the trigger and intercept chatter, and micro on the eyes to differentiate the explosives or find some of the stress faults in buildings."

"Total package," Gibb said.

"They had to up her processing to be sure she could take all that info in without exploding her damn self." Gibb tapped her temple, rolling her eyes. "Means she thinks we're slow."

"The word you're looking for is 'idiots,' Gibb." Turk performed an elaborate bow aimed at the cluster of them.

"Yes, but you're my idiots," Devra said, inclining her head in answer to his overdone gesture.

"Is everyone else on patrol or out on maneuvers?" Dix relaxed more into his chair, though his gaze moved quickly from each of them to the empty bunks lining the long walls of the packed-clay barracks.

"Everyone else." Gibbon laughed, longer and louder than it deserved, and flopped back on her bed. "Kid, we've been here for years. This is what's left of our unit. You're the first newbie we've gotten in...what's it been, Turk?"

"Two years," he replied cheerfully.

"Five-year tours, so they get their fuel money out of us. Maybe that's it, Dev." Gibbon rolled onto her side to stare at the other woman. "They're counting local time, not Galactic Standard."

"They know what they put in the contract." Dev shrugged, looking up at the cracks in the dry ceiling to better ignore the sympathy aimed at her. "Fuckers are late, and the least they could do is send a note."

"Maybe they don't have anything hot enough to send a three into. It's just Huvo and its never-ending mining scuffle with old colonists who claim-jumped and don't want to pay their taxes."

"Word in the training halls is that it's hot all over. Tax rates went up, and the colonies aren't liking it." While he'd stopped swallowing before every other word, Dix's blinking was still enough to rattle Devra's attempt at piecing her calm back together.

"Colonies never like anything." Turk sat on the edge of Shike's bed instead of making his way back to his corner. "Command gives them the speech—'you'll probably die! But if you live, you get a whole world that maybe your children's children can definitely survive on!' So Command only gets the crazies."

"I thought *we* were the crazies." Shike grabbed his pillow from under Turk and shook it out so fast Devra could hear the fabric snap. "We get the other speech—'We're going to make you better, stronger, faster, or at least one of them. You'll probably die if we try to do more than that! But if you don't, you get to keep your mods for life and can probably live on one of the colony worlds where the air doesn't want to eat you!'"

"We're not the crazies." Gibb pointed at Devra. "The threes are. The fours. We came out totally normal. The colonists are a little crazy, but hell, who wants to pay taxes for the honor of dropping dead on some shit rock?"

"Aaaanyway," Devra drawled, repeating her obscene gesture for Gibb's benefit. "Dix, you said there was word around training—you get any actual intel, or was it all rumor?"

"Rumor." He scratched the back of his neck, but met her eyes. "They don't tell us anything, but we trained over every kind of terrain. No one could figure out where we were getting sent because we were trained for all of the different worlds."

"Not very efficient," Shike acknowledged.

Turk frowned and glanced at Devra. She knew they were thinking the same thing—they'd been due a relief force since Turk, Gibbon, and Shike had hit the back half of their tour, but no one had come. Her second tour had been up weeks ago, but no ship or word. Then, still no word or actual force, but a quick buzz by a ship and a single newbie to train…

Did they all just…live here now? Had Command stretched itself too thin, or were they finally letting go of Huvo? Rumor had it the

Galactic Command had jettisoned colonies before, and for less antagonistic reasons than twenty years of Command and two waves of colonists blowing each other's shit to pieces.

Ten years ago, she would have told herself Command had too much invested in them to dump them on a planet and not look back, but even then she wouldn't have quite believed it. If the modded soldiers were term-complete, Command lost that investment either way. Why bother with the pickup fuel?

Devra shook her head slightly, playing it out in her head. Shit way to do business, and no matter how strung out the colony worlds were, word would get back to the training halls. Eventually it would hurt recruitment, which would hurt profits, and even Command...

Even Command wouldn't be that short-sighted.

The conversation turned again, to the regularities and familiar shared misery of training, and she dropped her hearing into radio. Still no chatter. It wasn't entirely unusual, but nevertheless added to her unease.

She pressed all the fingers of her left hand against her hip, letting the buzz of the feedback loop and the sharp pangs of the protesting nerves down her arm take over for her thoughts. Without another word to the group, she dropped back on her bunk and rolled over, putting her back to them.

Easier to go to sleep with her arm on fire than spiraling through the possibilities of Command fucking her over.

Her unit would educate the newbie, or they wouldn't. For the moment, she couldn't bring herself to care.

* * *

Part 2

A full decade on this rock and she'd never gotten used to the emptiness. Swathes of dry land, flat or sweeping into jagged hills that erased sight lines, covered in dust. Not enough cover, and even her eyes could only find so much of interest.

Underground was better for stalking, but the echoes were worse. Sound bounced for miles, whispering at her thoughts every time she tried to sleep.

She tried not to sleep.

Eventually they'd catch on to her tactics. She hadn't been able to erase every record of the cave systems, though she'd collapsed, rerouted, and mined enough stretches of it for some grace.

Only a few more targets.

Command didn't want to come back. They wanted it done.

She'd finish it.

Four Months Ago

"Oh, they remembered we're here?" Gibb had a knack for tying her boots with such sharp movements everyone kept an eye on her knives. "Fucking Command. How hard is it to crunch the numbers and send us somewhere worthwhile?"

"It's not an attack, it's a call from another unit." Devra checked the message's tags again. Unnecessary, but it gave her something to do while they finished getting suited. "The Diggers—"

A chorus of groans answered her. The Diggers were a bunch of barely-mods, all passive—enforced bones and beefed up hand-eye-coordination that made them good for drop and grabs.

It also made them good at calling for backup, which was really Devra's fault.

"Why'd you have to tell them anything could explode?" Gibb stood, stomping her boots and pulling the cords tight on her vest.

"Because these colonists are creative as hell, and anything *could* explode. First two years it was all—"

"If it has wires or there's a burning smell, call me." Turk and Shike chorused the rest of her sentence—even after their arrival, she'd still had to drill the directions into the other units.

It had nothing to do with the Diggers' processing capability and everything to do with the long stretches of time between colonist and Command skirmishes. Even her idiots got complacent.

"Turk, where's your vest?"

"Fuck a vest, Dev. It's hot. You've got the bombsuit, you're the bomb squad, I'm just lookout."

"Lookouts vest up too, Turk." Shike grunted as he checked his gear. "Just cause it's the Diggers doesn't mean they didn't find something, and it definitely doesn't mean there aren't collies holed up in the rocks."

"*Collies, really?*" Dix interjected into the team channel. "*They get nicknames now?*"

"Bored of calling them crazies. Or colonists. Or mentally empty assholes who got lost on their way to wherever and thought, hell, this dust planet looks great, Imma live here and fight about it for a hundred years." Shike's words all but ran together. He'd settle once they were in the shit.

"Twenty-one and point two standard, Shike." Gibb could never resist heckling him when the big man was at his antsiest. "You think they're going for the record?"

"*This is the record.*" Dix again, engine noise starting to layer over his words.

"C'mon, Galactic Command's been around almost two hundred years; you can't tell me there's not some longer fight out there they decided to drop from the records? That sound like them? You know those first hundred years were them duking it out with someone, until the science brains got mods straight."

"Gibb, you gonna talk all morning, or can I actually fly this thing somewhere interesting?"

"Dix is right, let's get loaded before we burn all the fuel." Devra squinted, pinging Lolly into her start-up mode.

"And Dix is wrong, because there isn't anywhere interesting to fly to on all of Huvo. Thought we learned you better than that, Newbie." Turk grabbed his vest and stalked out of the barracks, Shike on his heels.

Gibb looked back at Devra, and they both shrugged, following the men out.

"Dix stopped being Newbie when he took three hits at Coronus," Shike rebuked, though he would have known better if he weren't all early-action adrenaline.

"He's back to Newbie when he says dumb shit we trained him out of already, and they were all grazes. Vote's still out." Turk would have argued the point further—every one of them knew it—but Lolly tore ahead of them, kicking up an excessive cloud of dust in her path to their lift.

"Really, Dev?"

"Really, Turk. Shut up and follow the robot, there's a good boy."

He responded with her favorite gesture, and they all got loaded with a minimum of additional fuss.

"Flying us in low," Dix said, running through the checklist with easy confidence. Faint clicks in their channel indicated everyone else had switched to listening mode. Their team channel was designed not to screech feedback when they were in close proximity, but like everything Command gave, it had its moments. Better safe than crashed when it came to their pilot's concentration, so the conversation could wait until they landed.

The engine roared, and the lift lurched upward a hundred feet, allowing the stabilizing thrusters to level them before they shot forward. Dix flew with a slight downward tilt of the lift's nose—it made the most of his sight lines, but always made Devra's inner ear sure they were constantly, infinitesimally falling for the entirety of the ride.

She ran through Lolly's diagnostics as they flew to distract from the hint of ever-fall, closing her eyes as she commanded the implant to fully connect to the robot. Each system checked green across the board, from the secondary containment unit to the spectrometer.

The science arm of Command hadn't figured out how to get human eyes into the x-ray range—full infrared was still more of a hassle than just giving them goggles—and without that part of the spectrum even Devra couldn't fully analyze all the components of a potential explosive. Lolly had saved her ass more times than she'd chosen to count, and still hung in there. She couldn't ask more of their faithful robot sidekick, beyond maybe an additional containment unit. The colonists had gotten fond of cluster traps lately. Lolly had never played well with the drones, but Devra could hook another containment unit into the robot's system without affecting her processing if she did a little tweaking—

Gibb's elbow dug square between her ribs, and Devra's eyes snapped open. Turk and Shike, across from them, both had their heads back, their own eyes closed, and she shifted her head to glare a silent question at Gibb.

Gibb tipped her head back, as though Devra could see through the metal sheeting between them and the air ripping by outside. Glaring harder, Devra considered switching voice back on their channel—burning out all of their eardrums seemed super unlikely—then realized Gibb was calling attention to her helmet.

Notably, what wasn't coming through it.

Dix invariably kept up a patter of his favorite topics when he flew them, delighted with his captive audience and knowing they'd never be able to remember all the sharp comments they might have in response by the time they could talk to him again.

Last month he'd flown them through a small firefight and gave a credible summary of his favorite series at the same time, managing to both make Turk nearly wet himself and spoiling the ending of the show for Shike.

It was his proudest moment.

Now, he was silent.

They could see into the forward compartment, so he hadn't been shot or accidentally ejected, and the faint falling was unchanged from his usual lift orientation. Devra raised a hand to the harness restraining her against the wall in silent question, but Gibb shoved her hand back down with a quick headshake.

Devra turned her palms up to ask 'then what?' already knowing Gibb was going to shrug in response.

504 | IBSON & KENNEDY

The aisle between them and Shike and Turk was too far for her to kick them, so she dialed her channel way down and switched over to voice.

"Dix, you go fugue on us?" She pitched her voice low, just in case he had disengaged on them. He functioned with two mods, but that didn't mean he'd always be able to process them. Sometimes a modded soldier…broke, never to return to themselves again. Rare enough that she'd never seen it up close, but possible enough that their helmets tracked their brain activity.

Command didn't need to know as immediately if they fugued off-mission.

"Dix?"

"*Dev?*" His voice was hushed, and it wasn't just her volume settings.

"What's going on up there, Dix?"

"*How many colonists are on this planet?*"

"Official briefing has it in the tens of thousands, but the shitty ones didn't come in official Galactic Ships, so it's an estimate. Why?"

"*There are…a lot of heat signatures we're passing over. I can't see anything in visual, and I don't think it's…lava or hot water or anything, there isn't any volcanic activity here and—*"

"Dix." It wasn't the moment to ask why he was flipping out of visual to catch thermal signatures. He was a good enough pilot that he likely did it for added security at regular intervals, so she kept her tone level.

"*Yeah?*"

"Anyone targeting us? Moving toward us?"

The silence dragged on long enough that Gibb elbowed her again, and Devra elbowed her back harder than strictly necessary.

"*No.*"

"Keep flying. We'll talk about it on the ground." She switched back to listening mode and shook her head when she noticed Shike and Turk staring at her.

"*Dev?*"

"Yeah?" She sighed before she switched back to voice, keep her tone calm for his benefit.

"*Did you know someone who went fugue?*"

"No, Dix, I—"

"*I do. Thanks for checking on me.*"

The rest of their flight was disconcertingly silent. Devra caught herself wishing for some harebrained story about a magic fox and a stolen ship, or whatever had been going on in the kid's shows when Dix was growing up.

Confirmation codes exchanged with the Diggers broke through the steady roar of the engines, and within minutes, they'd landed neatly in a cove formed by a series of jagged rock towers. It was the most interesting landscape she'd seen in months on this dry stretch of planet, but they all knew better than to be distracted by something new. Turk dropped out of the lift first, signaling for Gibb and Dix to follow. Devra sent the command to Lolly to restart, then hopped off one side of the ramp while Shike took the other.

"They're in the center tower," Turk sent over their channel, voice too low to carry for anyone without ear mods. "Page is on point."

Devra turned slightly to observe the small opening at the base of the middle tower. Command was always sending the Diggers out to map cave systems, though it seemed like they came back with mineral reports far more often than enemy action intel.

Dix took the middling distance in a leap, engaging his rebuilt joints and tendons in what, for him, was basically a good stretch rather than any real effort.

"His face," Gibbon snorted, scanning the area. "Nobody told Page we had a runner now?"

"Who would tell Page anything?"

A chorus of suggestions for telling Page what to do with his anatomy answered Turk's rhetorical question, and Devra and Shike followed at a more moderate pace.

"Two lefts and a right," Page said by way of greeting, his eyes sliding away from the three of them even though he kept his face politely pointed in their direction.

"What's it look like?" Devra stared directly at him; intel was intel, even if it came from a squirm like Page.

"McCall said suspicious. Looked like a rock to me, but he swore he saw wires."

"*If it has wires or a burning smell—we called you.*" McCall joined the conversation through the channel. "*No smell, Specialist, but it's not attached to the wall like it formed there. Could be a weird Huvo thing, but we've been in and out of these caves for months, and the cols were going to figure our movements out eventually.*"

Devra kept her gaze focused on Page as she listened, and sure enough, the man started to shift in his tell-tale manner. Fucking squirms, still uncomfortable with the mods as though they hadn't saved his ass more times than he deserved. She should leave some poppers in his barracks, get some fun out of it and earn some measure of this distrust.

"Is it a tunnel, a chamber? Open or constrained?"

"Right on the inside as the corridor opens into a cavern. Iggs and Curry had already broken the plane when I noticed it, so if it's something, there's not a trip wire in the archway."

"No, if it's something it might be there to close the opening behind you. Everyone out?"

"We're a branch back. See you on the way in."

"Dix, you're with me, you're my cover for the other side of the cavern. Shike, stay with the Diggers when we meet up with them."

"A pleasure as always, Page," Shike said, causing the other man to look back at him briefly.

Dix blinked between them, and while it was clear he didn't understand all the interplay, he knew better than to ask. Coming to Huvo fresh out of the training halls and spending most of his time on Huvo training with them, he hadn't interacted much with the other kinds of units Command built. Usually better that way; separation while newbies got accustomed to their mods and their place in the Galactic Command structure.

The caves were the same yellow-orange as most of what she'd seen of Huvo; less dust, more solid, with bands of lighter yellow and darker orange, showing some sort of geological evolution to the unrelenting sameness of the planet over the billions of years since it formed.

Lolly chirped acknowledgement as it locked onto her path to follow, and she switched her eyes through their settings to scan as they walked. In the early days, she'd sent the robot ahead, but she'd lost two that way, and Lolly, her favorite, was running low on spare parts.

The humans didn't *have* spare parts, beyond the magic Shike could do, so she kept her head on a swivel. Nothing jumped out of the various spectrums she scanned, and Dix didn't jump, stutter, or mention anything.

"This part of Huvo is the Oven," Shike pronounced, tugging his jacket down even as he lifted his head. "Hot and smells like old food."

Devra often forgot about her sense of smell, as much of her processing went to other systems, so she paused to take a deeper breath. A hint of ancient meat, maybe, or stale hot air that didn't move much, baked into place as the dust had baked into rock.

"You a nose now?" Dix sniffed too, looking unconvinced.

"Every part of this planet looks like every part of this planet. Maybe it's hiding something interesting somewhere, but in the meantime, I like to name the pieces so I can keep them straight."

"It's hot all over this quadrant though. Why's this get to be the oven?"

"Dix, let me tell you something." Shike lifted a hand as though about to deliver a lecture, but Devra stopped him with a raised hand of her own.

"McCall, did you do any sampling in this tunnel? Cores or scrapes? Bring any heavy equipment through?"

"Negative, Specialist."

"Metal flakes." Devra gestured with a finger, but got no closer to the walls. "There are little sparks of them, and Lolly's picking up more on her way through. Someone dragged something through here."

"Like they made the tunnels?" Dix asked, halting entirely and staring around, trying to see what she saw. Infrared was his strength, and he registered it better than she did. But she had more than a decade of practice noting how light broke different elements, and could hold focus through the ranges better than any eyes she'd ever met.

"No, it'd be everywhere if that were the case. Tunnel is old dirt, same as everything else here. But something else has been down this way, and if it's not the Diggers, it's got to be colonists."

"But which group?" Shike asked, knowing none of them could answer. The colonists who'd 'earned' their charter mostly tried to stay out of the way of the claim-jumpers and Command soldiers best they could, though there was no telling who was who anymore when it came down to it.

"We're a turn away, McCall. Noise you hear should be us."

"*Confirmed.*"

Dix took the right turn first, checking around the corner. His runner reflexes gave him the best chance to get out of the way if it were all an elaborate ruse or one of the Diggers got jumpy with their trigger.

"We finally get to meet the new kid." McCall's voice lessened the tension in Dix's shoulders. "Can't imagine why you keep him cooped up in mod city."

"Page," Shike answered, following Dix without easing his own shoulders in the least. "And all his friends."

"Fair enough." McCall shrugged and gave a vague salute as Devra moved into the corridor with the rest of them. "You put my guts back in where they belong, and I'm gonna be nice to you, is all I'm saying."

"I'd rather not see anyone's intestines today." Devra considered smiling, but pulled the face mask down from her helmet instead.

"You do you, Specialist, and none of us have to worry about any of that."

"She don't do her, and none of us have to worry about any of that. Won't be any intestines left to speak of." The figure past McCall, facing outward into the cavern, moved closer against the wall to leave clearance for Devra and Lolly.

"Clear back to the first branch. I'll let you know if you need to be out of the tunnels entirely once I get eyes on it."

"You need cover, just in case?" A second head poked into the archway from inside the cavern.

"I brought my cover. Appreciate the offer." Even as Devra spoke, Dix crouched slightly and then exploded into motion, darting down the rest of the tunnel and into the cavern.

"Shit! I didn't know we had a runner these days." The closest figure flipped up their mask as they turned around, revealing a vaguely familiar face. Iggs then, not Curry, whom she hadn't met. Iggs used to be called something else, but she couldn't place it. Animal-related?

"New kid is new," Dev said, pushing the thought away and gesturing for them to fall back. Lolly tracked in on her treads, and Shike slapped one of her smaller appendages on his way by.

"Go get it, ladies." At the noise of protest from the cavern, he added, "You just stand there and look pretty, Dix. Let the ladies do all the work."

The world narrowed around her as Devra moved into the cavern. She bit down on her cheek and cycled her hearing through the ranges, listening for the taut string of a waiting receiver.

Nothing.

Nothing.

Nothing.

Noth—

Something. A burr in the silence, not quite noise or signal, but an almost hum that itched along her back teeth. She hummed back absently, blocking it, and sent Lolly ahead to the area McCall had marked.

The robot made no noise and barely disturbed the air as she worked through her analysis programs. Devra splintered her eyes and followed along the spectrum, matching her pace to Lolly's until the robot went beyond her reach.

The device had been mounted to the rough edge of the wall to look like a normal rocky protrusion. Lolly's smallest camera could barely get the angle, which meant her first option was out.

No way to move it somewhere else, including into Lolly's containment chamber. That left "defuse it here" or "blow it up," and if the colonials had set it to blow in this particular place, she could safely assume it would bring down a hell of a lot of rock on top of them. Command wanted the cave system that stretched ahead of them, so if she could defuse it, that was the best option.

Looked like standard ammonium nitrate, a little fuel mixed in. Nothing biological that either she or Lolly could pick up, nothing too dirty. *Definitely* enough to collapse the cavern. Remote trigger, which meant either there were eyes on them, or a signal would get sent at whatever time the bombers could assume enough Diggers would be through the cavern and trappable.

That depended on what their motive was—if it were simply blocking the path, it would have blown the second Iggs or Curry stepped in. Taking out a small force of Diggers would have been doable at any moment after they started waiting on her. The Diggers really should have known better than to wait so close to the device, but at least they'd learned her first lesson well enough to call for her.

Motives weren't her issue, so she redirected her thoughts again, throat vibrating in a silent offset to the wait signal from the device in front of her.

She dropped her eyes into micro and studied the fine blurrings of the fake rock's surface. At this level of detail it was clear the construct didn't line up quite the same as Huvo's rock, though the silica patterns indicated it was at least partly made of native materials. Lolly moved obligingly back so Devra could step up for a close scan. She found the stress fault near the center of the bottom bulge, but completed two passes to ensure there was no better entry point.

Taking a deep breath, she focused on her fingers, widening the inputs of the feedback loop and concentrating the bulk of her attention on the tens of thousands of sensory neurons loaded into her fingertips. She lifted her hands to the device smoothly, feeling the air drag against her skin, the inescapable grains of fine dust sparking needle-sharp bursts of bright pain. Another deep breath, and she made contact with the surface of the bomb, filtering out the unbearable grittiness of its surface to dig further into the makings of it.

Any pressure plate sensitive enough to be triggered by her barely-there touch would have exploded at vocal vibrations, so she crouched and craned her head back to let eyes and fingers work together, evaluating the layers of material and determining to the micrometer how Lolly should cut. Engaging the command, she stood and stretched her neck side to side, aware from only the stiffness how long that had taken.

Lolly extended one of her smaller arms, calibrated the laser, and sliced along the exact path Devra had marked, removing the newly loosed panel with a less finely pointed appendage.

Good girl. Dev crouched again, put her back to the purely stone wall, and gave herself a moment to wish they'd redone her quadriceps when they were mucking about with her system.

The wires were unsurprisingly all the same colors, but one vibrated with more energy than the rest. One at the end felt oddly slippery to her fingers, so she cycled her eyes again. Sometimes that meant primary and secondary trigger, sometimes it told her what order to cut. Getting that one wrong was a good way to lose her face, so she studied longer than usual, shifting each of the bundled cords slightly to peer further into the cuts of the device.

After that, it was snip, pause, didn't blow up, snip. The burr in her ears dropped away, and all sense of a waiting connection went with it. She swallowed, felt the roughness of her throat, and stopped humming.

"Time?" she asked, coughing as the dryness tried to choke off her words. She sent Lolly to finish scanning the cavern. There weren't any other remote triggers she could hear, but if the colonists were that good at blending materials, any part of the floor could be a mine, and part of the walls could have a tripwire. No need to get careless, even if Page was part of the crew.

"Forty-five minutes, Dev. Thanks for not blowing up."

"We're not done yet." Devra accepted the water Dix crossed over to hand her and flipped up her mask. There were no pockets in her suit, and no reason to carry anything that could become a projectile if things went sideways.

"If you're going to be there awhile, want me to take out the lookouts?" Gibb's voice was so casual, Dev almost laughed. With the one bomb defused and no other devices found yet, her de facto command was released, so she waited for Shike or McCall to answer.

"What do you have eyes on, Specialist?" McCall, unruffled.

"Looks like two, five kilometers out the flat way. No cover out there, but they're doing pretty good with camo. Took me a while to catch them—I think one got a cramp." For Gibb, taking a while meant she'd likely had eyes on them for most of the time Devra had worked on the bomb, and she and Turk had determined between the two of them to wait it out.

"Our orders were recon only." McCall didn't sound regretful, but he was the most professional of the Diggers, so Devra couldn't read too much into it.

She looked up at Dix, remembering his comment about the mass of heat signatures on their way in. If it was just Page, she might have been tempted to follow their orders to the letter and duck out, but McCall and Iggs weren't so bad. Command could still go fuck themselves, but she wouldn't lower herself to their level. She nodded at Dix, and he took a breath and broke into the conversation.

"McCall, be advised that about fifty kilometers out I caught a metric fuckton of heat signatures on infrared."

"You identify the source?"

"Underground city? Building something with a lot of moving parts? Unclear. Orders were to proceed to you."

"Understood, Specialist."

Chatter stalled, and Devra studied the openings on the far side of the cavern.

"Orders were to map. Can you all stick around while we knock it out?"

"Our orders were to secure your location, so we stay while you're here." Shike said it with confidence, but she knew he was full of shit. They were all curious. Beyond getting shot at, this was the most interesting thing that had happened in months.

"*Leave the lookouts unless they move. We don't need a hundred mole-men coming at us 'cause we kicked their nest.*" McCall grunted, and faint noises indicated they were coming back her way.

"*Will let you know if anything changes,*" Gibb replied by way of agreement.

"Cavern's clear as far as Lolly and I can tell." Devra stood, stretching out her legs. "Let us know if you need us in the tunnels."

"You don't want to go in?" Page, of course, wanted everything the mods could offer without needing to treat them as the superior soldiers they were.

"Orders," Devra replied with such sweetness she figured even Page had to hear the 'fuck you' she meant it as. With her number of successful mods, she was worth more than nearly every other soldier on Huvo combined. Maybe not worth enough for a ride home, but as long as she was stuck here, she might as well have some fun with the Pages of the universe.

* * *

Part 3

The number of colonists was staggering. There had to have been more ships than Galactic Command knew about.

Or.

She stopped, putting a hand on the smoothed wall of the cave to sense the vibrations of possible pursuit, and considered.

The subterranean cities she'd seen had taken more layers of this hole-ridden planet than twenty years accounted for. Even fifty.

How long ago had Command jumped their *claim?*

How many people lived here, fighting back against the couple hundred Command fielded against them? Hundreds of thousands? Millions?

She didn't care. Everything fell down if you blew the right anchor.

She'd replenished her supply, and she was narrowing in on the anchor.

Take the cities down.

Take Command *down.*

Let this planet return to the dust it was always meant to be.

Two Months Ago

"These orders don't make any shitting sense." Gibb shook her head hard, as though that would reorder the words on the screen.

"Diggers have been going missing, and I don't know if you noticed, but we're not getting newbies anymore." Shike shrugged, focused on his gear.

"We're not fucking Diggers." Gibb crossed her arms, pointedly ignoring the boots Turk threw to land near her. "What's the point of us going in the caves?"

"Off the top of my head, Gibbo?" Shike stared down at his assembled tools, movements jerky. "Orders. Gaping canyons only Dix can jump. Huge pockets in the ground that only you can cover. Landslides only Turk can unpack. Clusters of bombs for Dev to blow up or knock out. Spilled Digger-blood that only I can save. Or." He took a breath, forcing space between the words that had begun to run together. "It's just orders."

"Fuck orders." Gibb stopped, eyes widening as her own words landed, as they all turned to look at her. Then she set her shoulders and nodded once, the motion sharp. "Fuck orders. Command still hasn't answered any of us on why Dev is still here, or when the next troop drop off is. Even a damned computer can take the time to tell us why there are an uncountable amount of moving heat signatures on a planet that has a couple thousand colonists and us. What the fuck is going on in the caves? Why is Command so obsessed with them?"

"Maybe because there's an uncountable number of moving heat signatures in some of them?" Dix offered, nudging her boots closer to her and hopping back when she turned on him. "Even Command doesn't know everything. If the rest of the Galactic system isn't communicating, or there are blind spots in what the drones and satellites can put together..."

"Quantum computers stop communicating all the time," she huffed, but picked up a leg and slammed her foot into one of the boots. "Fucking Command."

Bile rose in the back of Devra's throat, and she swallowed it, spreading her fingers and breathing until everything settled. How many more of these runs before Command acknowledged she was well over tour?

There was no world in which she'd let her team go out without her, but if they refused...

Of course they wouldn't refuse. Gibbon's temper aside, they were all too thoroughly trained for that.

Still, no one felt much like talking as they suited up, nor for the long flight to their destination. She passed the time recounting the inventory, using Lolly to poke into a box when she couldn't recall the exact number. There was no explicit bomb threat, but they'd been told to bring the demolition suite, so it was likely she'd get to blow a few debris piles, or maybe a whole new passage. That usually cheered her, even as the days dragged on with no word on her ride home.

"It's just desert and dust," Gibbon noted, wrinkling her nose as she scanned their landing site. "The fuck is the cave? Dix, you land on it?"

"*Trap doors.*" Page's voice over the channel was almost welcome, after the ten minutes they'd spent looking.

"*They're getting good,*" McCall added. "*We'd gone too far under, missed your landing. You're a little early. Don't shoot, motion to the north of the LZ will be us.*"

"Damn well better be," Gibbon muttered, sighting over her rifle.

Dust billowed, and a section of the ground big enough to be a landing pad rose into the air soundlessly.

"Trap doors!" Shike laughed like a delighted child, and Devra felt her lips quirk in answer. McCall waved his hands over his head and steadily more of his body appeared over the lip of the opening.

"This pre-colony?" Shike asked, crouching at the side and staring at the mechanisms.

"How could it be pre-colony," Dix asked, staring, "when nothing lived here before us?"

"How can this only be a couple decades old?" Shike replied, pointing at the wear in some of the connections.

"Because Huvo dust is gross." Gibbon kept her eyes on, backing up toward them and surveying the area.

"Come on down, our orders were to wait on your team. All of you this time?"

"For some fucking reason," Gibbon replied, spitting to the side. "You sending anyone up for lookout while we're down with you?"

"Trap door locks from the inside with our program. Lock down the lift, Specialist, and let's do this." McCall dropped back into the opening as Gibbon hissed out her breath.

"Turk, carry Lolly, will you? These stairs are narrow, and I don't want her treads to stutter." Devra arched her back to loosen it and hoisted the pack holding her suit. Orders hadn't indicated bombs, but preparation never hurt.

"You want me to carry Lolly *and* all our gear?"

"You say that like two trips on a set of random stairs deep underground isn't the best thing to happen to you all day," Shike interjected, his delight in this new trick of Huvo's evident enough that even Devra laughed, answered by Turk's deeper one.

"Yeah, yeah. Gibb, you on watch while I do all the heavy lifting?"

"You know I like to watch you work." Even Gibbon's voice lightened.

It took Turk three trips, and by the end he whistled cheerfully. His pull-up sets had been interrupted, so Devra figured carrying a half ton of material nearly a hundred meters underground balanced him out. Gibbon came down last, having watched McCall set the lock. Until the last step she'd kept her eyes fixed on the door above them.

"I'd rather you were still up there too," Devra murmured, and Gibb knocked into her shoulder with a hint of a smile.

"We've been down here a few weeks and have mapped a fair amount, but we got dead ends in all directions. One tunnel's blocked, one cavern's got an uncrossable chasm, and one gets narrower over a kilometer until it closes, but sounds like there's an opening on the other side.

Shike's grin could have lit the caves. He didn't bother to say 'I told you so,' but he radiated it regardless.

This tunnel was a darker orange than the last one they'd found McCall in, smoother and well studded with light sticks. The rest of his team was camped out in the largest cavern they'd seen, at least ten kilometers from end to end.

A large crack split the natural room, almost perfectly centered from each arching wall. As they got closer, Devra stopped, distracted. The opening was studded with enough ridges and natural projections that it made a navigable path. Dark oranges and faded yellows studded the rock in almost-recognizable patterns.

"Have you mapped below?" Gibbon frowned at the crack. Three bodies wide, from their side to the other though each of the branching pathways would keep them single-file.

"A little. It gets deep fast. We reported this just after we'd sent back the rest of the dead-ends and got the order back to wait for you."

"Our orders were to map the system. Command didn't mention you'd been here." Shike glanced around, taking in the team of fifteen camped around the cavern. They were centered on the crack, and rightly so if there were no other ways in or out. "So I think it means down."

"Want to check the three blocked areas first? Down is a commitment." Devra leaned over, admiring the swirl of darkest orange that followed one of the potential paths. None of them were quite wide enough for Lolly, either, which made her want to stay up a little longer. Thoroughness.

"Our orders were just to wait for you, so I say we do both. I'll send a detachment down, with whoever you task to them. Specialist assignments are yours, so you tell me where each goes, and we'll see what we learn."

"We stashed food down all the branchings, just in case someone loses their head or there's a rock fall." One of the other soldiers, relaxing in half-dress indicating she was off duty, approached and nodded to them.

"Iggs," Devra said, placing the face and pleased with her recall. The non-specialists rarely made an impression unless they were far on the ends of the McCall-Page spectrum, but this one had been noncommittally pleasant enough times that her identity had stuck.

"Specialist." Iggs saluted, then turned to McCall. "You want to name assignments before meal call, or—"

Devra would never find out the 'or.' An explosion echoed from the depths of the opening in the center of the room, and in the moment they all froze, a second one answered it, shaking the entire cavern and knocking both McCall and Iggs off their feet.

Devra and Turk grabbed each other's arms and ducked, turning slightly away from each other to keep eyes on as much of the open space as possible.

With little additional warning, the ground around Lolly crumbled, sagged, and then gaped open, the robot plummeting out of sight.

"The fu—" Gibbon didn't finish her exclamation, a third explosion shaking dust and small debris from the ceiling above as four of McCall's soldiers lost the ground under their feet, disappearing after Lolly.

"Get to the door," Shike bellowed, command voice reaching them over the sounds of rocks collapsing and someone screaming.

Devra cycled through her hearing, but either all the remotes had blown, or they were too far down for even her to hear. How far could the signal go in this rock? She'd done the math and assumed all of Huvo would remain consistent to everything she'd seen so far, but this dark orange was composed—

Turk heaved her back toward the door and she snapped ears and eyes back to standard, focusing on the moment at hand, catching her balance to land with her feet under her. Page ran her way, gun out, as though he could shoot the ground and do any good.

She opened her mouth to snap at him, and his head cracked open.

It took her a full three seconds to realize she hadn't done anything to him, and then realized the shot had come from somewhere above and to her left.

All of the debris falling hadn't been the explosions, pieces of the wall above them had been removed, and were now filled with very human shapes.

They'd been herded into this cavern. Had left no one upside to cover them. What the hell had Command been thinking?

What the hell had *they* been thinking, to obey?

A blur of motion, Dix vaulted from the cavern floor to halfway up the wall, landing in one of the newly opened spaces. Screaming answered him, and belatedly Devra went for her gun, running forward to use Page's body for what little cover it could provide.

She pushed her vision up, focusing in on individual figures in the shadowed holes above.

Gunfire, from above and around her, varied in intensity.

Dampening her hearing, she imagined Gibbon's cool precision and did her best to take out one target after another. Despite her eyesight, she didn't have Gibb's adaptation, and she had three kill shots, eight hopefully serious wounds, and too many misses before she had to reload.

Quick glance around her to get her bearings.

Shike was pulling bodies and boxes toward the wall, aiming to create cover for the wounded. Gibbon darted and fired with exactly the attitude Devra expected, and Turk was hurling rocks into the openings fast and hard enough to slow some of the shooting from above. A body flew out of one of the openings in the rock face, telling her Dixon was still active.

Shooting wasn't her best offensive weapon, but most of what she had would take out allies as thoroughly as their enemy, and—

"Turk!" Shike shouted, having ripped the lid off a crate of grenades. He heaved a bandolier across the cavern, and Turk snatched it up, pulling pins and pitching them upward. Devra cycled through her vision, looking up, and the air above her sparked in warning.

"Turk, no—"

They'd flooded the cavern with gas. Devra ran full tilt toward the crack in the ground, useless, screaming for everyone to get down, the sound tearing her throat, too late—

Everything went white.

Had her eyes burned out? She didn't remember losing consciousness, but now there was only silence and darkness around her, the air still and cool. No gunfire. No answer on her channels.

Blood, sticky on her face.

Maybe it was Page's?

"Shike. Shike?" The slight shift in pressure that told her she still had ear drums, that she still cycled through the ranges.

The darkness grayed as she pushed her vision, then splintered. They were dead.

Command had killed them.

Command and colonists who fought endlessly, longer than Command had told them, longer than sane.

Her ears and eyes gave her nothing.

The endless fighting, over the dust of Huvo, for what?

She'd bring them an end.

* * *

Part 4

Now

She slammed into the ground, her hearing snapping back to aural as her head bounced off the rock below her.

"Grab her arms!" A voice from further back, not from whoever had her pinned—how many were there? Her eyes cycled through their settings, focus hard to find over the ringing in her ears.

"Get the trigger, there's a remote in her hands!"

A chorus of cursing, hard to separate as her head crashed against the cave floor *again*. She went limp as they ripped the small device away. Despite that, the force of the grab broke three of her fingers. She tried to dial back the feedback, but everything spun too fast for her control, and she screamed.

The weight on her released immediately, the other body rolling away, and the cursing became sounds of wordless pain.

One shuddering breath, two. A third and she wavered up to her knees, tucking her broken hand close against her chest.

Seven of them. Not Command's. Colonists then, struggling to get their own balance, blood streaming from ears or eyes. She couldn't get them all, but this? This was the largest pre-Command, subterranean city she'd found, and Command had built *right on top of it.*

WE DARE | 525

It would be enough. She could take out Command and as many colonists as could fit in one abnormal city.

She breathed again, got one foot under her, then the next. Made it upright.

The largest of them stopped writhing, eyes locking onto her movement. He pushed against the ground, starting to stand. She smiled, looked at him, and down at the remote in his hand.

"That isn't the trigger."

He was too slow. He was always going to be too slow.

The noise in her throat was one no human could have made, and few human ears could hear. She matched the pitch of the humming frequency of the bomb, *her* bomb. It had taken her a full month, stalking the underground, setting her charges. She felt the click of them coming together, her vibration and the bomb's waiting signal. It landed with a solid weight in her mind.

Fingers, eyes, ears, voice. Fours were always crazy. She didn't need to block the bomb's signal anymore, just meet it. Call it home.

She kept her eyes open to the end.

It was beautiful.

* * * * *

Marisa Wolf Bio

Marisa Wolf was born in New England, and raised on Boston sports teams, Star Wars, Star Trek, and the longest books in the library (usually fantasy). Over the years she majored in English in part to get credits for reading (this...only partly worked), taught middle school, was headbutted by an alligator, built a career in education, earned a black belt in Tae Kwon Do, and finally decided to finish all those half-started stories in her head.

She currently lives in Texas with three absurd rescue dogs, one deeply understanding husband, and more books than seems sensible. Learn more at www.marisawolf.net.

# # # # #

Now You See Me
by Kacey Ezell

I engaged the tactile feedback from my sim's shell and felt the thumping rhythm of the club's dance music reverberate deep in my chest. It wasn't quite the same as being out in my own body, but it was close. Plus, I've always liked that song.

One by one, my other sensory inputs flooded in: the club was dark, with red and blue colored lights flashing over the press of gyrating bodies. Some would be sims, like this shell, but most were actual living people out in the eternal pursuit of pleasure. More dance music flooded through my neural connection, and I made the shell move in time with the beat as it crossed the crowded dance floor toward the bar.

The bartender, Jhed, was another sim, but I'd never have guessed it if I hadn't already known. I magnified the sim's visual detection to see if I could catch sight of any tell-tale jerkiness or artificiality, but Jhed was a pro, and his sim piloting was seamless as always.

"Cary," Jhed said, giving me a nod as I approached. His hands wiped a glass clean with a cloth, and one of the flashing lights glinted off the rim. "The usual?"

"Yeah, Jhed, thanks," I said. I toggled my sim's lips into a curving smile and caught the appreciative flash of interest in Jhed's expression. It didn't mean anything, of course. It was just Jhed's pilot

528 | IBSON & KENNEDY

complimenting me on my shell control, but it was nice to feel like someone saw and appreciated my skills.

"Your usual table is free," he said, and then turned to pay attention to another customer, a young woman who careened drunkenly at the bar and laughingly ordered a popular drink laced with a mild stimulant.

I steered my shell to the right, back toward a marginally quieter section of the club. Low tables squatted between high-backed, round booths that offered a modicum of privacy. Especially when the music was jacked and loud. Like now.

The last booth before the swinging kitchen door had one occupant, and I switched the shell's facial expression from smile to scowl as I slid into the booth.

"Awww, why are you looking like that? You're so much prettier when you smile," the sim said. He was male, as was his pilot, but that and his name were all the personal details I knew. This time, the pilot had selected a shell that aped a middle-aged, overweight man with a hygiene problem. It was probably intended to be funny.

"You have no idea what I look like, Gage," I said, assuming a bored expression and blinking insouciantly. "Therefore, you haven't got the faintest idea whether I'm pretty, smile or not."

"You're always beautiful to me, sweetheart." Gage sneered with practiced, comical insincerity. I rolled my shell's eyes and stifled a laugh. I may not know much about Gage's identity details, but I knew his personality to a T.

"And you're always boring and predictable," I shot back. "What do you want?"

"Other than to see you? I like the blue hair, by the way," Gage said. "It suits the cat eyes you're sporting with this shell. Nice to see you stepping out of the normal, "beautiful human" trend everyone's been obsessed with lately."

"By lately, do you mean the last couple of millennia?" I asked. "Because that's about how long every single person has been fighting to be attractive to other humans. Well…everyone except you." I waved a hand at his current shell, cranking my expression over to indicate distaste.

"I'm beautiful on the inside, sweetheart, just like you. Speaking of the inside…" Gage leaned his shell's elbows on the table and scooted himself forward.

"Oh, finally. Have we gotten past the obligatory cute banter and can now get to the heart of this meeting you requested?"

"Cary! I'm hurt. I'm beginning to think you don't like me."

"I don't."

His shell grinned, and I cursed inwardly. I'd fallen into his trap.

"Awww, now we both know that's not true. You wouldn't have come if you didn't like me a little bit!"

"Can we just get on with this, Gage?" I sighed. "I have better things to do than waste my time talking to you."

"Oooh, busy woman! Prepping for a job, perhaps?"

Something in his tone warned me, and I magnified my vision again and looked closely at his shell's smug smile. A tiny flame of suspicion sparked and began to burn.

"Always. Why?"

"Word on the street is that you're after a big score. Trying to pay off Cybercorp for all of your upgrades?"

"Like you can talk." I snorted. "Everyone knows your ass is quite literally in hock to Bioinforma."

"Not for long." Gage smirked, and that tiny suspicion erupted into outright certainty.

"You're going after Neurovation's new interface," I said. I'd just gotten the job specs myself. No one knew the details of what it was, but this new tech was supposed to be groundbreaking enough to destabilize the holdings of both major cybernetic firms the minute it launched publically. Which was where I came in.

Because if my employers had their way, it *wouldn't*. And they were paying me very well to see that it didn't.

"Just like you," Gage said. He leaned back in the booth, crossed his arms, and threw her a wink. "Figured you'd want to know."

"Why?" I asked, leaning back and trying to appear mostly disinterested. I had the sinking feeling that I failed miserably. "Even if you steal the whole thing and bring it back to Bioinforma, you'll never get enough for you to be free of them. Not with that new electronic countermeasures suite."

"That's what you think," Gage said. "I've got it on contract that they'll release me if I bring back the info wholesale."

"And you believe that?"

"I've got it on *contract*. It's registered with the Hampson City archives and everything."

"Gage..." I said slowly, drawing the name out. Rival or not, irritating or not, Gage was one of my oldest acquaintances. "You know better. They'll find some way out of it; you know they will."

"I'm sure they'll try," he said, his grin never wavering. "But I've got a few tricks up my sleeve. I just wanted to let you know that if you're gunning for the interface...get ready."

"You've never beaten me, Gage. Every time we've gone after the same loot, we've both lost."

"And you've never beaten me, Cary. Every day is a new chance." He started to slide the bulky, fragrant mass of his shell across the booth's seat. "Good luck to you."

"I don't need luck," I said automatically.

"We all need luck, Cary; don't be cocky. That's my schtick." He reached the edge of the booth and pushed up to his feet. "See you around."

"Not if I see you first," I muttered. "And I *will* see you first."

"It warms my heart to see how much you care, Sweetheart."

"You mean that I don't, at all?"

Gage laughed and shook his head. "C'mon Cary, admit it. Your life would be so much less fun without me."

"That's debatable."

He laughed again and walked away. Not for the first time, I wished that I could just shoot him. But killing his shell wouldn't accomplish anything, and it was a terrible idea in this crowded club.

Damn it all, anyway.

* * *

"Gods of stars and rocks, Gage, you *are* getting predictable," I muttered as a cloud of icons flashed up on the tac display that overlaid my visual field. "Here you are, right on time."

As soon as I'd gotten my blue-haired, cat-eyed sim back to the storage garage after our meeting in the bar, a message from Cybercorp had pinged in my ear, asking for a status update on the neural interface job. I'd pulsed a terse message back, enough to remind them of who I was. My tech upgrades and track record spoke for themselves. Cybercorp had a reputation of being willing to pay for the best. I *am* the best, and I'd be happy to get on with things if they'd leave me the hell alone to *do* it.

They'd retreated happily enough, though not without reminding me that while they'd pay for destruction of the upstart technology, they'd really prefer to have the whole shebang, and could I please take extra care?

That pointed comment had reminded me of Gage, and his irritating habit of messing up my scores whenever we happened to go after the same target. Was that why he'd broadcast his intentions? Was he trying to scare me away?

Possibly. Though I'd be disappointed if that was his intent. Gage knew me well enough to know that warning me off was never going to work. In fact, it was likely to have the opposite effect, even if Cybercorp *hadn't* been chirping in my ear.

So here I was, on the roof of one of the highest buildings on Hel 2629A, waiting for Gage to show up and try to break into a much more secured building down below. I'd had a bet with myself as to how he'd make his approach, and, judging by the movement of the icons in my display, I was right. He'd taken the train.

"Ah, Gage," I said again, more for the fun of it than anything else. "All that money on your internal countermeasures, and yet you *still* haven't learned to vet your Gambit dealer properly." I used my tongue to depress one of the pressure triggers implanted into my back molar, which caused a burst of predatory data to radiate outward from the broadcast antenna embedded in the bones of my jaw. I tilted my head with a smile as a dark figure vaulted from the train over to the side of the building.

Two of the icons in my display winked out, making me sigh. I'd hoped to catch more of them with that data burst. It was practically untraceable. My other methods of destroying them weren't quite as subtle and might cast suspicion on my old friend Cyclo. Probably not, but it was possible. I'd have to be super careful.

Which was fine, because I was always super careful.

Thinking I'd probably have better luck inside the building, I turned and headed back to the roof access door. I leaned in so that the retinal scanner could do its thing. Sure enough, just as it had done before, the scanner chimed, and I heard the thick *ker-thunk* of the physical locks disengaging.

Retinal scan technology was about as old and as basic as it came, but its very simplicity ensured that it wasn't likely to go out of style anytime soon. Retinas were impossible to duplicate, short of birthing and raising a clone version of yourself. And even then, you'd have to create exact environmental factors throughout the raising process. They couldn't be stolen or misplaced, not and still work, and so they provided the perfect mechanism for determining an employee's identity.

So how did mine work?

Simple. I had my retinal information uploaded into this building's security database, via an innocuous inquiry about potential employment opportunities for a young, up-and-coming security tech. I'd included a resume—of course—and the resume had included my retinal profile encoded in the standard background check information that gets routed to security as a matter of course.

I think I had an interview set up for next week, actually. I'd probably have to call and reschedule.

The rev of a patrol boat startled me out of my admiration of my own cleverness, and I hunkered down next to the access door, trying to stay in the shadows. In the database or not, I wasn't supposed to be up on the roof at this hour, and especially not when I wanted them on alert and looking for Gage. They were up too high, damn them! They'd never see him from here. If this was going to work, I was going to have to do something drastic.

"Sorry, Cyc," I whispered, and keyed another trigger. Four of Gage's Gambits ignited in obedient response. On my tac display, I could see their icons turn red, and then wink out one by one as they presumably exploded. I heard the whine of the patrol boat's engines ratchet up in pitch and volume, then fade as she descended from the roofline down to the source of the trouble.

I exhaled, and slowly made my way back to the line of the roof. Why had they come up here? Had my retinal passcode not worked? It had gotten me into the building and up to the roof, so why...?

Unless the *timing* was an issue? Shit. Maybe I needed another way in.

Another one of Gage's Gambit icons winked out on my display. I pursed my lips and looked around for any other "eye in the sky" types and made a dash back to my earlier vantage point on the corner of this edifice.

I couldn't see him, but I was tracking the Gambits' control feed, and it led back to a spot on the side of Neurovation's headquarters, twenty stories down. He was probably going up the outside. Risky, with a patrol boat in the air, but it could be done.

If his Gambits continued to work.

Which they didn't. One blinked out as I formed the thought, followed closely by the other three. That left him all alone and exposed, stuck on the side of the building like an insect in fly-paper.

So sorry, Gage.

My turn.

I glanced down at the traffic flowing in the steel-and-glass canyons between the buildings. There—an Albatross-class transit shuttle, so-named because of the incredibly wide wingspan that saved on fuel and made them hard as hell to maneuver in tight quarters. My accelerated neural processes calculated a quick intercept trajectory, and I leapt, arcing outward with my arms spread and my chest thrown out in a swan dive.

Style counts, after all. Even if no one sees it.

But someone did see it.

"You just couldn't leave it alone, could you? Just couldn't do it."

"Why, Gage," I answered, drawing the words out as I tucked into a roll on the Albatross's wing. I came right back up to my feet and began to run along the leading edge. Less chance of damaging the wing that way. As I ran, I locked onto Gage's direct link. Without the Gambits running electronic interference for him, he could risk a little chat. I was happy to accommodate, if it kept him occupied. "Whatever do you mean, Sweetheart?"

"Knock off your shit," he growled. "This is my score."

"Not if I make it there first." I said, reaching the far end of the shuttle's wingspan and launching into another dive.

"You wouldn't even be here if it wasn't for me."

"Do me a favor would ya," I said, flipping over and landing feet first on the edge of the building's roof. "Take a couple of those curious shits with you when you go, if you don't mind. I'm sure they won't appreciate what I'm going to do next."

I cut the connection just in time to hear the revving of the patrol boat's engines as it started to rise up the side of the building toward the pinned, vulnerable Gage. Perfect.

Like the other, taller building, Neurovation's headquarters had a roof access door with a retinal scanner. Unlike the previous one, however, my retinal signature wasn't in this database. The ruse I'd used to infect the other database with my information would never fly with Neurovation; their information security was too good. If I wanted my retinal print in their file so it would open this door, I was going to have to use brute force to get it there.

Staying low so as not to highlight my movement, I crept over to the roof access hatch and the small scanner mounted on a short pole next to it. I leaned forward into the scanner, opening my eyes wide to allow the imager to see what it would see. At the first moment of flash, I slammed my right hand against the scanner. In my palm, I'd been holding a cylindrical object no bigger than a child's thumb. When the metal cylinder of the object met the hard plastic shell of the scanner, the shell cracked, and the cylinder was able to expel its nanowire contents inside the imager. I could tell the moment that my nanowires made contact with the information flow from the scanner's controlling server, because the flashing yellow light at the edge of my vision stilled. There wasn't a whir or a click, or any kind of noise at all, but that flashing yellow just simply flashed off and never came back on again. Instead, the light turned green and the hatch at my feet unlatched and popped up in invitation.

I slipped inside just in time to hear the patrol boat's engines revving. Out of curiosity, I opened the link to Gage again, just in time to hear him swearing under his breath. I didn't recognize the language and was fairly sure he didn't even realize he was speaking. The idea of it made me smile, even as a tiny worm of worry started to wriggle in the back of my head. Gage could take care of himself, and I wanted him occupied, didn't I? This was all part of the plan.

...but I didn't want him hurt...

Whatever. Like I said, he could take care of himself. I had a job to do. Still...

"Careful down there," I said as I dropped down to a crouch in the stairwell below the roof access hatch and took a moment to listen, dialing my audio receptors up to eleven. I heard the access hatch click closed above me and then nothing but the *whoosh* of air in the HVAC system.

Sweet.

I moved forward, pressing down the stairwell. If I was right— and I usually was—security would be busy with Gage for a minute, but when they came back, they'd head right for the roof. It was, after all, the most vulnerable spot, and my brute-force entry into the retinal database had left a mark. The upside was that it had corrupted the database as soon as it had let me in, however, so, while they knew that *someone* was in, they wouldn't necessarily know it was me. Not the most elegant solution, but hopefully a survivable one.

As long as they didn't catch me, anyway.

So I kept moving. The problem was that I didn't really know where I was going. Neurovation's security was so tight there were no building schematics to be had anywhere. I'd tried the usual information sources, and even the sketchier, less reliable options, but I'd come up completely empty. So I was flying blind, trusting to my instincts and hoping to get lucky.

If only luck were as easy to upgrade as other traits. I had the best sensory equipment and neural processing money could buy, but I could do nothing about the fickle hand of fate. Sometimes things just didn't work out, and sometimes...

I pushed through the door at the bottom of the stairs and stopped dead, frozen in surprise.

Well, shit.

Sometimes, they hung big directories on the wall that showed you exactly how to get to the laboratory complex.

I stepped forward, feeling like a tourist in the market sector as I blinked rapidly, storing multiple images of the directory in my short-term memory. Instantly, my processors started taking over, calculating the odds of security presence along the various routes to the goal and highlighting my best chance for minimal contact.

Good enough. I turned left and started moving. Now that I had an idea of my route, I needed eyes out ahead to run interference for me. Like Gage, I used Gambit drones. Unlike Gage, I knew who programmed mine...and I knew who paid him.

My Gambit readouts flashed into being on my display. With a thought, I pushed another layer of protection through my neural interface toward the handy little drones, just in case my old friend Cyclo got any ideas. I'd known him for years and trusted him with my life...mostly. It was the mostly that made me add the protection. If Gage had known to do the same, he'd be inside this building right now instead of me.

Friendship was one thing. Business was another.

My Gambit information came back clean, and suddenly I had situational awareness of my entire route down to the helpfully labeled "Laboratory Wing." I counted six security teams between there and here, some living, some drones. The living teams might have been shells, but drivers with enough skill to operate a shell in combat were few and far between. In fact, I could only think of two, offhand. I was one. The other was helpfully leading a patrol boat away from my present position.

I gave the Gambits the "disable" command and flipped between their visual feeds as they disabled the teams one by one, most of the time before the teams ever knew they were there. That was the other nice thing about being friends with Cyclo. My Gambits were next gen compared to Gage's and were therefore about the size of an infant's thumbnail. Hard to see coming, especially with their integrated active camouflage.

I stepped lightly over the last of the security teams—a live pair—and took a moment to crouch and let my scanner run over their forms. So far, luck had smiled on me. If that trend continued, I just might find...

Yes! The icon lit up bright blue in my visual display. It was a long, flat object with a rounded end and jagged, irregular teeth on one side. I'd seen security keys like this before, but no one had ever been able to explain the odd shape. Custom, I guess.

Whatever the reason, the object was exactly what I needed: a security bypass key intended to allow security teams quick access to sensitive areas in the event of a problem. This guy must have been a supervisor. He'd probably thought the lab would be safer with him to control the entry.

Poor guy.

I pulled the key out from the inside pocket of the security supervisor's tac vest and inserted it into the unobtrusive slot on the rear of the retinal scanner. The doors beeped, and then irised open, revealing a short hallway beyond.

The first of my Gambits shot past me in a near-silent whirr. As soon as I started receiving its data, I stepped over the raised doorway and into the lab complex.

"Complex" was a good word for it. "Ridiculous maze-like warren of rooms and hallways with no coherent plan" would be another way to put it. Whoever invested in this high-tech, state-of-the-art fortress of a building had obviously not saved many funds for a functional space designer or any kind. Or, more likely, they'd just let the scientists do what they wanted, and this was the result.

I sent my little eyes and ears fanning out down the various pathways, scanning for anything that would indicate the way to my target.

I found nothing.

Or rather, it was *nothing* that alerted me to what I'd found. I almost missed it. One of my Gambits stopped transmitting. It didn't break the link, and its icon remained a healthy green in my mental display, but it stopped giving me any new data. It took me a minute to notice, but when I did, I realized this had to be the score. Creating a security field that could stop a Gambit's transmissions without disabling it was seriously high-level tech and could really only be reliably imposed upon a relatively small area. So that had to be the crucial lab. I was close.

So close, my palms began to itch for the feeling of the...well...whatever it was. I just hoped it was something compact and easy to steal. If not, destroying it was an option, of course, but I *really* wanted that bonus.

And I wanted to prove that I could do it. That I could beat Gage. I wouldn't tell *him* that, of course, but it bugged me that whenever we both went for a score, I never got it. Of course, he never got it either, so it wasn't a total loss...but it wasn't a total victory, either.

I wanted total victory.

I wound my way to the frozen Gambit's position and tried to recall the tiny drone to my suit. It didn't respond, which rankled. This security field must be damn good. I finally solved the problem by leaping up and snatching it out of its hover above my head.

These things were expensive. I didn't want to lose one if I didn't have to.

I tucked it back into its pouch on my suit, and sent its fellows out to form a rough perimeter around the security field. Then I took a deep breath and walked in through the nondescript double doors.

In retrospect, it was strange that they weren't locked. At the time, however, I wasn't concerned. Maybe it was intended to be the trap it became. Maybe it was just an oversight. Maybe the scientists trusted to their groundbreaking security field. Whatever the reason, I got in and found myself in a darkened room with a single light source at the far end.

The room was outfitted with standard laboratory accoutrements—tables, terminals, and the like. I threaded my way through all of this stuff toward the light source. It took me a minute to figure out what it was, but as I walked closer, the light coming from a pair of huge, translucent glass cylinders strengthened. I put out a hand to touch one of them, and the glass cleared, revealing what stood within.

A sim shell. Human, but unfinished. It had no hair, and its skin was so pale I could see the tracery of red and blue veins beneath. It was nude, but sexless, which was odd but not unheard-of for humanesque shells.

As I stood there, the front panel on both of the cylinders slid upward. A voice came from everywhere and nowhere, and forever after, I wondered if I'd heard it with my ears, or just inside my head.

"Direct Neural Interface Protocol established. You may begin transference."

Transference? What could that possibly mean? And what under the countless stars was a "direct neural interface protocol?" Neural interface…something to do with the sims? What were these made of, anyway? They looked better than any shell I'd ever seen. Was that the top-secret new tech? A sim so lifelike that it almost looked biological? I reached out to run my fingertips over the forehead of the nearest shell. I expected to feel the cool sponginess of simflesh. Instead, the skin was warm.

Two things happened in that same moment, both of them impossible.

"Download commencing," the same everywhere/nowhere voice said, just as the shell opened its eyes.

* * *

It pulled me. Or pushed me. I'm still not quite sure which. I can't even really describe the sensation, to be honest. Just…I moved. But not because I wanted to. I had no choice. And it was weird because it wasn't my physical body moving. I don't know how I knew that, but it wasn't. It was like sending my awareness out with a sim, only I *was* my awareness…

I'm not making any sense. I know that. I'm sorry.

The point was, I moved. And it hurt. Bloody stars, did it hurt. All of my nerve endings ignited in pain, and I cried out, eyes screwing shut in agony.

Or tried to, anyway. My voice croaked, like I'd never spoken before in my life. I coughed, then doubled over and heaved. But nothing came out. Not even bile.

Stop. Stop panicking and just breathe!

I opened bleary eyes and looked down at my bare toes on the lit pedestal at the foot of the cylinder as I focused on the simple act of inhaling, exhaling. The searing pain began to recede, draining away to leave me sore, but coherent. I crossed my arms across my bare middle and straightened slowly, feeling the muscles in my back and legs stretch and contract. Another deep breath, and I reached out to steady myself on the edge of the cylinder as I stumbled down the step and out onto the cold concrete of the laboratory floor.

My knees buckled, and I came down hard next to a crumpled body...

...wearing my exosuit?

"What—?" I croaked, one hand coming up to my throat. "What is this?"

"Download protocol continuing," the voice said. "Wetware memory access granted."

And I knew. I *remembered*. Everything. I knew what the tech was, I knew how to use it, I knew what it meant and the horror of that knowledge dawned on me as I looked down at my hand, and then over at my own crumpled body on the floor nearby.

"Unknown error detected. Security network disconnected. Deadman switch enabled, commencing transfer reversal."

Just then, something flickered, and darkness closed in around the edges of my vision, too fast to avoid, even for someone as augmented as I had been.

* * *

My head lolled to the side, making my neck ache.

"Cary!"

Something stung against my cheek, snapping my head back the other way. Opening my eyes felt like clawing my way up through a pool of sludge, but eventually, I got there.

"Gage?"

"Cary! What the hell happened?"

My tac display flashed to life in front of my eyes, with four of my remaining Gambits screaming a silent warning in my head. Multiple parties moving in, weapons up in assault formation, closing in on the intruder in their inner sanctum. I was out of time. I had failed.

Or had I?

I shook my head and forced my eyes to focus on Gage's face. I'd never seen it before, but I knew him anyway. He wasn't bad to look at, actually. I liked the chiseled jaw and the promise of a beard. I liked the concerned look in his dark, serious eyes.

"Gage," I said again, my voice rough. "They're coming. We're blown unless..."

"Unless?" he asked, wariness replacing concern. He knew me so well. I smiled, and before I realized what I was doing, I reached up to brush my fingertips across his lips.

"Unless you work with me for a change. I can't explain, but if you can bring yourself to trust me, we might just both survive this." Sort of, anyway.

"Trust you."

"Gage, listen. They're coming. We don't have time. Either you're in or you're not. But this could be the biggest score of both of our lives." I let my hand drop down and pushed against the floor, trying to sit up and quit lying in his arms. I felt a bit too comfortable there, and we had things to do if this was going to work.

"Fine," he said, helping me sit up. "What's the plan?"

"You run," I said, pointing at the naked shell lying next to us. "And you take her with you. Just do me a favor would you, take the other one out for me. Just lay it on the floor there. I'll take care of the rest."

"What? Why are we dicking around with some sims? Cary, do you have the tech or not?"

"I have it, but you don't understand. The shells are everything, Gage. You don't...you don't understand what they *are*. Just...just do what I ask, okay? We're out of time. I'll meet you on the roof when I'm done."

Gage looked at me for a long moment, and then finally, finally, he nodded. And despite everything, I felt myself smile in return.

* * *

With Gage gone, I took stock. I still had my Gambits and a few similar surprises wired into my suit, as well as some other enhancements. The main things were to find and destroy any backup files that had been stored here in the lab and to buy Gage time to get clear.

I broadcast out a command to the Gambits to converge on my position. As they winged in one by one, I got a clearer picture of the teams working their way through the warren of laboratory rooms toward me.

I was right. There was no time. But I had to try. If Gage was clear...

I opened up a direct link and heard him muttering swear words in some language I didn't understand. His mutters became sharp curses as the distant rattle of an explosion echoed down the link.

"Gage?" I cried out as sudden fear gripped me. I needed him clear.

"Cary?" he came back, sounding befuddled. But the link was unbroken, which meant that he was okay. Mostly.

"Gage, get out of there!" I shouted. A banging commotion outside the lab area heralded the arrival of my combatants. I let out a swear word of my own and shoved the security key that had gotten me inside to wake the nearest terminal. The display flared to life in the darkened room, showing a simplified screen with only two menu options: <backup> and <liquidate>.

I didn't know what all was on the system, but I knew what was in my head. This was knowledge that Cybercorp and the rest of the world didn't need. Hell, I didn't need it, but I had it, and I was going to do my damnedest to protect it. I touched the second option and the screen flashed once in acknowledgement, then went dark.

"You know, that's a great idea, Cary. Why didn't I think of that? Sure, I'll just get out, one sec okay? I'm kind of in the middle of falling to my death at the moment."

Okay, he was okay. If he was being snarky, Gage was fine.

One of my Gambits flared in my vision, indicating the team approaching from that direction was almost in. I hopped back over the laboratory table and pulled out a small projectile pistol and fired it into the skull of the shell that Gage had left behind.

The shell twitched, then lay still as a pool of blood began to spread from underneath. Even with the teams bearing down on me, and even knowing what that meant, I found myself entranced by it. I used the toe of my boot to nudge its square, chiseled jaw over to the side. It had started to look like him, even in such a short time.

Fascinating.

An explosion rocked through the room behind me, throwing me forward onto the cooling shell. I rolled as I hit, pointing my little projectile gun as I came back up to my feet, and fired toward the hulking, armored figures that charged toward me out of the blinding light.

A sizzle of energy fire answered, searing the air around me and streaking through the plumes of dust and debris thrown up by the explosion. I dialed my visuals down to protect my eyes and threw one of the lab tables over on its side, then ducked down below it. Most of the Gambits hadn't survived the team's entry, but there were a few left, and I gave them a general attack command. They wouldn't be hard for the security teams to take out but they might buy me some time and that, in turn, might buy Gage some time.

"Gage!" I screamed down the link as I raised up enough to fire over my makeshift barricade.

"*What?*"

"You need to—"

Another explosion rocked through the room, throwing me to the floor and blotting out Gage's smart-assed response. A high-pitched ringing stabbed through my ears and into my brain, and I turned to fire in that direction as well.

"Listen, I don't mean to be rude, but unless you know how to power-hack a C74 Stallion, then I'd appreciate it if you just shut up for once!"

It was becoming clear that I wasn't going to make it to the roof. Time for Plan B.

"Gage," I said again, panting and squinting my eyes to try and resolve my suddenly doubled vision. "I'm not going to make it to the roof. Just run, okay? Just run and keep running. It's going to be okay. I'll explain later."

I pulled my last holdout device from the small pouch on my hip and armed it with the touch of a button. Then I pressed the "Hold" command tab on it and waited. If I could lure more of them in, I could create a bigger mess and a bigger diversion for Gage. Fear stabbed through me, but I shoved it down and away. This would work. I knew the data. It was imprinted in my memory as if I'd written it myself.

And if it didn't work…well. Then I guess Gage would finally win one over me.

Two more breaths, countless more bolts of energy fire, and a masked, armored face appeared over the top of my lab table barricade.

"Hands in the air!" he shouted, barely audible over the ringing in my ears. I clearly understood the meaning of his energy rifle barrel pointed at my face, however, and so I opened my hands and raised them up over my head. The detonator clattered to the floor next to my boot.

"Good luck, Gage," I whispered as the world folded itself down into a single pinprick of blinding white light.

* * * * *

Kacey Ezell Bio

Kacey Ezell is an active duty USAF instructor pilot with 2500+ hours in the UH-1N Huey and Mi-171 helicopters. When not teaching young pilots to beat the air into submission, she writes sci-fi/fantasy/horror/noir/alternate history fiction. Her first novel, MINDS OF MEN, was a Dragon Award Finalist for Best Alternate History. She's contributed to multiple Baen anthologies and has twice been selected for inclusion in the Year's Best Military and Adventure Science Fiction compilation. In 2018, her story "Family Over Blood" won the Year's Best Military and Adventure Science Fiction Readers' Choice Award. In addition to writing for Baen, she has published several novels and short stories with independent publisher Chris Kennedy Publishing. She is married with two daughters. You can find out more and join her mailing list at www.kaceyezell.net.

# # # # #

Now You Don't
by Josh Hayes

I probably shouldn't have told her what I was doing. I hadn't told any of the other spooks; why had I felt the need to tell her? It's because I'm a sucker for punishment, that's why. And, if I'm being completely honest with myself, I kind of like her.

The mag-lev train vibrated ever so slightly under me as it zipped along the track at a brisk four-hundred kilometers an hour. Actually relatively slow for a mag-lev, but Hampson's regulations were pretty damn strict on that point.

Which is kind of ironic considering the entire place was built because the major corporations funneled money away from legitimate Alliance projects to fund their little playground here on Hel 2629A.

I looked up as the mag-lev exited the tunnel and gazed up at the twinkling star field through the transparent panels of the geodesic dome that encompassed Hampson. The place had been carved out of the rock over a hundred years ago, creating an open crater out of the surface ten miles wide. Several tunnels connected various installations to the surface, deeper inside Hel 2629A and the various parts of Hampson.

The original companies had specifically excluded any Alliance contracts, effectively locking them out and allowing them to establish their own laws and regulations governing Hel 2629A. Since then, countless other corporations had established operations here. Now Hampson was owned, in part, by a conglomerate of companies, all of which were constantly involved in a high-stakes game of industrial espionage that no one would ever admit to.

But even if they had, the rules and regs of this place are a bit, shall we say, fluid. Trust me, I should know. I'm getting ready to break about twenty-seven of them in the next ten minutes.

I'm going to steal one of the most advanced pieces of technology in the known galaxy, but by extension, the most expensive. And that's not even the worst part. The worst part is, the people that hired me to steal it don't even know what it is. This has to be the strangest contract I have ever had, and because of that, it was also the best paying contract I'd ever had. It would've just been nice to know what, exactly, I was going to steal.

Does that make me a bad person? I guess that depends on how you look at it. I'm not Robin Hood by any means, but I'm not a selfish asshole either. Mostly.

The track curved around to the right, between several high-rise office buildings, their metal and glass façades covered with multicolored three-dimensional advertisements, selling everything from clean air to strap-on foot fetishes. What can I say? The population of Hampson really ran the gambit.

My matte-black chameleon suit absorbed the high-density neon lights reflected off the train as we passed. To anyone without an infrared scope I would appear as just another shadow in the night, which I know sounds trite, but it's true. Even without the suit, my new internal countermeasure system could ward off most passive sensors on Hel 2629A. The only ones I really had to worry about were active security measures meant to physically keep people out.

The suit's internal restricted intelligence program chimed as it identified the target building five-hundred meters ahead. My optical suite outlined the building in red, opening transparent text panels and locations of the building's active security fields. The Neurovation building was one of the newer additions to Hampson's cityscape, and from what I could tell during my initial research, it could quite possibly be the most secure building in Hampson.

No, not impenetrable, just difficult. And I handle difficult just fine.

Neurovation employed four roving aerial patrols, two roof-top spotters, and three underground patrols, not to mention the squad of guards assigned as a quick response force in the center of the building, just waiting to respond to any threat. I'd gotten a look at a couple of the guys a day ago, and I definitely would not want to go toe to toe with them. Steroids were definitely not illegal here, and they partook of more than their fair share.

The plan was to knock out the primary sensor suites on the south side of the building, masking my approach from the train, and enter through one of the unused offices on the eighteenth floor. Because the building was so new, all the spaces hadn't been leased out yet, though rumor was a legal firm had their eyes on the space. Couldn't blame them, really; the building was beautiful.

"Here goes nothing," I said, taking off at a run across the train's roof. The distance to target counted down in the bottom left corner of my visual field, my ocular implants displaying only the information I absolutely needed on this run.

I held the flap of my jacket open and a panel on the side of my exo-suit opened, shooting out a dozen Gambits. The tiny bots zipped away, twirling into the night, searching for their predetermined targets. I say night like it's ever day here. It was more cost-and-energy efficient to keep Hel 2629A stationary and provide artificial gravity. Otherwise, they would've had to build the dome so it would block the blue-dwarf sun's harmful radiation.

The track curved back to the left ahead, leading away from the Neurovation building and back into the interior of Hel 2629A. At its closest, the track was just under seventy-five meters from the south side of the building, not impossible for most people in our line of work, but barely even a challenge for me. With a running start, I leapt from the train, my cybernetically enhanced legs launching me high into the air.

At the apex of my jump another alarm chimed, automatic optical programs were zooming in on the corner of the building just to the north of the Neurovation building. A lone figure stood on the corner of the roof. I clenched my teeth together.

"Oh, you've got to be kidding me. What's she doing here already?"

Well, there was nothing I could do about it now.

Another optical display appeared, informing me that two of the twelve Gambits had lost connection, which meant two of the live targets wouldn't be incapacitated. What? I'm not a manic killer. I steal things and get paid, it's completely different than killing for hire. Yeah, sure I know some guys that make a killing at it—see what I did there?—but that line of work just wasn't for me. Too messy.

Cary had to have seen me. *Son of a bitch! I should've just kept my big mouth shut.*

I landed on the side of the building, and magnetic friction pads in my fingertips and boots held me to the enormous bay window as if I was part of the building itself. Like a spider crawling up his web. You know what, strike that, I fucking hate spiders. Bad analogy. How about…an ant? Let's go with that.

A second later, two of my Gambits clamped into the security suite on the roof and synced my exo-suit's chameleon field with the rest of the building. I froze there for a moment, watching as one of the patrol boats glided by, tendrils of blue energy from its repulsors trailing in its wake. It was an open top design, almost like a boat from back on old Earth. Four armed guards stood on the deck, scanning the building through their multi-spectrum goggles, looking for potential threats and intruders.

They didn't see me.

That was until Cary decided to get all crazy and ruin my plans.

Three more Gambit bots dropped out of my telemetry. No warning, no nothing. Just dropped off. Like I hadn't spent a couple hundred credits a piece on their anti-penetration skin and signal protection packages. The one-eyed freak who'd sold them to me had all but promised me they were indestructible.

Yeah. I guess fucking not. Well, you get what you pay for.

I had to forget about it now, though; I was about to be in deep shit.

Soon *all* the Gambit bots dropped off line, but not before the building's internal security suite detected the intrusion and began actively searching. Several different things happened then, all of which were extremely bad for me.

First, out of the corner of my eye, I saw the patrol boat flip-a-bitch and come back toward me. The armed guards moved to the gunwales, clearly looking for something, and I had a sinking suspicion it was me.

I sprinted up the side of the building on all fours, heading for the roof, but not really knowing what I was going to do when I got there. Why? Because the *second* thing that happened was that Cary made a running leap from her perch twenty stories up, hopped onto a passing shuttle, then ran along its wingspan like a *fairy*. Seriously, on her tiptoes and everything.

I sent her a direct link. "You just couldn't leave it alone, could you? Just couldn't do it."

"Why, Gage," she answered, giving me the best innocent Southern drawl she could manage. "Whatever do you mean, Sweetheart?"

I knew better. "Knock off your shit; this is my score."

"Not if I make it there first." She jumped from the tip of the shuttle's wing, spreading her arms out to the side in a gracious swan dive.

Eight out of ten. Definitely wasn't perfect. I'da done it better. "You wouldn't even be here if it wasn't for me."

"Do me a favor, would ya?" Cary asked, flipping over and landing feet first on the edge of the building's roof. She dropped down over the edge as I continued to climb. "Take a couple of those curious shits with you when you go, if you don't mind. I'm sure they won't appreciate what I'm going to do next."

I jumped over a window, still heading up the side, but knowing it was useless now, I couldn't beat her in. But if I could—

A spotlight flashed on, illuminating the building twenty meters below me. The patrol boat's repulsors flared as it lifted, bringing the light with it.

"For fuck's sake." I threw myself to the side again, trying to beat the light. My chameleon suit fooled sensors okay, but it wouldn't do shit about the human eye, enhanced or otherwise.

I didn't beat it.

The spotlight found me, and a second later I heard the distinct sound of a male voice shouting over a loudspeaker. "Halt! You're trespassing on private property! You're under arrest!"

Oh yeah, I'll just stop right here, that's a great idea. I continued to climb, but I angled sideways, heading to the corner of the building.

A bright red bolt of energy flashed off the building above me. For fuck's sake. Of course they weren't firing projectile bullets; they didn't want to run the risk of hurting anyone inside the building. Apparently that's frowned upon, but if they hit my exo-suit with those bolts, it could overload the suit and send me plummeting to the ground.

"Careful down there," Cary's voice said over the direct link.

There was another flash of red behind me, and I launched myself into the air, activating the small aero-thrusters integrated into the heels of my boots. The thrusters sent me arching away from the Neurovation building and right into the middle of a central air traffic lane.

I twirled in the air, looking up at the underside of a shuttle, so close I could read the registration number stenciled on its belly. I rolled to face down again; two slow-moving transport barges glided past underneath me. I disengaged the thrusters and dropped down to run across the open deck of the first, checking the location of the security boat over my shoulder.

It had turned away from the building, banking hard to pursue me. Two figures hunched over near the bow fired simultaneously, sending a barrage of red energy bolts through the mass of traffic between us. A small personal shuttle had to pull up hard to avoid slamming right into the side of the boat.

They were definitely going to catch flack for that. I jumped across the gap between the barges and landed on the second one just as it started to back away. I had to tiptoe along the edge with my arms out to keep my balance. It wasn't like I could fly or anything; the exo-suit wasn't designed for that, but in hindsight that was a pretty lousy design flaw. I was *definitely* going to have to have a conversation with someone about that.

A flash of red shot past my shoulder, smacking into the deck of the barge. I closed in on the bow, already looking for the next opportunity. It wasn't every day I had a chance to play Frogger in real life. Then again, jumping from car to car, trying to escape some really pissed off security guards wasn't something I generally woke up saying, *"Shit, that sounds like a really good idea; let's go do that."*

A horn blared as I jumped off the last aircar, a red, compact, sport model probably operated by some rich kid who never had to work a day in his life. The car dipped down as I launched off the hood. I corkscrewed and released a stream of dazzlers. The microbots sprayed high-powered sensor masks in all directions, scrambling any sensor cluster that might be pointing in my direction.

A little bit of my soul died every time one of the tiny machines burst into a brilliant flash of light behind me. At five hundred a pop, they weren't cheap, but they were a necessary evil of the job. It didn't matter how good you were at getting *in*to a place, if you couldn't get *out,* the job was pointless.

I landed on all fours on the side of another office building, just below the roof, magnetic grips activating on contact. My exo-suit's power was beginning to drop—still just above eighty percent—but you never can tell how long a mission is going to last until it's over, and I hadn't even *started* mine.

At the roof, I activated the thrusters embedded in my boots, throwing me over the edge. I flipped, landed on my feet, and ran. I checked over my shoulder and cringed as the security patrol damn near crashed into a skycab. Both vehicles peeled away at the last second, the security patrol angling down, the skycab pulling up.

Relieved, I slowed to a walk; I'm a thief, not a monster. I didn't want the deaths of innocent civvies on my conscience. That, and shit like that doesn't look good on a resume.

I moved back to the edge, scanning the traffic ways below for any sign of the patrol boat. It took me a moment to spot them, even with my optical enhancements, but I finally caught sight of the boat banking away from me, pulling away from traffic. Even without dazzler's, it was unlikely they'd spot me. I decided to throw them a bone.

"Let's see what you're really about," I muttered aloud, accessing their building's security array. Any security team worth its salt would be able to detect the link almost immediately, tracing it back to my location using Hampson's network grid. And by the look of things, Cary had done a bang-up job already.

Making it through the first few levels wasn't that hard; in fact it was relatively easy. For all the talk about the Neurovation's security, their counter-intrusion software was shit. At least until I hit Level 4; that's when things started to get a little tricky. It was also about the time the patrol boat turned, banking around in my direction.

"Not bad," I said.

I was interested to see how far they'd take this. Downtown traffic was horrendous, not to mention they were outside their patrol jurisdiction. If the Hel 2629A cops caught wind of what they were doing, they'd be facing some pretty heavy fines, maybe even the suspension of their security licenses.

Rules and Regs.

Time for Phase Two.

* * *

I killed my link to Neurovation's security network, then completely dropped off the network. I sprinted for the edge of the roof again, leaping back into the air. My jacket flapped in the air as my boot thrusters ignited, sending me rocketing through traffic. I kept a wary eye on the power consumption. The thrusters weren't necessarily designed for flight—more for use occasionally—but hey, adapt and overcome, right?

I spun between two oxygen haulers, their triple-sphere hulls making them look like peas in a pod. I flicked my wrist, producing a small coin-sized chip from inside my cuff, and held it between my thumb and forefinger. In less than a second, I'd transferred the codes to the chip and tossed it onto one of the oxy haulers. I didn't even wait to see if it had stuck before hitting the boosters on my boots and flying ahead.

Another two minutes of careful maneuvering landed me on the top of the Neurovation building. *About time.* I hadn't seen Cary come out yet, which was slightly troubling, but if she was still in there, it meant she probably hadn't found what she was looking for, which meant I still had a chance to find the interface before she did.

I charged for the door. The retina scanner had obviously been disabled. It was not what I would've done—not very clean—but it worked, I guess. I'd used the neural link I created when I'd accessed the building's security network earlier to disengage the security protocols when it detected my biometric signature approaching. The lock clicked as I pulled open the door and bounded down the stairwell, taking the steps three and four at a time.

"Oh yeah," I said aloud, jogging through the corridors. "Cary's been here all right."

Following the map I'd downloaded during my intrusion, I made my way through the building, stepping over several victims of Cary's handiwork along the way. To her credit, she hadn't killed any of them.

The door to the lab unlocked as I neared it. Inside was a maze of offices and work areas, clustered together in seemingly random order. I snaked through the main hallway, looking for Cary, but the entire place seemed to be empty. It was after hours, but there was always one or two pencil-necks that didn't have anything better to do with their lives but work.

To hell with that; I'm working to live, not living to work.

I passed office after office with no sign of her. I was beginning to think maybe she'd left and I'd missed it. But I was sure if she'd found what we were both looking for, she would've let me know about it. Especially knowing her. I was about to open a direct link to her when I came to large glass-walled office. I looked through the window and stopped dead in my tracks.

"Oh shit!"

Cary's body lay face down on the polished marble floor, not moving.

562 | IBSON & KENNEDY

I pushed through the glass double doors and rushed across the lab, taking a knee beside her. I didn't see any signs of a struggle. There wasn't any blood either. "Cary?"

She didn't answer.

I shook her shoulder. "Cary, are you okay?"

Still nothing.

"What the hell?" I said, looking around the lab, trying to make sense of it.

It was hard to believe that someone would've been able to sneak up on her without her knowing, especially a lab tech with no combat experience. Hell, I had my doubts that I could sneak up on her, even with full chameleon gear and the best Gambits credits could buy. But if she'd been caught by surprise by one of the security guards, why hadn't they taken her into custody?

She held a small, finger-sized cylinder in her palm. I didn't recognize the gear, which wasn't necessarily strange in and of itself; there was plenty of gear I couldn't afford, some things were outside my price range and skill level—not that I'd ever say that to Cary. The table was covered with data pads and various pieces of lab equipment, nothing to indicate why she was unconscious on the floor.

Then I saw something that gave me pause. On the far side of the lab I saw two naked shells, both featureless and hairless. One was obviously female, small breasts, and milk-white skin with absolutely no blemishes at all. The male was exactly the same. They didn't look like any shells I'd ever seen.

The female's eyes twitched.

"The fuck?"

I kept my eyes on the woman's face for a several long moments. The eyes twitched again, never opening, but moving like she was having a dream of something. They twitched again, then the female shell's body convulsed, as if it was having a seizure.

"For fuck sake!" I backed away from the table. I couldn't take my eyes of the shell, even after it stopped convulsing. I scanned the lab, searching for something…anything that would explain what the hell was going on.

"Cary!" I shouted. "You need to get up!"

A flashing screen along the wall caught my attention. The outline of two heads, red and orange and yellow lines flowing from one outline to the other. It reminded me of a data download graphic, complete with a percentage meter at the bottom of the screen.

I zoomed in with my optics to read the number. Ninety-five percent.

I walked around the table to the two shells. I leaned forward, inspecting the featureless one next to the female. I could see its veins underneath its skin.

"Creepy." I reached out and touched it, expecting to feel a rough shell job, instead it actually felt like human skin. It was smoother than any skin I'd ever touched before, but it didn't feel synthetic, it felt *real.*

A tactile feedback warning flashed over my optics, my exo-suit alerting me to possible intrusion. I took my finger away from the shell and the alert vanished. "What the hell?"

An alert chimed from the screen with two heads. The outlines flashed green, and all the data lines vanished, replaced by a text panel that read, TRANSFERENCE COMPLETE. An alarm sounded, and the lights in the lab began to flash amber.

"Son of a bitch."

I moved back over to Cary. She was still unconscious. I thought about leaving her there. I had a feeling this entire job had been one giant con. I looked around the lab again, searching for anything that looked like a neural interface, and saw nothing. Not even a standard connection.

"Fuck it," I said, kneeling beside Cary. "I'm going to feel really *really* bad about this." I slapped her. "Cary! Wake up!"

Her eyes flickered.

"Cary!"

Slowly, they opened. They stared up at me, confused and dazed. "Gage?"

"Cary! What the hell happened?"

"Gage, they're coming. We're blown unless…"

"Unless?"

"Unless you work with me for a change."

She had to be kidding, but the look on her face told me she wasn't.

She continued, "I can't explain, but if you can bring yourself to trust me, we might just both survive this."

I wasn't quite in line with the do-or-die scenario she seemed to be associating our current situation to, but I could see she was dead serious about it. Even so, we'd been opponents for so long, and with how sideways this whole mission had gone, I still wasn't entirely convinced.

"Trust you."

"Gage, listen. They're coming. We don't have time. Either you're in or you're not. But this could be the biggest score of both our lives."

I helped her sit up. "Fine. What's the plan?"

"You run," she said, pointing to the naked female shell, "and you take her with you. Just do me a favor would you? Take the other one out for me. Just lay it on the floor there. I'll take care of the rest."

She had to be joking. I didn't see any blood or bumps on her forehead, but my first thought was head trauma. She wasn't making any sense. "What? Why are we dicking around with some sims? Cary, do you have the tech or not?"

"I have it, but you don't understand. The shells are everything, Gage. You don't...you don't understand what they *are*. Just...just do what I ask, okay? We're out of time."

I stared into her eyes, trying to see if there was any bullshit there. The bio-readouts I was getting off her suggested everything about her was fine. I like to think I'm a pretty good judge of character in most instances. It's not very often anyone pulls one over on me, with the exception of Cary of course.

I took a long breath. I didn't have anything to lose. I nodded.

* * *

The shell was heavy. I could literally watch my exo-suit's power indicator drop as I ran through the lab. I didn't backtrack, the guards were busy trying to cut through the doors, but my downloaded building schematics told me there was a secure garage on the far side of the lab. Now the question was whether or not there'd be a car to jack. I knew damn well I wouldn't be able to carry this shell and fly at the same time.

It still didn't make any sense to me why I had to take this damn shell with me. Shells were a dime a dozen. Granted, none of the shells I'd ever encountered looked or felt so human, but I chalked it up to amazing innovation, but not, strictly speaking, ground breaking.

The run through the lab took longer than I thought. The entire time I weaved through the crisscrossing corridors, I couldn't help but watch the power level on my exo-suit drop lower and lower.

I turned a final corner and saw the entrance to the garage. With another flick of my wrist, I sent a small disk twirling through the air. It smacked again the opaque glass door with a click and, a split second later, exploded. It wasn't a large blast, just enough to shatter the glass. With the entire security team working to get through the doors on the other end of the lab I figured the time for subtlety was long past.

There were two cars in the garage, a small two-seat sprinter and a longer four-passenger cruiser. The sprinter would've been faster, but Cary damn well wouldn't fit in that with the shell taking up the passenger seat. I ran a quick hack on the car's simplistic security system and pulled the passenger door open.

I practically dropped the shell on her—its—head getting it into the backseat. Damn near threw my back out too, even with the exo-suit's enhanced power.

I slid in behind the wheel and worked through the startup sequence. The four repulsors on the underside of the car lit up; I could see their blue glow on the gray pavement around the car. "All right baby, what'd'ya got?"

The exterior doors were shut, but two more flicks of my wrist sent two more Wreckers flying and a moment later the floor to ceiling glass wall exploded. I threw the throttle forward, and the car shot out of the garage.

* * *

The first sign I knew I was fucked was when I didn't see any sign of Cary. The second was the three Neurovation thugs stepping out from the service entrance on the far side of the roof. Alarm tones in the car's cab started singing. I saw the reason almost immediately, and as soon as I did, I knew it was too late.

"Shit," I growled, throwing the throttle forward. The skycar's engines thrummed and whined as they powered up. I pulled back on the controls, bringing the car's nose up. I caught a split-second glimpse of the security guard bringing up his wrist rocket, then saw the flash as the weapon fired.

The explosion rocked the car, throwing me sideways and almost completely out my couch. My forehead smacked against the dash and stars danced in my vision as the world spun outside the car. It crashed back down to the roof, metal groaning and glass flying. I ducked, feeling the tiny pieces spray across my back and neck.

I glanced to the back seat where the shell was sliding like a passed out drunk. Even as the car spun across the roof—the world outside nothing but a blur—the sight of Cary in the back startled me.

What. The. Fuck?

"Gage!" Cary's voice came through my direct link.

"Cary?"

The car tipped up, the front pointing at the stars, and everything froze for a moment. I braced myself against the dash and seat. Hampson seemed to close in around me as the shuttle slid over the edge, like the whole damn thing was going to swallow me whole.

"Well fuck me." I dropped into the pilot couch, jamming my finger into the ignition override button, trying to jump start the repulsors as they flickered on and off, damaged by the blast. "Shit. Shit. Shit."

"Gage, get out of there!" Cary shouted.

"You know, that's a great idea, Cary. Why didn't I think of that? Sure, I'll just get out, one sec okay? I'm kind of in the middle of falling to my death at the moment."

The repulsors flared again, igniting briefly before winking out again. I tongued the molar at the back of my mouth, triggering a stream of andrenal-stims. Energy and clarity flooded my body, and time around me seemed to slow. My fingers danced across the cars' control panel, searching through menus, trying to bypass whatever hiccup was preventing the repulsors from kicking on.

"Come on, come on!" I swiped through the last menu, rerouted the primary power flow, and the flashing red icons on the screen switched to green.

"Yes!"

The repulsors fired, lifting me out of the couch. I laughed, weightless, looking back at the shell. Cary hung there like she was floating in space, as calm and peaceful as a sleeping baby, but she no longer looked like a shell—she looked like a real flesh and blood human being.

More alarms sounded as the repulsors failed again. Multiple red icons flashed across the cars' main displays, warning me of dropouts and disconnects throughout the system. The altitude warnings and proximity alarms blaring in my ears were extremely helpful.

I pushed everything to the back of my mind, forcing myself to focus on the only thing that mattered, keeping the car from smashing into the pavement three hundred meters below. The car's internal matrix was attempting to solve all the issues at once, effectively putting Band-Aids on gushing wounds, instead of closing off the one that was most life threatening.

The repulsors needed power, but it wasn't like I could just step outside and ask someone for a spare battery.

"But you have power," I said as the realization hit me. The power readout in my virtual vision said I had twenty-seven percent left. There was no way of knowing whether it'd be enough to fire the repulsors, my exo-suit wasn't designed to power a car. I pulled back my jacket sleeve, exposing the bottom of the exo-suit around my wrists. I pulled one of the charging wires free while frantically searching for a port on the dash. There had to be one.

Two hundred meters.

"Come on you bastard," I said, ripping back the console. "You've got to be here somewhere."

One-hundred and seventy-five meters.

I reached under the dash and ripped off the trim just to the left of the control stick. Using the boosted strength from my exo-suit, it almost took no effort at all to expose the car's innards, but every second I burned strength was that much less power I'd have to shunt to the repulsors.

One-hundred and fifty meters.

My fingers brushed over the internal components. I tried to visualize each part, seeing with my fingers instead of my eyes.

One-hundred and twenty-five meters.

"Gage!" Cary's voice in my head again.

"*What?*"

"You need to—"

"Listen, I don't mean to be rude, but unless you know how to power-hack a C74 Stallion, then I'd appreciate it if you'd just shut up for once!"

My fingers brushed against a small round outlet. There! I had to basically fold myself in half to get the cable into the outlet. I gritted my teeth as I stretched the cable out, praying the damn thing wouldn't just snap in half.

"Gage, I'm not going to make it to the roof. Just run, okay? Just run and keep running. It's going to be okay. I'll explain later."

Explain later? What the hell was she talking about?

The transmission terminated.

"Cary?" I shouted, yanking the controls to the right, swerving around a yellow skycab.

She didn't answer.

"*Cary?*"

Nothing.

I glanced over my shoulder and saw a brilliant ball of fire curling up from the Neurovation building, now fading into the distance. The explosion was right where the lab had been. The police had shown up now; their spotlights swept across the exterior of the building, illuminating the smoking holes made by the battle. I zoomed in on the roof, hoping maybe, just maybe, Cary would appear there. Every fiber in my chemically enhanced body yearned to turn the car around and head back. She had to be okay.

Cary can't die.

She's too good for that.

She's too stubborn to die.

I slapped the controls. "Son of a bitch!"

All right, get ahold of yourself, Gage. We still have to get off this rock. You're flying around with a billion credits worth of stolen tech in your backseat that looks like a dead mercenary and you're the only other suspect the cops are going to link to the theft. If they could tie me to the theft, they could tie me to Cary's death, which meant I'd be on the hook for murder, with no way to explain my way out of it.

First things first, kill the transponder, then reprogram it to broadcast a clean beacon. That would keep the cops off me for a while, but it didn't solve the problem of Cary's dead twin in the backseat.

I wondered briefly if a shell could actually be dead or not. Had it ever really been alive? If it could live, would it have a soul? Did that even matter? I couldn't just dump it, if this kind of tech ever got into the open...I didn't even want to think about it. A DNI that could literally turn a shell into an identical copy of someone, the implications were—

"Aaah!"

The scream made my heart stop.

I spun as the naked shell of Cary jerked up-right, grabbing the headrests of both seats in front of her. Her eyes were wide in terror, her breath coming in heavy ragged gasps.

"What the fuck?" I shouted, jerking the car straight as it drifted out of the lane.

A warning horn from a passing cargo hauler vibrated through my chest as it passed, the driver flipping me off, but then he hesitated when he saw what was in my back seat. His eyes lingered on the shell's body for a long moment, before flicking back to me, a smile creeping across his face. He nodded, then waved as he moved off.

I glanced over my shoulder, eyes locking with Cary. She closed her mouth, inhaling slowing through her nose. I didn't even know shells could breathe. After a couple minutes, her breathing relaxed. As her blue eyes stared into mine, the fear and confusion seemed to fade, replaced by—almost—serenity.

I couldn't help but raise my eyebrow at her. It? "Uh…" I didn't know what to say.

"That fucking hurt." She looked down at herself and realized for the first time she was naked. She covered her breasts and shot me an accusatory look.

I scoffed. "Seriously?"

Her hands rubbed a spot between her breasts.

I shifted to face front again, eyeing her in the rearview. "Are you…?"

"I'm okay. I think."

"Cary?"

She nodded and swallowed. "I'm thirsty as hell."

"I don't understand."

"I know; I'm sorry," Cary said. "Can I borrow your jacket?"

I slipped it off and handed it back. She put it on, then climbed into the front seat next to me.

"That's not just any shell is it?" I asked, pretty sure I already knew the answer.

"No." Cary ran her fingers through her hair, only a few centimeters long. "This isn't a shell at all. Not the way we understand them, anyway. Hell, *I* barely understand them, and I have the entirety of the program in my memory. They programmed it into this brain. I've got it all."

"And that new neural interface?"

"Wasn't an interface, it was a way to transfer consciousness between host and copy. They weren't just after a new weapon. They were after immortality. Can you imagine the things the corporations would do with that kind of power? The DNA replication process alone is revolutionary."

"They copied your DNA? That's why the shell morphed to look like you?"

"Yes. When I touched the shell back in the lab, it triggered the replication protocol. That's why I had you touch the other shell. When they dig out the lab, they'll find two bodies with our DNA signatures. As far as they know, we're really and truly dead."

I said nothing, the ramifications tumbling through my mind.

"We're free, Gage," she said then, and she reached over to take my hand. I glanced up at her, saw her lips curve. She really was prettier when she smiled.

"But, so…you're a copy of Cary?"

"No, Gage, this *is* me now."

＊ ＊ ＊ ＊ ＊

Josh Hayes Bio

A retired police officer, Josh Hayes is author of numerous short stories and co-author of the popular Terra Nova Chronicles with Richard Fox.

Ever since he watched his first Star Trek episode (TNG not OS), Josh has loved science fiction. Watching it, reading it, and writing it. He grew up a military brat, affording him the opportunity to meet several different types of people, in multiple states and foreign countries. After graduating high school, he joined the United States Air Force and served for six years, before leaving military life to work in law enforcement. During his time with the Wichita Police Department, Josh served as a patrol officer, bicycle unit, community policing officer, and was an assistant bomb technician on the Bomb Squad.

His experiences in both his military life and police life have given him unique glimpses into the lives of people around him, and it shows through in the characters he creates. You can find out more about Josh and his writing at www.joshhayeswriter.com.

Josh is also the creator and president of Keystroke Medium, a popular YouTube show and podcast focused on the craft of writing. For the best author interviews, news and craft discussion on the internet today, visit www.keystrokemedium.com or subscribe to their YouTube channel at www.youtube.com/c/keystrokemedium.

When Josh is not writing, he spends his time with his four children and his wife, Jamie.

# # # # #

About the Editors

Jamie Ibson is a new writer, originally from Ontario but now living in Western Canada. After joining the Canadian army reserves in high school, he spent half of 2001 in Bosnia as a peacekeeper and came home with a new appreciation for how amazing a place North America really is. After graduating college, he landed a job in law enforcement and has been posted to Canada's west coast since 2007. His first stories were published in 2018 with more to come in 2019 and beyond. His website can be found at https://ibsonwrites.ca, he is married to the lovely Michelle, and they have cats.

A Dragon Award finalist, Chris Kennedy is a Science Fiction/Fantasy/Young Adult author, speaker, and small-press publisher who has written over 20 books and published more than 50 others. Chris' stories include the "Occupied Seattle" military fiction duology, "The Theogony" and "Codex Regius" science fiction trilogies, stories in the "Four Horsemen" and "In Revolution Born" universes and the "War for Dominance" fantasy trilogy. Get his free book, "Shattered Crucible," at his website, https://chriskennedypublishing.com.

Called "fantastic" and "a great speaker," he has coached hundreds of beginning authors and budding novelists on how to self-publish their stories at a variety of conferences, conventions and writing guild presentations. He is the author of the award-winning #1 bestseller, "Self-Publishing for Profit: How to Get Your Book Out of Your Head and Into the Stores," as well as the leadership training book, "Leadership from the Darkside."

Chris lives in Virginia Beach, Virginia, with his wife, and is the holder of a doctorate in educational leadership and master's degrees in both business and public administration. Follow Chris on Facebook at https://facebook.com/chriskennedypublishing.biz.

* * * * *

The following is an
Excerpt from Book One of The Psyche of War:

Minds of Men

Kacey Ezell

Available from Theogony Books

eBook, Paperback, and Audio

Excerpt from "Minds of Men:"

"Look sharp, everyone," Carl said after a while. Evelyn couldn't have said whether they'd been droning for minutes or hours in the cold, dense white of the cloud cover. "We should be overhead the French coast in about thirty seconds."

The men all reacted to this announcement with varying degrees of excitement and terror. Sean got up from his seat and came back to her, holding an awkward looking arrangement of fabric and straps.

Put this on, he thought to her. *It's your flak jacket. And your parachute is just there*, he said, pointing. *If the captain gives the order to bail out, you go, clip this piece into your 'chute, and jump out the biggest hole you can find. Do you understand? You do, don't you. This psychic thing certainly makes explaining things easier,* he finished with a grin.

Evelyn gave him what she hoped was a brave smile and took the flak jacket from him. It was deceptively heavy, and she struggled a bit with getting it on. Sean gave her a smile and a thumbs up, and then headed back to his station.

The other men were checking in and charging their weapons. A short time later, Evelyn saw through Rico's eyes as the tail gunner watched their fighter escort waggle their wings at the formation and depart. They didn't have the long-range fuel capability to continue all the way to the target.

Someday, that long-range fighter escort we were promised will materialize, Carl thought. His mind felt determinedly positive, like he was trying to be strong for the crew and not let them see his fear. That, of course, was an impossibility, but the crew took it well. After all, they were afraid, too. Especially as the formation had begun its descent to the attack altitude of 20,000 feet. Evelyn became gradually aware of the way the men's collective tension ratcheted up with every hundred feet of descent. They were entering enemy fighter territory.

Yeah, and someday Veronica Lake will...ah. Never mind. Sorry, Evie. That was Les. Evelyn could feel the waist gunner's not-quite-repentant grin. She had to suppress a grin of her own, but Les' irreverence was the perfect tension breaker.

Boys will be boys, she sent, projecting a sense of tolerance. *But real men keep their private lives private.* She added this last with a bit of smug superiority and felt the rest of the crew's appreciative flare of humor at her jab. Even Les laughed, shaking his head. A warmth that had nothing to do with her electric suit enfolded Evelyn, and she started to feel like, maybe, she just might become part of the crew yet.

Fighters! Twelve o'clock high!

The call came from Alice. If she craned her neck to look around Sean's body, Evelyn could just see the terrifying rain of tracer fire coming from the dark, diving silhouette of an enemy fighter. She let the call echo down her own channels and felt her men respond, turning their own weapons to cover *Teacher's Pet's* flanks. Adrenaline surges spiked through all of them, causing Evelyn's heart to race in turn. She took a deep breath and reached out to tie her crew in closer to the Forts around them.

She looked through Sean's eyes as he fired from the top turret, tracking his line of bullets just in front of the attacking aircraft. His mind was oddly calm and terribly focused...as, indeed, they all were. Even young Lieutenant Bob was zeroed in on his task of keeping a tight position and making it that much harder to penetrate the deadly crossing fire of the Flying Fortress.

Fighters! Three o'clock low!

That was Logan in the ball turret. Evelyn felt him as he spun his turret around and began to fire the twin Browning AN/M2 .50 caliber machine guns at the sinister dark shapes rising up to meet them with fire.

Got 'em, Bobby Fritsche replied, from his position in the right waist. He, too, opened up with his own .50 caliber machine gun, tracking the barrel forward of the nose of the fighter formation, in order to "lead" their flight and not shoot behind them.

Evelyn blinked, then hastily relayed the call to the other girls in the formation net. She felt their acknowledgement, though it was almost an absentminded thing as each of the girls were focusing mostly on the communication between the men in their individual crews.

Got you, you Kraut sonofabitch! Logan exulted. Evelyn looked through his eyes and couldn't help but feel a twist of pity for the pilot of the German fighter as he spiraled toward the ground, one wing completely gone. She carefully kept that emotion from Logan, however, as he was concentrating on trying to take out the other three fighters who'd been in the initial attacking wedge. One fell victim to Bobby's relentless fire as he threw out a curtain of lead that couldn't be avoided.

Two back to you, tail, Bobby said, his mind carrying an even calm, devoid of Logan's adrenaline-fueled exultation.

Yup, Rico Martinez answered as he visually acquired the two remaining targets and opened fire. He was aided by fire from the aircraft flying off their right wing, the *Nagging Natasha*. She fired from her left waist and tail, and the two remaining fighters faltered and tumbled through the resulting crossfire. Evelyn watched through Rico's eyes as the ugly black smoke trailed the wreckage down.

Fighters! Twelve high!

Fighters! Two high!

The calls were simultaneous, coming from Sean in his top turret and Les on the left side. Evelyn took a deep breath and did her best to split her attention between the two of them, keeping the net strong and open. Sean and Les opened fire, their respective weapons adding a cacophony of pops to the ever-present thrum of the engines.

Flak! That was Carl, up front. Evelyn felt him take hold of the controls, helping the lieutenant to maintain his position in the formation as the Nazi anti-aircraft guns began to send up 20mm shells that blossomed into dark clouds that pocked the sky. One exploded right in front of *Pretty Cass'* nose. Evelyn felt the bottom drop out of her stomach as the aircraft heaved first up and then down. She held on grimly and passed on the wordless knowledge the pilots had no choice but to fly through the debris and shrapnel that resulted.

In the meantime, the gunners continued their rapid fire response to the enemy fighters' attempt to break up the formation. Evelyn took that knowledge—that the Luftwaffe was trying to isolate one of the Forts, make her vulnerable—and passed it along the looser formation net.

Shit! They got Liberty Belle! Logan called out then, from his view in the ball turret. Evelyn looked through his angry eyes, feeling his sudden spike of despair as they watched the crippled Fort fall back, two of her four engines smoking. Instantly, the enemy fighters swarmed like so many insects, and Evelyn watched as the aircraft yawed over and began to spin down and out of control.

A few agonizing heartbeats later, first one, then three more parachutes fluttered open far below. Evelyn felt Logan's bitter knowledge that there had been six other men on board that aircraft. *Liberty Belle* was one of the few birds flying without a psychic on board, and Evelyn suppressed a small, wicked feeling of relief that she hadn't just lost one of her friends.

Fighters! Twelve o'clock level!

* * * * *

Get "Minds of Men" now at:

https://www.amazon.com/dp/B0778SPKQV

Find out more about Kacey Ezell and "Minds of Men" at:

https://chriskennedypublishing.com

* * * * *

The following is an

Excerpt from Book One of the Salvage Title Trilogy:

Salvage Title

Kevin Steverson

Available Now from Theogony Books

eBook, Paperback, and Audio Book

Excerpt from "Salvage Title:"

The first thing Clip did was get power to the door and the access panel. Two of his power cells did the trick once he had them wired to the container. He then pulled out his slate and connected it. It lit up, and his fingers flew across it. It took him a few minutes to establish a link, then he programmed it to search for the combination to the access panel.

"Is it from a human ship?" Harmon asked, curious.

"I don't think so, but it doesn't matter; ones and zeros are still ones and zeros when it comes to computers. It's universal. I mean, there are some things you have to know to get other races' computers to run right, but it's not that hard," Clip said.

Harmon shook his head. *Riiigghht,* he thought. He knew better. Clip's intelligence test results were completely off the charts. Clip opted to go to work at Rinto's right after secondary school because there was nothing for him to learn at the colleges and universities on either Tretra or Joth. He could have received academic scholarships for advanced degrees on a number of nearby systems. He could have even gone all the way to Earth and attended the University of Georgia if he wanted. The problem was getting there. The schools would have provided free tuition if he could just have paid to get there.

Secondary school had been rough on Clip. He was a small guy that made excellent grades without trying. It would have been worse if Harmon hadn't let everyone know that Clip was his brother. They lived in the same foster center, so it was mostly true. The first day of school, Harmon had laid down the law—if you messed with Clip, you messed up.

587

At the age of fourteen, he beat three seniors senseless for attempting to put Clip in a trash container. One of them was a Yalteen, a member of a race of large humanoids from two systems over. It wasn't a fair fight—they should have brought more people with them. Harmon hated bullies.

After the suspension ended, the school's Warball coach came to see him. He started that season as a freshman and worked on using it to earn a scholarship to the academy. By the time he graduated, he was six feet two inches with two hundred and twenty pounds of muscle. He got the scholarship and a shot at going into space. It was the longest time he'd ever spent away from his foster brother, but he couldn't turn it down.

Clip stayed on Joth and went to work for Rinto. He figured it was a job that would get him access to all kinds of technical stuff, servos, motors, and maybe even some alien computers. The first week he was there, he tweaked the equipment and increased the plant's recycled steel production by 12 percent. Rinto was eternally grateful, as it put him solidly into the profit column instead of toeing the line between profit and loss. When Harmon came back to the planet after the academy, Rinto hired him on the spot on Clip's recommendation. After he saw Harmon operate the grappler and got to know him, he was glad he did.

A steady beeping brought Harmon back to the present. Clip's program had succeeded in unlocking the container. "Right on!" Clip exclaimed. He was always using expressions hundreds or more years out of style. "Let's see what we have; I hope this one isn't empty, too." Last month they'd come across a smaller vault, but it had been empty.

Harmon stepped up and wedged his hands into the small opening the door had made when it disengaged the locks. There wasn't enough power in the small cells Clip used to open it any further. He put his weight into it, and the door opened enough for them to get inside. Before they went in, Harmon placed a piece of pipe in the doorway so it couldn't close and lock on them, baking them alive before anyone realized they were missing.

Daylight shone in through the doorway, and they both froze in place; the weapons vault was full.

* * * * *

Get "Salvage Title" now at:
https://www.amazon.com/dp/B07H8Q3HBV.

Find out more about Kevin Steverson and "Salvage Title" at:
http://chriskennedypublishing.com/.

* * * * *

The following is an

Excerpt from Book One of the Earth Song Cycle:

Overture

Mark Wandrey

Now Available from Theogony Books

eBook and Paperback

Excerpt from "Overture:"

Dawn was still an hour away as Mindy Channely opened the roof access and stared in surprise at the crowd already assembled there. "Authorized Personnel Only" was printed in bold red letters on the door through which she and her husband, Jake, slipped onto the wide roof.

A few people standing nearby took notice of their arrival. Most had no reaction, a few nodded, and a couple waved tentatively. Mindy looked over the skyline of Portland and instinctively oriented herself before glancing to the east. The sky had an unnatural glow that had been growing steadily for hours, and as they watched, scintillating streamers of blue, white, and green radiated over the mountains like a strange, concentrated aurora borealis.

"You almost missed it," one man said. She let the door close, but saw someone had left a brick to keep it from closing completely. Mindy turned and saw the man who had spoken wore a security guard uniform. The easy access to the building made more sense.

"Ain't no one missin' this!" a drunk man slurred.

"We figured most people fled to the hills over the past week," Jake replied.

"I guess we were wrong," Mindy said.

"Might as well enjoy the show," the guard said and offered them a huge, hand-rolled cigarette that didn't smell like tobacco. She waved it off, and the two men shrugged before taking a puff.

"Here it comes!" someone yelled. Mindy looked to the east. There was a bright light coming over the Cascade Mountains, so intense it was like looking at a welder's torch. Asteroid LM-245 hit the atmosphere at over 300 miles per second. It seemed to move faster and faster, from east to west, and the people lifted their hands to shield their eyes from the blinding light. It looked like a blazing comet or a science fiction laser blast.

"Maybe it will just pass over," someone said in a voice full of hope.

Mindy shook her head. She'd studied the asteroid's track many times.

In a matter of a few seconds, it shot by and fell toward the western horizon, disappearing below the mountains between Portland and the ocean. Out of view of the city, it slammed into the ocean.

The impact was unimaginable. The air around the hypersonic projectile turned to superheated plasma, creating a shockwave that generated 10 times the energy of the largest nuclear weapon ever detonated as it hit the ocean's surface.

The kinetic energy was more than 1,000 megatons; however, the object didn't slow as it flashed through a half mile of ocean and into the sea bed, then into the mantel, and beyond.

On the surface, the blast effect appeared as a thermal flash brighter than the sun. Everyone on the rooftop watched with wide-eyed terror as the Tualatin Mountains between Portland and the Pacific Ocean were outlined in blinding light. As the light began to dissipate, the outline of the mountains blurred as a dense bank of smoke climbed from the western range.

The flash had incinerated everything on the other side.

The physical blast, travelling much faster than any normal atmospheric shockwave, hit the mountains and tore them from the bedrock, adding them to the rolling wave of destruction traveling east at several thousand miles per hour. The people on the rooftops of Portland only had two seconds before the entire city was wiped away.

Ten seconds later, the asteroid reached the core of the planet, and another dozen seconds after that, the Earth's fate was sealed.

* * * * *

Get "Overture" now at:
https://www.amazon.com/dp/B077YMLRHM/

Find out about Mark Wandrey and the Earth Song Cycle at:
https://chriskennedypublishing.com/

* * * * *

Made in the USA
Las Vegas, NV
01 November 2024